Sisters on
the Case

SISTERS ON THE CASE

Celebrating Twenty Years of Sisters in Crime

EDITED BY

Sara Paretsky

AN OBSIDIAN MYSTERY

OBSIDIAN
Published by New American Library, a division of
Penguin Group (USA) Inc., 375 Hudson Street,
New York, New York 10014, USA
Penguin Group (Canada), 90 Eglinton Avenue East, Suite 700, Toronto,
Ontario M4P 2Y3, Canada (a division of Pearson Penguin Canada Inc.)
Penguin Books Ltd., 80 Strand, London WC2R 0RL, England
Penguin Ireland, 25 St. Stephen's Green, Dublin 2,
Ireland (a division of Penguin Books Ltd.)
Penguin Group (Australia), 250 Camberwell Road, Camberwell, Victoria 3124,
Australia (a division of Pearson Australia Group Pty. Ltd.)
Penguin Books India Pvt. Ltd., 11 Community Centre, Panchsheel Park,
New Delhi - 110 017, India
Penguin Group (NZ), 67 Apollo Drive, Rosedale, North Shore 0632,
New Zealand (a division of Pearson New Zealand Ltd.)
Penguin Books (South Africa) (Pty.) Ltd., 24 Sturdee Avenue,
Rosebank, Johannesburg 2196, South Africa

Penguin Books Ltd., Registered Offices:
80 Strand, London WC2R 0RL, England

First published by Obsidian, an imprint of New American Library,
a division of Penguin Group (USA) Inc.

First Printing, October 2007
10 9 8 7 6 5 4 3 2 1

For Anna Katherine Green,
and all the other women who blazed a trail
for Sisters in Crime to follow

Contents

Sisters on the Case:
Introduction

Women writers and their detectives have been an important part of crime fiction since its beginnings. Who doesn't know Miss Marple or Peter Wimsey or Ebenezer Gryce and Amelia Butterworth? Wait: Butterworth? Gryce? Those aren't household names.

A century ago, they were. Both were detectives created by Anna Katherine Green, one of the most successful crime writers of the last hundred years. At a time when America's population was a quarter what it is today, Green's books usually sold around a million copies. She was President Wilson's favorite genre writer, she knew all the luminaries of the day, and her detective, Ebenezer Gryce, anticipated Sherlock Holmes by a decade.

Gryce did the same kind of forensic research as Holmes, examining medical evidence, typefaces, fabrics, buttons, and drawing conclusions based on physical evidence. Green was the first English-language writer to create that most beloved figure in crime fiction: the series character, whose insights and foibles are opaque to other figures in the story, but well-known to the reader.

In 1897, Green added Amelia Butterworth as an amateur aide-de-camp to Mr. Gryce. On more than one occasion, Ms. Butterworth's own insights saved Mr. Gryce from making a serious blunder. In 1915, Green created a bold new phenomenon, Violet Strange, a female private inquiry agent. Almost a century before V. I. Warshawski's arrival on the scene, Anna Katherine Green had created not one but two women detectives.

There are a number of differences between Ebenezer Gryce and Sherlock Holmes, but the biggest is this: Anna Katherine Green is out of print, while Conan Doyle never has been. Green is part of that long tradition of women whose voices fall off the margins of the page into obscurity.

In 1986, in a small room at a Baltimore hotel, twenty-six women came together over stale sweet rolls to discuss the hurdles we had to jump as we built our careers as crime writers. We were concerned that our own hard work and talent weren't enough to keep our own voices on the page.

The issues discussed ranged from the isolation that affects all writers, to the marginalization of novels by women—they stayed in print about a third as long as those of our male colleagues; they were reviewed (as we later learned) with a seventh the frequency. At crime conferences, we might be told that it was wonderful we had a hobby, so that we didn't make heavy demands on our husbands when they came home from work. Libraries with restricted budgets would buy works by men, because, as one librarian put it, women will read books by men, but men won't read those by women.

Many readers of crime fiction didn't know we were alive, let alone producing wonderful novels. Indeed, from 1960 to 1985, a woman had a better chance of winning the Nobel Prize in Physics than she did of winning the Mystery Writers of America's prize for best novel of the year.

I had been hearing about these issues for almost a year from women all over the country. With the support of my editor at Ballantine, Mary Ann Eckels, I convened the Baltimore meeting to see if my sister writers cared enough about these problems to organize and change them. Out of that meeting grew Sisters in Crime, and 2006–2007 marked our twentieth anniversary; this collection celebrates that milestone.

In 1987, when about a hundred women were involved, we decided we needed a structure to help keep people in touch with each other, and to make sure the concerns of all the members were heard. We formed a steering committee: Dorothy Salisbury Davis, Charlotte MacLeod, Nancy Pickard and I were writers; Kate Mattes owned a bookstore; Betty Francis, a corporate executive by day, was a reader with thought-provoking insights into both books and organizations.

That spring, we decided on our first two projects. One was tracking book reviews to see how women fared in the major national publications, and in our own regional papers and magazines; the other, the brochure *Shameless Promotion for Brazen Hussies*. Too many of us had been raised to think that only a brazen hussy tooted her own horn—and we knew that if we wanted people to hear about us, we were going to have to start shouting our names in public. A few years later, Carolyn Hart, Linda Grant, and Sharyn McCrumb undertook a heroic effort in creating Sisters' *Books in Print,* so we'd have a publication to take to bookstores and libraries.

In the last twenty years, the organization has grown to nearly four thousand members worldwide. What's truly wonderful is that readers have grown with us. At first, bookstores or libraries looking at our *Books in Print* would try a few books by our members. These disappeared off the shelves so quickly that they tried a whole shelf, and that grew in turn to an entire wall. Over and over, bookstores told us they heard from women who said, "I hadn't read a mystery since I outgrew Nancy Drew, because the characters just didn't speak to me. Now I'm finding dozens of books with characters I can identify with." We in Sisters in Crime feel proud of our role in growing the market for mystery readers.

Since 1987, we've had twenty presidents with very different profiles and ideas, but we've all shared one goal: the support and promotion of books by women, to make sure that we don't fall off the page again.

The stories in this collection are by the women who helped build the organization. We were honored from the start by Dorothy Salisbury Davis's involvement. A distinguished writer with a long history of important novels, she brought our voice to the larger mystery community; we received recognition and respect sooner than we might otherwise have found either. She has written another important story for this collection, "Dies Irae," set in her youth, during the waning days of Prohibition. As always, the voices of her characters bring them vividly to life: two sisters, living side by side but distinctly not in harmony.

Charlotte MacLeod, also on the original steering committee, died several years ago, but we are delighted to have one of her stories, "Lady Patterly's Lover," to include here.

Altogether, there are twenty stories. They show the different sensibilities of the women active in the crime-writing world of the last two decades. P. M. Carlson, with her sparkling homage to Chicago's theater scene in the 1880s; Nancy Pickard, always taking new risks, showing us an unusual twist on the mob; and Linda Grant, pushing maternal love to its extremes. Libby Fischer Hellmann turned to Grant Park during the 1968 riots over the Democratic convention for inspiration, while Susan Dunlap's "Hearing Her Name" shows some of the legacy of those turbulent times. Sue Henry's elegiac prose is awe-inspiring in

"Sister Death," while Barb D'Amato chills in a different way in "Steak Tartare."

Dive in; see for yourself what sisters who are on the case can accomplish.

Sara Paretsky
Chicago, February 2007

Sister Death

by Sue Henry

I am grown old now and weary, and speak more often with Death, though we have yet to strike a bargain, she and I. Still, she comes at times to sit on the low, three-legged stool by my small fire and croons to herself under her breath.

Then we may trade memories for a space, before she goes out again, for, given a cup of herb tea, she is willing to share rambling reminiscences, half forgotten. And I am comforted, if a bit nostalgic, at recalling past times and company.

She is well acquainted with Fate, for they are cousins. Time and again I see them together, like shadows in their long, gray dresses, the lace edges of their windblown petticoats repeating the color and rhythm of the ivory foam on the leaden sea, as they move slowly along above the cliffs of the cove to watch the tide come in over the jagged reef beyond the harbor.

Quiet and unassuming is Death, and has a refined and exquisite sense of timing and taste. She patiently does not initiate, but responds in serenity and forbearance to inevitabilities. She has a liking for old familiar things—songs, tales, her few living acquaintances—

1

especially those of us on whom she must soon lay her cool hand.

I think she is reluctant to treat with me because she has grown fond of my hearth and companionship. Few enough there are willing to keep company with Death, and she is lonely. Unseeing, most villagers pass her on the road, for she is invisible to the incredulous. They go by with a small shudder, or perhaps a gasp of self-conscious laughter like a sob. She turns her head to watch them, a stoic patience in her clear gray eyes, acknowledging their fear with tolerant understanding and sympathy.

Some are intuitively aware of her presence. A crippled veteran of the last war once mentioned a figure he feels keeping pace beside his slow, uneven gait, but who is never there when he turns his head. Soon he will recognize and welcome her, I think.

It must be a disappointment and a burden to be feared, and it is sad that most cannot understand that Death is not the dreaded calculating haunt they imagine, but generous and gentle as a mother, well acquainted with grief.

She has a lovely, poignant smile. Out of her solitude she values compassionate company of an undemanding kind. Some nights I shake off the shades of sleep to find she has slipped in out of the dark to sit contemplating the coals of my banked fire, elbows on thin knees, chin and hollow cheeks cupped in the graceful curve of her palms and long, slender fingers.

She has the hands of a young woman, does Death, soft, comforting, and as beautifully translucent as old porcelain.

Once, when I was far gone with a winter fever, she laid one of them on my brow. It was cool, compelling, and she smiled faintly, but then swiftly removed it and shook her head a little as the hint of a frown drifted across her face. Willing I was, for, as I said, I am weary of being lame and as wrinkled as one of last autumn's leftover apples. But she refused me and has since touched me not, careful never to brush so much as a fingertip against my hand in accepting a cup, so she must find some value of her own in our relationship.

I am not impatient, for I know that one day soon her gray cousin will follow Death in at my door and there will be no hesitation in the matter. For the time being, we are sisters of a kind and strangely closer than husband or kin. Sometimes, when the pain flares up in an evil lump and flutters like a bird within the cage of my ribs, she reaches one thin, pale finger to draw a slow circle through the tea in my cup. When I have drained it, if I sit very still, the agony slides away and I grow drowsy in the comfort of my own fire, glamoured by its flickering ribbons.

The winter was long and dark this year, and spring laggard to appear. But lately there have been a few days warm enough to go out into my greening patch garden of herbs and sit on the bench in the sun to watch the gulls float high over the cliffs of the cove. There I rest, and sort through my memories like an old gypsy with a bag of bright buttons. I recall days and hours, and people I have loved and lost into the long passage of my years, and find that often I can remember them more clearly than those of last week, or even yesterday. It is at times more difficult to recall the name of the boy who brings my wood, or to decide if it was two days or two weeks ago he last knuckled cheerfully on my door.

I was sitting there this afternoon, warming my brittle bones and watching a redbreast hop along the low garden wall after a beetle, when I heard a merry whistle and the boy came swinging up my path, a bundle of sticks on one shoulder and a grin of greeting on his crooked mouth.

"How be you, auntie?" he asked, laying the bundle by the door and a gentle hand upon my shoulder.

I glanced up and was sad and cross to see, among

the old, fresh bruises on his face, and worse than usual. One eye had swelled near shut and a split in the corner of his lower lip still oozed a bright bit of crimson.

As he wiped it away with the back of a hand, his sleeve fell back to reveal dark bluish purple discolorations—clearly the result of his stepfather once again taking out spite where he was able, leaving the marks of his cruel fingers in the flesh of the boy's forearm.

I sucked breath through my few remaining teeth and, recognizing the helpless anger in my eyes, he gave me a smile, shook his head, and shrugged shoulders already well muscled from rowing the boat and hauling nets out of the sea.

"Ah, auntie, they are but trifling and petty things, already mending. Shall I carry you up a fish when we return?"

I turned my gaze down to the harbor and narrowed my eyes to pick out the figure of the brutal man who stood by the boat, shaking a fist and hallooing an impatient demand for the boy's attendance.

"Best you be off, or he'll make the next blow even less to your liking," I suggested. "And be you cautious, for he would care little if you came not home, but drowned out of reach of shore."

He gave me only another quick smile for answer, but I caught a hint of thoughtful anger and resentment in his eyes as he turned to scramble away down the steep path to the crescent of sand below, then trotted along to join his tormentor, earning another clout for his trouble.

With an ache of fury and fear hard under my breastbone, I watched them cast off and turn the boat for open water, the boy spending all possible effort to keep even the sweep of the long oars, while his persecutor rested in the stern of the heavy craft. As they cleared the reef and headed into the stronger waves of open water, a hint of motion drew my eyes back

to the shingle and told me I was not alone in my
concern for that particular departure.

Not high on the cliffs, but close together where the
boat had rested and the incoming tide lapped the narrow beach, stood those two familiar cousins, petticoats
aflutter in the breeze, each with a comforting arm of
reassurance about the other's waist. Patiently, their
consideration focused on the pair in that small shell
of a vessel moving inexorably away over the rocking
surface of the endless gray sea. When it disappeared
around the headland, they turned and paced away
slowly, stepping together, growing smaller to my sight
until, far along the shingle, the cliffs loomed between
us and they too were gone.

A long time later, clouds, dark and growling a heavy
threat of oncoming rain, slid across the sun and it
grew cool and breezy, even in the shelter there beside
my cottage door. Unwilling to surrender my vantage
point until I saw the boy home safe, I grasped the
stick that I keep against the bench beside me to pull
myself, stiff as a rusty gate, to my feet and tottered
inside in search of my old blue shawl and a cup of
water to soothe my throat, parched with disquiet.

Back on the bench once more, I felt my concern
increase to see that the now howling wind of the approaching storm was assisting the incoming tide to
hurl massive waves over the reef, all but hiding it with
their assault and its resulting spray. The gulls that earlier had coasted circles in the air above the cove had
fled away to some shelter of their own, leaving the
sky empty of all but a blackish green wall of cloud
moving rapidly toward land and casting ragged lines
of lightning into the watery maelstrom beneath.

Narrowing my eyes and sheltering them with a hand
to my brow, I peered seaward, yearning to see the
boy in the boat pulling hard for the safety of the cove,
but there was nothing among the huge, endless waves
rolling one after another onto the reef and shingle

below. From the few huddled cottages that make up our small village, a number of folk had hurried down to haul their boats higher on the sand and secure them from the greedy fingers of the rising sea. I could make out the widow Kale, hair and skirts a-toss in the blow, and her two tall sons as they struggled to drag their old dory up over the wet sand. Lost at sea in just such a storm three years before, her good man had left her little but helpless dread at the need to send her boys out as fishermen in his wake.

As soon as the boats were made safe as possible, the shingle quickly emptied as they all rushed back to shelter, except for the widow, who hesitated and swung slowly around to have one last look at the on-coming storm. Then, suddenly, she turned her back on the writhing sea, lifted her face and, following the direction of her gaze, I saw that she had marked the two gray-clad figures of Death and her cousin, as they slowly made their way along the cliff top, now hand in hand as they watched the sea. So the widow too was familiar with the pair. But it was apparent that she bore them no acceptance as she made a quick sign against evil in their direction, whirled and caught up her skirts to hasten to the consoling shelter of her hut.

Not long after her disappearance, as the first fat drops of rain began to fall and splash dimples in the dust of my yard, before seeking my own shelter I took another look beyond the waves dashing over the reef and was at last rewarded for my watchfulness by the sight of two figures in a boat as it rose on the crest of a wave, then was whirled out of sight into the trough that followed. It was only a glimpse, but I could tell that both were now rowing, hard, and had not far to go to gain the shelter of the cove, though that was now little calmer than the open sea that poured and pounded into it. A sudden lump of fear in my chest bent me half over with concern for them.

Again the craft rose, a bit closer, and I could tell that the rowers were making an attempt to ride the crests whenever possible in endeavoring to reach safety. Very slowly they pulled nearer and, as I could see them even in the troughs now, I could tell that the man, rowing closest to the bow of the boat, was angrily shouting something at the boy in the stern, but it was impossible to hear his voice over the roar of the wind and crash of the waves. There was no response from the boy, his back to his stepfather, struggling to pull the heavy oars evenly and keep the boat headed for shore.

Again the man moved as if he were shouting, leaning forward, letting both oars drag through the water from the oarlocks. There was still no answer from the boy, intent on his rowing, who had little chance of hearing within the fury of the storm that had swept over them in a deafening curtain of rain.

As it reached me, I hauled myself partially erect, fighting a stab of pain in my chest, to gain the shelter of the door to my cottage, and saw that the cousins had reached the foot of my path and hesitated there to join me in watching the pair in the boat. Though the wind still tossed their skirts and the lace of their petticoats, the rain that had half soaked me through in a moment seemed to have no effect on the shadowy fabric of their dresses.

I was more concerned with the two in the boat, who were silhouettes against a sudden flash of lightning, and I could see that the craft had now almost gained the cove. That gain must have been made from the efforts of the boy alone, for the man had slid forward onto his knees and taken one of his oars from its oarlock, ignoring the other. He held it raised high over his head, clearly meaning to bring it down on the head of the unsuspecting boy with murderous intent.

"No-o-o," I cried, clutching at the air between us with the gnarled fingers of one hand. The other dangled strangely unresponsive at my side when I attempted to draw it up to hold against the pain of panic in my chest. The pain turned suddenly to a fire that ran down that arm and a great weakness came over me. Only by leaning against the frame of the door was I able to tell what happened next, for it occurred so very quickly.

Frowning, and shaking her head slightly, Fate withdrew her hand from that of her cousin and raised it toward the boat we could just make out in the distance and made a swift and subtle gesture.

With a last stroke of the boy's oars the boat was caught by a rogue wave that came out of nowhere, unexpectedly catching it sideways and flinging it forward to stop abruptly, hard on the stones of the reef now hidden by the tide. Their jagged sharpness tore a hole in the hull, crushing it like an eggshell, ruining the precarious balance of the man and tossing him, oar still raised above his head, out of the boat and onto the rocks as well. There for a moment or two he lay quite still, then was washed off into the outer waters of the sea and sank from sight, leaving only the oar to rock and spin in the foam of the turbulent surface.

The boy had been cast backward into the bottom of the boat, but I saw him scramble up in the sinking vessel and look about in confusion for his stepfather, seeming dazed at seeing no one.

Now completely awash in the sea, the boat began to slip and disappear as the steep outer side of the reef lost its hold. Slowly, inexorably, it sank, following the man into the depths, threatening to take the boy as well. But at the last moment he rose and, leaping nimbly out of it onto the sharp stones of the reef, threw himself over into the slightly calmer waters of the cove, where he began a determined swim toward shore.

Gasping and faint, I sank to my knees in my cottage doorway, apprehension fading along with anger in the relief of knowing he would easily reach the safety of the shingle with no more trouble.

*   *   *

A long time later, I woke to find myself in my own bed.

The sharp pain was still there in my chest, but it was less, and I lay still in concern that I might wake it again.

The storm had passed and through the window I could see that the night was full of darkness and welcome silence. A small fire crackled and I could see the kettle steaming gently over it. Near it was the boy, peacefully asleep on a rag rug near the hearth.

I closed my eyes, deeply glad to see him alive and whole and, best of all, free, then opened them again, feeling the presence of someone else.

The door, which at times complains, opened without so much as a whimper and enough moonlight slid into the room to define the pair of shadows that fell across the floor. I looked up to see not only Sister Death, but also her cousin, Fate, standing together in the doorway, as I had long expected them to appear one day.

"Come in and welcome," I whispered as well as I could through my twisted mouth and beckoned with the fingers of my one good hand.

They came in together and closed the door.

Fate said not a word, but smiled and nodded before crossing to the three-legged stool where she sat, slim and graceful, by the fire, staring intently into its bright, compelling ribbons.

Sister Death stepped close to the bed, stood looking down at me patiently, and, saying nothing, said everything.

Without words, she had asked and I answered.

At last we had struck that long-anticipated bargain, she and I.

Slowly, she reached one pale hand with its slender, translucent fingers and laid its coolness with infinite gentleness on my brow.

The pain disappeared and I took a deep breath.

You are weary, she told me silently. *Sleep.*

Obedient, I closed my eyes and was content, but for one thing.

Care . . . for the boy, as thought faded.

Yes.

Hearing Her Name

by Susan Dunlap

They didn't look at her. Not one of them. "That's a bad sign, right, Dennis?"

"Means zip. And anyway, it'll all be over soon." Dennis Haggarty flipped back the pages of his yellow lined notepad, dropped it in his briefcase and pushed himself up from the defense table. "Elizabeth—"

"Carla! Call me by my real name. Carla," she snapped, then relented. "Despite everything, it's just good to be called who I really am." She looked over her too-thin, too-unkempt lawyer and wondered yet again if she had made a mistake hiring a man who couldn't even remember her true name. When the media latched on to the breaking story it was FEDS CAPTURE FUGITIVE IN HIDING FOR 24 YEARS, and she was Elizabeth Amanda Creiss, her fugitive name. Carla Dreseldorf meant nothing to them or their readers. It was Elizabeth Amanda Creiss and her two decades on the run that made the front page. For the eight months run-up to this trial every shabby room Elizabeth Amanda Creiss had hidden in, every menial job, every guy she had spent a night with was a day's hot story. It was impossible to turn on the radio or television without hearing "Elizabeth Amanda Creiss."

Even her high school graduation pictures had run over the caption ELIZABETH AMANDA CREISS 25 YEARS AGO. Carla Dreseldorf was merely a footnote. Before Carla went underground, no one bothered with her name. And when the other conspirators were caught and created their own rounds of publicity, the news stories often didn't mention her. As Dennis repeated every time she worried aloud, she had been the most peripheral conspirator, present at only one meeting of the much-more-radical-than-she-realized group before they attacked the power plant. She hadn't even known what kind of explosive they were using. They were making a statement with their smoke bombs, they had told her; never had they said they were trying to blow up the plant. "Everybody has endgames," her mother would have told her. "You don't pay enough attention to see them." True. And way too late now to think about that. Better to remember what Dennis said, that to the conspirators, she was akin to the political campaign worker who dropped off the doughnuts and trotted on home. Besides, Dennis concluded every single time, no one had been killed, and all the evidence against her was circumstantial.

Still, when they filed out the jurors hadn't looked at her.

Dennis turned to her. "Look, juries are ecstatic that testimony has finally ended and they will never have to sit in those chairs again. They're like kids heading for the playground. They don't waste time looking at you. They've had weeks of you. They're sick of the sight of you, and me, and Jefferson K. Markoff over there, not to mention the judge. Trust me, I have never seen a jury pause for a last look." He stood, yanked ineffectually at his ill-fitting tweed jacket and turned toward the door. "Come on, let's get some coffee."

The speed with which the courtroom gallery emptied had increased with each week. Already, reporters would be outside calling in their updates. Lawyers who turned up for the summations and the judge's final instructions fled as soon as the last word was out. The groupies knew the routine after these three weeks. Even the sensation junkies raced out. Carla was shocked at how much the trial, her every action, affected people. She would never have guessed.

She walked through the double door that Dennis always held open for her—"to remind viewers that you are a person worthy of caring about"—and to the kiosk. "Just juice, Dennis, I don't think my stomach can handle coffee anymore."

"Hang in there, Elizabeth, we're coasting now."

She didn't bother to correct him. Instead, she took the plastic bottle of orange juice and stood against the wall. Orange juice—that was an unfortunate color. How many years would she be wearing orange? Or do prisoners only wear those ugly-on-everyone jumpsuits in court? Conspiracy for malicious explosion: fifteen to twenty years. She shivered so violently the orange juice shot over the side of the bottle and she just caught the flow with her napkin. In prison, would they call her Carla? Or Elizabeth? Or just seven nine nine oh four eight?

All the regulars had their spots in the gray marble hallway. This corner for defense. In the far corner Jeff Markoff angled his bald head to say something to his assistant, a newbie in the DA's office who must have been a basketball star in college. From the near corner a blond woman in her early forties offered a timid smile. Carla sucked it in as if its hope could fill her. The blonde had been at trial almost every day. Carla felt a bond and wondered if the woman felt it, too. Sometimes out here when the wait went on and on, she made her eyes go blank like she had learned to do in the subway in New York, and fantasized about the woman's life, a life that could have been hers if only she had said no to the seduction of saving the world. The woman's blond hair fell just at her shoulders with the ease of alignment only a stylist could achieve. She wore a wedding ring, probably had children in college now, maybe one still in the last year of high school. She took notes every day on an unruled pad. Maybe she'd gone back to college herself now that her kids were older. Taking notes for a law class, or a journalism seminar? After court let out each day she could call her friends—she would have friends, old friends, friends she could speak to without monitoring every sentence lest something give her away. Or she could fly to Paris, London, Saigon, using her utterly legitimate passport in her real name. If Carla had ever imagined the last twenty-four years, she would never have guessed how important a name was, how much she would miss her own, how she would loathe hearing "Elizabeth Amanda Creiss." She swallowed, and tried to smile back at the blond woman.

The defendant was looking at her! Laura Powley felt a tingle right down her spine. But she wouldn't write that, not "tingle," too trite. She was trying to be a writer; she needed to be able to come up with a more original word to describe emotion. Rush? Shiver? Quiver, maybe? No. Still trite. Besides, *her* reaction didn't matter. What was important—key?— was to "get" Elizabeth Amanda Creiss now, because everything would be over so soon. She was a mere observer, not one who had joined the club of the brave, not like Elizabeth Creiss who had risked all because she believed in something so much. Her essay assignment merely allowed her to peek in the door.

Look at Elizabeth Creiss leaning against the dark wood panel, shoulders so straight she could be holding up the wall rather than vice versa—nice. Keep that. She wasn't afraid to let gray muddy her brown hair, didn't waste time on expensive cuts. Laura knew that her dark blue sweater, plaid wool skirt, and flesh-color stockings must have been chosen to give the appearance of wholesomeness. Bet she'd tear them off the minute she could. She was so strong on the stand, never made excuses for herself, but never let that slime of a DA twist her words either. It was her testimony that set the groundwork for her pound dog of a lawyer insisting that to even be called "circumstantial" the DA's accusations had to have some relation to evidence. Look at her! Never once did she have family or friends to support her here; she stood tall on her own. Laura Powley tried to sip her orange juice, but she was too anxious, too excited. She just wished she could tell her how impressed she was.

The jury could be walking back to the court right now. It could end any minute. But Elizabeth Creiss wasn't nervous; she was so cool. Look at her!

In the far corner Carla noted the older couple. They made no eye contact, not with her or anyone else. Some days they didn't even speak to each other. There was a bench in the middle of the lobby, but they never used it, as if that would be an admission that they were part of the whole soap opera. Once, a week or so ago, Carla had caught the woman's eye; the woman had jerked her head away before there was time for reaction. But there had been plenty of time after for Carla to wonder about them, if they were like her mother. How would it have been to telephone them whenever she wanted, to tell them what she was doing, where she was? Tell them she missed them so much she ached from the hollowness of it? They had winced with her when Dennis failed to remember her name, or maybe she just wanted to believe that.

That first night after the explosion, she got off the bus somewhere in Nevada by a thirty-dollar-a-room motel. She had been desperate to call home, just to tell them she was okay, alive, that it was all an awful mistake. But she didn't dare, not then. She had thought she was just postponing the call, that she'd find a safe time. She hadn't known the chance wouldn't come for twenty-four years, that by then not only would she have created identities, one after another, but her mother had created one for her—the girl who had lied, abandoned her family and disgraced them. The girl who didn't care.

"Elizabeth, do you want to walk outside in the courtyard? The bailiff will call us."

She jerked back to the gray marble hallway. "That's okay, Dennis. For now. How long do you think the jury will be out?"

"The longer the better. If they're going against you, they've already decided. The vote will be a formality."

Icy cold shot down her spine. She stared at the juice, the orange. Years in prison. The rest of her life, till she was old, way older than the old couple, till no one at all remembered her real name. She had never, not once, allowed that thought in, but now it was smothering her. "How long, if they go . . . against me?"

"An hour, three hours. Like I say, it could go very fast. You should take that walk."

"Then—" Her voice was a squeak. She had to swallow and start again. "Then you think it will go bad?"

"I'm not saying that. Just that a walk outside in the air, under the blue sky, would be a good idea."

A walk in a walled enclosure was worse than standing here. She wanted to run into the jury room and beg them to understand that she not was a conspirator. The guys who planned the explosion didn't want her advice, didn't tell her their plans; most of them didn't even know her name.

After an hour she did go out, sat on the steps, looked up at the sky she might never see any other way. The courtyard reminded her not of the outdoors but of the motel rooms where she huddled time after time creating new identities, forcing herself to give up the things that could reveal her as her. Her streaked blond hair, her violet toenails, the silver snake bracelet the boy who could have become her boyfriend had just given her. She had watched her swimmer's muscles go to flab as she avoided even motel pools. At the sight of a bookstore she had crossed the street to avoid the temptation of lingering in front of the window. Those abandonments were painful, but manageable. They were the top layer. She had ripped off the next layer like a bandage off too-raw skin: good coffee, marzipan, steak very rare. And the next: the way she automatically stood when waiting, arms crossed over her chest, her quick retorts that brought a laugh; that was the hardest, to never ever say anything that made her other than bland. To become next to nothing.

Each time she plunked down her duffle and watched the town she had called home for a year or for three months shrink to nothing outside a bus window, she had mourned her attachment to her life there. Each time she had sworn that her next identity would steer clear of the telltale link to Carla Dreseldorf that forced her to abandon this town and her few acquaintances who passed as friends.

The marble courtyard reminded her of the county record rooms and libraries she visited one after another, till she found the name of the dead baby who would have been about her age, born in the United States, died in another country. Elizabeth Amanda Creiss had allowed her to get a birth certificate, a driver's license, a passport she hadn't been quick enough to use. The legitimate name had made her a person again. A Frankenstein of herself. Still she had never dreamed she would come to hate it.

"The jury, they're coming back."

"Omigod, Dennis. Is it too soon?"

"It's okay. It'll all be over in a minute. Come on."

Carla Dreseldorf walked stiff-legged up the steps. In the lobby she saw the blond woman start toward her, stop and just give her a thumbs-up, but she was too scared to respond. The old couple stepped back as she passed. It was them she felt the bond to, they who walked as tensely, stiffly as she. She passed through the bar. Dennis had to tell her twice to sit, and then pull her arm when the bailiff said, "All rise."

The judge spoke but his words didn't penetrate her ears. The foreman spoke. She swallowed hard, forced herself to hear her future.

"Ladies and gentlemen of the jury, have you reached a decision?"

"We have, Your Honor. We find the defendant not guilty on charge number one, not guilty on charge number two, not guilty on charge number three."

Carla slumped into her chair, hearing nothing but her heart pounding. Dennis' arms were around her. "Free! Free! We won! You're free! Let's go celebrate! Let's have the most expensive meal two people have ever eaten. Come on, don't you want to get out of here?"

She let him pull her up and guide her through the bar, down the aisle toward the double doors. Free! To go anywhere, to call anyone, to answer the phone without fear, open the door without peering through the peephole. Free to say, "Hello, I'm Carla Dreseldorf." Free to call Mom, to go to Mom's house, make her listen to the real story. Free to ask, to demand why she hadn't come to the trial, hadn't done as much as the blond woman, the old couple, these strangers who supported her by their presence. She pushed through the double doors and walked across the lobby. "Free to—"

Dennis opened the courthouse door.

She stood there, letting the sunlight coat her body, looking out past the reporters at the tiny green leaves of the live oaks, the deep green pine needles, the pale, soft green grass. The gray buildings sparkled silver; cars danced in jelly bean colors. A sweet breeze rippled her collar. Gray gulls rode the winds.

On the landing below, the blond woman threw her arms up in victory. "Oh, Elizabeth, you were so smart, so brave! I'll always be so impressed by you, Elizabeth Amanda Creiss!"

"Don't call me that *name*!"

"Don't call *her* that name!"

The shot knocked Carla onto the marble steps. Her chest burned; she was freezing. Blood was over everything, her blood. "Why?" she whispered. "Why?"

The old couple was standing over her. The gun hung from the woman's hand. As the bailiff reached in, the woman bent closer. "My baby died. We had nothing left of her, nothing but her name, Elizabeth Amanda Creiss. Every time we hear her name on the news, see her name in the papers under your picture, it tears us up. All we had left was her name. And you made a travesty of it."

Frighted Out of Fear; or, The Bombs Bursting in Air

by P. M. Carlson

The problem with diamonds is that when a young lady sells one, she receives a lovely large amount of money, and in 1886 Chicago was filled to the brim with fashionable bonnets and delicious cakes and expensive Parisian scents—in short, as Shakespeare says, it was a surfeit of the sweetest things. So I knew that the money would have disappeared quick as a wink.

I had just come from St. Louis, where my darling little niece Juliet, not yet four years old, lived with my friend Hattie in a home that was pleasant but with a roof that was beginning to leak. As there were only five diamonds remaining of the ones Juliet's father had left, I had resolved to keep them for her future use. For safekeeping I'd had them set into a cheap theatrical bracelet, interspersed with flashy paste jewels, to disguise their value. Oh, I know, rich people prefer to keep their valuables in bank vaults. But an actress on tour never knows when money might be needed, and if the diamonds are far away in a vault they aren't much help. Besides, when men like Jay Gould decide it's time for their banks to fail, everything disappears except for Mr. Gould's share. The bracelet had proved much more convenient for me.

Not that I planned to use it, except of course as part of my costume. It was boom times in Chicago. Just a few steps north of the train station I saw the brand-new Home Insurance Building and lordy, it must have been nine or ten stories high! The April breezes were alive with the smells of the lake, the smokestacks, the bakeries, the stockyards, but to me it seemed the scent of money. I reckoned I'd soon be joining the ranks of the rich folk like Marshall Field and George Pullman.

There were a great number of shows playing, and in the normal way of things a few cast members would have succumbed to sciatica or a catarrh by now. But unfortunately, actors in Chicago all enjoyed superb good health that week. Even when I showed managers the Kansas City clipping calling me "Bridget Mooney, the Bernhardt of Missouri," one after another informed me that replacements were not required.

Well, hang it, what's a poor girl to do, when even her fellow actors conspire against her? To avoid having to pry one of Juliet's diamonds from my bracelet, I was reduced to performing my comic impersonation of Lillie Langtry in a variety show at Kohl and Middleton's Dime Museum, the one on Clark near Madison. That week the program also included a local pair of jugglers called the Flaming Flanagans and a troupe of ten trained Saint Bernard dogs. "Thoroughbred canine heroes!" said the advertisements. Shakespeare must have been thinking of a manager when he wrote, "He has not so much brain as earwax," because the dogs received top billing, even though I was appearing in an olive green figured sateen dress with handsomely draped bustle that had once belonged to the rich and beautiful Lillie Langtry herself.

The giant dogs were amiable but slavered copiously. As we were preparing for the first show that afternoon, one of them drooled into the Flanagans' box of juggling balls backstage. Johanna—the female Flanagan—fetched the huge dog such a whack that he turned tail and ran for his trainer. Her eyes blazing bright as the torches that she and her brother juggled at the finale of their act, Johanna advanced on dog and trainer. The trainer babbled confused apologies and Johanna quickly relented. "Oh, the dear puppy, I didn't hurt him, did I?" She petted the animal's massive skull, and I decided she had a warm heart after all.

My judgment was confirmed after the show, when she learned I was looking for lodging and promptly offered me a cheap bed. I was quick to accept, and Johanna looked pleased. "Good! You can share my room in my mother's house," she said. "Mutti charges less than a boardinghouse, and you won't have to pay till we get our money."

As Kohl and Middleton paid very little, and not until the end of the week, this was welcome news to me. "Johanna, you are so very kind! Will there be space for my costumes?" I gestured at the trunk I'd had brought from the station.

"Yes, at the foot of your bed."

"But did you say 'Mutti'? Are you German, then?" I asked. It was true that Johanna was blond and tall in stature, and looked more German than Hibernian despite being a Flanagan.

"I'm half German," she explained. "Da is Irish, but we haven't seen him these fifteen years. And when my brother Peter and I went on the stage with our blazing torches, we thought 'The Flaming Flanagans' was a good name." She finished removing the rouge from her cheeks, closed her box of paints, and said, "Let's go, then. Peter's off to the beer hall with his friend Archie tonight, and—oh!" She looked apologetic. "I forgot to say, I promised to call on my friend Mabel on our way home. Do you mind? Just for a short chat. You must come too, she's ever so nice, and good at finding bargains, and we won't be long."

"I would be honored to meet your friend."

"Oh, good! Here, let me help you get your trunk down the steps."

We pulled it out the stage door into the balmy April night. I hailed a porter, a hollow-eyed fellow in a yellow checked cap who gave his name as Peebles and clumsily bumped my arm as he lifted my trunk into his barrow. Then I hurried up Clark Street toward Johanna, who had strolled ahead a few steps toward the crowds spilling from the Grand Opera House. Suddenly a strong hand seized my arm. "Stop in the name of the law! Your kind aren't permitted here!"

I turned to see a man with a mustache and a derby hat. Despite his ordinary clothes he was wielding the weighted cane used by police detectives, so I said most politely, "Why, sir, I have done nothing wrong! I am but a visitor to your city."

He seemed taken aback by my excellent speech, as well he might be. My tutor had been the great actress Fanny Kemble. But he blustered on, "You're new in town, that I believe, if you think you've done nothing wrong! Red hair, clothes beyond your means—you're a tart!"

Lordy, was there ever such an insult? True, my hair is red, and I was still wearing the dress that had been the notorious Lillie's, but those are not good reasons to arrest a perfectly innocent young lady who only rarely is forced to resort to the line of work he mentioned!

Johanna had finally looked back and now came striding up, nearly as tall as my captor. But her voice was girlish as she simpered, "Why, Detective Loewenstein, what a coincidence! I was just taking my friend to meet your wife! Bridget, let me introduce Detective Jacob Loewenstein, my dear friend Mabel's husband, and one of the finest policemen in Chicago. Detective Loewenstein, this is Miss Bridget Mooney."

Hang it, he didn't seem such a fine policeman to me! But he had finally released me, and it appeared that I was about to call on his wife, so I followed Johanna's lead and said loftily, "I'm delighted to meet you, Detective Loewenstein. It is indeed reassuring to know that you are protecting the citizens of Chicago with such zeal."

"Yes, er, happy to meet you too." He gave me a little bow, looking a bit flustered.

"And how is your friend Officer Degan?" Johanna asked him.

Loewenstein answered, "I believe he is well, Miss Flanagan. As auxiliaries to Captain Bonfield, his unit is very busy these days."

"As you must be, I'm sure! Let's be on our way, Bridget," Johanna said, sliding her arm into mine. "Mrs. Loewenstein will be waiting for us."

I looked to make certain that Peebles the porter was following and we joined the jostling throngs before the brightly lit opera house and courthouse. We crossed a drawbridge and continued on Wells Street. The crowds thinned as Johanna led me north to a handsome three-story corner building, adorned with a tower at the entrance. I instructed Peebles to wait and we ascended a well-kept staircase to the third floor, where the Loewensteins had their rooms.

Of the two Loewensteins, I much preferred Mabel. She was short in stature with dark hair and lively eyes, and her stylish dress was of lilac-colored foulard with flounces of ecru lace. "Johanna, it's good of you to come! We haven't had a good gossip for quite a while! And you've brought a friend, what a pleasure!"

Johanna made the introductions and Mabel sent her nephew to purchase some cakes for us while she went into the next room for tea. The sitting room was well-appointed with Turkey carpets, lace at the windows, soft upholstered chairs, and a handsome parlor stove. I murmured to Johanna, "The city of Chicago appears to pay Detective Loewenstein well for his efforts."

"A thousand dollars a year!" whispered Johanna, eyes round at the prospect.

As Mabel returned with the tray, she said, "Miss Mooney, that is such a lovely sateen!" She cast an admiring glance at me and my Langtry dress. I murmured my thanks and she added, "If you ever wish to sell it, I have a friend who loves that shade of green. Tell me, are you Irish too? I was a Keenan before I married Jake."

"Yes, I'm Irish. And your husband is German?"

"He speaks it, and that's very helpful these days with all the unrest. Do you know how many German immigrants are in Chicago? Four hundred thousand! Poor Jake has a great deal to do." I could see the tenseness around her eyes. "Besides the usual problems with gambling and unsavory women, he says those dreadful German anarchists are trying to take over the labor organizations, and turn the workers against all the decent people."

"Oh, he should know better than that," Johanna said. "The German workers Mutti knows are decent people too. Of course when Pinkerton men shoot striking workers some of them talk about defending themselves. But it's all talk."

Mabel frowned. "Still, I worry about Jakey. He's given some special assignments, because he's a favorite of Captain Schaack."

"What kind of assignments?"

"He won't say, but— Come look," said Mabel abruptly, taking something from under the leg of the stove. We followed her into a velvet-draped bedroom. She pulled a box from under the bed and unlocked it. "You mustn't tell because he doesn't think I know where the key is. But can that be what it seems?"

In the box, sitting among gloves and watches on layers of lace and velvet, was a round iron object. Emerging from one side was a thick cord perhaps five inches long. Johanna peered at it and gasped, "Oh, Mabel, how thrilling! It looks just like the pictures in the *Tribune,* when they wrote about how the anarchists make bombs!"

Mabel shuddered. "It's horrid! I've hardly slept since I saw it there."

"But how splendid that Jake has found an anarchist! He'll be a great hero," Johanna declared.

"You look on the bright side." Mabel locked the box and slid it back under the bed. "Johanna, you'll be an excellent policeman's wife."

Johanna blushed pink as a rosebud. "Oh, Mabel, don't tease!"

Mabel smiled at me, explaining, "Officer Degan is sweet on Johanna. I expect wedding bells any day."

"What good news, Johanna!" I exclaimed in my most sincere tones, although I have never been enthusiastic about marriage to anyone, not even for a thousand a year. "This Officer Degan must be a good man."

"Oh, yes, Matt is a dear fellow!" Johanna said earnestly. "And he has promised to escort me to the park Monday, when we both have free time."

Mabel clapped her hands. "Oh, Johanna! This puts me in mind of the days when Jakey was courting me! Such a happy time!"

Well, I couldn't imagine being pleased by the attentions of a fellow like Detective Loewenstein, who hid bombs under his bed and tried to arrest perfectly innocent young ladies. But in the past I too have had moments of being blinded to the truth by a manly shoulder or a twinkling eye, and Mabel was right, it was a happy time. So for a few moments we all three praised the qualities of Johanna's Matt and Mabel's Jakey and my dear departed Slick, and wondered if Matt would be asking for Johanna's hand Monday.

After this pleasant half hour, Johanna and I awakened Peebles the porter and continued to Johanna's more modest home. "Mutti" was tall and of sturdy physique like her daughter, and she seemed pleased to have a paying visitor. The little bed in Johanna's room was narrow but clean and warmed with a featherbed, and I would have had no complaints except for one thing. I had quietly checked the contents of the pocket I'd sewn into my bustle, because a couple of handsome gentlemen's hunting watches had found their way into it as we jostled through the throngs of opera patrons this evening. But as I removed my Langtry dress I gasped.

"What is it, Bridget?" Johanna, already in her white nightdress, was brushing out her long blond hair.

I took a deep breath, as I confirmed that nothing had caught in the lacy sleeve of the dress. "A trifle. Part of my Langtry costume is missing."

"Oh, dear!" Johanna turned from the little mirror over her table and looked at me with consternation. "What is it?"

"A trifle," I repeated, keeping the despair from my voice. After all, Johanna was possibly guiltless—though I remembered her slipping her arm through mine as we walked toward the Grand Opera. "I suppose the clasp broke and I dropped it along the way. Just a bracelet with a dozen paste jewels."

Well—seven paste jewels. The other five had been my little niece's future.

Next morning, as soon as Johanna left our chamber to assist her mother, I did a thorough but fruitless search of her vanity table and clothing—although I couldn't truly believe that Johanna had it. For all her skill as a juggler, she didn't seem clever enough to remove a bracelet from under the sleeve of a young lady as alert and knowledgeable as I. I donned a simple walking dress and went in to a hearty breakfast. Afterward I thanked her mother, told Johanna I would see her at the theatre, and set off to retrace my steps.

I did not have high hopes of finding my bracelet. Johanna had not been the only one who had been near me the night before. The porter, Peebles, had bumped my arm as he lifted my trunk into his barrow and numerous people had brushed by on the crowded streets. As I walked I tried to remember the details of our journey the night before. Here was a corner where I'd paused to look back at Peebles and my trunk; here Johanna had met a German relative of her mother's on the street; here was Mabel Loewenstein's home. I paused; could I have dropped it on that Turkey carpet? It was too early to call on her, but later I would.

I continued down the street and across the drawbridge. If the hasp had broken there the bracelet might have fallen through the steel grid into the busy Chicago River below, which teemed with scows and shouting rivermen. But when I reached Clark Street and remembered the jostling throngs outside the Grand Opera, I had to admit that even a young lady as clever as I might have missed a master pickpocket if distracted, and hang it, I had been distracted. I'd been conversing with Johanna, and watching for gentlemen with hunting watches, and making certain that Peebles, in his yellow checked cap, was following with my trunk.

Peebles, who had nudged my arm. He could so easily have taken my bracelet.

It was time to hunt for Peebles.

It was not easy.

Though I watched for him every day, Peebles did not appear near the theatre where I had first found him, nor around the train stations. Johanna was no help, being all atwitter about her upcoming Monday walk in the park with the peerless Officer Degan. Toward the end of the week Kohl and Middleton asked us all, even the slobbering hero dogs, to play for a week at their second theatre, a mile west on Madison, and Sunday was spent moving and rehearsing in the new space.

On Monday I wished Johanna a happy day with Officer Degan and returned to question the porters at the railroad station. At last I found a spiky-haired fellow who knew Peebles. "He's not really one of us, mum, he's a machinist. Worked for McCormick Reaper, see, but got locked out back in February along with the other union men," he explained. "To put bread on the table he works as a porter when he can get the use of a barrow."

"Do you know where he lives?"

My informant shrugged. "Moves from one relative to another. If you want to find him, try looking at the McCormick works."

"But you said he'd been locked out."

"A lot of the union men picket outside the gates and holler at the scabs."

When he'd given me directions to McCormick's, out Blue Island Avenue, I rewarded the unkempt fellow with a few pennies, then took the streetcar, as the McCormick works were some three miles from the city center.

I did not ride the full distance, because when we reached Twenty-second Street I saw a large crowd of workers, Peebles perhaps among them. The workers were gathered around a boxcar, and atop it stood a man perhaps thirty years old, with a handsome light brown mustache and a gaze that might have inspired Shakespeare to cry, "Look on me with your welkin eye!" He was speaking in German when I first approached, and about half of the large crowd was nodding, but he soon shifted to pleasantly accented English. As I wandered through the crowd searching for Peebles, I couldn't help but hear some of what the handsome gentleman was saying. "Wherever we cast our eyes," he declared with a sweeping gesture, "we see that a few men have not only brought technical inventions into their private ownership, but have also confiscated for their exclusive advantage all natural powers, such as water, steam and electricity. They little care that they destroy their fellow beings right and left." The blue eyes blazed and indignation radiated from his honest face.

"Who is the speaker?" I murmured to a grizzled man who was nodding enthusiastically.

He looked at me with pity. "You don't know? He is the editor of the best German newspaper, the *Arbeiter-Zeitung,* and one of our most popular speakers. His name is August Shpeece." Later I learned that, in the peculiar way the Germans have, it was spelled Spies, but I always thought of him as August.

"We must progress to cooperative labor for the purpose of continuing life and of enjoying it," August told us. "Anarchy does not mean bloodshed, does not mean arson or robbery. These monstrosities are, on the contrary, the characteristic features of capitalism."

Well, having recently been robbed, I certainly agreed that it was a monstrosity, and I was ready to do away with whatever had caused it, though I wasn't certain what this dreadful thing "capitalism" was. And August had mentioned anarchy favorably—but surely he couldn't be one of the horrid anarchists that the newspapers told us we must fear! I couldn't believe it of such a kindly, well-spoken man.

"Do not be slaves! Your toil produces the wealth, it is yours, not the bosses'!" August cried. "Workers must stand firmly together, then we will prevail!"

Oh, they were splendid words, as stirring as Shakespeare's "Once more unto the breach"! I was on the verge of running up to Kohl and Middleton and pummeling them for higher wages! But on reflection I wasn't certain that the other workers would stand firmly with me, as August advised. Johanna might, and perhaps her brother if he wasn't at the beer hall. But those giant hero dogs were more likely to rescue the managers than attack them. I decided I'd best wait for better troops.

There was no sign of Peebles, and I could see another clump of men farther along Blue Island Avenue near the McCormick works. So I left August and his enormous crowd behind me, and moved on toward the pickets outside McCormick's. Suddenly a loud bell clanged. A man called, "Here they come!" and as workers began to emerge from the door the men who'd been locked out began to holler "Scabs!" and "Shame!" and some German words that sounded even worse. I thought I saw a yellow checked cap on the far side of the little crowd and started toward it eagerly. But a few among the picketers picked up stones and threw them at the strikebreakers, and suddenly there was a melee. One of the two policemen on duty fought his way to a patrol box to call for help.

Well, my aunt Mollie always said that a lady should never get involved in anything as low-class as a riot, so notwithstanding August's inspiring words I ducked around the corner of a building, and a lucky thing I did! When I peeked I saw a patrol wagon full of policemen, drawn by two galloping horses, careening up Blue Island Avenue and straight into the crowd. "It's Black Jack Bonfield!" cried a picket, and a few stones were thrown at the police. The officers laid about with their nightsticks and bloodied many heads, and soon were joined by dozens of officers on foot. The strikebreakers had run back into the building but a few picketers continued to throw stones. Although the police had the upper hand, whenever I glimpsed a face under a helmet it looked frightened. Captain Bonfield, a squinty-eyed fellow, yelled something I couldn't hear above the shouting, and the officers pulled their revolvers.

Well, in my experience revolvers make a situation a sight more dangerous than stones and nightsticks. I dove back to safety and pulled my Colt from my bustle pocket. I heard gunshots and screams and in a moment the pickets were dragging their wounded friends away, some to the haven where I stood. The groans of the bleeding men were piteous indeed.

At last the gunshots stopped, and I peeked again, but could not see Peebles. I heard a familiar voice and saw August come running toward the factory, looking as shocked and sickened as I felt.

The picketers had scattered, and the police arrested the stragglers while shouting congratulations to each other for winning such a glorious victory. Yes indeed.

When they'd left I put away my Colt and tore strips from my petticoat to hand to those who had crept out to help the wounded. Peebles was not among them. My chance to find him was gone, and even the handsome blue-eyed August had left. Frustrated, I kicked a stone into the street and made my way back to Kohl and Middleton's.

At the theatre I found Johanna too in a dark mood. She wore a terrible scowl, and was distracted and clumsier than usual, dropping a ball once and almost lighting her poor brother's hair on fire with a poorly aimed torch. Afterward he drew me aside. "Please, Bridget, walk home with her! The only thing she said to me was, 'You men are beasts!' "

Well, I had to agree with her opinion of men after seeing all the pelting and shooting at McCormick's. I followed her out the door and murmured, "Johanna, what did that dreadful Officer Degan do?"

"Nothing!" She strode up Halsted Street and I had to trot to keep up.

"Nothing? You mean some other horrid man has hurt you?"

"No! I mean he did nothing! He didn't meet me in the park!" She began to weep.

I offered her a handkerchief, patted her arm, and asked, "Didn't Detective Loewenstein say that Officer Degan worked with Captain Bonfield's men? They were in action today, so perhaps Matt couldn't—"

"But he promised!" Johanna sobbed.

I suggested, "Why don't we go speak to your friend Mabel? She can tell you if Officer Degan had adequate reason for such a terrible breach of courtesy."

Johanna nodded and allowed herself to be guided toward the Loewenstein home. I was pleased, for I too had questions.

"I'm delighted to see you!" Mabel, in a violet jacket dress, hugged us both. "Jakey is so busy these days. I dined alone again tonight—" A shadow darkened her lively features. She looked more closely at Johanna and added, "But Johanna, what is wrong?"

Though red-eyed from weeping, Johanna was listening carefully to Mabel's words. She asked, "You say Jake is busy these days? Abandons you?"

"Sometimes it seems that way! Captain Schaack assigns him to these secret meetings—oh, I shouldn't be telling you this—"

Johanna sank into a plush armchair, sniffled into my handkerchief, and asked, "Do you think Matt Degan was assigned to a secret meeting?"

Mabel looked surprised. "I wouldn't think so. He's not a detective. If he had to stay on duty to help Captain Bonfield, it wouldn't be a secret assignment like Jake's. Matt should have got word to you!"

"He didn't," Johanna sobbed.

"Let me get you some tea," Mabel soothed.

I followed her into the butler's pantry. She frowned back at Johanna and murmured to me, "Poor Johanna! She should not bestow her heart so easily."

"Do you mean Officer Degan is not reliable?"

She shrugged and placed the teapot on the tray. "When I mentioned Johanna's hopes to Jake, he laughed and said Degan had more than one young lady at his beck and call."

"Oh dear, poor Johanna. Mabel, I had another question. I may have dropped a bracelet while I was visiting here." I described it as we carried the tea back to Johanna, who had risen from her chair and was pacing about the parlor.

"I will look very carefully," Mabel promised with a little frown. "Sit down, Johanna, have some tea!"

We finally convinced Johanna that Matt might yet apologize and she stopped sobbing. Mabel maintained that Jake and the others were upset because of the labor unrest, and would be kind and loving once again when the work was not so frightening. "Jakey hates to feel frightened. He much prefers being angry."

I couldn't help thinking of wise old Shakespeare, who said, "To be furious is to be frighted out of fear." Captain Bonfield's order to shoot had helped his men feel fury instead of fear; but laborers were men too, and Bonfield had given them cause to be more frightened than ever, and I wondered if their fear would turn to fury too.

Instead, they called another meeting.

At breakfast Johanna was silent, probably brooding on Matt Degan, but her brother Peter was reading the *Arbeiter-Zeitung* and I asked if it mentioned the shots at the McCormick works. "Oh, yes!" he said. "They write about the injustice of the police firing on un-armed men, and say workers should carry dynamite or revolvers in self-defense. They've called a meeting tonight. Look, it's at the Haymarket, very close to the theatre! Our show will be over in time to hear the last speeches."

"This is strong language," his mother cautioned, pausing teapot in hand to frown over his shoulder at the paper. " 'Avenge the atrocious murder that has been committed upon your brothers today'—Do be careful, Peter."

But like Peter, I wanted to go. Peebles might well be there with answers about my bracelet—and per-haps the handsome, fiery August as well.

It was after nine and dark when Johanna and Peter and I departed from Kohl and Middleton's, leaving the Saint Bernards to finish the evening performance. We walked a block to Desplaines and turned north toward the meeting, where Peter met his ruddy-faced friend Archie, a reporter for the *Chicago Times*. "Look at all the police Captain Bonfield has mus-tered," Archie said.

"Why do they call him Black Jack?" I asked.

"He can be brutal. Like yesterday's shooting," Archie said. "Or last year during the streetcar strike, when he clubbed everyone in reach, even store owners who came out to see what was happening. A gas company worker named Kerwin is still laid up from that beating."

"They ought to replace Bonfield," Peter said.

"The mayor might, but Marshall Field and his rich friends are nervous with this talk of dynamite, and they think Bonfield can frighten the eight-hour supporters. Look, he's lining up reinforcements." Archie gestured at the alley we were passing and made a note.

Johanna said nothing but I saw her crane her neck to look for Matt Degan among the massed officers. I tugged her arm and we moved on up Desplaines.

There was a large crowd ahead, and several men including the welkin-eyed August up on a wagon. The man speaking was nearly as appealing as August, but had coal black hair and mustache. His beautiful English had a hint of a Southern accent. "It's Albert Parsons," Archie told us. "He edits the English-language anarchist paper. That's his wife and children on the next wagon, see them?"

Parsons was saying, "I am not here for the purpose of inciting anybody, but to speak out, to tell the facts as they exist, even though it should cost me my life."

I was beginning to think that the rich folks had it all wrong about the anarchists, who claimed to be filled with the noblest of sentiments: truth-telling, cooperation, and love for family. Parsons mentioned Jay Gould, who owned railroads now instead of banks, and someone shouted, "Hang him!"

"No," Parsons replied, "this is not a conflict against individuals, but for a change of system. Kill Jay Gould, and like a jack-in-a-box another or a hundred others like him will come up in his place."

"Hang him!" cried a boy, and the huge crowd laughed.

Archie seemed disappointed and snapped his notebook closed. "Won't sell any papers with that peaceful stuff."

But it was my bracelet that I wanted to find. I excused myself and slipped into the crowd to search for Peebles.

After introducing the next speaker, a bearded British fellow named Fielden, Parsons left the speakers' wagon and joined his family nearby. I continued searching through the crowd. There was a low rumble of thunder in the north, and a gust of wind blew papers about. Parsons called to Fielden, "It's going to rain! Do you want to finish in Zepf's Hall?"

Fielden said, "I'm nearly done. Then we can all go home." Parsons nodded and gathered his children to take them to Zepf's for shelter.

Many people were glancing at the sky and leaving. Fearing that I would miss Peebles, I made my way up the entry steps of a building for a better look. At last, in the glimmer of the streetlight, I saw his yellow checked cap! He was making his way toward Lake Street, not far behind Parsons' family. I started after. It seemed now that there was a faint thunder in the south as well, but I didn't take my eyes from him until I heard a loud voice call out, "Disperse!" and Peebles stopped to look back.

I looked too, and hang it, I'd never seen so many policemen! The street was inky with them, rank on rank, filling Desplaines Street from the speakers' wagon back toward the police station. At the head of the wall of police was Captain Bonfield, facing Fielden on the speakers' wagon. Fielden said, "But we are peaceable!"

"Disperse!" insisted Bonfield's spokesman.

Fielden didn't argue. He said, "All right, we will go," and jumped down from the wagon. The others shrugged and began climbing down, even August. I was about to turn back to Peebles when I saw a bright spark like a shooting star sizzle through the air from the east edge of the street into the center of the police ranks.

And then, lordy! A fearsome thunderclap. A flash as bright as noon. A blast of wind that blew me against the wall. Around me windows cracked.

For just an instant, silence quivered in the air. I looked for Peebles and he was standing there bedazzled, like the rest of us.

Then a woman shrieked, and a man groaned a spine-chilling groan, and others began screaming and swearing, and the terrified police began to fire, round after round after round.

I lit out of there quicker than a rabbit.

Oh, I know, I know, a proper lady would have stood there weeping prettily until rescued by a noble officer of the law. But hang it, I didn't much like loud blasts, and I didn't like wild shooting by frightened men, and frankly I hadn't found Chicago policemen to be all that noble. Besides, Peebles was hightailing it away, so I followed.

The riot bell from the police station began to clang. As I chased Peebles past Zepf's saloon I heard August call to someone, "It was a cannon, wasn't it?"

Well, I'm just a poor girl from Missouri, but my brother fought for the Union and he described a bomb to me, a bright flash and a thunderclap, and I wondered if these anarchists of noble sentiment knew what their audiences might do.

The firing stopped. It had lasted only three or four minutes. Around a corner I finally reached Peebles and put my hand on his arm. "Mr. Peebles, do you remember me?"

"What?" His sunken eyes rolled with terror.

"Last week you carried my trunk in your barrow."

"What?"

The fellow was so stunned and terrified he could hardly think. I finally caught his attention by tapping his nose with a coin. "Peebles! We're safe, the police have stopped shooting! Get hold of yourself and think. You carried my trunk from Madison and Clark up Wells Street." I waved the coin. "If you can answer my questions there may be something for you."

"Yes'm." There was still a little hitch in his voice but he seemed to be listening now.

"On that night, someone took my bracelet. Was it you?"

"No'm, of course not!"

"The truth, Peebles! What did you do with it?"

"I never took it, don't lay it on me! You gave it away!"

"*I* gave it away?"

"Yes'm, when that detective stopped you. Ladies allus give that detective something before he lets 'em go. Most times it's money, but you already told me you didn't have much, and I saw him looking at the bracelet and putting it in his pocket afterwards. So it warn't me took it!"

I remembered the locked box Mabel had shown us, the lace gloves and brooches—all extorted? Was my bracelet there now? Was the bomb? I asked Peebles, "Why didn't you tell me?"

"I thought you gave it to 'im! All the ladies do!"

I sighed. "Well, here's something for telling me at last," and gave him the coin.

I went back to Desplaines. No one was in the street now, but a block away I could see policemen helping wounded officers up the steps of the police station. I didn't see Johanna or Peter, so I decided to go to the Flanagans' home. As I turned back, the glimmer of the streetlight showed me a telegraph pole peppered with bullet holes. All of them were on the side that faced the police. I shivered, for I had passed that pole just moments before the frantic shooting.

On my way back, there were several drugstores filled with wounded people buying medicines. In the third I saw Johanna and hurried in to greet her. She was shaky and weeping and had a gash on her back, not very deep. I helped her get a sticking plaster onto it, and arrange her torn dress, then led her home.

"You're bleeding! What happened?" demanded her mother, and when we explained she asked, "Where's Peter?" But we didn't know. I left the two of them to wait up for him and went to sit on my bed and have a good think.

I wanted to get out of Chicago. In the week I'd been here I'd seen too much shooting, too much bleeding, and much too much bombing. But first I had to get my bracelet back from Detective Loewenstein. How? After what I'd just seen I didn't want to cross a policeman anytime soon. I decided to lie low until things calmed down again, then check with Mabel to see if she could help me.

Things didn't calm down. They got worse. Lordy, I've never seen anything like it!

Policemen had never before died and been wounded in such numbers. Maybe they'd never before been ordered to shoot when in such close formation. But of course they wouldn't admit they'd shot each other. They blamed it all on the foreign anarchists, and worked Chicago into a frenzy of fear. I was glad my hosts were named Flanagan, because everyone turned on the Germans. Marshall Field's favorite paper, the *Tribune,* suggested restricting immigration to keep out "foreign savages," and even Archie's paper, the *Chicago Times,* said the bombers were not Americans; they were "cutthroats of Beelzebub from the Rhine, the Danube, the Vistula and the Elbe." The Knights of Labor ran for cover, saying they hoped the anarchists "would be blotted from the surface of the earth." The whole nation agreed. A New York reporter said the mob "poured volley after volley into the midst of the officers." I reckon he hadn't seen the telegraph pole that proved the volleys came from the police, maybe because he lived in New York, maybe because the telegraph pole disappeared the next day. Jakey's superior,

Captain Schaack, explained that the telegraph company had removed it in the common course of business. Yes indeed.

The courts backed up the police, of course. The state attorney told the police, "Make the raids first and look up the law afterward." They did. Hundreds of people were arrested. Fielden, the speaker who had obeyed the captain's order and agreed to leave, was one.

Handsome August was another.

The mayor consulted with Marshall Field and other notable citizens and made a proclamation to forbid crowds from gathering in public places, but of course they could gather to spend money in big stores like Mr. Field's, and luckily in theatres too, because we had other problems. Poor Johanna's sore shoulder prevented her from performing, and when we learned that Officer Degan had been killed by the bomb she sank into a fever and could barely move. I learned a few juggling tricks from Peter so that I could pretend to be a Flaming Flanagan, though I balked at the blazing torches. I was glad for the extra few dollars, for I would soon have enough for a ticket to New York.

But hang it, I needed my bracelet.

As the week drew to a close, I risked calling on Mabel. I embraced her and she winced, but said, "Bridget! How good to see you!"

"Dearest Mabel, I have a favor to ask."

"Of course! It's so lonely these days—Jakey is very busy and out of sorts, trying to find that anarchist Lingg, and he has all these secret projects."

"Yes, I don't want to bother your husband, that's why I came to you. It's about the box you showed us, under the bed."

"No! Please!" Mabel fell into a chair and burst into tears. "Don't even mention that horrid box!"

"Oh, my—what happened?" I pulled a slipper chair to face her and dabbed at her wet cheeks with my handkerchief. When I brushed her arm she flinched.

"I don't know what happened!" she sobbed. "Jakey looked in the box, and the bomb was gone. I don't know where! But he shouted I was only to sell what he gave me, and became furious!"

Gently, I turned back the lace of her sleeve, where a yellowing bruise marred her pale skin. No wonder she'd been wincing. I said, "He struck you!"

"No, no, he loves me, I know he does!" She gave me a brave smile.

I touched the scar on my cheek. "Slick loved me too, yes indeed."

Her eyes locked onto mine. "And you left him?"

"Yes. A little afterwards he was shot. I don't like to think about it. But tell me, did you look in the box to see why Jake was angry?"

"No, I mustn't. It's his." She sniffled and added, "Besides, he's started hiding the key somewhere else, I don't know where."

Well, hang it, my chance to regain my bracelet had slipped away for now. When payday came, I took the train to New York, and had better luck, eventually joining a national tour with dear Mr. Booth.

Of course I read the news from Chicago wherever my tour took me. Jakey became a hero when he helped capture Lingg, who was put on trial with seven other anarchists, including dear August. The charge was the murder of Officer Degan, the only one killed by the bomb instead of bullets. The police hadn't caught the bomb-thrower but said the eight had conspired to cause someone else to throw a bomb. They even got one witness to claim he'd seen August light the fuse, though he'd been half a block away on the speaker's wagon. Clearly the police wanted to be the heroes of this melodrama and they'd cast poor August as a villain. Everyone knows villains must be punished, whether the plot makes any sense or not. I wasn't surprised when the jury decided to hang them.

There were appeals, and three of the eight ended

up with prison terms instead of a death sentence, but in November of 1887 dear August was hanged. I have to admit I shed a tear.

The next time I saw Mabel was the autumn of 1888. I'd just returned from a horrid stay in London, and was on my way to St. Louis to see my dear little niece, but I didn't want to arrive empty-handed, so again, I stopped in Chicago. I found a temporary role at the Columbia Theatre because one of the young ladies in *The Bells of Haslemere* had turned her ankle.

I knew there was little hope of recovering my bracelet but for Juliet's sake I was obliged to try. It was evening, after the show, when I called on Mabel Loewenstein.

The boy who'd brought us cakes before took up my card, and in an instant Mabel herself, in mourning, appeared on the steps to welcome me upstairs. "Mabel, what is it?" I asked, concerned by her distraught appearance.

"Oh, Bridget, you are just the one to tell me what to do! Please come in!"

I followed her into the parlor. It was as richly appointed as before, with a few additions in the form of new lamps and paintings.

As she prepared tea she explained, "Ever since he helped capture that anarchist Lingg, Jakey has been praised by all. Captain Schaack continues to favor him—seems almost afraid of him! I think both of them are—well, not entirely honest."

"What makes you think—oh! Did you find the key to the box?"

"Keys," she corrected me. Tears glistened on her lashes as she handed me a cup. "Now there are three boxes. And one of them holds your bracelet."

"Oh, thank you, Mabel! It's just a trifle but I'm fond of it. How can I ever—"

"No, wait! I can't return your bracelet! He'd know

that I'd been nosing about, and he'd—" The sobs broke out. "I'm so afraid he no longer loves me!"

I asked, "He still strikes you, then?"

"He comes home so late, and so drunk—and he says it is my fault our dear baby did not survive! But how could I protect the little one when I can't—" She dabbed at her eyes.

I said, "Mabel, I'm so sorry. How can I help?"

She reached tentatively toward the little scar on my cheek. "You said you left him. Please, tell me how!"

Well, hang it, there was a poser! It's easier to up and leave a fellow when you're a traveling artiste, and have friends around the nation. But Mabel seemed so settled here. I asked, "Do you have family in other cities?"

"No, my sister and brother are here. Oh, I don't want to leave town!"

I waited for a fresh spasm of sobs to subside, and finally said, "I see a way you can leave Jake yet stay in Chicago, but first I must ask if you can bear a bit of scandal."

"Oh, must I? That Captain Schaack already says I'm disreputable. Liar!"

"I promise you, in the end it will fall on Jake and not on you."

"He would hate that!" she said with a damp smile.

"The first thing to do is count up our strengths. We must look in the boxes." I raised a palm to quiet her fearful protest. "Will Jakey be back soon?"

"No, he'll be late and drunk, but he'll know!"

"We can replace everything just as before." She still hesitated and I added, "Do you want to be safe?"

"Yes. No, I want him to love me!"

"But does he?" When her face fell, I added, "The keys. Hurry!"

With fearful steps, she went to the boot stand in the entry and, picking up a man's polished boot, pulled three keys from the toe. We pulled the boxes from under the tall carved bed, opened them, and there, clumped with other jewelry in a corner of the second box, was my bracelet! My heart danced a happy jig.

The rest was even better than I'd hoped. There were watches. There was a fine silk scarf. There were handsome dresses—"Oh, that's the one stolen from Mrs. Hill!" Mabel said, warming to our task. "The thief was arrested, but Mrs. Hill never got her dress back." There were rings and brooches. "Look, remember the anarchist Lingg left a brooch to his sweetheart, and after he died they couldn't find it? There it is!" Best of all, there were official papers. "Yes, that's the man who testified he saw August Spies light the bomb!"

I frowned at the page. "That's not what he says here."

"This is the man's original testimony. Captain Schaack and Jakey pay people to say what they want them to, so in court this man swore August Spies lit the fuse."

"And then Jake hid the original statements." I flipped through the rest of the papers. No wonder that low-down Schaack was afraid of Jake. And it looked as though Black Jack Bonfield had reason to fear exposure as well. I beamed at Mabel. "Mabel, your future is bright! Bring a little valise or carpetbag."

Looking hopeful, she complied, and protested only a little as I slid the papers, the silk scarf, and Lingg's brooch into the little black valise she brought. My bracelet, of course, was already safe in my bustle pocket. I was closing the valise when the downstairs door slammed and we heard a heavy tread on the stairs.

Mabel gave a terrified squeal. I grabbed her arm. "Hush! You must act as you always do! Don't mention me!" I finished relocking the three boxes and kicked them under the bed.

From a floor below came a muffled, sleepy Scandinavian voice. "Yakey, be quiet, yah?"

Mabel whimpered, "Don't leave me!"

"Don't worry. Just help him to bed, all the usual things." I gave her arm a little shake. "Are you listening?"

"I help him to bed?"

"Yes, good!" I ran into the parlor. Jake's heavy steps sounded very near now, so I dove behind a settee that was angled across a dusky corner of the room. I held my skirts close about me and trusted to the shadows and to Jake's inebriation to protect me.

"Jakey, dear!" Mabel said as the door opened. She was trying, but I could hear the quiver in her voice. "Do you want a beer?"

He tossed his coat onto a peg, his gun peeking from its pocket. "Nah, I'm tired. Move!" And he added an oath that no lady should be forced to hear, although Mabel did not seem surprised. He tugged off his boots and staggered to the bedroom to fall onto his pillow.

When he began snoring Mabel tiptoed to the entry to hang up his jacket and looked around, but didn't see me as she turned down the lamps.

It was not a night for rest. Jake snored, Mabel sobbed, and in my head Aunt Mollie was whispering to me that Mabel was not strong enough; I should take my bracelet and skedaddle and never see Mabel or Jake again. But hang it, I could also hear the piteous groans of the men Bonfield had shot at McCormick's and at Haymarket, and the cries of panic afterward that Bonfield and Schaack and Jake had created and thrived on, and especially the idealistic voice of August of the welkin eye, hanged because the police didn't want to admit they'd shot each other. So I told Aunt Mollie to hush up, crept out to empty Jake's Smith and Wesson, then returned to hide behind the settee and doze off with my Colt in my hand.

I woke to morning light and the sound of an oath from their room. I hurried silently to stand by the hinge side of their closed door. "Where's my watch? Stupid woman!"

"Jakey, it's in your jacket." Mabel, in her wrapper, emerged to fetch his coat from the entry hall. She didn't see me because I was behind the door she'd just opened. Through the gap between the hinges I could see Jakey stumbling to his feet, fumbling in the pocket of the jacket she brought back.

"Pour the water!"

"Yes, Jakey." She poured water into the basin for him and handed him a towel. Apparently seeing him at his ablutions inspired tender feelings, for she added, "Dear Jakey, it's not too late, if you would only love me as you once did."

"Stupid woman!" He elbowed her away to wash his neck.

Just then the boy knocked and called, "Do you want pastries today?"

"Yes, please!" Mabel hurried to the door and gave the lad some coins, then returned to the bedroom and said, "Jakey, do you love another? Tell me!"

"I'm tired of your jealous nonsense, Mabel! Stop it or we'll have to split up!"

She cried, "But I've kept quiet! I've only sold what you told me to! I've been a good wife!"

"Shut up!" He grabbed his Smith and Wesson from his jacket and waved it about.

Well, I was pleased, though Mabel wasn't. "Jakey, no! I'm a good wife!"

Just then I got the perfect angle through the gap between the hinges. Jake was in profile, and I could have hit him square in the temple, but instead, as a favor to Mabel, I aimed a bit forward and took off his left eyebrow.

I know, I know, proper ladies are not good marksmen, but growing up in St. Louis I'd learned to hit a squirrel in the eye from thirty paces, and some days it's hard to give up the old ways. Jake was much nearer and much slower than a squirrel. And how can a poor girl resist when fate provides her with one of

the finest Colts in the nation, once the favored gun of
Jesse James?

Jake bellowed and fired twice, and I shot him in the
hand because if he kept firing he might realize that
someone had emptied his Smith and Wesson. Blood
streamed down his face, blinding him, and his cries
grew weaker. Mabel was still whimpering, "Jakey,
no!" when he fainted and fell on her.

I rushed out and down the stairs, clutching the valise, passing the old Scandinavian neighbor on his way
up. "Help! They need a doctor!" I gasped.

He began to shout, "Doctor, come quick!" while I
ran down the front steps and melted into the morning crowds.

My first stop was at the lawyer Kern's office on
LaSalle Street. When I sent in word that my business
had to do with Lingg's missing brooch, he consented
to see me. He was intrigued by the brooch and the
papers and the keys to three boxes of further evidence. When I explained that Mabel would need a
good defense lawyer because his fellow policemen
would try to claim that she was trying to kill Jakey
instead of the other way around, he agreed to take
her case if she requested his help, and meanwhile he
would deposit the evidence into the vault at Mer-
chant's Bank.

Next I found Mabel's sister and told her that Mabel
was in trouble and would have to move out, and to
be sure to take the three locked boxes under the bed
along with her gowns and clothing, and that a lawyer
named Kern was prepared to defend her for a reasonable fee.

But the police moved fast too. Mabel was in jail
almost as soon as Jakey was in the hospital. Captain
Schaack wouldn't let family or friends see her, and I
knew he was trying to get her to agree to his story.
But as Jakey recovered he and Schaack must have
realized that Mabel held all that evidence and they

became more respectful. I decided it was safe to go on to St. Louis, especially since the actress with the sprained ankle was recovering and wanted her role back.

Mr. Kern did well by Mabel and got Jakey to withdraw the charges; but I grew impatient for action against those who had hanged dear August so unjustly. Marshall Field's pet *Tribune* was hopeless as usual because it favored the police version, but when I returned to Chicago after the holidays I left an unsigned note for Archie at the rival *Chicago Times,* telling him to talk to Kern and keep a close eye on the Loewenstein shooting case.

Within days the *Times* had published Mabel's side. "Her home was turned into a warehouse for stolen goods!" "Captain Schaack and 'Jake' Loewenstein were in the game!" "Other and higher members of the force said to be implicated!" Schaack and Bonfield sued the *Times* for libel, but the editors had seen the proof and didn't back down. Heaps of newspapers were sold to a public eager to read about Lingg's brooch, Mrs. Hill's dress, and manufactured evidence in trials. A month later Mayor Roche suspended all three officers.

They never caught the Haymarket bomb-thrower. A few years later in Colorado I happened across a traveling carnival that featured a tall blond lady juggler called Anna the Anarchist. I watched a moment, until sensible Aunt Mollie began to whisper in my head that it might be best not to recognize Johanna, so I slipped out the side way; but not before I'd seen that the gray balls she was juggling had been fitted out with burning fuses to look like the bomb she'd stolen from the box under Mabel's bed, the one that had landed with such precision on the faithless Officer Degan.

Others were also chipping away at the police story, and in 1893 Governor Altgeld looked at the trial record and fully pardoned the three anarchists who were still alive, with scathing words for police and court alike. But, hang it, life is not as neat as melodramas. Governor Altgeld was not reelected, and a new mayor reappointed Schaack and Bonfield to the force, and rich businessmen erected a statue in Haymarket Square to the police, the "heroes of Haymarket." Yes indeed.

Guardian Angel

by Rochelle Krich

Although Belinda believed that everything would turn out for the best (it always did), she couldn't help feeling anxious. In part it was the exhaustion, which she hoped would diminish as her body adjusted to the new schedule.

When the baby was finally asleep, she took a quick shower and wrapped herself in the one-size-fits-all, gray and navy striped velour robe that she'd bought in the men's department at Macy's. Bracing herself for the chill of the January morning, she opened the door to take in the *Times*.

The phone rang. She had turned off the ringer in the bedroom, but she hurried to the kitchen extension, taut with apprehension that twisted inside her stomach and eased only a little when she saw the caller's name in the receiver's window. Her mother.

Belinda didn't want to talk to her mother, not today. "Doing anything special, Linnie?" her mother would ask in the carefully cheerful tone Belinda hated, as if Belinda were about to break into tiny pieces, like the cup she'd thrown against the wall—only one time, but no one would let her forget it. Her mother would

want to come over ("I haven't seen you in weeks,
Linnie. Is everything okay?"), and Belinda would have
to invent another reason for turning her down. And
what if the baby started crying?

In her yellow kitchen, commandeered by bottles,
nipples, brushes, and a phalanx of baby formula cans,
Belinda slid the newspaper out of the plastic bag that
she added to the others under her sink. The bags were
two-ply, perfect for disposing of eggshells and vegeta-
ble peels and chicken innards and overripe fruit ooz-
ing sticky liquids, and for masking the ammonia and
fecal odors belonging to the mass of soiled diapers
that was growing at an alarming rate.

There was nothing of note in the *California* section.
Belinda read it twice, then checked on the baby. She
was still sleeping. Savoring the stillness, Belinda relaxed with a mug of hot coffee and the crossword
puzzle, which she finished in less than ten minutes, in
ink. The one time she had mentioned the ink to her
family, her father had said, "Don't preen, Linnie."

That had stung. Belinda never drew attention to
herself. She never boasted about the acts of kindness
she performed, some of which she could never reveal,
much as she was tempted. Like feeding meters about
to expire, and visiting the ill and doing their chores.
And dropping off groceries anonymously, in the middle of the night, for Mary Iverson, a widowed friend
of the family who couldn't make ends meet but was
too proud to ask for help.

"My guardian angel was here again," Mary would
tell Belinda, her voice quavering with delight.

Being called a guardian angel did make Belinda feel
special, but it was unfair to say she was preening.

Her mouth stretched into another yawn. The baby,
whimpering throughout much of the night, had slept
fitfully and only in short bursts. So had Belinda. And
while the coffee, robust and deliciously bitter, had
taken the edge off her weariness, sleep tugged at her

eyelids, which felt like sandpaper. If not for the baby, she would crawl back under her comforter and stay in bed forever.

She did that sometimes, when she was between projects. Well, not *forever,* but for hours. There was nothing wrong with that, though her family would disagree. (One time she stayed in bed for three days, getting up only to relieve herself. She didn't like to think about that dark period. She had promised herself it wouldn't happen again.)

"Kind of self-indulgent, don't you think, Linnie?" her father would say, a smirk playing around his thin lips. "Slothful, in fact. Your sister wouldn't do that. Alicia's raising two boys, but she still finds time to chair committees and help others. You don't find *her* lolling in bed."

"Now, Arnold." Her mother would shush him with a gentle shove. "Linnie is helpful in her own way. And she does have a job." Then she would urge Belinda, again, to move back into the room she'd shared with Alicia. "This old house is *way* too big for your father and me, and why do you want to live all alone, anyway?"

And of course, Alicia ("the pretty twin"), married to a successful (and shady) real estate developer, and mother to two bratty toddlers, would throw Belinda a pitying look before imparting some of her sage advice.

"You need to get a life, Linnie." Alicia would sigh while studying the acrylic finish on her nails. "Why don't you let me fix you up with one of Martin's colleagues? Or I can help you write your profile for eHarmony or another Internet site."

"Every pot has its lid," her father would say. "Every roaster, too," he'd add with a sly wink, enjoying his cruel reference to Belinda's large frame.

Belinda *had* a life, thank you very much. She enjoyed copyediting the steady stream of manuscripts that provided her with security and some luxuries and allowed her to set her own schedule. And she excelled at what she did: finding the perfect word, correcting diction or grammar or inconsistencies or clumsy phrasing. In her desk drawer she kept notes from editors complimenting her thoroughness and expertise, and from authors thanking her for saving them from embarrassment. Some authors listed Belinda's name in their acknowledgments. Belinda flushed with pleasure each time she saw her name in print, but she didn't fault authors who hadn't thought to include her. She didn't mind the anonymity. Sometimes, she preferred it.

Helping people, making things right. That's what life was about, really. Whether it was fixing an author's words, or providing groceries for a lonely widow, or making sure Megan Conway was chosen class valedictorian in Belinda's senior year—not that pothead Jeffrey Ames, who had earned top class ranking with four years of cheating. Jeffrey had been the faculty and administration favorite, until they found the marijuana Belinda had placed in his locker.

No, it was Alicia who deserved pity. Belinda knew for a fact that Martin was having an affair, and not for the first time.

Careful not to make noise, Belinda opened the door to the bedroom and tiptoed to the crib. The baby had maneuvered herself into a corner and wriggled free of the blanket Belinda had taken pains to wrap her in tightly. She was fast asleep, sucking on the thumb she had worked out of the covered sleeve on the pale yellow nightgown.

"Lilly," Belinda whispered. She loved the name more every time she said it. "Lilly" made her think of whiteness, of all things beautiful and pure.

Leaving the bedroom door open, and the bathroom door, too, Belinda slathered her face with moisturizer and coaxed her damp hair into shape with her fingers. She would have liked to use her hair dryer, just as she would have enjoyed luxuriating earlier under the shower's stinging hot spray. But what if the baby woke and Belinda didn't hear her? She had learned to her dismay how quickly a whimper could become an ear-splitting cacophony of shrieks that would turn the baby's face a dangerous red and set her arms and legs flailing.

Even if Belinda took Alicia up on her offer to fix her up with one of Martin's colleagues, nothing would come of it. And what could she put in a profile for one of those Internet dating sites?

> *Guardian angel, solid, dependable, compassionate, loves word games, looking for same.*

Men weren't looking for guardian angels. They weren't looking for "solid" or "dependable" or "compassionate." They wanted sirens. They wanted "voluptuous" and "vivacious" and "sexy," like her neighbor Melissa, a mother in name only to little Carrie, the precious child she neglected and had probably never wanted. Melissa never took the baby out of the apartment, never strolled her down the block. It was as though the child didn't exist. From what Belinda had observed, Melissa was more interested in the men she invited into her bed. The bed thumped against the wall Melissa and Belinda shared. The noises made Belinda cringe and had brought her close to phoning the police several times.

So, no, Belinda would not be posting her profile on a dating site. She knew she was dull. She knew she was plain. Her face was flat and wide. Her thin brown hair was limp and without luster. Her chin was too square, her pale brown eyes too small, the lids almost lashless even with mascara, which she rarely used because it irritated her eyes. She had learned at an early age from her father, and later from her classmates, that she would never be anyone's favorite. She had seen disappointment on the faces of the blind dates for whom she had opened her door.

(Even plain, unexciting women found husbands, so she had to be lacking something else. What?)

Alicia, younger than Belinda by two minutes, had thick auburn hair that framed her heart-shaped face and green eyes that sparkled when she laughed her tinkling laugh, which she did often, especially around men. When the twins were toddlers, passersby would stop in front of the double stroller and coo at "the pretty one." Belinda's mother would say, "*Both* my girls are pretty." She would pinch Belinda's cheeks. "You're a love, is what you are. You are the sweetest little girl in the whole world. Mommy's angel. And you're pretty, just like your name. That's what Belinda means, pretty."

The name was a jinx, Belinda had decided, directing her bitterness at her parents and sometimes at God, who had participated in the joke. She couldn't remember when her parents had started calling her Linnie, probably to put an end to the lie.

But now the baby had come into her life. Lilly was a gift, a miracle. Belinda would shower her with love and make certain no one ever harmed her.

Her family would be shocked when they learned about Lilly. ("Adopting a child? What were you *thinking,* Linnie? How do you plan to take care of that baby on your own?") They wouldn't understand. They wouldn't have understood about Megan Conway, either. That's why Belinda hadn't told them about Megan, or about her friend Jim Langdon. He wouldn't have believed that his wife was cheating on him if Belinda hadn't followed her several times and taken compromising photos that she'd left in an envelope at Jim's office. Jim had a right to know. He had left his wife, and yes, he was miserable, but ultimately his life would be better, because of Belinda.

She hadn't decided when to let Alicia find out about Martin and his latest. Soon, she thought. Alicia had a right to know, too.

Belinda was zipping her jeans when she heard the

doorbell. Shutting the bedroom door behind her, she walked to the front door and glanced through the privacy window at a uniformed policeman.

"LAPD," the officer said. "We're looking for information about the woman who lives next door. Melissa Heckman?"

"Did someone complain about her?" Belinda asked. "Ma'am?"

"About the noise from her apartment. I don't like it, either. I thought about calling the police, but I didn't. You can tell her that."

"Actually, that's not why I'm here. Can I come in?"

Belinda asked to see his ID before she allowed him into her living room.

"If you're not here about the noise . . ." She caught her breath. "Did something happen to her? To Melissa?" Her voice sounded shrill to her ears. She hoped she hadn't woken the baby.

"I'm sorry to have to tell you Ms. Heckman is dead. We're talking to people in the neighborhood, hoping someone saw or heard something."

Belinda stared at him and sank onto the sofa cushion, which whooshed under her weight. "Oh, my God. Oh, my God."

"When was the last time you saw her? What's your name, ma'am, by the way?"

"Belinda Ellinson. I can't believe she's dead."

"The last time you saw her?" the officer prompted.

"Last night, around seven. I saw her drive off, with a man."

Melisssa had left the baby without a sitter, again. Belinda had rung the bell and knocked on the door. No one had answered. Melissa had left Carrie alone several times, even though Belinda was right next door. Just for half an hour or so while she went to the market, but still . . . Belinda had considered calling Child Services, but what was the point? They would warn Melissa. She would promise to do better. And then she'd go back to her selfish ways.

"What happened?" Belinda asked. "How did she . . . ?"

"We're trying to figure that out," the officer said. "We received an anonymous call from a man about an hour ago. You mentioned hearing noises, ma'am. What kind of noises?"

Belinda felt color creeping up her neck and face. "She has lots of men friends. And, well, you know . . . There's a lot of screaming, and other sounds."

Night after night she had covered her ears to block the sounds and the accompanying images. Night after night she had tried not to think about the innocent child sleeping not ten feet from her mother's bedroom. Belinda had seen the baby the day Melissa moved into the apartment a month ago. She had brought a bundt cake and offered to babysit, especially since there were no grandparents or other family to help out.

"It's just me and Carrie," Melissa had said. "Her daddy's not keen on babies. He's not thrilled about paying our bills, either."

"This man you saw her drive off with," the cop said. "Do you know his name?"

Belinda shook her head. "Melissa and I aren't close. She'd borrow a cup of sugar or a few eggs. We'd say hi when we saw each other. I don't know much about her personal life." Belinda hesitated. "I *did* hear yelling Tuesday night, when she came back. She and this man were fighting."

"About what?" the officer said, his interest quickened.

"I couldn't hear what they were saying. She sounded angry. And she was crying. I've heard her cry before, though. I asked her about it once, and she said it was nothing, she was fine. If I had known . . ."

Belinda's father would say that she *should* have known, that she was to blame. Alicia would, too, of course, and maybe even her mother. ("Oh, Linnie. What have you *done*?")

It wasn't her fault.

Belinda had assumed Melissa would be frantic when she came home and found the baby missing. That was the point, to teach her a lesson. She couldn't have known that Melissa would call Carrie's father, that he would drive over. She couldn't have anticipated that Melissa would attack him the minute he stepped into the apartment. ("You never wanted her born!" Melissa had screamed, her anguished cry penetrating Belinda's wall. "You took her, didn't you? You sold her! Or did you kill her? Is that what you did, you bastard?")

"Did this guy abuse her?" the cop asked.

"I saw her once with a black eye, but she said she bumped into something. And like I said, she had a lot of men friends. I don't know who she was with last night."

Belinda couldn't have known that Melissa would grab a knife ("Put down the knife, Melissa! Put it down, I said! Are you crazy?"), that he would slap Melissa, that she would fight him ("Baby killer! You killed my baby. *Why?*"). She couldn't have known he would slam Melissa's head against the wall ("Shut up! Shut up, I said!"), slam it again and again and again until Melissa was suddenly, awfully, quiet.

How could Belinda have known any of that? How could she have stopped it?

"You saw her get into a car," the officer said. "Can you describe it?"

"No." Belinda sighed. "I wish I'd paid attention. It was a black car. Or maybe blue or dark gray. I'm sorry, I'm not good with cars."

She hadn't wanted Melissa *dead*. She had wanted to frighten her, to make her realize how reckless she was every time she left little Carrie alone, even for five minutes. Last night after Melissa left, Belinda had let herself into the apartment with the spare key the former tenant had given her in case she ever locked herself out or if there was an emergency, which most people would say this was. The baby had been asleep in the Pack 'n Play. Belinda had scooped her up, blanket and all, and taken her to her own apartment.

"Did you see the license plate?" the cop asked. "Even the first few letters or numbers would help."

"I didn't think to look."

The officer hadn't asked about Melissa's baby. Belinda had been in a near panic at first, wondering what she would do if neighbors mentioned Carrie to the police. But she had reminded herself that really, no one ever saw the baby. Melissa never showed her off, never took her out. And there had been nothing in the *Times* about Melissa or the baby.

"What about the man? Can you describe him?" the officer asked.

"I only caught a glimpse. I'm sorry," she said again. "I'm not much help, am I?"

She had seen Carrie's father more than once and could describe him accurately, and his car. He should pay for what he had done. He had taken a life. (She was surprised that he'd phoned the police—he was obviously the anonymous caller. Guilt, she decided.) But if Belinda helped the police find him, he would tell them about the baby, and how long before they would be back here, questioning Belinda?

And what would happen to the baby then? They would put her in foster care, where she would never receive the love she deserved. Belinda had heard horror stories about foster homes and orphanages.

"If you remember anything about this man, or about the car, or anything else, please call right away." The officer handed Belinda a card.

"Of course."

She would never tell anyone how terrified she had been, waiting for Melissa's boyfriend to leave, wondering if he would realize that the baby was next door. Her heart had pounded when she had entered the apartment, and she had truly prayed that Melissa was alive. But she had found Melissa on her bed, slumped against the wall, which was streaked with blood. Her eyes were lifeless, her skin was gray. Belinda knew without touching her wrist that there was no pulse.

She had tried not to think about Melissa while she transferred the baby's things. The Pack 'n Play, bottles, brushes, formula, diapers, receiving blankets, clothing, ointments, liquid baby aspirin. She had almost forgotten to empty the hamper, and the trash, which was filled with soiled diapers.

She hadn't touched anything of Melissa's. She had taken only what belonged to Carrie.

To *Lilly*. A new life deserved a new name.

"It's terrible what happened," Belinda said, meaning it. "Just terrible."

And really, could anyone say with certainty that if she hadn't taken the baby, something horrible wouldn't have happened? If not last night, then another time? Melissa had said her boyfriend didn't like babies. . . . Sooner or later he would have grown tired of supporting Melissa and the baby.

Melissa's *killer,* not her boyfriend. Because that's what he was.

Belinda looked at the card and nodded. She had done the right thing, for the baby.

It was for the best.

Never Too Old

by Linda Grant

Sophia Diamante was worried about her mother. "You know how she frets," she told her sister, Cara. "You should never have told her about the Russian. It's just upset her."

"Mother does not fret," Cara said. It was the mildest retort she could think of.

"What?"

"Mother does not fret," she repeated. "Doesn't now, never has. When she's worried, there's a good reason." Like the fact that a mafiya thug up for murder one has just told her oldest daughter she won't live long enough to go to trial.

Sophia's sigh was audible, even over the weak cell phone connection. "I told you, he's just blowing off steam. These guys don't go after cops or prosecutors. You know that."

Cara knew that the Italian mafia did not go after cops or prosecutors. She did not know what the Russian mafiya might do, and she was pretty sure that Sophia didn't either. Still, she was sorry she'd told her mother. There wasn't anything that she could do, and it just worried her. Not for the first time, she vowed to play dumb from now on when her mother grilled her about her sister's life.

"She doesn't look well," Sophia continued. "I'm worried about her. She doesn't take good care of herself."

It was Cara's turn to sigh. This was a rerun of a conversation they'd had before. It was true that their mother had aged noticeably. When they were young, their friends had considered her the prettiest mom in their group. Now she looked at least ten years older than the other women. "Just because she doesn't go to the gym or get her hair dyed doesn't mean she doesn't take care of herself," Cara said. "She's still plenty sharp."

"I don't know. She's getting forgetful. Remember that fancy orchid I bought her? She forgot to water it, and it died. And she makes appointments and forgets them."

Cara could have pointed out that their mother did not like houseplants, especially ones that required special attention, and the appointments she forgot were weekly luncheons with Sophia. Cara suspected that her mother found it easier to "forget" than to deal with her eldest daughter's inability to take no for an answer.

"I think she's acting rather erratic," Sophia continued. "First she develops such a fascination with orchids that she has to rush off to a convention in Chicago, then she loses interest and forgets the one I got her. And how about that distant cousin in Denver she had to visit last month? She can't remember whether the woman was related to Aunt Silvi or Uncle Phil."

Cara had her own theory about her mother's trips. She was fairly sure that there was a man involved. Their father had died when they were children, and while their mother had never admitted to having a boyfriend, there were always men happy to take care of household and automotive repairs. Of course, it helped that Tony Diamante had been a close friend of the local mafia don, and that that same don seemed to have a fondness for their mother, but neither factor explained why the men seemed anxious to hang around long after the job was done, or to drop by to see if anything more needed doing.

She understood why her mother wouldn't want to tell Sophia if she had a male friend. Her sister would drive them both wild with her suspicious nature. She'd probably run a background check on the poor guy and badger the local cops into checking him out.

"She needs some outside interests," Sophia said, "something to stimulate her mind and get her out of the house. I keep telling her you're never too old to try new things."

"She's fine," Cara said. "You worry too much about her." And too little about yourself, she thought. "What's happening with the Russian, by the way?"

"He's in lockup," Sophia said. "There'll be a bail hearing, probably Monday. It's too late for them to get to him today."

"Will he get bail?" Cara asked. "I mean, he's up for murder and he threatened you. They won't let him out, will they?"

Sophia laughed, but there was no mirth in the sound. "Depends on the judge. Whether they think he's a flight risk. Whether they accept his apology about the threat. I don't think he's a risk. I doubt the judge will."

"They might take it more seriously if you did," Cara said. "You're making it easy for them to dismiss the danger."

"There is not much danger," Sophia assured her. "I'd just look like a wimp if I made a fuss."

There was no point in arguing, Cara realized. Sophia would rather put herself at risk than chance damaging her status as "one of the boys." She'd worked hard to make her way in the DA's office, and it hadn't made it any easier that her father had had close friends in the mafia.

* * *

If Sophia was worried about her mother, Bianca Diamante was even more worried about her daughter. She was taking the Russian's threat entirely too lightly. Sophia was sure that a criminal wouldn't go after a prosecutor, but that was naïve. When the stakes were high enough, anyone was fair game. And in this case the stakes were the highest. The Russian, one Yuri Reznikov, was up for murder one, and it was Sophia who'd convinced his girlfriend to testify against him. The girlfriend was in protective custody. What better way to convince her of the high cost of testifying than to kill the woman who'd promised her the cops could keep her safe?

Bianca wasn't about to gamble with her daughter's life. If anyone had earned a trip to the boneyard, it was this guy. And no one was better equipped to punch his ticket than Bianca Diamante. While she'd always made it firm policy never to mix personal and professional matters, she was prepared to make an exception for the Russian.

That's what Tony would have done. He'd never have stood for a thug threatening one of his girls. A hit man does not have to put up with poor behavior.

Tony had been a real pro, not a mob thug who blasted away with the biggest gun he could find. He'd worked freelance. The money had been good and he was his own boss. But there's no retirement program for hit men, and when he got the cancer and knew he wouldn't be there to see his kids grow up, he'd provided for them the only way he knew how. He'd taught their mom the family business.

In the early days Bianca had let Tony's contacts believe that his brother had taken over. Even now, only the man who acted as her agent knew her true identity. He hadn't liked the idea of repping a woman, but she'd convinced him that she had unique assets that suited her for special jobs. When she was younger, she'd used her looks to gain access to powerful men. But in her late forties, she'd discovered an even better cover. Instead of trying to look younger, she'd aged herself.

As an older woman, she was invisible. People paid no attention to her. A homeless woman talking to herself could stumble into a mobster without arousing suspicion. A nicely dressed church lady could chat up guys who'd never let a stranger get close.

"You'll need a niche," Tony had told her, "something you do better than anyone else, so when a job comes up that's right, they call you, and they pay extra."

Bianca's niche was the convenient accident, death by natural causes. Or unnatural ones that left no trace. She was an expert in poisons. It wasn't a subject they offered at the local JC so she'd had to teach herself. Once she had the basic knowledge, it was a matter of locating experts who possessed information not found in books. It was surprisingly easy to get them to talk; they were delighted to find someone who shared their passion. Especially when that someone was a woman adept at flattering their egos.

Could they send her a specimen of this or that poisonous mushroom so she might see it for herself? Did they know where she could get a small bit of that amazingly potent toad-skin toxin? In recent years, with the expansion of the Internet, just about anything was available if you knew where to look.

The Russian posed several problems. The first was timing. Bianca needed to set up the hit before he got out of jail; then she needed to execute it before he could act on his threat. The chance that the cops would keep him under surveillance made things even dicier.

The second problem was that she knew almost nothing about the thug. A hit that didn't look like a hit required planning. You needed background on the victim if you were to design a proper exit for him. And research was the best protection against dangerous surprises. This was not a job she'd have accepted for any amount of money. But then, it wasn't about money.

She called Marty, the guy who handled her business dealings, and asked him to find out what he could. "I need quick and dirty here," she said. "An address, whether he lives with anyone, if he uses drugs and which ones, anything you can get that might be useful."

Marty whined when she told him she needed it in a couple of hours. "It'll cost double," he said. "And that's whether I get anything or not, 'cause with so little time, I might not get much."

Not much was exactly what he got—an address and word that the guy lived alone. "He's midlevel," Marty said, "and a nasty piece of work. I have to tell you that I thought you were being maybe a bit too worried. I mean, why hit a prosecutor? They just bring in a new one. But this Reznikov has a real temper, plus he don't like women, and he *really* don't like a woman taking him down.

"You know you don't have to do this one. I could get someone to take care of it for you. Guys like him have enemies. He gets whacked, no one's gonna be too surprised."

Bianca considered it. Hiring the job out was safer, but it was also less sure. She didn't want to risk a screwup. While the cops might not look too hard for the killer, if Sophia decided the Russian was hit to shut him up, she'd start digging around, and Bianca didn't want to think where that might lead.

The best way to learn about the Russian was to search his house. And the time to do it was now, while he was safely locked away. The address Marty had given her was in a town about twenty minutes from her house. She wasn't familiar with the neighborhood, so she took a drive to check it out.

September had brought a break from the summer's

humidity, but the air was still warm in the late afternoon. Only a few trees showed the first signs of color. Otherwise, it was summer without the stifling heat.

Reznikov's home was a fairly new two-story brick on a quiet street in an affluent neighborhood. It was a family house, but Marty had said he lived alone. Bianca would have bet an ex-wife and kids lived in less spacious digs somewhere else. The street was deserted. Several garages had basketball hoops, but there were no kids banging balls off the backboards. Not for the first time, Bianca reflected that the more valuable the real estate, the fewer people you saw enjoying it.

In neighborhoods like this, the easiest way in was the cleaning lady ruse. An older woman lugging cleaning supplies barely registered. No one got suspicious when she went into a backyard or fumbled with a lock. Most people forgot they'd even seen her.

As she drove home, Bianca formed a plan. If she'd had more time, she'd have opted for an accident. But you couldn't count on an accident to be fatal, and she needed to nail the Russian on the first try. That left poison as the weapon of choice. Something fast acting that would incapacitate him before he could call for help. A faked suicide, perhaps. Feed him the poison, let it do its work, then come back and leave a bottle next to the body. The police would figure he saved them the expense of a trial. If his friends suspected otherwise, they wouldn't be talking to the cops about it.

For faked suicides, she had a special cocktail of a barbiturate and a drug prescribed as a sleeping medication. Each magnified the effect of the other, and alcohol gave them an even bigger boost. Best of all it was colorless, odorless, and tasteless, and she had it in both liquid and pill form. It cost plenty, and she had to put up with its producer, Alvin, a brilliant chemistry student who was either bipolar, schizophrenic, or both.

Conversations with Alvin were always trying since he assumed they shared the same paranoid universe and got agitated if she muffed her lines. But once she plugged into his fantasy, he was delighted to provide whatever she asked for and to tinker for months to get it to meet her specifications.

The major problem with poison was targeting. You had to be sure to get the victim without exposing anyone else. You couldn't just lace his favorite snack with poison because he might share that snack with a bystander. And one of Bianca's cardinal rules was that you never hit a bystander.

At home she donned her cleaning woman disguise—shapeless housedress, apron, sensible shoes, heavy support hose. She collected a mop, bucket, blue plastic gloves, and assorted cleaning supplies. Studying herself in the mirror, she decided to add a wig of tight steel gray curls and thick glasses.

There was no way to know whether the suicide plan would work until she'd had a look inside the Russian's house, but it was worth taking the poison with her, on the chance she'd get lucky. For that, and for the wig and glasses, she turned to the cabinet.

Tony had built the cabinet when she pointed out that he couldn't have guns around with children in the house. He'd closed off about eighteen inches at one end of their bedroom closet and installed the cabinet there. With the clothes pushed up against it, the opening was all but invisible. There were only two keys to the tiny lock hidden near the floor in the darkest corner. Bianca kept one and had given the other to one of Tony's old friends who had promised to empty the cabinet if anything happened to her.

The guns had been replaced with Bianca's tools—wigs, glasses, specially designed canes, and of course, poisons and the means of administering them. She took a bottle of clear fluid from the cabinet and two unlabeled brown bottles secured to each other with a heavy rubber band. One bottle held a common variety of sleeping pill that matched the fluid in the bottle, the other a barbiturate. They weren't an exact match for the fluid, but that wouldn't show up on any tox screen the coroner was likely to use.

Before she left, she took one final precaution. She called Sophia to make sure that Reznikov was still in jail. "I know you think I'm a worrywart," she said, "but I just wanted to know what was happening with that Russian fellow."

"He's in jail, Mom. Really. He's in jail. His bail hearing isn't scheduled until Monday."

"But that doesn't really mean you're safe. I mean, he could arrange for someone else to go after you. I've heard that happens."

"He's made his one phone call, Mom. And he'd have to be a real fool to arrange a hit from inside the lockup. But, just so you can relax, the police are taking his threat seriously, and they're keeping close watch on him."

"Well, then, that's a good thing. A very good thing."

"Mom, I'm sorry if I've been short with you about this," Sophia said, her voice softening. "I understand why you're worried, and I appreciate it. I'm sorry to put you through this."

Bianca experienced the odd mixture of warmth and sadness she always felt when Sophia let down her tough façade. She was a sweet kid, always had been, but from the time she was in grade school, she'd needed to appear tough. Bianca had never understood why. She'd hoped that someday her eldest daughter would feel safe enough to let her softer side show, but now that she was a prosecutor, there was little chance of that.

Sophia was not lying to her mother when she said that Reznikov was in jail and that the police were paying special attention to him, but she was stretching the truth when she mentioned the bail hearing on

Monday. It had been scheduled for then, but his attorney had requested that it be moved up. Ordinarily she'd have objected, and that would have been enough to keep him in the lockup, but the cops had decided that it fit their interest to cut him loose. They had plans for Yuri Reznikov, and they needed him on the outside for those plans to work.

As she hung up the phone, Sophia felt a moment's guilt about misleading her mother. She valued her mother's trust. When she was a teenager and the other girls' moms had treated them like whores or criminals, her mother had accepted her word. But, she told herself, technically, she hadn't lied. The hearing wasn't for forty-five minutes, and it was worth shading the truth to give her mother some peace of mind.

Bianca parked her car up the street some distance from Reznikov's house. There was no fence, so she didn't have to worry about a dog in the yard. She checked for an alarm system, though she'd have been surprised to find one. Guys like Reznikov figured they were so tough that no one would dare break into their house, and the last thing they wanted was to give the cops an excuse to enter without a warrant.

Out of sight of any neighbor, she pulled on thin surgical gloves. The back door had a ridiculously simple dead bolt. Bianca had it open in less than a minute. Inside, the house smelled slightly stale and the kitchen had the off odor of garbage going bad. She set down the mop and bucket of cleaning supplies and did a quick reconnaissance.

The house was fairly tidy, too tidy for a bachelor. Mob thugs didn't vacuum or mop floors. He'd have a cleaning service. No one had cleaned since he left, though. There was a scattering of grounds spilled next to the coffeemaker and bits of dried food on the counters.

A check of the kitchen suggested that Reznikov

didn't do a lot of cooking. There was more beer than food in the refrigerator, and the freezer held frozen dinners and a bottle of vodka.

The living room was set up for a single guy who didn't have a lot of company. A huge plasma TV with mammoth speakers on each side dominated the room. A dark brown leather lounger sat squarely in front of it, a small table to the side of the chair. The guy probably lived in that chair, Bianca thought.

The dining room looked like it hadn't been used in ten years. There was a china hutch but no china, further proof of Bianca's theory that there'd been a wife who'd stopped putting up with the thug.

She checked out the upstairs bedroom, hoping to find a stash of junk food or treats that might be doctored, and the bathroom, looking for prescriptions, but she struck out on both counts. A second bedroom held weights and expensive exercise equipment, but nothing to eat or drink.

She was checking the medicine cabinet in the downstairs bathroom when she heard the click of a key in a lock. She froze. She heard a lock turn, and a door open. The sounds came from the front of the house.

Reznikov was supposed to be in jail. There was no sign that he shared the house with anyone, no cat to be fed or plants to be watered. But someone had just come in the front door. It could be a friend. Or—the realization hit her with a shock—it could be that Sophia had lied to her.

The door slammed shut. A man coughed.

It took only seconds for Bianca to react. "Mr. Reznikov?" she called out. "Is that you, Mr. Reznikov?" There was no response.

She pulled on heavy blue plastic gloves over the thin surgical ones as she headed for the front door. She shifted her gait to a shuffle, rolled her shoulders forward to hunch her back, and thrust her head out. By the time she reached the entry, she was inches shorter and years older.

The man she confronted there was at least six feet tall and heavy—broad shoulders, substantial gut, thick black hair flecked with gray. He wore dark pants and a thigh-length black coat. He had one hand inside the coat, as if he might be reaching for a gun.

"Who the fuck are you?" he demanded in a low, slightly raspy voice. His heavy accent muffled the words, but their hostility came through loud and clear.

"I'm Irma, the cleaning lady," Bianca said, giving her voice a nasal quality. "Your regular's sick. I'm filling in. Didn't they tell you? They was supposed to call." She shrugged, the put-upon employee. "They said the house'd be empty." A note of complaint in the last part. "What're you doing home?"

The man stared down at her. Not a guy hired to do any heavy thinking, Bianca decided. Slowly, he withdrew his hand from his coat. "You're not supposed to be here till next week," he said, but he didn't sound suspicious, just surprised.

Bianca pursed her mouth and shook her head. "It's that Mary Louise in the office. That girl has spaghetti for brains, and since she's started dating the delivery guy, she can't keep nothing straight. I can go if you want, or I can finish up now. I won't get in your way." She paused, but not long enough to let him answer. "You look tired, Mr. Reznikov," she said, now a picture of maternal concern. "You should rest. Can I get you a cup of tea or something?"

If the Russian was aware that it was odd to find a strange woman in his house offering him tea, he didn't show it. He lumbered into the living room and collapsed in the recliner.

"No tea," he said. "Vodka. It's in the freezer."

"Vodka, sure," Bianca said and headed for the kitchen. She pulled the frosted bottle from the freezer, chose the biggest glass in the cupboard, and poured a hefty slug of the vodka into it. Then she retrieved her bottle of liquid from the bucket of cleaning supplies, and added some to the vodka. She'd have liked to measure, to make sure she had the right amount for the man's weight, but she made a guess and added enough extra to guarantee the desired result.

Reznikov took the glass without comment. She'd worried he'd complain that she'd poured too much, but from the size of his first gulp, that wasn't going to be a problem. He'd turned on the TV and was watching football.

She retreated to the kitchen before he could tell her to leave. She'd never been present to see the effect of this particular combo of drugs, so she wasn't sure how long it would take, but Alvin had assured her that taken together they'd work in less than an hour. She decided to pass the time by cleaning. There was always the off chance that someone would remember seeing a cleaning lady go into the house. If it hadn't been cleaned, the cops would get suspicious.

As she washed the dirty dishes, cleaned the counters and mopped the floor, the commentary from the football game played in the background. After about twenty minutes, she walked quietly to the entry hall where she could see the table next to Reznikov's chair. The glass was almost empty.

As she turned to go back to the kitchen, the sound of the TV went dead. The word "muted" flashed on the screen. She froze, fearing that Reznikov had heard her, but he didn't get out of the chair.

He shifted position enough so that she could see he was holding a cell phone. Damn. She'd taken the house phone off the hook in the kitchen to make sure he couldn't call out, but she'd forgotten that he might have a cell phone.

"Max, this is Sam," he said. Bianca tensed. The fake name was a sure sign of trouble. He was calling a hit man!

"I got a job for you, needs to be done soon, like tomorrow." There was a pause as he listened to the response. Bianca's mind was racing. She had to interrupt the call, and fast. "What'dya mean, half now, half after? What kind of bullshit is that?"

There was no time for planning. She had to stop him before he gave the hit man Sophia's name. She rushed forward, banged into the table and fell toward Reznikov, crashing into his right arm with all her weight. The table tipped forward and the almost empty glass landed on the rug. The cell phone popped out of Reznikov's hand and flew across the room, bounced off the wall, and dropped to the floor.

The angle of Bianca's body when she hit Reznikov's shoulder sent her sprawling into his lap. He stared down at her, stunned; then his face twisted into a furious scowl.

Bianca was up and out of the Russian's reach much more quickly than an old lady should have been able to manage. "Oh, Mr. Reznikov," she squeaked. "I'm so sorry. That was so clumsy. I'll clean this up right away."

"You stupid cunt," he snarled. "Get me that cell phone." He started to rise from the chair.

Bianca hurried to get the cell phone, praying it would be broken. Her cell had died when she dropped it on a granite counter. Surely . . . But the cell didn't look broken. The call had been cut off, but the screen displayed the time. She picked up the phone, stammering apologies. "Oh, Mr. Reznikov, I'm so sorry. I broke your phone. I'll pay for a new one. Please don't tell the service. They'll fire me sure."

Reznikov was on his feet, his hands balled into fists, his face contorted with fury. "You're not . . . Who the fuck *are* you?" he bellowed.

Bianca assessed her escape routes. The chair sat in the middle of the room, blocking the path to the front entry. That left the way through the dining room to the kitchen and the back door, but Reznikov would only have to move a few steps to intercept her. If the poison had slowed him down, there was a chance she might make it, but not a good one.

"I said I was sorry. I'll pay for it, honest," she repeated. "Oh, I made such a mess. But I can take care of that. I gotta get the dustpan, then I'll clean that right up." She began to edge her way toward the dining room, moving slowly, giving him no reason to grab for her.

He took a step toward her. "What the hell . . ." But his voice was less forceful, and he had a strange expression on his face. Bianca hoped desperately that the drugs were taking effect.

It was all a matter of time now. She took a step backward. He took another step toward her. If she could get him to move far enough from the chair, she could make a dash for the entry, putting the recliner between her and the Russian.

Reznikov weaved slightly. His face was no longer knotted in a scowl. The features seemed to have loosened. His jaw had slackened and his mouth hung slightly open. He looked more confused than angry.

"You don't look so good, Mr. Reznikov," Bianca said. "I think maybe you should sit down." She took a step toward him.

He raised his arm to take a swing at her, but he couldn't follow through and it fell useless to his side. Bianca let out her breath and felt a rush of relief. She waited, watching him closely.

"You . . . you . . ." He was mumbling now. It seemed to take all his effort to stand. He stumbled backward and collapsed into the chair, but his eyes were still fixed on her. The color had drained from his face, leaving it a sickly white.

Bianca realized that this was the first time she'd watched a man die. For all the deaths that she had arranged, she'd managed to be absent for the actual passing. She felt a kind of animal sympathy for the man in the chair. Not for Reznikov, the thug, but for a fellow being who was dying and knew it. A strange feeling. There was no temptation to intervene, no guilt really. She had no doubt that the world would be a better place without this man. It surprised her that she had any feeling for him at all.

As she watched the Russian, she remembered Sophia's description of attending the execution of a particularly brutal killer she'd convicted. She'd had the same confused reaction, emotions she didn't understand and couldn't explain.

Bianca backed out of the room and stood behind the chair for long enough to satisfy herself that Reznikov was not getting up, then returned to cleaning the house. The mess in the living room could wait.

It was full dark by the time she was sure Yuri Reznikov was no longer breathing. She set the stage for his final scene by the light of the giant television. It was not the first time she'd done this. The first time she'd feared having to confront the sight of a man whose life she'd ended, but then, as now, she'd felt little remorse. When she'd decided to go into the business, she'd drawn up a set of rules covering who was fair game and who wasn't. Tony had laughed at her; Marty had been incredulous and infuriated, but she only took jobs that let her sleep at night.

The glass lay on the rug where it had landed when she knocked over the table. What liquid there'd been in it had soaked into the carpet. Bianca righted the table and picked up the glass, holding it by the rim and bottom so as not to smudge Reznikov's fingerprints. She took it to the kitchen, added a bit of fresh vodka to rinse it out, then replaced it on the rug. She wrapped Reznikov's hands around each of the two brown bottles, to provide the crime lab with decent fingerprints, and dropped them near the glass so that it looked like the Russian had knocked them off. She stepped back and surveyed the scene.

It was then that she noticed the cell phone. She

picked it up and checked the call history to see what the Russian had dialed. The number was Marty's.

She stared at it, shocked and shaken. Surely, Marty wouldn't have . . . She shook her head, refusing to consider it. The half-now-half-later demand was no doubt because Marty knew Reznikov wouldn't live long enough to pay off, but under other circumstances, she wouldn't have trusted his loyalty.

One thing was sure: she didn't want the police having Marty's phone number. Put him in a cell, and he wouldn't hesitate to give her up for a lighter sentence. She aimed the phone at the brick fireplace and threw it as hard as she could. It broke apart and fell to the floor. Bianca wished she knew enough about cell phone technology to be sure that the memory was erased but decided that any further damage to the phone risked raising questions with the cops.

It occurred to her as she was packing up to leave that the police might be keeping tabs on Mr. Reznikov. The house behind the Russian's was dark, so instead of leaving the way she'd come, she walked through the backyard and down the neighbor's driveway.

Sophia came by the next morning. Bianca had never been able to break the girls of the habit of dropping in. She'd hinted that such unannounced visits could prove embarrassing for all concerned, but to no avail. "We're all grown-ups," Cara had said with a knowing smile. It would be nice, Bianca thought, if getting caught with a lover was the worst that could happen.

Sophia had stopped at the bakery to pick up Bianca's favorite pastries, and she brought flowers, a sure sign that she was feeling the need to make up for some misdeed. As they sat over steaming mugs of coffee in the sunny kitchen, Sophia said, "I wanted you to know that you don't have to worry about the Russian. He killed himself last night."

"Really?" Bianca said; then remembering that she

was not supposed to know of Reznikov's release, she added, "In jail?"

"Actually, he was at home," Sophia said, looking a bit abashed. "After I talked with you, the judge set bail, and we had to let him out."

"Oh," Bianca said. "Well, good riddance. It'll save the taxpayers the cost of a trial."

Sophia laughed. "That's what my boss said."

"I imagine it's a relief to you all," Bianca said. Sophia hesitated just long enough to tell her mother that she was holding back. "There's something you aren't telling me, isn't there, dear?"

Sophia gave her tight little caught-out laugh. "Boy, I could never keep anything from you. Okay, it's over now, so I guess there's no harm in telling. This was a sting, and the Russian was the bait. Losing him cost us the target."

Bianca was getting a bad feeling about this. "The bait? I don't understand, dear."

"I wasn't really honest with you about Reznikov's threat. I knew he was serious, and so did the police. We let him out so he could order a hit. With traces on his phones, we'd have a straight line back to the hit man, or maybe if we got really lucky, to an even bigger fish, a guy who arranges hits. As soon as he made the call, we . . ." Sophia stopped midsentence. "Mom, is something wrong? You're really pale."

Bianca was having trouble catching her breath. A chill had spread through her body at the memory of Marty's number on Reznikov's phone. "I don't like the idea of them using you for bait," she said, working to keep her voice steady. "Something awful could have happened."

"I was perfectly safe. I was with the cops the whole time. We'd have been in his living room as soon as he hung up, and a second unit would have been on its way to the hit man's place. I was never in danger."

Not in danger of dying, Bianca thought, but definitely in danger of watching your mother led off in handcuffs. In all her years as a professional, this was the first time she'd come even close to getting caught. "What happened?" she asked.

"It was really weird. He put in a call, said he had a 'job,' and it looked like they were about to negotiate price when he hung up. We waited for him to call back. But he never did."

"But if you had a trace, you must have gotten the number of the person he called," Bianca said, knowing her daughter would ascribe her knowledge of such things to her fondness for reading and watching police procedurals.

Sophia shook her head. "The call was too short to trace," she said, "and it appears he threw the phone across the room and broke it. The cops think maybe he got cut off and smashed the phone in anger."

Bianca laughed, more from relief than amusement. "I've felt like doing that after a dropped call," she said.

Sophia nodded and was silent for a few moments; then she said, "It doesn't fit. I mean, why would he start to order the hit, then change his mind and commit suicide? I tried to get them to go in when the connection was cut. I knew there was something funny going on."

Good lord, my own daughter would have brought them down on me, Bianca thought. "What do the police think?" she asked.

"They're not thinking," Sophia said, her tone sharp with aggravation. "With the cell phone smashed, we have no leads on the hit man. There's no evidence to suggest murder, and they want to close the case. If it's suicide, they're done."

"It's too bad you lost the hit man, but at least you're safe now." She studied Sophia's face for signs of her intentions. "Are you going to pursue it, to investigate this man's death?"

Sophia shook her head. "No, the case is closed. It's over. I just wish I knew what happened in that house last night."

No, you don't, Bianca thought. You really don't.

Murder for Lunch

by Carolyn Hart

Madeleine Kruger held up the menu to hide her face. It would be embarrassing if Mike saw her, although surely his lunch with that gorgeous young woman was perfectly aboveboard and Meg knew all about it.

Madeleine had a quick vision of Meg's tight-drawn, slick face. Surgery makes a difference, no sags, no bumps, no lines, but plastic skin is as great a tip-off to age as wrinkles. Not that Meg was all that old. She was in her early thirties, but that's old in Hollywood.

Madeleine wriggled uncomfortably. Was she being unkind? Madeleine hated to be unkind. If she had a husband as young and appealing as Mike, perhaps she'd try to wipe away wrinkles too. Willy had been dead for years, but she knew he would love her just the way she was, with untidy gray hair and nearsighted blue eyes and a shapeless bosom and plump hips.

Madeleine heard a thump in the next booth. Mike and his friend were right behind her. She'd stay quiet as a mouse until they left. She wouldn't breathe a word about seeing them to Meg. Just in case. It seemed odd that Mike brought a guest to the Cosy Café. It was a modest little place away from Main

Street, not the sort of restaurant young people preferred.

The waitress brought Madeleine's tomato soup, so cheerful and warming on a rainy February day. Even Southern California had its off season but this was nothing like the cold in Kansas. Sometimes Madeleine missed the crunch of snow underfoot and the frosty wreath of her breath—

". . . have to kill her. Otherwise we're stuck." Mike's clear baritone was brusque.

Madeleine's plump hand wavered. Soup splashed onto the Formica tabletop. She hunched forward, struggling to hear over the roaring in her ears. Her blood pressure . . .

The girl answered, but her voice was soft and low. Madeleine could make out only a few words. ". . . when a wife dies . . ."

Madeleine watched all the detective shows. A husband was always the prime suspect when a wife died.

Mike sounded irritated. ". . . have to kill her. Murder's the only solution. It ruins everything if . . ."

Madeleine put down her spoon. She used her napkin to swipe at the spilled soup, then grabbed the check. She struggled out of the booth and hurried to the cash register. Oh dear, oh dear. She hadn't left a tip. At the register, she put down a bill, twice the total, and said breathlessly, "So sorry. Must leave. Please see that the waitress gets the tip." She walked as fast as she could to the exit and didn't stop until she was a block away, her legs aching and wobbly.

She couldn't escape the sound of Mike's voice: ". . . have to kill her . . . Murder's the only solution . . ."

Madeleine shuffled the deck of cards with practiced ease. She arched the cards in a high curve, caught them expertly. She'd played cards since she was a little girl and was adept at everything from bridge to Texas Hold'em. Faster than a croupier sorting chips, she slapped cards facedown, one after another. Solitaire helped her think.

Dandelion's orange paw flicked out and the first card slewed toward the edge of the table.

Madeleine caught it in time. "Bad girl." But her tone was loving.

The orange cat hunched her shoulders, waiting for another card to be played.

When the cards were down, Madeleine began to play, occasionally righting a card from Dandelion's attack, but her thoughts darted like minnows. She should call the police. Would they listen? Mike would deny everything. Maybe she could warn Meg.

She'd never really talked much with Meg. It was Mike who was friendly. He seemed like such a nice young man. And to think he and Meg had moved to Castle Point because of her. The block of flimsily built condos had been thrown up in the sixties. Each condo had three floors that had later been made into separate apartments. An exterior stair served each unit. Apartments were scarce in the Hollywood area. She'd told her best friend, Mia, that the apartment beneath her was empty and the ad hadn't yet run. Mia's nephew Mike was looking for a place. Mike and Meg moved in the next week. Both had jobs on the fringes of the business, but they wanted to write movies. Didn't everyone in Hollywood have a script to sell? Everyone but her. She was a reader and hardly ever gave a thought to the fact that she lived in Hollywood, though occasionally she went to a show with Mia.

Madeleine felt a pang of sorrow for Mia. She and Mia loved to play bridge. They made good partners, Mia bold and aggressive, Madeleine with an uncanny card sense. Their regular foursome ended with Betty Bailey's heart attack and her husband's move back to Texas after the funeral. Now Mia and Madeleine played bridge with Mike and Meg every Wednesday in Madeleine's apartment.

Mike and Meg were pretty good players. Madeleine

suspected that the young couple agreed to play to
keep on his aunt's good side. Mia had no family other
than her sister's son. Mia wasn't rich but her house,
once a modest bungalow, had appreciated in worth to
almost a million and someday would come to Mike.

Madeleine didn't find the evenings with Mike and
Meg as cheerful as the old days with the Baileys. She
had to put Dandelion in the bedroom because Meg
didn't like cats. Mia said Meg hated cats and she was
sure it was because she was deathly afraid of them.
"You'd think anyone would know a pet cat wouldn't
hurt them. But some people . . ." That was as near as
Mia ever came to criticizing Meg, though Madeleine
was sure that Mia and Meg didn't like each other and
were pleasant only because of Mike.

Oh, how awful that Mike would plan to murder—

Dandelion reached out, snagged a card.

Madeleine caught it before it fell. She drew her
breath in sharply. The ace of spades. Here she was
thinking about murder and she held the ace of spades
in her hand. She had to do something, because she
knew well enough what she'd heard and what it meant,
but the police would think she was a silly old lady. It
wouldn't do any good to call Crime Stoppers. She had
no proof.

Madeleine gripped the ace so tight, it bowed under
pressure and the edges hurt her fingers. If only there
were some way to frighten Mike . . .

She stared at the card. Tomorrow was Wednesday.
They'd be coming here to play bridge.

Slowly a plan took shape.

Madeleine clutched the phone with a hand that
shook. She hated to lie and especially to imperious
Mia, a former Latin teacher with a clear-eyed view of
human frailty. Madeleine tried to keep her voice ca-
sual, though she was afraid she sounded utterly false.
". . . running late. Could you be here at seven thirty
instead of seven? That's fine with Mike and Meg. I'll

have everything under control by then." Oh dear, that wasn't what she'd meant to say at all. It sounded absurd.

There was the tiniest pause before Mia responded. "Seven thirty it is. Is there anything I can do to help?"

"Oh no, no, it's a family thing. Thank you, Mia. I'll see you then." She hung up quickly.

Madeleine added another swath of blush to her cheeks. Twin patches of red glowed like beacons. She smoothed and smudged and ended up looking as if she had a rash. That was all right. Young people never looked at old people, and anyway· the red smears would hide a flush if her blood pressure soared. She must remember to focus on the cards and not think about Mike and Meg, not for an instant.

At ten to seven, she made sure Dandelion was in the bedroom, the door closed. She patted the pocket of her loose blue smock, scanned the card table, checked the serving tray. Everything was ready.

The bell pealed promptly at seven.

Madeleine pulled a fluffy white handkerchief from her pocket and clutched it in her left hand as she pattered to the front door. She opened it, her welcome effusive. "Come in, come in. I have our drinks ready. A light beer for Mike and scotch and soda for Meg." She offered them easy chairs on one side of the coffee table, brought the drinks.

Mike looked around. "Mia usually beats us here." He had a long scholarly face with bright blue eyes and an easy grin. His lanky frame made the chair look small.

Meg's expression was remote, although some of its blankness might have been caused by stretched skin that emphasized a heart-shaped face. She took the drink with a murmured thanks.

Madeleine patted her face with the hanky, dropped onto the sofa. "Mia's running a few minutes late. The traffic. But she'll be here before we know it." Madeleine tucked the handkerchief into the wristband of her smock and picked up a deck of cards. "We can have fun while we wait. I love to read the cards." She looked coy. "I used to pick up some extra money telling fortunes, but I don't do that anymore. I'll do yours for free." She lifted the deck, shuffled, shuffled again, shuffled a third time. "Have to start fresh to find out the truth."

Suddenly her nose wrinkled. She sniffled and reached for the handkerchief. She sneezed into it, murmuring, "Oh, that Dandelion, sometimes she makes me sneeze."

Meg's head jerked around in search of the cat.

As Madeleine fluttered the hanky and thrust it in her pocket, the shuffled deck disappeared, replaced by a deck that looked the same. But this deck had been very carefully arranged.

Madeleine glanced at the clock. "We have time to do the magic square. We'll do Mike first."

She placed one card—the ten of spades—in the center of the coffee table and snapped, facedown, three cards in a top row, three in a center row, three in a bottom row.

Mike grinned and casually draped one leg over the side of the chair. "How about this. We come for a game of bridge and instead we're going to find out what the future holds." His tone was genial, but his glance at Meg was amused.

Meg smoothed back a lock of dark hair and bent forward in curiosity.

Madeleine frowned at the card she turned faceup, spoke in a low hoarse voice. "There may be trouble ahead. Some barrier. Something will go wrong." She took a deep breath, hesitantly began to turn over the cards, her voice deeper and deeper. "Disaster is ahead. The cards are dark, dark. Spades and clubs. A relationship may be ended."

Mike's smile slipped away. He frowned.

Meg's eyes narrowed. Her hands closed into claws.

Madeleine gave a moan. "There's a warning of danger and deceit. The nine of diamonds is light but it is the symbol for a coffin. I see a letter. I can't quite make it out. Oh yes. It's an M. M as in money? No, it's a name. Some name begins with M. Death will touch an M. The jack of spades means someone here— No, surely not. Here's a figure of authority. A judge? The police? The death is supposed to be an accident but it isn't. The police will find out. Oh, here's the four of clubs. It isn't too late for everything to change. Oh." A gasp. "The ace of spades." Abruptly, she swept the cards together. She was breathing hard, her face shiny with sweat. "I'll get us a snack. I don't know what to think. . . ." Her words trailed off as she struggled up from the sofa and hurried to the kitchen.

She stopped out of sight, but she could hear.

Mike's voice was uncertain. "Do you think she's all right? She looked sick."

Meg spoke lightly. "More silly than sick. Superstition's absurd. Oh Lord, how long do you suppose we'll have to stay tonight?"

The doorbell sounded.

Madeleine bustled to answer, welcoming Mia. Within minutes, the bridge began. It might have been any Wednesday evening. Madeleine wished her head didn't hurt. She didn't win a single hand.

Mike looked over his shoulder, punched in Cindy's phone number. He was a third assistant to the executive assistant in a start-up development company. His boss snarled like a junkyard dog if you made personal calls on company time. Mike was relieved when Cindy picked it up on the first ring. He had to convince her . . . "Cindy—"

The soft voice interrupted. "I rewrote the scene last night. You're right, Mike. We have to get rid of Kelly's wife to increase the pressure on him. Now he's backed into a corner . . ."

The tight muscles in the back of Mike's neck eased. Cindy was a swell writing partner. They'd met in his script class at UCLA and been going like gangbusters ever since. He wished he didn't have to sneak around to meet her, but Meg would flip if she found out. Cindy didn't like things not being aboveboard but she understood when he explained that Meg wanted to co-write everything. He'd tried for a while, but he'd soon realized that Meg didn't have the magic. He thought he did, especially with Cindy. A tiny thought darted in the back of his mind. Meg always acted like she knew so much about the business. He'd been excited when she assured him he was going to make it big someday. That's why he'd married her. Even though she could be fun and exciting, sometimes he wondered if he'd done the right thing. But he'd made his choice. He'd thought she had more contacts than she really had. Still, she knew some people. Maybe when this script was finished, if she didn't get mad, she'd help him sell it. Could he ever tell her about Cindy? Well, he'd worry about that later.

"Great. Listen, we're almost there. In the last scene . . ."

Meg was good at computers. She'd easily broken into Mike's. The new script was almost finished. God, it was good. It should have been hers too. She'd teach him to double-cross her. That was the only reason she'd married him, a long-haired kid with about as much attraction for her as a missionary. But he could write, that was for sure. This script could hit it big, really big. She knew an A-list producer who'd kill for a script like this.

Just like she would.

She clicked off Mike's computer, rose and paced to the kitchen. She poured a drink, leaned against the counter. She'd had it all planned. As soon as the script was done, they'd go sailing. A crack with the tiller and off he'd go. The script would be hers and her fortune would be made.

How did the old bitch upstairs know? How could she possibly know? Meg had a dim memory of her ancient aunt Ida, hunched over a table, reading cards and saying a death was coming—and the next day Meg's mother was hit by a car as she crossed La Brea.

Meg felt cold as ice. How could cards know anything? But Madeleine knew. Those cards and that shaky voice . . . Now if Mike died in an accident, Madeleine would run to the police.

Meg looked up toward the floor above. Madeleine saw the letter M and somebody dead.

Meg said it aloud. "M. M for Madeleine."

Meg waited until the front door slammed, Mike hustling out for his morning run. What a Boy Scout.

Meg slipped out of bed and glanced in the mirror. The red silk shorty nightgown emphasized her long slender legs. She was proud of her legs. She pulled on a T-shirt and jeans over the nightgown. It would take only a minute to return to the apartment, strip them off. She'd tell the police she heard a scream. She'd be distraught. She smiled in anticipation. The old bitch always went down and got her paper first thing in the morning. Out of those boring sterile nights of bridge, Madeleine had droned on and on about her breakfast, that hideous cat, the wonderful paperboy always coming early, the cost of milk, and on and on and on. More, Meg thought sourly, than she'd ever wanted to know, but now it was paying off.

Meg hurried to the cupboard above the broom closet. She pulled on plastic gloves and picked up a small paper sack.

Outside the door, she slipped in the shadows to the stairway, nice steep steps with a metal-edged tread. Birds twittered as the first hint of dawn added a rosy glow to the horizon. She started up the steps, moving fast.

In the third-floor apartment, Madeleine hummed as she poured a cup of green tea and spread cream cheese on a bagel. Certainly Mike looked uneasy last night. Perhaps she'd send an anonymous letter too. That should be enough to keep Meg safe.

The sound of shredding cloth brought her to her feet. Oh dear. Dandelion was a love, but she was ruining the sofa. Why didn't she meow?

Madeleine rushed to the front door, aware she'd forgotten to let Dandelion out. This was her safe time to roam, before the street was busy with traffic.

Madeleine opened the door, cautioned, "You be careful now. Stay out of the street."

The cat slipped out into the grayness of dawn. The door shut behind her.

Meg froze on the steps, the hammer tight in one hand, a slender strip of wire in the other. The head of a nail protruded five inches from the wall to her left.

Dandelion, amber eyes glowing, trotted toward the steps.

Meg's heart thudded. She flung the hammer toward the cat.

Dandelion slipped sideways. Her tail puffed. She hissed, launched herself forward, claws extended.

Meg recoiled. She flailed away, twisting, turning, trying to evade the cat, the sharp-edged steps forgotten. Her balance gone, she arched backward, scream rising. She plummeted down, her head smacking against the risers. She crashed onto the landing to lie in a bloodied crumpled heap.

When the police arrived, they found the strip of wire still clutched in a plastic-gloved hand, the hammer on the upper landing, and the protruding nail.

That night Detective Lieutenant Miguel Mendoza shook his head as he told his wife about his day. ". . . so go figure why this dame wanted to kill the old lady who lived upstairs. Maybe she played her music too loud. Guess we'll never know."

The Whole World Is Watching

by Libby Fischer Hellmann

" 'The whole world is watching.' " Bernie Pollak
snorted and slammed his locker door. "You wanna
know what they're watching? They're watching these
long-hair commie pinkos tear our country apart.
That's what they're watching!"

Officer Kevin Dougherty strapped on his gun belt,
grabbed his hat, and followed his partner into the
squad room. Bernie was a former marine who'd seen
action in Korea. When he moved to Beverly, he'd
bought a flagpole for his front lawn and raised Old
Glory every morning.

Captain Greer stood behind the lectern, scanning
the front page of the *Chicago Daily News*. Tall, with
a fringe of gray hair around his head, Greer was usually a man of few words and fewer expressions. He
reminded Kevin of his late father, who'd been a cop
too. Now Greer made a show of folding the paper and
looked up. "Okay, men. You all know what happened
last night, right?"

A few of the twenty-odd officers shook their heads.
It was Monday, August 26, 1968.

"Where you been? On Mars? Well, about five thousand of them—agitators—showed up in Lincoln Park

yesterday afternoon. Festival of Life, they called it."
Kevin noted the slight curl of Greer's lip. "When we
wouldn't allow 'em to bring in a flatbed truck, it got
ugly. By curfew, half of 'em were still in the park, so
we moved in again. They swarmed into Old Town.
We went after them and arrested a bunch. But there
were injuries all around. Civilians too."

"Who was arrested?" an officer asked.

Greer frowned. "Don't know 'em all. But another
wing of 'em was trying to surround us down at head-
quarters. We cut them off and headed them back up
to Grant Park. We got—what's his name—Hayden."

"Tom Hayden?" Kevin said.

Greer gazed at Kevin. "That's him."

"He's the leader of SDS," Kevin whispered to
Bernie.

"Let's get one thing straight." Greer's eyes locked
on Kevin, as if he'd heard his telltale whisper. "No
matter what they call themselves—Students for a
Democratic Society, Yippies, MOBE—they are the
enemy. They want to paralyze our city. Hizzoner made
it clear that isn't going to happen."

Kevin kept his mouth shut.

"All days off and furloughs have been suspended,"
Greer went on. "You'll be working overtime too.
Maybe a double shift." He picked up a sheet of paper.
"I'm gonna read your assignments. Some of you will be
deployed to Grant Park, some to Lincoln Park. And
some of you to the Amphitheater and the convention."

Bernie and Kevin pulled the evening shift at the
Amphitheater, and were shown their gas masks, helmets, riot sticks, and tear gas canisters. Kevin hadn't
done riot control since the Academy, but Bernie had
worked the riots after Martin Luther King's death.

"I'm gonna get some shut-eye," Bernie said, shuf-
fling out of the room after inspecting his gear. "I have
a feeling this is gonna be a long night."

"Mom wanted to talk to me. I guess I'll head
home."

Bernie harrumphed. "Just remember, kid, there's more to life than the Sears catalogue."

Kevin smiled weakly. Bernie'd been saying that for years, and Kevin still didn't know what it meant. But Bernie was the patrolman who broke in the rookies, and the rumor was he'd make sergeant soon. No need to tick him off.

"Kev . . ." Bernie laid a hand on his shoulder. "You're still a young kid, and I know you got—what— mixed feelings about this thing. But these . . . these *agitators*—they're all liars. Wilkerson was there last night." He yanked a thumb toward another officer. "He says they got this fake blood, you know? They holler over loudspeakers, rile up the crowd, then pour the stuff all over themselves and tell everyone they were hit on the head. Now they're threatening to pour LSD into the water supply." He faced Kevin straight on. "They're bad news, Kev."

Kevin hoisted his gear over his shoulder. "I thought they were here just to demonstrate against the war."

"These people want to destroy what we have. What do you think all that flag burning is about?" Bernie shook his head. "Our boys are over there saving a country, and all these brats do is whine and complain and get high. They don't know what war is. Not like us."

Kevin drove down to Thirty-first and Halstead, part of a lace-curtain Irish neighborhood with a tavern on one corner and a church on the other. When he was little, Kevin thought the church's bell tower was a castle, and he fought imaginary battles on the sidewalk in front with his friends. One day the priest came out and explained how it was God's tower and should never be confused with a place of war. Kevin still felt a twinge when he passed by.

His parents' home, a two-story frame house with a covered porch, was showing its age. He opened the door. Inside the air was heavy with a mouthwatering aroma.

"That you, sweetheart?" a woman's voice called.

"Is that pot roast?"

"It's not ready yet." He went down the hall, wondering if his mother would ever get rid of the faded wallpaper with little blue flowers. He walked into the kitchen. Between the sultry air outside and the heat from the oven, he felt like he was entering the mouth of hell. "It's frigging hot in here."

"The AC's on." She turned from the stove and pointed to a window unit that was coughing and straining and failing to cool. Kevin loosened his collar. His mother was tall, almost six feet. Her thick auburn hair, still long and free of gray, was swept back into a ponytail. Her eyes—as blue as an Irish summer sky, his father used to say in one of his rare good moods— looked him over. "Are you all right?"

"Great." He gave her a kiss. "Why wouldn't I be?"

"I've been listening to the radio. It's crazy what's happening downtown."

"Don't you worry, Ma." He flashed her a cheerful smile. "We got it under control."

Her face was grave. "I love you, son, but don't try to con me. I was a cop's wife." She waved him into a chair. "I'm worried about Maggie," she said softly.

Kevin straddled the chair backward. "What's going on?"

"She hasn't come out of her room for three days. Just keeps listening to all that whiny music. And the smell—haven't you noticed that heavy sweet scent seeping under her door?"

Kevin shook his head.

His mother exhaled noisily. "I think she's using marijuana."

Kevin nodded. "Okay. Don't worry, Ma. I'll talk to her."

*   *   *

As he climbed the stairs, strains of *Surrealistic Pillow* by the Airplane drifted into the hall. He knocked on his sister's door, which was firmly shut.

"It's me, Mags. Kev."

"Hey. Come on in."

He opened the door. The window air conditioner rumbled, providing a noisy underbeat to the music, but it was still August hot inside the room. Kevin wiped a hand across his brow. Her shades were drawn, and the only light streamed out from a tiny desk lamp. Long shadows played across posters taped on the wall: the Beatles in Sgt. Pepper uniforms, Jim Morrison and the Doors, and a yellow and black sunflower with WAR IS NOT HEALTHY FOR CHILDREN AND OTHER LIVING THINGS.

Maggie sprawled on her bed reading the *Chicago Seed*. What was she doing with that underground garbage? The dicks read it down at the station. Said they got good intelligence from it. But his sister? He wanted to snatch it away.

"What's happening?" he asked, managing to control himself.

Maggie looked up. She had the same blue eyes and features as her mother, but her hair was brown, not auburn, and it reached halfway down her back. Today it was held back by a red paisley bandana. She was wearing jeans and a puffy white peasant blouse. She held up the newspaper. "You want to know, read this."

She slid off her bed and struck a match over a skinny black stick on the windowsill. A wisp of smoke twirled up from the stick. Within a few seconds, a sickly sweet odor floated through the air.

The music ended. The arm of the record player clicked, swung back, and a new LP dropped on the turntable. As Maggie flounced back on the bed, another smell, more potent than the incense, swam toward him. Kevin covered his nose. "What is that awful smell?"

"Patchouli oil."

"Pa—who oil?"

"Pa-chu-lee. It's a Hindu thing. Supposed to balance the emotions and calm you when you're upset."

Kevin took the opening. "Mom's worried about you."

"She ought to be worried. The country is falling apart."

Bernie had said the same thing, he recalled. But for different reasons. "How do you mean?"

"Idiots are running things. And anytime someone makes sense, they get assassinated."

"Does that mean you should just stay in your room and listen to music?"

"You'd rather see me in the streets?"

"Is that where you want to be?"

"Maybe." Then, "You remember my friend Jimmy?"

"The guy you were dating . . ."

She nodded. "He was going to work for Bobby."

"Who?"

"Bobby Kennedy. They asked him to be the youth coordinator for Bobby's campaign. He was going to drop out of college for a semester. I was too. It would have been amazing. But now . . ." She shrugged.

"Hey . . ." Kevin tried to think of a way to reach her. "Don't give up. What would Dad say?"

"He'd understand. He might have been a cop, but he hated what was happening. Especially to Michael."

Kevin winced. Two years ago their older brother, Michael, had been drafted. Twenty-fifth Infantry. Third Brigade. Pleiku. A year ago they got word he was MIA. Their father died three months after that, ostensibly from a stroke. His mother still wasn't the same.

"Dad would have told you that Michael died doing his job," he said slowly.

"Launching an unprovoked, unlawful invasion into a quiet little country was Michael's job?"

"That sounds like something you read in that—in that." Kevin pointed a finger at the *Seed*.

Maggie's face lit with anger. "Kevin, what rock have you been hiding under? First Martin Luther King, then Bobby. And now we're trying to annihilate an entire culture because of some outdated concept of geopolitical power. This country is screwed up!"

Kevin felt himself get hot. "Damn it, Mags. It's not that complicated. We're over there trying to save the country, not destroy it. It's only these—these agitators who are trying to convince you it's wrong."

"These 'agitators,' as you call them, are the sanest people around."

"Throwing rocks, nominating pigs for president?"

"That's just to get attention. It got yours." Maggie glared. "Did you know Father Connor came out against the war?"

Kevin was taken aback.

She nodded. "He said it's become the single greatest threat to our country. And that any American who acquiesces to it, actively or passively, ought to be ashamed before God."

Kevin ran his tongue around his lips. "He's just a priest," he said finally.

She spread her hands. "Maybe you should have gone into the army instead of the police. What good is a deferment if you don't understand why you got it?"

"I'm the oldest son. The primary support of the family."

"Well, then, start supporting us."

He stared at his sister. "Dad would be ashamed of you, Maggie."

"How do you know? Mother came out against the war."

"What are you talking about?"

"You should have seen her talking to Father Connor after church last week. Why don't you ask her how she feels?"

"I don't need to. I already know."

Maggie shook her head. "You're wrong. It's different now, Kevin. You're gonna have to choose."

He averted his eyes and gazed at an old photo on the windowsill. Himself, Mike, and Maggie. He remembered when it was taken. He and Mike were eleven and twelve, Maggie seven. Mike had been wearing mismatched argyle socks. He was scared his father would notice, and he begged Kevin not to tell. Kevin never did. It was their secret forever.

Monday night Mayor Daley formally opened the 1968 Democratic National Convention. Marchers set up a picket line near the Amphitheater, and thirty demonstrators were arrested. But there was no violence, and it was a relatively quiet shift. Kevin didn't touch his riot gear.

It was a different story at Lincoln Park, he learned the next morning, as he and Bernie huddled with other cops in the precinct's parking lot.

"They beat the crap out of us," Wilkerson said. "See this?" He pointed to a shiner around his left eye. "But don't worry." He nodded at the sympathetic noises from the men. "I gave it back." He went on to describe how hundreds of protestors had barricaded themselves inside the park after the eleven o'clock curfew. Patrol cars were pelted by rocks. Demonstrators tried to set cars on fire. When that didn't work, they lobbed baseballs embedded with nails. The police moved in with tear gas, the crowd spilled into Old Town, and there were hundreds of injuries and arrests. Wilkerson said the mayor was calling in the guard.

"What did I tell you?" Bernie punched Kevin's shoulder. "No respect. For anything." When Kevin didn't answer, Bernie spat on the asphalt. "Well, I'm ready for some breakfast."

They drove to a place in the Loop that served breakfast all day and headed to an empty booth, still wearing their uniforms. Two men at a nearby table traded glances. Kevin slouched in his seat.

One of the men cleared his throat. "Look . . ." He folded the newspaper and showed it to his companion.

Even from a distance, Kevin could see photos of police bashing in heads. "Listen to this," the man recited in a voice loud enough to carry over to them. " 'The savage beatings of protestors were unprecedented. And widespread. Police attacked without reason, even targeting reporters and photographers. For example, one reporter saw a young man shouting at a policeman, "Hey, I work for the Associated Press." The police officer responded, "Is that right, creep?" and proceeded to crack the reporter's skull with his nightstick.' "

Bernie drummed his fingers on the table and pretended not to hear. When their food came, Kevin pushed his eggs around the plate. "My parish priest came out against the war," he said.

Bernie chewed his bacon. "I'm sure the father is a sincere man. But has he ever seen any action?"

"Not in Nam."

"What about Lincoln Park? Has he ever dealt with these—these *demonstrators*?" Bernie lowered his voice when he spoke the word, as if it was profane.

Kevin shrugged.

"Well, then." Bernie dipped his head, as if he'd made a significant point.

I'll call your shiner and raise you an MIA? How could you compare Vietnam to Lincoln Park? "Maybe they have a point," Kevin said wearily.

"What point comes out of violence?"

"Couldn't they say the same about us?"

"We're soldiers, son." Bernie scowled. "We have a job to do. You can bet if I was on the front line . . ." He threw a glance at the two men at the next table, then looked back at Kevin. "Hey, are you sure you're up for this?"

"What do you mean?"

"You seem, well, I dunno." He gazed at him. "I got this feeling."

Kevin tightened his lips. "I'm fine, Bernie. Really."

*   *   *

The cemetery hugged the rear of the parish church. It was a small place, with only one or two mausoleums. Unlike the Doughertys, most Bridgeport dignitaries chose Rosehill, the huge cemetery on the North Side, as their final resting place. Kevin avoided going inside the church; he didn't want to run into Father Connor.

Despite the blanket of heat, birds twittered, and a slight breeze stirred an elm that somehow escaped Dutch elm disease. He strolled among the headstones until he reached the third row, second from the left. The epitaph read: HERE LIES A GOOD MAN, FATHER, AND GUARDIAN OF THE LAW.

Life with Owen Dougherty hadn't been easy. He was strict, and he rarely smiled, especially after he gave up drinking. But he'd been a fair man. Kevin remembered when he and his buddy Frank smashed their neighbor's window with a fly ball. Frank got a beating from his father, but Kevin didn't. His father forked over the money for the window, then made Kevin deliver groceries for six months to pay him back.

He sat beside his father's grave, clasped his hands together, and bowed his head. "What would you do, Dad?" Kevin asked. "This war may be wrong. It took Michael. But I'm a cop. I have a job to do. What should I do?"

The birds seemed to stop chirping. Even the traffic along Archer Avenue grew muted as Kevin waited for an answer.

Tuesday night Kevin and Bernie were assigned to the Amphitheater again. The convention site was quiet, but the rest of the city wasn't. On Wednesday morning Kevin heard how a group of clergymen showed up at Lincoln Park to pray with the protestors. Despite that, there was violence and tear gas and club swinging, and police cleared the park twice. Afterward, the demonstrators headed south to the Loop and Grant Park. At three a.m. the National Guard came in to relieve the police.

Greer transferred Bernie and Kevin to Michigan Avenue for the noon-to-midnight. Tension had been mounting since the Democrats defeated their own peace plank. When the protestors in Grant Park heard the news, the American flag near the band shell was lowered to half-mast, which triggered a push by police. When someone raised a red shirt on the flagpole, the police moved in again. A group of youth marshals lined up to try and hold back the two sides, but the police broke through, attacking with clubs, Mace, and tear gas.

As darkness fell, demonstration leaders put out an order to gather at the downtown Hilton. Protestors poured out of Grant Park onto Lake Shore Drive, trying to cross one of the bridges back to Michigan. The Balbo and Congress bridges were sealed off by guardsmen with machine guns and grenades, but the Jackson Street Bridge was passable. The crowd surged across.

The heat had lost its edge, and it was a beautiful summer night, the kind of night that begged for a ride in a convertible. When they were teenagers, Kevin's brother had yearned for their neighbor's yellow T-Bird. He'd made Kevin walk past their neighbor's driveway ten times a day with him to ogle it. He never recovered when it was sold to someone from Wisconsin.

"Hey, Dougherty. Look alive!" Kevin jerked his head up. Bernie's scowl was so fierce his bushy eyebrows had merged into a straight line. About thirty cops, including Kevin and Bernie, were forming a barricade. Behind the police line were guardsmen with bayonets on their rifles. A wave of kids broke toward them. When the kids reached the cops, they kept pushing. The cops pushed back. Kevin heard pops as canisters of tear gas were released. The kids covered their noses and mouths.

"Don't let them through!" Bernie yelled. Kevin

could barely hear him above the din. He twisted around. Bernie's riot stick was poised high above his head. He watched as Bernie swung, heard the *thwack* as it connected with a solid mass. A young boy in front of them dropped. Bernie raised his club again. Another *thwack*. The boy fell over sideways, shielding his head with his arms.

The police line wobbled and broke into knots of cops and kids, each side trying to advance. Kevin caught a whiff of cordite. Had some guardsman fired a rifle? The peppery smell of tear gas thickened the air. His throat was parched, and he could barely catch his breath. He threw on his gas mask, but it felt like a brick. He tore it off and let it dangle by the strap around his neck. Around him were screams, grunts, curses. An ambulance wailed as it raced down Congress. Its flashing lights punctuated the dark with theatrical, strobe-like bursts.

Somehow Kevin and Bernie became separated, and a young girl suddenly appeared in front of Kevin. She was wearing a white fluffy blouse and jeans, and her hair was tied back with a bandana. She looked like Maggie. Young people streamed past, but she lingered as if she had all the time in the world. She stared at him, challenging him with her eyes. Then she slowly held up two fingers in a V sign.

Kevin swallowed. A copper he didn't know jabbed her with his club. "You! Get back! Go back home to your parents!"

She stumbled forward and lost her balance. Kevin caught her and helped her up. She wiped her hands on her jeans, her eyes darting from the other cop to Kevin. She didn't seem to be hurt. She disappeared back into the crowd. Kevin was relieved.

A few yards away a group of cops and kids were shoving and shouting at each other. Rocks flew through the air.

"Traitors!" An angry voice that sounded like Bernie rose above the melee. His outburst was followed by more pops. As the tear gas canisters burst, a chorus of screams rose. The protestors tried to scatter, but they were surrounded by cops and guardsmen, and there was nowhere to go. The cops closed in and began making arrests.

Coughing from the gas, Kevin moved in. He was only a few feet away when the girl with the long hair and peasant blouse appeared again. This time she was accompanied by a slender boy with glasses. He was wearing a black T-shirt and jeans. The girl's bandana was wet and was tied around her nose and mouth. She was carrying a poster of a yellow sunflower with the words WAR IS NOT HEALTHY FOR CHILDREN AND OTHER LIVING THINGS.

The boy looked Kevin over. He and the girl exchanged nods. "What are you doing, copper man?" His eyes looked glassy.

Kevin kept his mouth shut.

"You don't want this blood on your hands. She told me how you helped her up. Come with us. You can, you know." The boy held out his hand as if he expected Kevin to take it.

Wisps of tear gas hovered over the sidewalk. Kevin tightened his grip on his club. He stared at the kids. The girl looked more and more like Maggie.

Suddenly, Bernie's voice came at them from behind. "Kevin. No! Don't even look at 'em!"

Kevin looked away.

"Don't listen to him, man!" The boy's voice rose above Bernie's. "You're not one of the pigs. You don't agree with this war, I can tell. Come with us."

Kevin looked down.

"Get back, you little creep!" Bernie moved to Kevin's side and hoisted his club.

The boy stood his ground. "You know you don't belong with"—he waved a hand—"him."

A commander in a white shirt at the edge of the barricade yelled through a megaphone, "Clear the

streets. Do you hear me, men? Clear the streets.
Now!"

Someone else shouted, "All right. Grab your gear.
Let's go!"

A line of police pressed forward, but the boy and
girl remained where they were. Everything fell away
except the sound of the boy's voice. In an odd way it
felt as silent as the cemetery behind the church.

"Time's running out, man," the boy said, his hand
half covering his mouth. "How can you defend the
law when you know it's wrong?"

Bernie's voice slammed into them like a hard fist.
"Kev, don't let him talk to you like that."

Kevin spun around. Bernie's face was purple with
rage. Brandishing his riot stick, he swung it down at
the boy's head. The boy jumped, but the club dealt a
glancing blow to his temple. The boy collapsed.

"Bernie, no!" Kevin seized Bernie's arm.

Bernie snatched his arm away. "Do your job,
Dougherty." He pointed to the kids with his club.
"They are the enemy!"

The girl turned to Kevin with a desperate cry.
"Make him stop!"

Kevin strained to see her face in the semidark. "Go.
Now. Get lost!"

"No! Help me get him up!" She knelt beside the
boy.

"What are you waiting for, Dougherty?" Bernie's
voice shot out, raw and brutal. He clubbed the boy
again. The boy lay curled on his side on the ground,
moaning. Blood gushed from his head. His glasses
were smashed.

"Do something!" the girl screamed at Kevin.
"Please!"

Her anguish seemed to throw Bernie into a frenzy.
His eyes were slits of fury. He raised his stick over
his head.

Kevin froze. Everything slowed down. Images of

Maggie floated through his mind. She could be in the crowd. Maybe Father Connor. Even his mother. He thought about Mike. And his father. What Bernie was doing. What *his* duty was. His duty was to serve and protect.

The moment of clarity came so sharply it hurt. His chest tightened, and his hands clenched into fists. For the first time—maybe in his entire twenty-three years—he knew what that duty meant.

"Dougherty." Bernie kept at him, his voice raspy. "Either you do it, or I will!"

Kevin stared at his partner. Then he dropped his club and threw himself over the girl. She groaned as his weight knocked the wind out of her. Her body folded up beneath him, but it didn't matter: she was safe. Kevin twisted around and caught a glimpse of Bernie. His riot stick was still raised high above his head.

Kevin wondered what his partner would do now. He hoped the whole world was watching.

I Killed

by Nancy Pickard

When the second man sat down, the green metal park bench groaned and sank into the dirt. He took the left side, leaving a polite foot and a half between his arthritic, spreading hips and the wide hips of the man leaning on the armrest on the other side of the bench.

They glanced at each other. Nodded heavily, like two old bulls acknowledging one another's right to be there. Then they turned their beefy faces back to the view. Each man inhaled deeply, as if his worn-out senses could still detect the burnt-grass, baked-dirt scent of autumn.

They both wore baggy gym suits that looked as if nobody had ever run in them.

Behind them stretched an expanse of golden grass, and then the elegance of Fifty-fifth Street. On the opposite side of Fifty-fifth, the big windows of large, well-maintained houses looked out over the same beautiful vista the two men faced. In front of them, there was a cement path, then trees, then the golden-green, rolling acreage of Jacob L. Loose Park. If they'd hoisted their aching bodies up, and limped to the right, they'd have come to a pond where swans paddled in bad-tempered glory all summer, but which

Canada geese owned now that it was late November. If they'd hobbled left, instead, they'd have come to tennis courts, wading pool, rose garden, playground. Mansions and high-rise, high-priced condos ringed the big park in the middle of Kansas City, Missouri. To the north was a private school, then the Country Club Plaza shopping center; to the south were the neighborhoods of Brookside, Waldo, and a short drive to the suburbs.

It was a tranquil, wealthy, civilized scene in the heart of the city.

The man on the right side of the bench said, in a voice made gravelly from time and the cigars he no longer smoked, "You come here often?"

After a long moment, as if he hadn't much liked being spoken to and was considering ignoring it, the second man said, "No."

His voice sounded as if he, too, had been a heavy smoker in his day.

"I do." The first man coughed, deep, racking, phlegmy. "I come here every day." When he was finished hacking, he said, without apologizing for the spasm, "This bench, every afternoon, regular as clockwork."

"That right." His bench companion looked away, sounding bored.

"Yes, it is. You know the history of this park?"

"History?" Now the second man looked where the first man was pointing him, with a finger that looked like a fat, manicured sausage. He saw a black cannon, a pyramid of cannonballs, and what looked like a semicircle of signs for tourists. "No, I don't know it."

And don't care to, his tone implied.

"This was the scene of the last big Missouri battle in the Civil War. October twenty-third, 1864. The Feds had chased the Rebs all across the state from Saint Louis, but the Rebs kept getting away. Finally, they took a stand here. Right here, in this spot. Picture it. It was cold, not like today. They were tired, hungry.

There was a Confederate general right here, where that big old tree is. It's still called the General's Tree. His graycoats were standing here, cannons facing across the green. Then the bluecoats suddenly came charging up over that rise, horses on the run, sabers glinting, guns blazing."

He paused, but there was no response.

"Thirty thousand men in the battle that day."

Again, he paused, and again there was no response.

"There was a mass grave dug afterwards, only a few blocks west of here."

Finally, the second man said, "That right?"

A corner of the historian's mouth quirked up. "Mass graves always get people's attention. Saddam would still be alive without 'em. You just can't kill too many people without somebody noticing."

"Who won?"

"Feds, of course. Battle of Westport." Abruptly, he changed the subject. "So what'd you do?"

"What did I *do*?"

The question rumbled out like thunder from a kettledrum.

"Yeah. Before you got here to this park bench. I'm assuming you're retired. You look around my age. You'll pardon my saying so, but we both got that look of being twenty years older than maybe we are. And not to mention, you're sitting here in the middle of a weekday afternoon, like me."

"Almost."

"Almost what? My age, or retired?"

"Both, probably."

"I figured. You always think so long before you speak?"

There was a moment's silence which seemed to confirm it, and then, "Sometimes."

"Well, retire quick, is my advice. I was a salesman."

The other man finally looked over at him, but skeptically. A slight breeze picked up a few strands of his thin hair, dyed black, and waved it around like insect antennae before releasing it to fall back onto his pale skull again.

"You weren't," he said, flatly.

"Yeah, I was. I don't look it, I know. You expect somebody smooth looking, somebody in a nice suit, not some fat goombah in a baby blue nylon gym suit. Baby blue. My daughter picked it out. Appearances are deceiving. I don't go to any gym, either. But ask anybody who knows me, they'll tell you, I was a salesman."

"If you say so."

"I do say so. So what were you? In your working days?"

Instead of answering, his park bench companion smiled for the first time, a crooked arrangement at one corner of his mouth. "Were you good at selling stuff?"

"You look like you think that's funny. It's serious, the sales business, and supporting your family. Serious stuff. Yeah, I was good. How about you?"

"I killed."

"No kidding. Doing what?"

The other man placed his left arm over the back of the park bench. His big chest rose and fell as he inhaled, then exhaled, through his large, pockmarked nose. "Let me think how to put this," he said, finally, in his rumbling voice. "I never know what to tell people. You'd think I'd have an answer by now." He was silent for a few moments. "Okay. I was a performance artist, you might say."

"Really. I'm not sure what that is. Comedian?"

"Sometimes."

"No kidding! Where'd you appear?"

"Anywhere they paid me."

"Ha. I know how that is. Would I have heard of you?"

"You might. I hope not."

"You didn't want to be *famous*?"

"Hell no." For the first time, the answer came fast. "That's the last thing I'd ever want."

"But—"

"Fame can be . . . confining."

"I get you." The first man nodded, his big, fleshy face looking sage. "Paparazzi, and all that. Can't go anyplace without having flashbulbs go off in your face."

"I hate cameras of any kind. Don't want none of them around, no."

"Imagine if reporters had been here *that* day . . ."

"What day?"

"The Battle of Westport."

"Oh."

"Embedded with the troops, like in Iraq. Interviews with the generals. Shots of the wounded. What a mess."

"And no TVs to show it on."

The first man let out a laugh, a booming *ha*. "That's right."

His companion took them back to their other topic, as if he'd warmed up to it. "Lotsa people with lotsa money aren't famous. You'd be surprised. They're rich as Bill Gates, and nobody's ever heard of them."

"I wouldn't be so surprised."

"Yeah, probably not. You look like a wise guy."

"You wouldn't think I was so wise, not if you'd ask my son."

"What's the matter with him?" The second man was talking faster now, now that he was asking questions, instead of answering them. They were getting into a rhythm, a pace, a patter. "He think you're an idiot?"

"He says I'm a fool, ought to mind my own business."

"But you retired from that, didn't you?"

"From what?"

"Minding your own business."

That earned another explosive *ha*, followed by some coughing. "That's right, I did."

"So the only business you got left to mind is his."

"Ha! You're right. That's pretty funny."

"But he doesn't think so. Your son, he's not so amused by you?"

"A serious guy, my son." The man in the baby blue gym suit sniffed, the corners of his mouth dropped into a frown. He settled his body more heavily into the bench. If he still smoked, it was a moment when he'd have puffed reflectively, resentfully, on his cigar. After a moment, he pulled himself up and alert again. "So. Tell me. You make any money being a comedian who didn't want to get famous?"

"I made plenty."

"Clubs?"

"I did some of those. And private jobs."

"That's how you got to know the rich people who aren't famous?"

"Some were famous. Some got famous after I met them. I'd see their pictures and their names in the papers."

"Those ones—they ever call you again after they got famous?"

"No." He smiled slightly. "They were beyond me by then."

"Really. Stupid shits. People get big heads, that's what fame'll do. They think they're too good—"

"They're dead to me now." He smiled to himself again, as at a private joke.

"Sure. So what was your act?

"My act?" He frowned.

"Your shtick. You know, your routine."

"I didn't have no set routine. That's dangerous, to be too predictable like that. You don't want people to know what's coming, you want to keep your edge, keep *them* on edge, so you take them by surprise, startle them, come at them out of the blue where they're not expecting it. It's intimidating that way. You shock 'em. Knock 'em off balance and never let 'em get back up straight again. Then you just keep knocking 'em down—"

"Knockin' the jokes down—"

"Until they're bent over, pleading and gasping for you to stop, 'cause it hurts so bad."

"Been a long time since I laughed like that. That's as good as sex. If I recall."

The second man smiled at that. "Yeah, it's real satisfying. I guess you'd say I have a talent for shocking people. And for improvisation."

"Like George Carlin? Or that black kid with the mouth on him, Chris Rock? Not everybody can get away with stuff like that."

"I've gotten away with it for a long time."

"Good for you. So that was your act? Improv?"

"Sometimes. It varied."

"Depended on the venue, I suppose. You're smiling. Did I say something naive?"

"No, no, you're right. A lot depends on the venue, whether it's in the open air—like this, like a park, for instance. Or maybe it's inside. Could be a great big room, even as big as a stadium, or could be as small as a bathroom. Size of the audience makes a difference, too, now that you mention it, now that you've got me talking about it. Some things will go over well in a big crowd that are just overkill when there's nobody around. And vice versa. That was part of the improvisation."

"You get hecklers?"

"If I did, I took them out."

"Pretty good audiences, though?"

"I had very attentive audiences. Very."

"What's your secret?"

"You want to get their full attention immediately. Don't give them any time to adjust to your appearance. Hit 'em upside the head."

"A big joke right off the bat, huh?"

"A two-by-four. A baseball bat. *Bam.* Get their undivided attention. I'm not a subtle guy."

"Pretty broad comedy, huh?"

"Pretty broad . . . there was one of those in Pittsburgh."

"Ha ha. Vaudeville, like. Slapstick. That you?"

"Slapstick. I coulda used one of those."

"Ha ha. Borscht belt comedy. You Jewish?"

"Me? No way. I was circumspect, not circumcised."

"Ha! You're a wise guy, too."

"That I am."

"What about costumes? You ever wear costumes?"

"Yeah. Hairpieces. Teeth. Mustaches. Canes, crutches. I got a closet full of them, or I would have if I'd kept any of it."

"Your own mother wouldn't have recognized you?"

"My mother's dead."

"Oh, I'm sorry."

"It was a long time ago. I killed her, too."

"That's nice, that she appreciated your humor. Your dad, you get your funny bone from him?"

"Oh, yeah, he was hilarious." It sounded bitter, as if there was jealousy. "He killed me. Nearly."

"Is that unusual?"

"What?"

"A comic from a happy family? I thought all comedians came from bad families, like they had to laugh to keep from cryin', that kind of thing."

"I don't know about that."

"Not much of a philosopher, like you're not much of a historian?"

"Hey." Defensive. "When I was workin', I knew what I believed, and what I didn't. That's philosophy, ain't it?"

"Like, what did you believe?"

"I believed in doing my job, and not cryin' over it."

"Me, too."

"That right?"

"Yeah, do your job and fuck the regrets."

"Or fuck the pretty broads in Pittsburgh."

"I think maybe we're kind of alike, you and me."

"A salesman and a comedian."

"You still don't buy it that I was a salesman, do you?"

"You said it yourself, you don't look the part."

"I look the part as much as you look like a comedian."

"You bought it. Askin' me all about it."

"I was sellin' you. You think I'm no salesman, but I sold people down the river all the time. But you already know that, don't you? What? Gone silent again? Nothin' to say? So who sent you? One of those wise guys I ratted out? My son? Somebody else in the Family? And where's your two-by-four? You got a reputation for takin' 'em by surprise, knocking 'em flat first thing, you said so yourself. So why the conversation first before you take me out?"

"The conversation was your idea."

"What about the two-by-four?"

"Not as quick as the gun in my pocket."

"What about the noise?"

"Silencer."

"Witnesses?"

They both looked around, both of them taking note of the two young women with baby carriages over by the historical markers, of the middle-aged male jogger moving their way from the west, of the young couple leaning up against a tree.

"Witnesses to what? I get up and stand in front of you to continue our conversation. You slump over, but nobody sees past me. I grab your shoulder to say good-bye. When I leave, you're an old man in a baby blue tracksuit, asleep on a park bench, and I'm an old man walkin' back to my car."

"And then what?"

"Then you go to hell. I go home and retire."

"You're retiring, all right. See this wire on my baby blue jacket? And see those young women and that jogger coming our way? They're FBI. If you looked behind you, you'd see a few more, including a sniper in the bedroom window of that nice house back there. He's aiming at your head, so don't think you can take a shot at mine. I just made my last sale, Mr. Comedian. And you're the product."

He stood up, slowly, heavily, and then turned and looked down at the fat man with the gun in his pocket.

"You should have paid more attention to history when I was trying to tell you.

"You want to know why the Confederates lost? Because the greedy fuckers stole a farmer's old gray mare, which pissed him off, and so he told the Feds where they could sneak over that ridge." He pointed north and a little west, as the first two agents laid hands on the shoulders of the other man. "It took the Rebs completely by surprise. Then they got surrounded, and they never had a chance." The agents hoisted his audience to his feet. "Just like you were going to steal my life, which pissed me off, so I told the Feds how to sneak up on you, so they could surround you, and you wouldn't stand a chance. You know the old song? 'The old gray mare, she ain't what she used to be'? Your life and mine, they ain't what they used to be, but my life is still mine." He banged his meaty right thumb on his chest. "I'm hanging on to it, like that farmer and his old gray mare.

"You know what they say about history," he called out, raising his voice to make sure the other man heard as they led him away. "If you don't pay attention to it, you're bound to repeat it!"

Maubi and the Jumbies

by Kate Grilley

A roach coach is the closest St. Chris comes to an after-hours joint.

When the restaurants and bars in Isabeya are shuttered and silent, the last of the weekend revelers—mostly local boys-going-on-men in their late teens—head for the waterfront parking area near Fort Frederick to cluster around a shiny aluminium-sided Grumman Kurbmaster step van labeled in foot-high red letters, MAUBI'S HOT TO TROT. The Os sprout dancing yellow and orange flames like the garish hair colors favored by MTV punk rockers, a hairstyling trend rarely seen on our tiny patch in the Caribbean.

A construction worker forced into early retirement by an accident that shattered his left leg—leaving him with a permanent limp and occasionally dependent on a cane—Maubi sells cold sodas, homemade ginger beer, and maubi from ice-filled coolers, and takeout platters from the foil-lined containers of West Indian snacks and fried chicken kept hot under infrared lamps.

Late one Friday night in early April, I stopped for a take-home snack. Maubi sat inside his van, elbows resting on the serving counter, chatting with a handful of lingering customers. Michael's voice crackled over the airwaves from an old boom box radio sitting up high on a back shelf. Maubi ended a ribald story with a thigh-slapping belly laugh to greet me with a warm smile.

"Morning Lady! What carries you to town so late?"

"Last-minute parade stuff and the memory of your wife's pates. Got any left?"

"Beef or saltfish?" I never ordered saltfish, but Maubi always asked just the same.

"Two beef, please."

"I got beef roti tonight."

"I'll take one. And a chicken leg for Minx." I knew from experience a cat will forgive any slight if there's a food bribe involved. In the five years we've been together, Minx has become hooked on Maubi's fried chicken.

"Something to drink?"

"Your specialty," I said, smiling. "A large one."

Maubi grinned. "Brewed it fresh myself this week in my big enamel kettle. Best maubi batch ever." He kissed the tips of his fingers as a sign of his own approval, chortling as he packed my food and drink in a cardboard box.

"Is your quadrille group ready for the *Navidad de Isabeya* parade next weekend?" I asked, digging in my fanny pack for cash.

"My band's been practicing every evening with the dancers at the legion hall."

"The parade wouldn't be a success without you. I've put your group at the end of the lineup."

"Saving the best for last," said Maubi with a broad smile. "Where you parked?"

I pointed to my ten-year-old hatchback a short distance away.

"That's too far to go by yourself. The jumbies could get you." He leaned toward me, lowering his voice. "It's not safe like the old days. We got drug dealers and lowlifes limin' around the fort. That's why I come to rest my van down here so late. Keep my boy and his friends out of trouble."

"You've done a good job," I said, putting the change in my coin purse. "He's a fine boy. He's graduating this year, isn't he?"

"First in his class." Maubi beamed with pride. "He got a scholarship to Cornell to study hotel management. He works at Harborview on weekends, they want him full-time this summer."

He called to his son. "Quincy! You take this food and see Miss Kelly gets to her car safe. Then come back and help me close up. It's time we go home."

Quincy and I were at my car when we heard a clopping sound like horses' hooves, followed by Maubi's cry, "Jumbie be gone!"

We quickly turned toward the van to see Maubi throwing salt in the air through the serving window.

Maubi pointed at Kongens Gade in the direction of the Anglican church on the western edge of town. Quincy sprinted up Isabeya's main street against the sparse one-way traffic while I stayed at the van.

"Maubi, what happened?" I asked.

"I feel a chill. A sure sign there be a jumbie about."

I looked around and saw nothing out of the ordinary. The salt under my feet rasped like sandpaper against the rubber soles of my flip-flops.

"Why the salt?"

"Jumbie cure. If you throw salt on the skin of a jumbie, it can't harm you. I always keep my salt close."

I thought of my grandmother's tales of spirits in her native Ireland, and the luck stone with a hole in it she'd given me when I was a child that now hung from a leather thong over my bed with my collection of dream catchers. The Irish tradition said if anyone looked upon you with an evil eye, looking back at them through the hole in the stone would ward off any harm they might wish you.

Quincy jogged slowly back to the van, panting from his fruitless exertion.

Maubi took his cane from a hook and pounded it against the floor of the van. A sound reminiscent of horses' hooves. He began to laugh. He laughed until he was gasping for breath and tears were streaming down his face.

"I fool you," Maubi said when he was able to speak.

Quincy and I were not amused.

The next afternoon I took the ferry from the Dockside Hotel on the Isabeya waterfront over to Harborview on Papaya Quay where Quincy was working at the water sports pavilion.

The history of Papaya Quay includes a ghost.

Until the fire that destroyed Isabeya in 1764, Papaya Quay was uninhabited.

After the fire, the Danish government was homeless with only Fort Frederick left standing to house the soldiers and dispossessed town residents. Temporary Government House quarters were established on Papaya Quay.

When the first phase of the new Government House at the foot of Kongens Gade was completed five years later, Papaya Quay became the governor's private retreat.

Island legend tells us that the governor had a mistress—an enchanting beauty who claimed descent from the original Arawak Indians—whom he stashed at Papaya Quay until her death one night during an early spring yellow fever epidemic. She was buried on the quay, but her grave has never been found.

It is said she haunts her former home to this day, walking back and forth along the Harborview terrace waiting and watching for her lover to come to her by boat.

Quincy and I sat on the terrace drinking iced tea. We decided to bring the legend to life that very evening.

We enlisted the help of two of the Mocko Jumbies—gaily dressed dancing figures on stilts, a highlight of every St. Chris parade.

Shortly after midnight, Isabeya was again shuttered and silent, the quiet broken only by chirping crickets near the gazebo bandstand on the green between the fort and the library, the slap of waves against the boardwalk, and twanging boat lines. The Harborview ferry was docked for the night at Papaya Quay, the boat captain snoring in his bunk in the harbormaster's quarters.

Maubi sat in his van facing the harbor, chatting with the last of his customers. He stopped in the middle of a story to stare wide-eyed at a wooden rowboat approaching the seaside boardwalk from the direction of Harborview. He began to shiver.

In the boat were a man and woman in eighteenth-century clothing. The man wore a Danish officer's uniform, with the scarlet sash across his chest favored by the governor for formal occasions. The woman was dressed in a resplendent ball gown, a gossamer shawl covering her head and shoulders.

Maubi grabbed the salt.

The man extended his hand to help the woman alight from the boat. As they passed silently arm in arm in front of Maubi's van, salt showered the couple like wedding rice.

The electric lights in front of Government House blinked once, then went out. Flickering candle flames were visible in the windows of the Government House ballroom. The couple passed through the locked iron gates separating the Government House driveway from Kongens Gade, up the broad set of outside stairs to the double doors at the formal entrance on the second floor. As they slipped through the doors, the strains of a minuet were heard from the candlelit ballroom. Once the couple was inside, the music ceased and the candles were extinguished one by one until

Government House was again darkened. A woman laughed merrily. Then all was silent. The lights in front of Government House slowly brightened to normal.

Quincy and I bit our fingers to keep our guffaws in check. My luck stone dropped from my hand to rest on my chest like a pendant suspended from the leather thong around my neck.

As we were ready to leap from our hiding place to yell "Fooled you!" at Maubi, a second boat approached the boardwalk. A rogue wave caught the boat broadside, spilling the occupants into the sea. We heard familiar voices cursing as they thrashed about in the shallows, weighted down by their heavy clothing. Quincy and I ran to the boardwalk to help our sodden friends out of the water.

When we talk about that night, which isn't often, we always have shakers of salt in our hands.

"Maubi and the Jumbies" was originally published in the Fall 1999 issue of Murderous Intent *magazine. In 2000 it was an Agatha nominee for Best Short Story and received a Best Short Story Macavity Award.*

Estelle Is Dead

by Medora Sale

TEMPTATION

Kate Brady tossed her keys on the table and began sorting rapidly through a week's worth of mail. The brightly colored flyers landed in the basket in the hall; everything else, no matter how unpromising it looked, went into the dining room with her. Once she had trashed a check for eighteen hundred dollars because it had come in an envelope that looked like a begging letter. Now she opened everything.

Bills and financial statements went into a pile. Requests from charities and classier advertising glided into another wastepaper basket. The last envelope was from a university, probably raising funds. She slit it open impatiently, glanced at the single sheet of paper inside, and paused.

Her hand hovered over the basket, drew back, and set the letter down on top of the bills and statements, to be taken into her tidy little office.

She disposed of the bills and statements rapidly and efficiently, checking every item, prepared—if necessary—to spend the rest of the day disputing an interest charge or error. She had fended off poverty and eviction for too long after leaving home to turn careless over money.

Only the letter remained. It demanded a decision. She was between books. Worse yet, between contracts. An irritating restless lethargy enveloped her, prodding her into useless activity and keeping her from sleep. And yesterday a set of royalty statements had arrived, confirming what she already knew. Sales of her type of fiction—the romantic-sadistic thriller—were falling. People were tired of bodice slashers. She lay awake at night thinking of a long old age and no new income. When that onetime windfall, the film rights to *Death on a Double-Edged Blade,* had come in twelve years before, her accountant had pointed out that she had better figure on living at least until eighty-five. Forty-seven more years, it was then. She had bought her house, paid cash for it, and started salting away her money. But it wasn't going to be enough.

Why ask her—of all people—to come and speak at Sight and Sound: The Windsor Festival of the Arts, surrounded by poets, artists and scornful intellectuals. At least she wouldn't run into any old friends, she thought grimly. If she went. No, she couldn't. Still . . . She picked up the letter again. How much were they paying?

The hotel lobby was small and gleaming with polish on the brass and dark wood. The plump, pretty woman behind the desk greeted her with the enthusiasm of a long-lost friend and Kate wondered for a moment if she was. She looked at her again. Not a chance. When Kate had moved to Chicago, this bouncing creature hadn't learned to ride a tricycle yet. She smiled and checked in.

"I almost forgot, Ms. Brady," said the desk clerk. "There's a letter for you."

She walked into the dimly lit room, swung her suitcase up on the bed, and dropped her shoulder bag on the floor. She peered into the dimness for a light switch. "My God, Kate, you're going blind," she muttered and yanked back the heavy curtains covering one wall. Light flooded the room.

The window was the width of the room and overlooked the river. From where she stood, she could see all the way upriver to the bend in the east and downriver to the bridge and islands to the west. It was even better than the view from the tiny room in her grandmother's attic. At that moment, as if it had timed its arrival for her benefit, a lake boat came into view, on its stately progress down from Lake Superior in the golden sunshine. During how many nights of her stormy childhood had the melancholy, reassuring sound of the lake boats' foghorns lulled her to sleep? Her face softened. Maybe tonight there would be fog.

She turned and kicked her shoulder bag. "For chrissake, Kate," she muttered to herself. "You're pathetic. In a minute you'll be sobbing over this shitty town and all your shitty little friends. Friends. I bet they're fat as pigs with six kids each, living on welfare."

Then she noticed that she was still clutching the letter.

"Dear Estelle," it began. She froze for a second, unable to think, hardly able to breathe. She took a deep breath and started reading again.

Welcome home! I was thrilled to discover that you had agreed to speak at Sight and Sound. I know you'll be a great addition to the weekend's entertainment. I've been following your career as closely as I could since we were all in school together. In those days, I admit, I worshipped you from afar. Alas, you've been even further from my grasp since then.

There is so much that I would like to talk to you about, and even more that I would like to tell the world about your varied talents.

I am writing an article about your life and exploits for the *Star*. If you wish to discuss what ought to go into it, meet me tonight at nine o'clock at the east end of the sculpture garden. There is a bench in between the four pillars standing alone and the plump, self-satisfied gentleman on the horse. A fitting spot, I thought. I will be there.

You still look pretty athletic these days. It's not far from your hotel, and you'll find there's enough light for walking. E.

"Who in hell is E.?" she said, crumpling up the paper and then smoothing it out again over her thighs.

The telephone rang and she jumped like a frightened cat. "Yes," she said in a cracked, uncertain voice.

"Ms. Brady? Kate Brady?"

She murmured agreement.

"Rob Martin, from the Sight and Sound committee. I hope you had a good trip. Look, most of the others came in yesterday and we laid on a dinner for them. We thought you deserved a good meal as well. How about tonight? Can I pick you up at the hotel at six thirty? Or have you made other plans?"

It was like talking to a bulldozer. By the time he gave her a chance to answer, it was too late. She had agreed to meet him downstairs, said she would be wearing black with a red leather jacket, and hung up.

Rob Martin appeared to be in his late thirties or early forties. He was balding slightly, but that suited his rangy, athletic-looking frame. His smile was friendly, his grey eyes cool and assessing. If he hadn't been a little young for her, she might have considered him as possible—very possible—light relief during the next four days. She still might, she thought, glad that she had dressed with care.

"Where are we going for dinner?" she asked, bracing herself for the worst. She couldn't remember there being a whole lot of decent restaurants around here.

"To the Art Gallery," he said, with a quirky smile that—annoyingly—reminded her of someone.

"Isn't that carrying the idea of the weekend a bit far? Do we bring sandwiches and munch as we troop through the exhibits? Or are there benches to sit on?"

"There's definitely someplace to sit," he said coolly. "The gallery has a restaurant with interesting food, artistically presented, of course. I thought you might like it. If you prefer a burger somewhere, we can do that, too. But the Art Gallery is just along the street. We can walk there in two minutes."

Kate brooded over the menu, hovering between the venison *espiritu* and the duck breast *vestido de fumar*. "I have to admit that I wasn't expecting this sort of food," she said. "It doesn't fit exactly with my image of the city."

"Try the venison. It might change your image," said Rob. "Ms. Brady will have the venison," he murmured to the waitress. "And I'll have the duck." He turned back to Kate. "But haven't people around here always appreciated good food?"

"Do you come from here?"

"I grew up in a town near London, came here to go to university and never left. What about you? Have you always lived in Chicago?"

"Winnetka," she said. "It's not quite Chicago. But it's on the lake as well. I like living near water."

"So do I," he said. "Sometimes. It's fascinating. It has its dark and destructive side, though, don't you think?"

The arrival of the wine relieved her from having to respond to that one.

Lunch had been a cup of coffee and the venison was superb. She ate everything on her plate except for a sprig of fresh herbs and the flower, and sat back, turning her wineglass around and around, staring at it. "Why invite me to speak?" she asked abruptly. "Along with the pretentious arty types. My junk doesn't exactly fit the image. I write 'bodice slashers,' as my editor calls them—pink perfumed scary porn— to make a living."

"We all have to make a living," he said smoothly. "I suppose someone on the committee likes your books and thinks it'll be fun to have you on the list. I don't know. I'm a messenger boy, that's all—not one of the powerhouses. Why did you come?"

"Curiosity, I suppose," she said.

"Killed the cat," he replied with a lazy grin. "What are you up to tonight? I could take you around to the nightspots, or if you prefer, there's a poetry reading at the Capitol Theatre."

"I'd love to," she said, injecting all the sincerity at her command into her voice, "but after driving all day and eating this spectacular dinner—you know, it really was terrific," she added, in normal tones. "But I'm going for a walk along the river with a friend. Like I said, I have a thing about rivers."

"I thought you didn't know anyone here."

"He's from Detroit. I said I'd meet him at eight thirty."

JUDGEMENT

Kate went back to her hotel room and put on the pale yellow outfit she wore for her daily two- to three-mile walks. It showed off her legs—still one of her real assets—making them look even longer than they were. She flicked a comb through her shiny hair, snapped her pouch with cab fare and room key around her waist, and set off.

She crossed the broad drive that separated the hotels and the Art Gallery from the riverside park and plunged from light into darkness. Trees blocked out

the streetlights, swallowing up the ambient glow of the
city and the water. She had forgotten how dark it
could be down here and ran down the broad path in
a mild panic. When she reached the riverbank, she
slowed to catch her breath. The water ran smoothly
along beside her, murmuring reassuringly, giving her
back her strength and courage. She stretched her legs
out and began walking quickly and confidently toward
the meeting place.

She passed the four pillars and looked up the hill-
side. There was the wooden bench, halfway up the
hill. A figure on the bench was silhouetted in the light
from the street above, arms spread out, head tipped
back, long legs, crossed at the ankles, stretched out in
front of him—the essence of relaxation.

She stopped dead halfway up the slope and gasped.
"Omigod." It came out between a squeak and a
scream. "Jack! No—it can't be." She clapped her
hand over her mouth to keep herself from saying
more. The man looked over at her. The headlights
of a passing car swept over his face and she laughed.
"Oh. It's you. For a minute there, I thought you were
someone else. You really gave me a turn. What are
you doing here?"

"Waiting for you, Estelle."

"Sorry. The name is Kate, or Katie, if you must."

"That's up there, on the other side of the road.
Down here by the river you're Estelle. Beautiful Estelle Leblanc. You know, in this light you look almost
the same."

"Almost?"

"Lithe, slender, graceful as a deer. And strong."

"I still am," she protested. "I haven't gained a
pound in thirty years."

"Maybe. But you've turned from a schoolboy's fantasy into something nasty, hard and stiff. It's sad. But
no matter. We're not here to talk about the ravages
of time. I saw you that night with Jack, you know.
Down there. On the far side of the railing."

"I don't know anyone named Jack," she said. "You're crazy. And I think I've heard enough." She tried to move away and found that her wrist was caught in a grip of steel.

"I don't know how you got him down there on the rocks. Remember how terrified he was of water? But you did, and you pushed him in. I saw you."

"That's crazy. Why would I push him in?"

"Because he was hard to get rid of, Estelle. Because you promised to marry him and he believed you. He told me that."

"That's a lie. I never said I'd marry him."

"He bought you a ring—he showed it to me. You accepted it and promised to be his forever. But why say you'd marry him and kill him a month later?"

"I never killed him. He slipped," she said quickly. "He did. It was awful. It had been raining and the rocks were slippery. I tried to save him but I couldn't."

"No—*I* tried to save him, Estelle," he said. "You ran away. I jumped in after him, but it was dark and I couldn't find him."

"That's not true." She slumped down on the bench beside him. "I thought I was pregnant," she said, in a vague, faraway voice. "My dad would've killed me. But I wasn't, after all. When I told him, he wouldn't take his ring back."

"You'd got rid of the baby. Jack's baby."

"So? Big deal." She shrugged her shoulders. "You can't print any of this, you know. I'll sue you and I'll sue the paper for all it's worth. Okay. We were engaged. Then we broke up. Jack drowned trying to rescue his little brother who came to get him and fell in the river. The little brother got out, but he didn't. Tragic, but by then I'd gone home. That's what they said. And as far as I'm concerned, it's the truth."

"But I'm not a journalist, Estelle. I'm not even on the committee."

"What are you, then?" Her eyes widened in alarm.
"Call me an avenging angel."

REVELATION

A pair of early-morning joggers, their backs warmed
by the rising sun and their sweaty faces cooled by a
light breeze off the river, saw her first.

She was lying on a wooden bench near the paved
walkway. It was not far from a children's playground,
bright with swings and slides. Birds chattered and
quarrelled in the lush, neatly trimmed trees. The dap-
pled sunlight flirted with a patch of dried blood caked
in her expensive blond hair.

Chiselled into the wood of the seat back was the
inscription ERECTED IN MEMORY OF JOHN WILLIAM MAR-
TINEAU BY HIS LOVING BROTHERS, EDWARD AND
NORMAN.

"Look at that."

"She's drunk. Leave her be."

"She might be hurt." The young woman walked
over. "There's blood on her head." She leaned over.
"Kevin, come here," she said unsteadily. "I think
she's dead."

A laker, heavily loaded and riding low in the water,
slipped downstream toward Lake Erie, indifferent to
the lives and deaths of the land-dwellers. The river
lapped gently against its walls.

"Sergeant, do you think she could've been carrying
a thousand bucks in twenties in that pouch around her
waist?" He eased himself into the room, standing
more or less at attention.

"No, Al, I don't. She was just out for a walk."

"Maybe she was looking to buy drugs."

"I doubt it. Why do you ask?"

"Because there's a John Doe downstairs. He came
into emergency this morning, unconscious, with . . ."
He pulled a notebook out. "Nine hundred and sixty-

seven dollars on him and a thirty-dollar bottle of scotch, almost empty. He could have bashed her over the head last night and taken the thousand."

"He hits her over the head, he strangles her, takes a thousand bucks, leaving her the twenty we found in that pouch thing? He wanted to send her home in a cab, maybe? No, Al, I don't believe it."

"The guys who found him in the sculpture garden had a look around. They found blood on a bench near him and down by those horses' heads."

"He kills her and carries her body all the way up the river? Why? So she'll be closer to her hotel?"

"You were the one who said the body'd been moved, Sergeant."

"Not me. The doctor did. Where did they pick the drunk up?"

"On a bench near the horses' heads. He's been there before, they said."

"We'd better see him. Bring him up when he can talk."

It was not until five o'clock that the committee in charge of Sight and Sound realized they were missing a speaker and began to make serious inquiries.

At eight o'clock a miserable-looking man, small, thin and dishevelled, was brought upstairs to be interviewed. An ineffectual attempt had been made to clean him up for the ordeal.

The sergeant looked up. "Hi, Billy. How'd you get mixed up in this?"

He blinked. "Hey, Paul. How's it going? You talking about the couple down by the river?"

"Probably. Al? It's your John Doe. You take it."

"Name?" asked Al.

"Billy. Everyone calls me Billy."

"Full name. Your real name."

"Oh. William Sampson."

"We'd like to know how you laid your hands on

almost a thousand bucks," said the sergeant, yawning. "In your own words."

"It was like this, see. I had half a bottle I was saving from the night before . . ."

"Yeah, sure," said Al.

"Let him talk, Al."

"And I come down to sit on the bench behind those horse heads. It's dark there and no one's gonna bother you, mostly. Well—there's this guy sitting there, staring down at the ground behind the bushes, like, and so I look to see what he's staring at. There's a woman lying there wearing light-colored clothes. I didn't notice anything else about her. I ask him if she's drunk and he says, 'Yeah, she is, and she's sleeping it off.' "

"Did you go look at her?"

"Why would I? She was his problem. We shared the bottle and talked."

"What about?"

"Everything," he said vaguely. "Finally he said he'd better take her home to her husband—"

"He used those words?" asked the sergeant. "To her husband?"

"Yeah. And he went down and got her on her feet, sort of. I came along to help but I slipped and fell and he just picked her up and carried her away. Before that he handed me this big bundle of money and said, 'Thanks for everything, Billy. You're a good friend. We'll say good night. Say good night, Estelle.' "

"Did he happen to say who he was?"

"Why would he do that? It was Eddie Martineau."

"Are you sure?"

"Of course I'm sure. I wouldn't never forget Eddie. Remember? We were pals, like, until we were twelve or thirteen. Lived next door to each other and went to the same school. When his brother, Jack, died, he left and nothing was ever the same." His eyes began to tear up and his nose dripped. "Nothing ever the same," he mumbled. "We knew Estelle pushed Jack off them rocks. Eddie almost died from diving down trying to pull him out. Poor Eddie. But he's happy now."

"Why do you say that?"

" 'Cause Estelle is dead. Yeah. Estelle is dead. He told me that."

"And nothing else? He didn't tell you anything else?"

"No. I would have remembered if he had, because it was Eddie. Can I go now?"

"Why not? We know where you live, don't we?"

"I still live with Ma at the old house. Can I have the money back? Eddie gave it to me. He said Ma and me, we needed it more than he did."

"Come back tomorrow when you're sober and you can have it. Go on home to your ma, Billy."

"Are you really going to let him have that money?"

"Why not? No one's reported it stolen. He probably took it out from under his ma's mattress. I've known him for years. He's harmless."

"But he was talking to the bastard who murdered that woman. You can't just let him go."

"He was talking to a ghost, Al," said the sergeant, yawning. "I don't know who this Estelle is, but his friend Eddie Martineau is long dead. And the dead woman is a writer from Chicago, named Kate Brady, here to give a talk. Two people have identified her. The waitress where she had dinner heard her say she was meeting a friend from Detroit to go on this walk—it's time we got on to that, don't you think? We've already lost a day because we didn't know who she was. Get rid of Billy and find me the guy from Detroit."

As soon as Al left, Paul leaned back in his chair, closing his eyes. He saw the three of them, clear as could be, Billy, Eddie and his wide-eyed younger self, sitting on the grass in the dark outside Billy's house. Eddie crying and swearing as he shivered with the cold water dripping off him, saying if he ever saw

Estelle again, he'd get her good for what she'd done. And they swore, solemnly, that they'd help.

But no one believed Eddie when he told them she'd killed Jack, because he was sick and running a fever and they thought he'd been hallucinating. He went wild and the day he got out of bed, he ran off to live with his aunt. As far as anyone knew, he never came back and the word was that he had died.

Paul opened his eyes. "We swore we'd help him, Jack," he whispered to the sad drowned ghost. "And a promise made is a debt unpaid, isn't it? So now we're quit. Because if Eddie can't disappear again in the twenty-four hours we've given him, I'll be very surprised."

Two days later, on the bench where Kate Brady's body had been found, someone had printed in a neat script using black paint and a narrow brush, "Estelle is dead, too, Jack."

Steak Tartare

by Barbara D'Amato

If you drive north from Chicago along Lake Michigan, you will pass through several increasingly wealthy suburbs. The first and oldest is Evanston. Then Wilmette, Kenilworth, and Winnetka. Winnetka is one of the richest municipalities in the United States. It may be that the average income in Kenilworth, nestled next to it, is higher than Winnetka, but Kenilworth is so small that it hardly counts.

Basil Stone had therefore been thrilled to be hired as resident director of the North Shore Playhouse, located in Winnetka. It wasn't Broadway, of course, but it was a very, very prestigious rep house. And you rubbed shoulders with nothing but the best people.

Like tonight.

He spun his little red Lexus around the curves of Sheridan Road, which ran right along Lake Michigan and therefore was the Place des Vosges of Illinois, *rue de la crème de la crème,* the street that accessed the highest-priced real estate in an already high-priced area. And the Falklands' mansion was on the lake side of Sheridan, the east, which meant beach frontage, of course, and was far tonier than living across the road.

These things mattered to Basil.

Pamela had given him the street number and told him to watch for two brick columns supporting a wrought-iron arch and elaborate iron gates. And there they were. He swung in, spoke his name into the post speaker, and the gates majestically opened.

God, the place was a castle. The drive wound in a lazy S up to a wide pillared veranda. Pamela stood on the lip of the veranda like a midwestern Scarlett O'Hara, framed among acres of flesh pink azaleas that swept away on both sides of the fieldstone steps.

"Welcome, Basil," she said, giving him a quick kiss on the cheek. He pulled back fast, not wanting her husband to see. Although everybody hugged and kissed when they met, didn't they? It didn't necessarily mean anything.

She drew him in the front door.

Basil stopped just inside, trying not to goggle at the immense foyer. A tessellated marble floor flowed into a great entry hall, stretching far back to a double staircase, which curved out, up, and in, the two halves joining at the second floor. The ceiling was thirty feet overhead. The chandelier that dimly lit the hall hung from a heavy chain and was as big as a Chevy Suburban turned on its end.

Basil looked around, found that they were alone, and whispered, "Pamela, I *don't* think this was such a good idea."

"Oh, please!" she said. "Don't be so timid."

Timid! He didn't want her to think he was timid. He was bold, romantic. Still . . . "But what if he guesses?"

"He won't." She patted his cheek, leaving her hand lingering on the side of his face. Just then, Basil heard footsteps coming from somewhere beyond the great hall, and he backed sharply away from her.

Pamela laughed. She touched him with a light gaze, then spun to face the man who had just entered. "Darling," she said, "this is Basil. Basil, my husband, Charles Falkland."

Gesturing with his drink, Charles Falkland said, "I know she'll make a wonderful Kate."

"I'm very grateful that she wanted to do the show. With her background in New York. Of course, Pamela is a brilliant actor. And as Kate, she has just the right combination of bite and vulnerability."

"Absolutely," Falkland said, placing his hand possessively on the back of Pamela's neck. "She is extremely accomplished."

Basil studied the room, taking time to answer. Must be cautious here. "Of course, you know we're an Equity house, so all the actors are professional. They'll support her beautifully."

"But why *The Taming of the Shrew*?"

"You'd rather we did a drama? Don't you feel that it's important for the general public to realize that Shakespeare can be light? Humorous? People are so deadly serious."

"Well . . ." Falkland said, drawing the word out, "some issues in life *are* serious, of course. Aren't they?"

"Of course, but—"

"But enough of this. Let me just mix us all a drink."

Falkland busied himself with the bottled water, lime, and lemon wedges that the silent butler, Sloan, had brought in, and decanters of some splendid bourbon and Scotch, which the Falklands were too well-bred to keep in labeled bottles, but which to Basil's taste in his first drink seemed like Knob Creek or possibly the top-of-the-line Maker's Mark. Not the kind you buy in stores, even specialty shops. You had to order it from the company.

"Here, darling," Falkland said, turning to Pamela. "Basil's and yours."

Pamela carried Basil's drink to him, reaching out to put it in his hand. Her fingertips grazed his as he reached for the glass, and her thumb stroked the back of his hand. Basil's breath caught. How beautiful she was. He could scarcely believe his luck. Their affair had started the first day of rehearsals. Seeing her husband, and this mansion, knowing that she had been an actress of some considerable reputation, he could imagine that she might be bored in this big house, with a husband who looked chilly and austere.

Pamela left her hand next to his just half a second too long. Basil resisted pulling back. Surely that would only make it more obvious. But he thought Falkland had seen. Or maybe not. He'd been pouring his own drink, rather a stiff one. But he'd been casually looking toward them, too, over the lip of the glass. Did he notice? After all, what would he see? A woman hands a man a drink. Just ordinary hospitality. Just what was expected.

Abruptly, Falkland said, "Pamela?"

"Yes, dear?"

"I just realized I've not chosen a dessert wine. I have a lovely Médoc for dinner. We're having a crown roast of lamb, and the dinner wine should be just right. But we need something to go with the sabayon and raspberries, don't we?"

"Yes, I imagine so, dear."

Basil noted that Sloan was waiting near the door that led from this great room to some unspecified back region. Briefly, he wondered why Sloan hadn't poured and passed the drinks.

"Well, go to the wine cellar with Sloan and find something special, would you?"

"Of course, darling." An expression of mild puzzlement passed over Pamela's face, not rising quite to the level of a wrinkle across her lovely brow.

"We want something beyond the ordinary for Basil, don't you think? Something that sings. A finale! A last act! After all, he is an artiste."

"Uh, yes, darling. It's just that you usually make the decisions about wine."

"Yes, but Basil is *your* friend."

"Of course."

"Help Mrs. Falkland, please, Sloan," Falkland said.

Pamela went out the door, and Sloan, after nodding to Falkland, followed her.

                              *   *   *

It was just a bit awkward with Pamela gone, Basil
found. He rose, strolled about, stopping at the French
windows facing the back, admiring the lake view, the
private dock, and the yacht anchored there, sleek,
long, and bright white even in the dying daylight. He
tried a few questions about Falkland's line of work,
but when the man answered at length, he realized that
he didn't know what e-arbitrage was and couldn't in-
telligently carry on that line of conversation. Pamela
was taking entirely too long with the dessert wine. She
should have stayed here to protect him. After all, this
damned dinner had been her idea. He wondered
whether maybe she was a risk taker and liked to skate
close to discovery. He'd had hints of that when he saw
her drive out of the playhouse parking lot at highway
speed. Perhaps tonight she was teasing her husband.
Well, Basil would have to be doubly careful, if so.

Then Falkland quoted, "'And bonny Kate, and
sometimes Kate the curst; but, Kate, the prettiest Kate
in Christendom, Kate of Kate-Hall, my super-dainty
Kate.'"

"You know the play."

"Oh, yes. I was quite a theater scholar once upon
a time. In fact, I met Pamela through the theater."

"Oh?"

"I was a backer for one of her shows. She, of course,
was the star."

"But she doesn't act outside of rep anymore."

"Oh, I need her all to myself. 'Thy husband is thy
lord, thy life, thy keeper, thy head, thy sovereign; one
that cares for thee—'"

"Shakespeare has Kate present some good arguments against that point of view."

"Ah, but 'such duty as the subject owes the prince,
even such a woman oweth to her husband.'"

Basil did not respond. How had he gotten drawn
into this discussion anyhow? And where the hell was
Pamela?

Sloan appeared in the arch between the great hall and the dining room. Basil was startled for a second to see him, and he realized how very soundproof the back regions were. One heard no sounds of cooking, or plates rattling, or glasses clinking.

"Dinner is ready, sir, whenever you are."

Basil had not studied Sloan before, since Basil had been fully occupied with other problems. But now he realized that the man was extremely sleek. His suit was as well made as Falkland's, or nearly so. His cheeks were pinkly smooth-shaven. His hair, thin on top and combed down flat with no attempt to cover the bald center, was rich brown and shiny. Therefore it was a bit of a surprise that, apparently unknown to Sloan, a small tuft, no bigger than the wing of a wren, was disarranged in back. Perhaps he had brushed against something while cooking, if indeed he was the person in the ménage who cooked.

Falkland murmured, "What say you to a piece of roast and mustard?"

Basil winced. He was getting bloody damned tired of Shakespeare. "We should wait for Pamela, shouldn't we?"

"We'll just start on the appetizer, I think," Falkland said.

Basil sat across from Falkland, himself to the right and Falkland to the left of the head of the long table, a wide pond of shiny walnut between them. Candles were the only lights. The head of the table apparently had been left for Pamela, which made some sense, since it put her between them and she was the only woman present. Or absent, as was the case currently. Basil regarded the silver at his place setting with dismay. Why five forks? There were also three spoons, but he was sure he could figure those out. One was likely for coffee. Or dessert? There was a rounded soupspoon. A fellow director had once told him on a shoot, where they were doing a two-shot of the happy couple at dinner, that a small round soupspoon was for thick soup and a large oval soupspoon was for clear soup. But five forks, only one perhaps identifiable as a salad fork? Now that he thought about it, the setup was probably designed to intimidate him. Well, he wasn't going to let that happen.

He said, "Where is Pamela? We'll be done with the first course before she arrives if we're not careful."

"She might be—quite a while. Pamela has always had a difficult time making up her mind."

Basil had no idea what to say to that. He sat unhappily in his chair, wondering why Falkland kept the dining room so dark. It would make a wonderful set for—oh, hell. The kind of atmosphere Falkland had prepared would only be good for a show with a supernatural element. Or a murder. *Gaslight, Macbeth, Deathtrap.*

But, of course, it was just the natural dining behavior of the very rich. For the thousandth upon thousandth time Basil reflected that he should have been born rich. Candles at dinner were probably a nightly ritual at the Falklands'. He'd used them in his production of *An Inspector Calls.* And of course *Macbeth.* Thank God he hadn't uttered the name of the Scottish play aloud. Very bad luck.

With the darkness crowding his shoulders, and the flicker of the candle flames causing the shadows of his five forks to undulate as if slinking slowly toward the plate, Basil resolved to look upon the whole evening as a set of suggestions for his next noir production. Use it, don't fight it, he told himself.

Sloan entered. He carried two plates of something that surely must not be what it looked like. Surely it was just the low candlelight that made the lumps appear reddish and bloody and undercooked.

As the plate touched down in front of Basil with scarcely a sound, he saw it was indeed raw meat.

"Steak tartare," Falkland said. "A small portion

makes a perfect appetizer. As a main dish it becomes a bit much, don't you think?"

"Uh, is he serving just us two? What about Pamela?"

"Oh, Pamela won't be long. As I was about to say, as an appetizer I have Sloan serve it without the raw egg. Although if you can buy fresh new eggs from green-run chickens, there is really no danger. And of course with these new methods of preventing salmonella in chickens—something about the properly inoculated feed—you can be quite confident. Nevertheless, for the sake of my guests' equanimity, I forgo the egg and serve the steak tartare as an appetizer.

"Traditionally, of course, it is chopped fillet steak or sirloin, twice run through the grinder. Then mixed with chopped onions and garlic and capers and raw egg. Salt and pepper. And the patty is shaped with a depression in the center. Into that depression is dropped a perfect golden yolk. It is a beautiful presentation, really, the yolk a deep cadmium yellow, and the meat around it rich red. Well, like this, actually. So fresh it glistens. Do you see?"

"Uhhh, yes."

"Of course," Charles said, steepling his fingers as the manservant stepped back, "it can only be the very, very freshest meat."

"Uh, yes indeed."

"And never, never ground beef from the supermarket." He uttered the word "supermarket" the way another person might say "latrine." The man, Basil thought, should have been an actor himself. He certainly got all the juice out of a word.

"You're not eating. Now, these are the traditional accompaniments around it—capers, chopped onion, and minced parsley."

"Mmm-mm."

"Not used to steak tartare, Basil?"

"No."

"Some chefs mix in cognac as well, and garnish it with caviar. The Swiss even add anchovies. But it seems to me if you're going for the taste of fresh, raw meat, tarting it up with extraneous flavors is a waste. Don't you think so?"

"Uhhh."

"Still, to revert to our earlier topic, I wonder why it had to be *The Taming of the Shrew*. There are more interesting Shakespeare pieces you could do."

"Uhhh. The trustees, actually."

"The trustees wanted it? Well, then I suppose you're stuck with it. They do hold the purse strings. But I wonder, as time goes on, if you could convince them to do Shakespeare's unappreciated masterpiece. I'm speaking of *Titus Andronicus,* of course."

"Mmm."

"It's reassuring to me, as a Shakespeare enthusiast, that the Julie Taymor film of it is coming out, at least. But there isn't any substitute for the immediacy of the stage."

"I agree, of course," Basil half whispered.

"Real human beings near enough to touch. And *Titus Andronicus* is so Grand Guignol. It was Shakespeare's breakout play, you know. Made his name. Although at the time people claimed to be upset at all the violence."

"Media violence—"

"Fascinating to think that without it, without all that excess, we might never have known the name Shakespeare."

Basil picked up a heavy Francis I fork. He touched the chopped meat. It was lumpy and bright red, with tiny flecks of gristle or fat. He wondered whether he could tell anything if he touched it with his finger. If it was warm—? Had it been in the refrigerator, or was it body temperature?

But he couldn't bear to touch it.

Falkland went on. "And what a story. The son of

Tamora, queen of the Goths, has been killed by Titus. For revenge, she has her other two sons rape Titus's daughter and cut out her tongue."

"I know," said Basil in a strangled voice.

"Then Titus, in an antic burst of exquisite revenge, invites Tamora to dinner and unknown to her, serves her a pasty—we'd call it a potpie, I imagine—made from her two sons' heads."

"I'm familiar with *Titus Andronicus,* dammit!"

"Oh, of course you are, dear boy. You're a director. Terribly sorry."

"Uhhh."

"My word, Basil, you aren't eating."

"Auuhhh—"

"You haven't touched your steak tartare."

It could not be what he thought. It could not. How long had they been down in that cellar? And how would Falkland dispose of the—of the rest? But then he recalled the dock, the boathouse. The mansion backed directly onto Lake Michigan. Well, of course it did. It was on the high-rent side of Sheridan. But what about Sloan? Could Falkland possibly have Sloan so much in his pocket that he would do anything Falkland asked?

Inadvertently, Basil glanced up at Sloan, standing silent and lugubrious just left of the dining room door.

Falkland caught his glance. "Sloan is such a gem," he said. "He's been with me for twenty-three years now."

"Oh, yes?"

"Since I agreed to accept him from the parole board. You see, they would only let him go if he had permanent residential employment."

"Oh, yes, I see."

"In a home with no children."

Basil stared at his plate. If he so much as sipped a smidgen of water, he would be sick. Staring at his plate was worse. He averted his eyes. But it was too late. Perspiration started up on his forehead and he could feel sweat running into his hair. His face was hot and his abdomen was deeply cold.

Basil threw his napkin down next to the army of forks. He half rose. "I don't think I'm feeling very well—"

"Oh, please. We were so looking forward to this evening."

"I think I'd better go."

He gagged out the words and could hardly understand what he himself had said. It sounded like "guh-guh-go."

The swinging door from the pantry opened. Pamela stood in the spill of kitchen light, holding a dusty glass bottle.

"It's a terrible cliché, I know," she said, smiling apologetically, "but I picked out everything else and finally went back to the Château d'Yquem."

"Uh-uh-uh," Basil said, trying to stand upright, but bent by the pains knifing through his stomach.

"Basil! Are you ill?" she said.

Basil ran at a half crouch out of the dining room, through the long hall and the marble foyer, and pushed out the front door into the glorious cool night air.

"Oh dear," Pamela said, still smiling.

Falkland said, "Fun, darling?"

"Fun? The best we've ever done."

Animal Act

by Claire McNab

"G'day," I said. "I'm Kylie Kendall. I'm here to see Arnold."

The bloke who'd opened the door of the flamboyant Beverly Hills mansion looked at me without enthusiasm. "Oh, yes. The Australian. Lisette told me you'd be coming by."

With his thick, curly black hair, deep brown eyes, straight nose, and jutting jaw, he was handsome, and he knew it. "Where's the blonde?" he asked. "She's the one who usually does the inspection." His expression warmed slightly as he added, "Good-looking woman."

He was referring to my partner in Kendall & Creeling Investigative Services, Ariana Creeling. "She's out of town on a case," I said. "You'll have to make do with me."

He grunted and stood aside. "I suppose you'd better come in."

I blinked at the entrance area. Two stories above, light flooded in from a huge circular stained-glass window set into the ceiling. Multicolored patches of light were splashed over the black marble floor and chalk white walls. A wide curving staircase with bloodred carpet led to the next floor. Scattered, apparently at random, were life-size sculptures of various animals— dogs, cats, a llama, a potbellied pig—displayed on white marble bases. The one closest to me depicted a huge bear rearing up on its hind legs. Engraved on the pedestal were the words LEONARD, DANCING.

"Crikey," I said.

I became aware the bloke was watching me with a sour smile. It was apparent he wasn't intending to introduce himself, so I said, "And you'd be Paul Berkshire."

"Proper little detective, aren't you?"

Actually, I wasn't. I'd inherited fifty-one percent of Kendall & Creeling from my father, but wasn't a private eye's bootlace yet, just a trainee. There was no need to blab this to Paul Berkshire, of course.

He set off for the rear of the house down a wide hallway, not bothering to see if I was following. Even from the back he was a bonzer-looking bloke, with a strong neck, wide shoulders and a narrow waist. Paul Berkshire was the nephew of Rhea Berkshire, who before her death had been a crash-hot animal trainer for movies and TV. She'd been a heavy drinker, and six months ago—just before I came to the States— had died from an accidental overdose of bourbon and sleeping tablets. The very specific provisions she'd made in her will for her menagerie of animals at her ranch outside LA ensured that all went to good homes, many with other professional trainers. The ranch itself was sold, the proceeds going to animal charities.

One of her charges, however, received special treatment. This was Rhea's most adored and successful subject, Arnold. Her will specified that no expense was to be spared. Her nephew, Paul, was to ensure that Arnold lived a life of luxury in Rhea's Beverly Hills estate for the rest of his days.

Everyone knew Arnold's story. Rescued from a

shelter when just a puppy, he was what we Aussies call a bitser—a bit of this and a bit of that. He was a pepper-and-salt charmer, incredibly photogenic and very smart. And he loved performing. He'd become a household word as the cute psychic dog—also called Arnold—in the paranormal hit comedy series *Professor Swann's Spooks*. Even before I'd come to the States, I'd been a fan of the show. Most people in my outback hometown, Wollegudgerie, watched the program on Wednesday nights. Even my mum, who wasn't what you'd call a fan of television—addled your brains, she always said darkly—always made sure the program was on the screen above the main bar of her pub, the Wombat's Retreat.

Ahead of me, Paul Berkshire had reached a black lacquered door, and was looking impatiently over his shoulder. "I haven't got all day."

I suppose in his place I'd resent being regularly checked to ensure that the conditions set out in his aunt's will were being followed to the letter. Rhea Berkshire had cause to use Kendall & Creeling's services long before I turned up on the scene. She'd become a fast friend of my father's, so she'd instructed her lawyers, Frogmartin, Frogmartin & Flye, to include in her will a generous payment to our company to visit Arnold once every two months—or more often if it seemed indicated—to make certain he was being treated in the manner a megarich canine should expect. We were to liaise with his vet, his walker, his dietician, his groomer, and his round-the-clock companion, Lisette, who had been in Rhea's employ for many years. And Paul Berkshire, of course, as he had inherited his aunt's business and so was Arnold's trainer.

I'd heard a new series of *Professor Swann's Spooks* was in the works, and was going to ask if that was true—Mum would love to know—when the bloke threw open the door. "Arnold's beauty parlor," he said with a bit of a twist to his lip. As he spoke, I noticed these three words were engraved in ornate script on the door's lacquered surface.

"Gets up your nose, does it?" I said.

"What?"

"Not sure I approve, myself. Not very macho, is it?" He looked at me blankly, so I added, "I reckon a dog like Arnold would prefer something more masculine. How about 'sprucing room'? What do you think?"

"I think Arnold can't read," he said, "so he doesn't give a rat's ass what the room's called." Opening the door, he said, "Lisette? This is the Kendall from Kendall and Creeling, here to check we're not mistreating the dog."

He'd said "the dog" with such a flat tone that I looked at him with surprise. Recently I'd read an article in *Hollywood Reporter* where Berkshire had spoken glowingly of Arnold's sweet nature and his ability to master new routines.

"Lisette will call me when you're finished," he said, turning away and stalking off back down the hallway before I could respond.

I stepped into the room, and found myself grinning at Arnold, who cocked his head and waved his stubby little tail. Even more adorable in person than on the screen, he was standing patiently on a table while a young bloke with a pale face and lifeless fair hair groomed him.

"G'day, Lisette," I said to the woman who was smiling at me warmly. "I'm Kylie." She was much older than I expected, small and wiry, with a cloudburst of white hair.

"Hello, dear. Ariana's told me all about you." She had the faintest suggestion of an English accent.

"Crikey. All good, I hope."

"Mostly," said the young bloke with a bit of a smirk.

Lisette introduced him as Gary Hartnel. "G'day,

Gary," I said. I couldn't resist adding, "And g'day to you, too, Arnold." Arnold blurred his little tail.

"Friendly," I remarked.

"Not to everyone," Gary declared. "Arnold has his likes and dislikes."

"Righto," I said, whipping a folder out of my bag. "I've got a checklist here. Let's go through it and then I'll get out of your way."

Lisette took me to meet the rest of the staff. Arnold came, too, trotting along beside us with a delightfully cheerful demeanor. As we walked down the hall's thick carpet, I said to her, "Does he miss Ms. Berkshire, do you think?"

"Rhea? I'm sure he does. Look at him."

When she said her late employer's name, Arnold's tail drooped and he gave me such a pitiful look my heart turned over.

"I'm sorry I mentioned it."

"That's okay, dear. Arnold's very sensitive. We found him snuggled up in bed with Rhea, her being dead and all and him softly whining. He was in mourning. Near brought me to tears."

Soon I knew rather more about Arnold's day-to-day schedule than I'd ever intended to know—his dietician went into such detail about the measurement and preparation of Arnold's food that my eyes glazed over, and his walker insisted on describing at length the variety of routes Arnold covered every week.

"Is everything satisfactory?" Lisette asked when I'd finished going through her duties as Arnold's companion.

"Too right," I said, giving her the thumbs-up. "She's apples."

She shook her head. "You Aussies."

Lisette, Arnold, and I headed back to the front of the house. "All I need to do is to check a few things with Mr. Berkshire."

"Paul will be in his office—no, wait, here he is now."

I've got pin-drop hearing, or I wouldn't have heard the soft growl Arnold gave. I looked down at him. He was staring fixedly at Paul Berkshire. His body language was a puzzle—I'd heard a growl, but he wasn't stiff with aggression; he was unnaturally still, waiting. Then he glanced up at me, with the oddest expression on his face.

"You're done?" Berkshire asked me.

"I've got a few more areas to cover with you."

"Lisette, take Arnold to his gym. He doesn't need to tag along with us."

When I looked back over my shoulder, Arnold hadn't moved.

The bloke's office was huge, being more what I'd call a library, with shelves and shelves of impressive-looking books and lots of maroon leather furniture. Paul Berkshire plunked himself behind a massive antique desk and answered my questions about Arnold's training regimen with cool economy. It seemed there *was* to be a new series of *Professor Swann's Spooks* and Arnold was already learning new routines for the show.

"Nothing too risky?" It was one of our duties to make sure Arnold was never involved in hazardous situations.

"Of course not. Arnold has a stunt double who looks exactly like him."

"But not as talented?"

Berkshire gave me a thin smile. "More talented, in my professional opinion. A pleasure to work with the animal. Dopp is Arnold without the attitude."

"Dopp for doppelganger?"

Berkshire raised his eyebrows. "My little joke."

I raised my eyebrows right back at him. "I'm surprised you say Arnold has an attitude. I found him a bonzer dog."

"He's temperamental at times. Difficult. Could be he's getting close to the end of his performing life."

"Maybe he's grieving for your aunt."

A fleeting emotion flickered across Berkshire's face. Just that morning at breakfast I'd been reading in my invaluable reference source, *Private Investigation: The Complete Handbook,* about microexpressions. These only lasted for a split second, but exposed the true feelings of a person before they could hide them. In this case, I reckoned he'd revealed a pretty disturbing mix—sneering anger, tinged with arrogant triumph.

"If there's nothing else, I'll get Gary to escort you to your car," he said, clearly wanting to get rid of me.

Gary, a limp strand of pale hair flopping over one eye, arrived. Once outside the front door, he gave me a conspiratorial look. "I don't know if you're the one I should go to, but lately Arnold's been trying to tell me something. I swear he has."

"What sort of something?"

"You know about Rhea—her dying like that? Well, of course it was a stupid accident, but it's odd how Arnold's changed. Like, he used to love Paul, but lately he just goes quiet when Paul comes in the room. Arnold watches him, weird-like, if you get what I mean. And then Arnold looks at me . . ."

"What do you think he's trying to tell you?"

"I'm not sure." He glanced around furtively. "Gotta go."

Gary went. I climbed into my car, feeling a bit weird-like myself. I couldn't shake the idea that Arnold had tried to tell me something, too. Something bad.

Earlier I'd seen Dr. Stanley Evers, veterinary surgeon to the stars—Arnold was one of his most valuable celebrity clients—so I had everything I needed to write my report for Frogmartin, Frogmartin & Flye.

Turning off Sunset Boulevard I got my customary little thrill when I drove through the gates and past the sign reading KENDALL & CREELING INVESTIGATIVE SERVICES. I still had thousands of hours of supervision ahead of me, plus an exam, but one day I'd become a fully fledged PI, and be worthy of my dad's company.

Our building was a pseudo-Spanish house converted into offices. I still wasn't quite used to its pinkish ocher color, but I rather liked the black, brass-studded front door.

"G'day, Melodie," I said to our receptionist—at least until her acting career took off.

Green eyes wide, Melodie gave a practiced swirl of her long blond hair. "Kylie! It's real urgent!"

"Not Mum again?" My mother was always trying to persuade me to return to the outback and help her run the pub.

"No, not your mom. It's Lonnie. Julia Roberts has been in his room for the fourth time this week. He says he's desperate. This time he means it—he's calling the authorities."

I was outraged. "What? And have her taken away, just because he sneezes?"

"Lonnie says it's impacting his quality of life. He's real serious, Kylie." She clasped her hands and added soulfully, "He says it's him or Julia Roberts."

As we were speaking, Julia Roberts herself sauntered into view, her tawny tail held high. She was followed by the plump, indignant form of Lonnie Moore, our technical wizard and sufferer of severe feline allergies.

"Jules, have you been wicked again?" I asked her. "You know very well you're not supposed to go into Lonnie's office." Julia Roberts gave a quick, contemptuous flick of her tail. She never took criticism well.

Lonnie sneezed, blew his nose on a tissue he snatched from Melodie's desk, then declared, "Either that cat goes, or I do." His soft face was grim. "I really mean it."

This was a true dilemma—I loved Jules dearly, but Lonnie was absolutely invaluable to Kendall & Creeling. I had talked Lonnie around before, but this time his militant expression showed I had my work cut out for me.

"Injections," I said.

Lonnie looked horrified. "I don't want her killed—just out of my hair."

"I'm talking about desensitization. For you. It's a course of injections giving you a tiny bit of what you're allergic to, and your body gets used to it so you don't get a bad reaction anymore. I'll spring for the cost, and any time off you need, if you give up the idea of getting rid of Jules."

"Kylie, you know I don't like anything medical. I can't stand the sight of blood."

"There won't be any blood. You'll hardly feel a thing."

"Well . . ."

Melodie said helpfully, "And Lonnie, you wouldn't have to be looking out for Julia Roberts every moment of the day, and you wouldn't be sneezing all the time and you wouldn't—"

"All right! All right! I'll do it." He glanced at Julia Roberts, who had one foot up in the air as she washed her nethers. "It's not that I hate her or anything. It's her rotten personality. I swear it amuses her to torment me."

"Speaking of personality," I said, "I was at the Berkshire mansion this morning, checking on Arnold. He's a bonzer little dog."

"*Love* that show!" Melodie exclaimed. "Larry, my agent, says when auditions open for the new series of *Professor Swann's Spooks,* he guarantees I'll get a part. Like, with my psychic abilities, I'll be in sync with Arnold."

"Arnold is no more psychic than you are," Lonnie snorted. "He's just a dog doing whatever his trainer tells him to. Anyway, I hear he's on the way out. Taking early retirement."

"I am too psychic," Melodie snapped. "And Arnold's so cute, no one could replace him."

Lonnie was an authority on showbiz gossip, so he probably had the good oil. I had a sinking feeling that Arnold was in danger. "He's got a stunt double called

Dopp," I said. "Paul Berkshire spoke very highly of him when I was there this morning."

Lonnie smiled cynically. "If that's the case, I don't need to be clairvoyant to predict that Arnold's retirement will be a short one. And when he dies, the Beverly Hills estate and all the funds dedicated to Arnold's welfare will go to Berkshire. The sooner the guy bumps the dog off, the sooner he gets his hands on it."

Melodie, scandalized, said, "Are you saying he's going to murder Arnold?"

"As long as Arnold is unique, and working in the biz, he's raking in the dollars big-time, so Berkshire can afford to wait. But if Arnold can be replaced—it's good-bye doggie."

I told them about Arnold's change of attitude towards Paul Berkshire.

"Awesome," said Melodie, impressed. "Like, it's practically mystic."

"So what about Rhea?" I asked Lonnie. "Is it definite her death was accidental?"

He shrugged. "At the time there was lots of smoke but no fire. It could have been an accident—she was a heavy drinker and could have got confused about how many sleeping tablets she'd taken. Maybe the dog knows for sure, but he's the only witness, and he can't tell anyone."

"I think he's been trying to," I said. "I'm going back there, right now." They both stared at me. "Premonition," I announced. "Psychic flash."

Melodie nodded wisely. "I have those all the time."

I left Lonnie chortling and marched back to my car. "I'm coming, Arnold," I said.

When Berkshire opened the front door he was scowling. "Forget something?"

" 'Fraid so. I missed filling out a whole page of my checklist. Can't write my report until I've got all the info."

"Jesus," he said, "can't anyone do anything right these days?"

"Sorry. I'll only be a mo."

"Lisette!" he yelled over his shoulder. "Get up here, fast."

He beckoned me in and closed the door. "I'll be upstairs if you want me, but I'm not expecting you to."

I watched him mount the long curving stairway. It was like something out of *Gone with the Wind,* except, of course, Clark Gable had been even more good-looking.

"Yes, dear?" said Lisette, hurrying up to me. "What's wrong?"

"Do you get the feeling Arnold's been trying to tell you something?"

She seemed uncomfortable. "It's just my fancy."

As she spoke, Arnold appeared, trotting down the hall towards us. He had a determined, focused manner, and when he reached us, he sat down and fixed us with an unblinking stare.

"Would Arnold be telling you something about what happened to Rhea?"

Lisette's lips trembled. "I'd be lying if I said I wasn't worried sick about it all. I took Rhea's death hard— we'd been together for so many years—so I think I've exaggerated things in my own mind, to the point of believing Arnold was a witness to murder."

She said the last word in a harsh whisper. It was almost melodramatic, the way we both looked up the stairway. On cue, Paul Berkshire appeared at the top. "What the hell's going on?"

"Arnold," I said, "I'm sorry. I can't do anything. If only there'd been someone else there to bear witness."

Arnold shook himself, as though he'd been dunked in water, then dipped his head at me. Paul Berkshire had started down, swearing. "Get the hell out of here."

Arnold sighed, then shot like a furry bullet up the

stairs. Paul Berkshire yelled, "Fuck!" then tumbled down, a flaccid doll bouncing obscenely until he came to rest on the marble floor, his neck at an unnatural angle.

Lisette rushed over to him. "Oh, my God! He's dead!"

Arnold came down at a leisurely pace, stopped to sniff the corpse, then came over to me. I said, "That wasn't an accident, was it, Arnold?"

Fair dinkum. That little dog cocked his head—and smiled at me.

Lady Patterly's Lover

by *Charlotte MacLeod*

"We'd be doing him a kindness, really," said Gerald. "You do see that, Eleanor?"

Lady Patterly ran one exquisite hand idly through the thick, fair hair of her husband's steward. "I'd be doing myself one. That's all that matters."

Born beautiful, spoiled rotten as a child, married at twenty-one to the best catch in England, wife at twenty-three to a helpless paralytic, bored to desperation at twenty-four; that, in a nutshell, was Eleanor, Lady Patterly. When old Ponsonby had retired and her husband's close friend Gerald had come to manage the Patterly estates, Eleanor had lost no time in starting an affair with him. Discreetly, of course. She cared nothing for the world, but she was vain enough to care greatly for the world's opinion of her.

Gerald had been only too willing. As handsome as Eleanor was lovely, he had the same total lack of scruple, the same cold intelligence, the same passionate devotion to his own interests. He took the greatest care of his old friend Roger Patterly's property because he soon realized that with Eleanor's help he could easily make it his own. It was Gerald who suggested the murder.

"The killing part is the easiest. A pillow over his face, a switch of medicines, nothing to it. The big thing is not getting caught. We must make sure nobody ever suspects it wasn't a natural death. We'll take our time, prepare the groundwork, wait for exactly the right moment. And then, my love, it's all ours."

Lady Patterly gazed around the drawing room with its priceless furnishings, through the satin-draped windows to the impeccably tended formal gardens. "I shall be so glad to get out of this prison. We'll travel, Gerald. Paris, Greece, Hong Kong. I've always had a fancy to see Hong Kong."

They would do nothing of the kind. Gerald was too careful a steward not to stay and guard what would be his. He only smiled and replied, "Whatever you want, my sweet."

"It will be just too marvelous," sighed the invalid's wife. "How shall we go about it?"

"Not we, darling. You."

After all, it would be Eleanor, not he, who would inherit. Unless he married her afterwards, he hadn't the ghost of a claim. And suppose she changed her mind? But she wouldn't. With the hold of murder over her she could be handled nicely. If he were fool enough to do the job himself . . . Gerald was no fool.

"I shall continue to be the faithful steward. And you, my dear, will be the dutiful wife. A great deal more dutiful than you've been up to now."

Lady Patterly inspected her perfect fingernails, frowning. "What do you want me to do?"

"I want you to start showing some attention to your husband. Don't overdo it. Build it up gradually. You might begin by strolling into Roger's room and asking him how he's feeling."

"But I do, every morning and evening."

"Then do it again, right now. And stay for more than two minutes this time."

"Oh, very well. But it's so depressing."

"It's not all jam for old Roger either, you know."

"How sententious of you, darling. Shall I hold his hand, or what?"

"Why don't you read to him?"

"He loathes being read to."

"Read to him anyway. It will look well in front of the nurse. That's our objective, Eleanor, to create the impression of devotion among the attendants. You must be able to act the bereft widow convincingly when we . . . lose him."

His mistress shrugged and turned toward the stairs.

"Oh, and Eleanor." Gerald lowered his voice yet another pitch. "We'd better postpone any further meetings until it's over. We mustn't take any risk whatever. And don't be surprised if I start a flirtation with one of the village belles."

She arched one delicately pencilled eyebrow. "Have you picked out anybody special?"

"One will do as well as another. Protective camouflage, you know. It's only for a few weeks, darling." He turned the full force of his dazzling smile on her, and went out.

Eleanor stood for a moment looking after him. It was hard on Roger, of course. Still, she had her own future to think of. Her husband had offered her a divorce as soon as the doctors had told him the sports car smashup had left him paralyzed for life. Naturally she had refused. It wouldn't have looked well, and besides, the settlement he'd offered was not her idea of adequate support.

No, she would have it all. She and Gerald. It was clever of Gerald to have found the way. She arranged her features in exactly the right expression of calm compassion and went to visit her husband.

Day by day she increased the length of time she spent in the sickroom. It was less tedious than she had anticipated. For one thing, Roger was so glad to have her there. She took to bringing him little surprises:

some flowers, a few sun-warmed strawberries from the garden. She had the gramophone brought into his room and played the records they had danced to before they were married. Nurse Wilkes beamed. Marble the valet scowled distrustfully.

Eleanor found herself looking forward to her visits, planning the next day's surprise, thinking of new ways to entertain the invalid. The weeks went by and Gerald began to fidget.

"I say, don't you think we ought to be getting on with it?"

"You said we mustn't rush things." And she went past him into Roger's room, carrying a charming arrangement of varicolored roses she'd got up early to pick with the dew on them.

As had become her habit, she took up the book she was reading aloud to him and opened it to her bookmark. Her eye, now attuned to Roger's every expression, caught a tightening of the muscles around his mouth. She put the book down.

"You hate being read to, don't you, Roger?"

"It's just that it makes me feel so utterly helpless."

"But you're not. There's nothing the matter with your eyes. From now on, you'll read to yourself."

"How can I? I can't hold the book, I can't turn the pages."

"Of course you can. We'll just sit you up, like this—" Eleanor slid one arm around her husband and pulled him up. "Nurse, let's have that backrest thing. There, how's that?"

She plumped a pillow more comfortably. "Now we'll prop the book up on the bed table, like this, and lift your arm, like this, and slip the page between your fingers so that you can hold it yourself." A pinching between the right thumb and forefinger was the only movement Lord Patterly could make. "And when you've finished with that page, we just turn it over. Like this. See, you've managed it beautifully."

"So I have." He looked down at his hand as though it were something miraculous. "That's the first thing I've done for myself since . . . it happened."

For the next half hour, Roger read to himself. Eleanor sat at his side, patiently moving his hand when he signalled that he was ready, helping to slide the next page into his grasp. She found the monotonous task strangely agreeable. For the first time in her life, she was being of use to somebody else. When Marble brought in the patient's lunch and Nurse Wilkes came forward to feed it to him, she waved the woman away.

"He'll feed himself today, thank you, Nurse."

And he did, with Eleanor setting a spoon between his thumb and forefinger and guiding his hand to his mouth. When he dropped a morsel, they laughed and tried again. At last Lady Patterly left Nurse Wilkes clucking happily over a perfectly clean plate and went to get her own lunch. Gerald was waiting for her.

"I've got it all figured out, darling," he whispered as soon as they were alone. "I've been reading up on digitalis. The doctor's been leaving it, I know, on account of that heart of his. All we have to do is slip him an extra dose and out he goes. Heart failure. Only to be expected in a helpless paralytic."

To her own surprise, Eleanor protested. "He is not helpless. He's handicapped."

"Rather a nice distinction in Roger's case, don't you think, sweet? Anyway, there we are. You've only to notice which is the digitalis bottle, watch your chance, and slip a tablespoonful into his hot milk, or whatever they give the poor bloke."

"And what happens when Nurse Wilkes notices the level of the medicine's gone down in the bottle? Not clever, Gerald."

"Dash it, you can put in some water, can't you?"

"I suppose so." Eleanor pushed back her chair. "I'll have to think about it."

"Think fast, my love. I miss you."

Gerald gave her his best smile, but for some reason her heart failed to turn over as usual. She got up. "I'm going for a walk."

She started off aimlessly, then found herself heading toward the village. It was pleasant swinging along the grassy lane, feeling her legs respond to the spring of the turf under her feet. Roger had loved to walk. For the first time since the accident, Eleanor felt an overwhelming surge of genuine pity for her husband.

She turned in at the bookshop. It was mostly paperbacks and greeting cards these days, but she might find something Roger would enjoy now that she'd found a way for him to manage a book.

That was rather clever of me, she thought with satisfaction. She liked recalling the look on Roger's face, the beaming approval of Nurse Wilkes, the unbelief in old Marble's eyes as he watched His Lordship feeding himself. "There must be any number of things I could help him do," she mused. "I wonder how one goes about them?"

She went up to the elderly woman in charge. "Have you any books on working with handicapped people? Exercises, that sort of thing."

"Physical therapy." Miss Jenkins nodded wisely. "I do believe there was something in that last lot of paperbacks. Ah yes, here we are."

Eleanor rifled through the pages. "This seems to be the general idea. But don't you have any that go into greater detail?"

"I could always order one for you, Lady Patterly."

"Please do, then, as quickly as possible."

"Of course. But—excuse me, Lady Patterly—we all understood His Lordship was quite helpless."

"He is not!" Again Eleanor was startled by her own reaction. "He was sitting up in bed reading by himself this morning, and he ate his own lunch. You can't call that helpless, can you?"

"Why . . . why no, indeed. Good gracious, I can hardly believe it. Nurse Wilkes said—"

"Nurse Wilkes says entirely too much," snapped Eleanor. She would have a word with Nurse Wilkes.

She walked back slowly, studying the book page by page. It seemed simple enough. Manipulating the patient's limbs, massage, no problem there. If only they had a heated swimming pool. But of course Roger wouldn't be ready for that for ages yet. And by then she and Gerald . . . Gerald was getting a bit puffy about the jawline, she'd noticed it at lunch. Those big, beefy men were apt to go to flesh early. He ought to start exercising, too. No earthly good suggesting it to him. Gerald made rather a point of being the dominant male. Roger was much more reasonable to deal with.

He was positively boyish about the exercises. When the doctor dropped around for his daily visit, he found them hard at it, Roger pinching on to Eleanor's finger while she swung his arm up and down.

"See, Doctor, he's holding on beautifully."

"She's going to have me up out of this in a matter of weeks."

The doctor looked from one to the other. There was color in Lord Patterly's face for the first time since the accident. He had never seen Her Ladyship so radiant. Why should he tell them it was hopeless? Life had been hard enough on that young pair. Anyway, who knew? There was always the off chance the long bed rest had allowed some of the damaged nerve endings to mend themselves.

"By all means go on as you're doing," he said. "Just take it a bit slowly at first. Remember that little heart condition."

Eleanor suddenly thought of Gerald and the digitalis. Her face became a mask. "I'll remember," she said tonelessly.

Her husband laughed. "Oh, nonsense. Everybody's got these idiotic heart murmurs. My father had and he lived to seventy-nine. Gerald has, and look at him. Shoots, swims, rides, all that."

"Gerald had better watch himself," said the doctor. He picked up his bag. "Well, the patient appears to be in good hands. You're doing splendidly, Lady Patterly, splendidly. Don't be discouraged if progress is a little slow. These things take time, you know."

"Time," said Lord Patterly, "is something of which we have plenty. Haven't we, darling?"

His wife smoothed his pillow. "Yes, Roger. All the time in the world."

"I'll leave you to it, then." The doctor moved toward the door. "Watch his pulse, Nurse. Give the prescribed injection of digitalis if it seems advisable after the exercises. You keep the hypodermic ready, of course?"

"All in order, Doctor. Right here on the medicine tray if need arises."

Gerald was right, Eleanor thought as she gently kneaded the wasted muscles of her husband's arms. It would be easy. Too easy. She drew the covers up over him. "There, that's enough for now. I don't want to wear you out the first day. Shall I put on some music?"

"Please."

She had taken to playing the classical records he liked. It whiled away the time for her, too, sitting beside the bed, letting the long waves of melody sweep over her, daydreaming of all the things she would do when she was free. Today, however, she found her mind dwelling on more homely pictures. Miss Jenkins's face when she'd dropped her little bombshell at the bookshop. The doctor's, when he'd found her giving her husband therapy. Her husband's now, as he lay with his eyes closed, the long afternoon shadows etching his features in sharp relief. He was as good-looking as ever, in spite of everything. That jaw would never be blurred by fat. What would it be like, living in this house without Roger? She tried to imagine it and could not.

*   *   *

After dinner the following evening, Gerald suggested a walk. "You're looking peaked, Eleanor. Needn't stay cooped up with your patient forever, you know."

His double meaning was plain. She rose and followed him out the french windows to the terrace.

"Rather an inspiration of yours, that therapy thing."

"What do you mean?"

"Easy enough to overdo a bit. Make the heart attack more plausible, eh?"

She did not answer. He went on, confident of his power over her.

"You were right about the digitalis, I decided. I've thought of something even better. Potassium chloride. I was a hospital laboratory technician once, you know. One of the jobs I batted around in after they turned me down for the army. Rum, when you come to think of it. I mean, if it hadn't been for my wheezing heart I shouldn't have drifted into this post, and if it weren't for Roger's I shouldn't be . . . getting promoted, shall we say? Anyway, getting back to the potassium chloride, it's reliable stuff. Absolutely undetectable. Do an autopsy and all you find is a damaged heart and an increased potassium rate. Exactly what you'd expect after a fatal coronary attack."

"Gerald, must you?"

"This is no time to turn squeamish, Eleanor. Especially since it's you who'll be giving it."

"Don't be a fool. How could I?"

"Oh, I don't mean directly. We'll let Nurse Wilkes do that. She keeps a hypodermic of digitalis on the bedside table, ready to give him a quick jab if he needs it."

"How did you know that?"

"I'm the dear old pal, remember? I've been a lot more faithful about visiting Roger than you ever were until your recent excess of wifely devotion. Nurse Wilkes and I are great chums."

"I can imagine." Men like Gerald were always irresistible to servant girls and barmaids and plain, middle-aged nurses. And rich women who thought they had nothing better to do.

"I took careful note of the type of hypodermic syringe she uses," Gerald went on. "Yesterday when I was in London, I bought one just like it at one of the big medical supply houses, along with some potassium chloride and a few other things so it wouldn't look too obvious. I'd dropped in beforehand to visit some of my old pals at the hospital and pinched a lab coat with some convincing acid holes in it. Wore it to the shop and they never dreamed of questioning me. I ditched it in a public lavatory and got rid of the rest of the stuff in various trash bins on my way back to the station."

"You think of everything, don't you, Gerald?" Eleanor's throat was dry.

"Have to, my love. So here we are. I give you the doings all ready for use. You watch your chance tomorrow morning and switch the syringes. Then you put old Roger through his paces till he works up a galloping pulse, back off and let Nurse take over, and get ready to play the shattered widow. The stuff works in a couple of minutes. And then this is all ours."

"It's all ours now," Eleanor told him. "Mine and Roger's."

"I say! You're not backing out on me, are you?"

"Yes, I am. I won't do it, Gerald."

No woman had ever refused Gerald anything before. His face puckered like an angry baby's. "But why?"

"Because I'm not quite the idiot I thought I was. You're not worth Roger's little finger."

It was astonishing how ugly Gerald could look. "And suppose I go to Roger and let him know the loving-wife act was just a buildup for murder? Suppose you're caught with the evidence? You will be, Eleanor. I'll see to that."

"Don't be ridiculous. What would you get out of it?"

"You forget, my love. I'm the boyhood chum and devoted steward. I'll be the chap who saved his life. I'll be in charge here, far more than I am now. And with no wife to pass things on to, Roger just might be persuaded to make me his heir."

"How long would he survive the signing of the will?"

"That won't be your concern, my sweet. You'll be where you can't do a thing about it."

Eleanor stared at him, frozen-faced. He began to wheedle.

"Oh, come on, old girl. Think of the times we'll have on dear old Roger's money. You don't plan to spend the rest of your life in that bedroom, do you?"

"No," said Eleanor, "I don't."

Her mind was forming pictures, of Roger being carried down to a couch on the terrace to get the sun, of Roger being pushed around the garden in a wheelchair, of Roger taking his first steps on crutches. And someday, of Roger and herself walking together where she and Gerald were walking now. It would happen. She knew it would because this was what she wanted most in all the world, and she always got what she wanted.

"Very well, Gerald," she replied. "Give me the syringe."

"Come down into the shrubbery first so we can't be seen from the house."

She hesitated. "It's full of wasps down there."

He laughed and steered her toward the dense screen of bushes. Once hidden, he took the hypodermic out of his pocket. "Here you are. Be sure to handle it with your handkerchief as I'm doing, so you won't leave any fingerprints. Now have you got it all straight?"

"Yes, Gerald," she said. "I know exactly what to do."

"Good. Then you'd better go back to the house and tuck Roger in for the night. I'll stroll around the grounds awhile longer. We mustn't be seen going back together." He blew her a kiss and turned to leave.

"Wait, Gerald," said Eleanor sharply. "Don't move. There's a wasp on the back of your neck."

"Well, swat it, can't you?"

Lady Patterly's hand flashed up. "Oh, too late. Sorry, that was clumsy of me. Did it sting you badly?"

She left him rubbing his neck and walked easily across the terrace. The hypodermic barrel felt pleasantly smooth in her hand. She lingered a moment by the garden well, idly dropping pebbles and listening to them plop into the water far below. If one plop was slightly louder than the rest, there was nobody but herself around to hear it. She went in to her husband.

"How are you feeling tonight, Roger?"

"Like a man again. Eleanor, you don't know what you've done for me."

She slipped a hand over his. "No more than a wife should, my darling. Would you like to read for a while?"

"No, just stay with me. I want to look at you."

They were sitting together in the gathering twilight when the gamekeeper and his son brought Gerald's body back to the house.

"How strange," Eleanor observed to the doctor a short time later. "He mentioned his heart again this evening. It kept him out of the army, he told me. But I'm afraid I didn't take him all that seriously. He always looked so healthy."

"That's always the way," said the doctor. "It's these big, hearty chaps that go in a flash. Now, His Lordship will probably live to be ninety."

Lady Patterly smoothed back her husband's hair with a competent hand. "Yes," she replied. "I don't see any reason why he shouldn't."

Not Just the Facts

by Annette Meyers

A POSSIBLE HOMICIDE

They call it the High Line. It's an elevated meadow
that rises some thirty feet above the streets of Chelsea
on the far west side of Manhattan. In the spring and
summer the High Line is a rich blanket of green, dot-
ted with wildflowers. When Francine Gold goes missing, it is here among the wildflowers on a sunny June
afternoon that her body is found.

The High Line used to be a railroad route running
from Gansevoort Street in the meatpacking district all
the way to 34th Street, and the tracks are still visible
cutting through the flora that has grown around them.
People climbed the mound and strolled through the
meadow, marveling that such a wonderful place ex-
isted in the city.

So the city, after much debate about tearing it down,
actually listened to the protests, decided to convert the
High Line into a public park, and closed it to the public,
pending renovation. Now of course, as happens in New
York, architects and landscape experts are being consulted without end, and there is no sign that any work
will be done on the project in the near future.

This being the case, were it not for Chopper 6, the

WNYS weather and traffic helicopter doing a sweep to report on sailboating traffic on the Hudson this summer morning, decomposition would have been more extensive.

"What a sight! Let me tell you, it's a great day for the tall ships," chopper pilot Phil Vigiani reports. "Just enough wind to fill those beautiful sails. Boy oh boy, wouldn't you like to be tacking the mainsheet right now? I would." He smiles at the photo of Jen and the twins propped next to the one of him and Dwayne and Fred in their gear in front of Dwayne's Apache. Fred, poor bastard, comes all the way through Desert Storm, then, drunk as a skunk, tops a hundred into a concrete barrier outside of South Bend. Phil pushes it from his mind. What's the fucking point?

"Water looks a little choppy there, Phil," Wanda Spears comments from the studio.

"Maybe a little. But there's not a cloud in the sky. What a day." He pauses, adjusts his goggles. "I'm looking down on the High Line now, Wanda. From up here she looks like a wide green carpet. Hey!" Engine surges.

"Phil?"

"Holy sh—"

Wanda doesn't like where this is going and cuts him off before they're all in trouble with the FCC.

Phil calls 911 on his cell. "Phil Vigiani, Chopper 6. I'm low over the High Line and I see what looks like a body lying in the grass. Not moving."

"Hold on, sir."

"Listen, babe, don't put me on hold. I'm in a chopper. Get some medics and cops to the High Line, around 18th or 19th Street. What I'm seeing down there hasn't moved though I made two low passes over it."

THE 911 OPERATOR

Doris Mooney doesn't like being called babe, but she's a pro. She's been taking 911 calls for five years now. Before that she spent twenty-five years teaching fourth grade. Ask her which she likes better, she says right away, being a 911 operator.

"Sir, I'm routing you through to the police and the fire department."

"Tell them Phil Vigiani, Chopper 6. They'll get it."

His name and phone number appear on her screen. "Stay on the line, Mr. Vigiani." Doris hears the excitement in his voice. It's like a drug, this adrenaline thing. She wonders if that's really a body up there on the High Line.

Doris knows the High Line because she lives in a tiny one-bedroom apartment on 8th and 25th, part of the Penn South Houses, a middle-income housing development. She and Walter, her nine-year-old calico she realizes she loves more than she did her late husband, for whom the cat was named.

The High Line is very much part of the neighborhood. She'd buy a rotisserie chicken, make biscuits and potato salad, Walter would pick up a bottle of wine, and they'd have a nice picnic up there in the tall grass. It was like being in another world. But that was a long time ago. Walter was gone and she was no spring chicken anymore, though she still had her wits about her and the new copper color she'd washed into her hair looked really nice. If it was a body up there, how had it gotten there? The High Line was closed off till the city got around to renovating it. Heck, it's New York. Anyone who wants to get somewhere bad enough finds a way.

She hears and sees on her screen that Phil Vigiani is connected to the 10th Precinct on West 20th. In short order, the area's going to be crawling with cops, firemen, and EMTs. Doris disconnects, freeing the line for another call.

THE 10th PRECINCT

The 10th Precinct is an old-fashioned lime-and-brownstone precinct building on West 20th Street between 7th and 8th avenues. You can't miss it because of the large number of unmarked and radio cars, plus SUVs slant-parked on the sidewalk in front of the House, which pisses off some of the environmentally conscious locals. Not so much the parking all over the sidewalk so you can't walk, but all those gas-guzzling SUVs with no thought to global warming.

The precinct covers a wide area from Chelsea into Hell's Kitchen, combining both a large commercial industrial area and varying socioeconomic, multiethnic residential communities, including three housing projects: Fulton Houses, Chelsea-Elliot Houses, and Penn South Houses.

The precinct house's claim to fame is that it was featured in the 1948 film *The Naked City*.

THE COPS

Officers Mirabel Castro, a twenty-eight-year-old redheaded Latina with a nice nose job, a booming voice, and a deceptively relaxed manner, and Anthony Warbren, thirty-four, former Little League pitching champ, who got as far as a Yankee farm team and is still recognized with a lot of *Yo, Tonys* around Fort Greene in Brooklyn, have just come off cooling a couple of hot tempers in a parking dispute in front of Loehmann's.

They are already on 18th and 7th, three long blocks from the area where the body was sighted.

"So whadja say then?" Tony said, making tracks. He intends being First Officer on the scene.

"Said, Felipe, you gotta respect my career." Mirabel's sweating like a fool in this heat, taking three steps for his every one to keep up. Felipe's her live-in boyfriend. He has a good job with Home Depot in the Bronx and's been bugging her about kids. "Tell the truth, Tony, you see me wiping asses?"

Tony laughs. "You already dealing with crap on the Job." He's crossing 9th Avenue, leaving her behind. What's she got to bitch about? All these women on the Job get special attention and it burns a lot of guys. But he has no complaints. He's gay and out and no one at the 10th says boo to him about it. He and Larry, a dental surgeon, have been together for nine years. They're in the process of adopting a multi-racial kid.

They get beat to the scene by the fire department. An EMT fire department bus, lights swirling, is pulled up next to the red fire emergency vehicle in a parking lot below the thirty-foot rise. Metal stairs lead up from the lot to the High Line. Two EMTs are taking the stairs fast. An FDNY fire marshal is on the top of the rise, waving the medics up. He sees Tony first and draws his hand across his throat, like he's slicing.

"See that?" Tony says. "I'm calling it in." He talks into his cell. "Yeah, looks like something. FDNY beat us to it. Better get someone from Crime Scene over before they fuck it up."

"Hey, up there," Mirabel yells. "Don't mess up our crime scene." Her voice is so loud they all turn.

On his cell, Tony says, "Gotcha, Sarge. Everyone stays till the detectives get here, and no one else goes up there." He clicks off. "You heard?"

"Yeah." Mirabel folds her arms across her chest.

Pigeon crap coats everything, including the staircase, which is fenced off at entry by a gate with a padlock. It wouldn't be easy to get to the top of the rise without climbing over the fence, unless someone has a key to the padlock of the gate. The padlock hangs loose now, either broken by the perp or by the FDNY.

The EMTs come back down the stairs, hauling their kits. First, black woman, her curves almost, but not quite, hidden under the regulation uniform. Simone Norwood, Corporal, National Guard, served two tours in Iraq as a medic and could be called back any day now, which doesn't make her happy, her being a single mother with two kids under ten and her own mother whining all the time about taking care of kids again at her age. Simone's wire-rimmed glasses have slid down her nose on beads of sweat. She pushes them up and gives her gear to the probie Ryan Moore to load into the bus.

"You gotta hang out till the detectives get here," Mirabel says. She has her notepad out.

"Yeah." Simone leans against the bus and gives Mirabel her name, serial number, time of arrival, time of pronouncement of death, then motions for Ryan to do the same. Boy, she'd like a cigarette, except she's trying to quit. Pack she carries in her pocket is burning a hole in her Windbreaker.

"What's the word?" Tony says. He's unrolling the yellow crime scene tape around the staircase area.

"Not a pretty sight."

Fire Marshal Richard Fergussen comes clanking down the stairs. He ducks under the tape. He's done. He hates this kind of call, dead girl, beaten to hell and back. Nothing he can do for her. Makes him worry about his Anna Marie, who's going off to Boston College in August. Wouldn't listen about Fordham and living at home. At least he could protect her from some of the bad stuff out there. She's such a sweet, trusting kid. The ulcer starts grinding his gut. He's got his bottle of Maalox in the car. He can't hold back the shudder, can't shake the image of that poor girl up there, something he can't do a goddam thing about. His job is saving lives. Now it's up to the NYPD.

An unmarked screeches to a stop next to the FDNY bus. A radio car follows.

Fire Marshal Fergussen joins the patrol officers.

"Homicide?" Officer Castro asks.

"Possible," Fire Marshal Fergussen replies.

THE DETECTIVES

"What do we have?" Detective First Grade Molly Rosen, wearing a white shirt, black linen pants, climbs out of the passenger side of the unmarked, while her partner, Greg Noriega, pops the trunk and collects camera and booties. She's sweating right through the shirt she paid too much for at Banana Republic, even though it was on sale.

"First Officer?" she says.

"Foot Patrol Officer Anthony Warbren."

Rosen tilts her Mets cap upward. She takes in the scene. The EMTs, the fire marshal, the staircase to the High Line, the loosened padlock. The sun like a fucking ball of fire overhead. The parking lot with scattered vehicles. "Okay," she says. "Let's have it."

Tony Warbren reads from his notepad. "Call came in at nine twenty. Chopper 6 reported what looked like a body on the High Line, around 19th Street. Castro and I were three blocks away and arrived on the scene at nine forty-two. Two FDNY EMTs, Norwood and Moore, running up the stairs." He nods to Norwood and Moore, who lean against the bus. "Fire Marshal—"

"Richard Fergussen," the fire marshal says. "Got here first. Dead woman. Face down. Didn't touch anything except her wrist for a pulse. EMTs turned her on her back." He blinks as Noriega begins taking photos.

"I want the scene extended," Molly Rosen tells the two uniforms from the radio car. She points. "There. There. There." Barriers are set up and the taped area is widened. "The plates on every car. Get me a printout."

"The padlock was hanging loose," Warbren continues.

"Like it was when I got here," Fire Marshal Fergussen says.

"In order to preserve the integrity, Castro and I didn't climb the stairs or enter the crime scene," says Warbren.

"Good. Warbren, you stay here. Castro, canvass these buildings." She nods at the commercial buildings and a tenement across 10th, facing the High Line. "See if you can round up a few witnesses." She eyes the gathering group of the curious held back by the wooden horses and yellow tape strung around by the patrol officers. "Let's get some additional personnel here to make nice with the crowd and maybe come up with something valuable."

Molly Rosen slides the latex gloves on heat-swollen hands and ties the booties over the black pumps, which have begun to pinch. She opens the gate and climbs the rattling stairs. She's sweating buckets. Doesn't like that she has to stop at the top to catch her breath, for chrissakes, and to quiet her stomach. Her mouth tastes like raw fish. She is forty-one, a fifteen-year veteran NYPD, gold shield eight years. Anyone would tell you, she's tough, knows her stuff. Worked her way up butting heads with the good old boys in the department. Has great kids—Josie three, Del Jr. five, and Mary eight. Great kids thanks to Del, who quit his teaching job to be a stay-at-home dad. It was a case of who wanted what more.

Noriega's flash goes off. Rosen wobbles. "You okay?" he says. Rosen doesn't look okay. She's got this pasty look on her face. She's tough as nails with this rep of chewing up rookie homicide detectives and spitting them back to narcotics, and he for sure doesn't want to go back there.

"Yeah, why wouldn't I be okay?" She wipes the oily sweat off her face with a tissue. Okay if being fucking pregnant again is okay.

"Looks like all that's missing are the cows," Noriega says. He snaps what may or may not be the path to the vic made by the perp and/or the fire marshal and the EMTs.

Dr. Larry Vander Roon from the ME's office appears on the stairs. He's overweight and only months from retirement, but everyone else is busy. He could do without this, but they can't do without him. They don't have enough on staff. Cutbacks all the time, now they're talking about his retirement as attrition. If it was up to him, he wouldn't retire. It's Joanne who wants it. She's got her eye on a condo in Fort Myers. What the hell would he do there, sit by a pool and listen to the jabber? Not him.

When he gets to the top of the stairs, the sun bakes right down on him. It's an oven up here. The body is going to stink something awful, the corruption difficult. Give him a winter body anytime.

THE CRIME SCENE

The meadow is green, almost lush in the late morning heat. The sun is high and there are no clouds to offset the glare. A faint breeze barely moves the blades of tall grass and the wildflowers. The footfalls of the fire marshal and the two EMTs are unmistakable, marking a passage of approximately twenty feet from the top of the stairs to the body. It is understood that this may have obscured the path left by the killer, should this prove to be a homicide.

Because of this probability, the body has been left uncovered.

Scattered along the way from the top of the stairs to the body are various articles of clothing. A black T-shirt lying on a clump of daisy-like wildflowers, black pants and a stained white blazer closer to the body. A lacy black bra and black bikini panties, tossed to the right and to the left. Noriega marks each spot.

The vic is female, late twenties, early thirties, slim, long blond hair. Her eyes half-open slits, one side of her face obscured by dried brown blood, purple bruising. She is naked, brutally beaten. Rigor has set in.

Noriega snaps dozens of pictures of the vic from all angles, then circles around taking care where he steps, taking more photos of the area. He narrowly misses tripping over an empty wine bottle. "Wine bottle. Empty."

"Mark it."

He drops a marker, slings his camera over his shoulder, and sketches out the scene in his notepad. The air reeks with decomposing body smells.

Molly Rosen steps aside so Larry Vander Roon can get to the body. She calls down to the patrol officers. "I want the body isolated and this whole area of the High Line around the body, a block both ways, uptown and downtown, cordoned off."

THE MEDICAL EXAMINER

"She was spotted by Chopper 6 at nine twenty this morning," Rosen says. "The fire marshal got here first, then the EMTs, who pronounced her. They flipped her over on her back."

"I can see that. Lividity's on her butt." Vander Roon is old-school. Gloves on, he crouches beside the body, nostrils twitching. "Poor little thing." He takes his thermometer from his bag, rolls the body onto her side.

"We've got her clothes, tossed around like someone was having a good time."

Vander Roon grunts. "Value judgment?" He checks the vic's eyes for hemorrhages.

"Not me, Larry. Just an observation."

He squints up at her. "You look a little green around the gills, Rosen. You—?"

"Larry, just deal with the vic." Regrets the snappish tone. "Sorry. Can you estimate time of death?"

Vander Roon shifts his weight. His bad knees will have him limping when he gets up. "Some of this is old stuff."

"Antemortem?"

"That and ante antemortem. I gotta get her on the table." He checks the reading on the thermometer. "Given loss of body heat, even taking into account roasting up here, the stage of rigor, lividity, I'd say twelve to fourteen hours."

"Gunshot wound? Asphyxial? What? Beating? That head wound looks bad."

"Even minor head wounds bleed a lot. Like this one."

"Can you tell if she died here or was dumped?"

"She died here."

"Found something," Noriega says. "Looks like what's left of a pill. You want to see it up close?"

"Let's have a look," Vander Roon says. He removes his gloves and drops them into a container in his bag. "Give me a hand, will you, Rosen?"

Molly takes his elbow and he leans into her. The old guy weighs a ton. Good thing she's a big girl. "Mark the place and bring it here," she tells Noriega. "Then see if anyone even vaguely of her description's been reported missing."

Vander Roon looks at the mashed remains of a pill in Molly's palm. "If it's hers, and it's important, we'll find it in the tox screen."

Molly's cell rings. "Rosen." She sees Crime Scene unloading their gear in the parking lot. "Crime Scene just got here."

"I'll stick around," Vander Roon says. "When they're through, my people will take her away."

"Noriega, you, too. When the body is removed, get pictures of the area around and under where she was." Molly's distracted, phone to her ear. "What? Where? Okay, I'm on my way." She pockets the cell. "Patrol found two EDPs on 14th under the viaduct fighting over a woman's purse."

THE FIRST BREAK

Emotionally Disturbed Persons.

Zachary lives in a cardboard box under the viaduct. He's been on the street in New York since he left the VA hospital in Baltimore. Tossed the pills they gave him for the voices the minute he got out. Can't remember how he ended up in New York, but what the fuck difference does it make anyway? He's got a home here, fixed up real nice, with a mattress he found outside a brownstone on 20th. He sits all day in front of the Chelsea Hotel on 23rd. That's his place. People put money in his bowl, which says Purina. He gets real mean if someone tries to move in on him.

Sometimes when it's real hot, he climbs the fence to the High Line and sleeps in the grass. The grass is sweet. But then it's not. He smells it. He goes looking for it, though he doesn't want to. He never leaves his platoon, even when it's real bad. He isn't going to run now. It's a girl. Not a gook neither. They took her out. She smells like Nam. Rotting dog meat. Nothing he can do. He backs away and falls on his ass. Lays still a long time, waiting for the blast. Nothing happens. He sits up and there it is. A purse. He grabs it up and takes off.

When he gets to his crib, there's filthy bare feet sticking out of it, laying on his mattress. He goes nuts. It's that acidhead been hanging out under the viaduct.

"Hey!" He kicks the feet hard. "Get the fuck outa my crib."

The feet pull back. Otherwise, nothing. Zachary reaches into his box and grabs one skinny ankle and pulls the piece of shit outa his crib. "What the fuck you doing?"

"You wasn't using it," the acidhead screams, scrambles to his feet. He calls himself Shane. Mooches from the moochers. He's twelve when his mother remarries. Every time his stepfather gets him alone, the slug sucks his dick and more. First chance Shane gets, he cleans out all the cash in the house and leaves. He hangs in the Port Authority the first winter turning tricks. Hash, acid, even coke, easy to come by. A rapper faggot drops some acid on him once outside a Village club. The AIDS killed that life, but he's managing. Finds plenty to eat out of the trash baskets, still turns a trick now and then.

"You come back and I'll throw you in the river," Zachary screams, laying punches on Shane. He drops the purse.

Shane covers it with his mangy body. "I got it, I got it. Finders keepers."

"Get up. Let's see what you got there." Patrol Officer Gary Ponzecki pokes Shane with his baton.

"Fuck!" Zachary screams. "It's mine. He's stealing it."

Shane gets up, smirking, swings his scrawny hips. "Oh, so Mister Tough Nuts is carrying a purse now. Everybody knows it's my purse."

"Back off," Ponzecki says. He's testy, having had a fight with Ellie again this morning. Her asshole father's forever with the negative comments about the Job. And he can see Ellie's beginning to go along. Ponzecki always wanted to be a cop. Loves the patrol. Really loves it. He's not going to give it up and work for the old fart in his grocery store. He sees Rosen coming fast down 10th Avenue. "You heard me. Both of you. Back off. Don't touch the purse."

"I'll take it from here," Molly Rosen says. She points to the purse. "Bag it."

"Not fair! Not fair. I found it." Zachary is dancing around, fists clenched, like he's prizefighting. "She don't need it no more."

"No! No! It's mine."

Ponzecki says, "This one calls himself Shane. The ballet dancer is Zachary."

"I ain't no faggot," Zachary screams. "I was in the ring."

"This purse is evidence in a murder investigation. Maybe you both want to go to Rikers for a little vacation." Molly flips through pages in her notepad till she finds a clean one.

THE WITNESS

"She stepped on a mine," Zachary says. "She don't need it no more." He's got the shakes, doesn't like that they brought him into the precinct house and he's not sitting in front of the Chelsea in his place. Though the lady cop in the Mets cap promised they'd drive him there if he told them everything he knew. Even though he don't know nothing. And they let that prick-face liar Shane go and he's probably on his mattress again.

"What time was it?" Rosen puts a cardboard container of coffee on the table in front of Zachary.

"I don't got a watch." He likes the smell of coffee, but not the taste. At least there's plenty of milk. "You put five sugars in like I told you?"

"Yes. Drink up. The sooner you tell me everything you know, the sooner you'll get back to your place in front of the Chelsea. What time did you go up on the High Line?"

"It was dark. That's all I know. I sleep up there when it's hot. The grass smells good. But not last night."

"What was different?"

"Smelled like in-country. She was took out. Almost got me." He grimaces, takes a big gulp of coffee.

"Whoever killed her tried to kill you?"

"Yeah. Whole place was mined."

"Did you see anyone besides the dead woman?"

"No."

"Where did you find the purse?"

"Fell on it."

THE IDENTIFICATION

"They took her away. Crime Scene is finished," Greg Noriega says, coming into the interview room. "Jeez, what a stink."

"The EDP." Rosen comes up behind him with a spray can and sprays the room. There's an intense flowery smell. She looks at the label. "Magnolia is better than EDP." She puts on gloves and removes the purse that Ponzecki bagged. It is peach nylon fabric with leather handles, zipper closure. She empties its contents on the scarred and dented table. "Let's see what we got."

Noriega, gloves on, begins separating the items. He takes out his notepad and writes each item down. "Black wallet. Lipstick." With the back of his pen, he pushes the cylinder to Rosen. "Glasses case. No glasses. Kleenex. Cell phone. Postal receipt: priority mail, twenty-one dollars and fifteen cents. Five thirty p.m. yesterday."

"Francine Gold," Rosen says. She holds up a driver's license. "Thirty-one. Five two, blue eyes. Could be our vic. Address: 400 West 12th Street."

"Those new loft conversions."

"See if anyone reported her missing."

Noriega takes a printout from his back pocket. "Manhattan missing persons. No one fitting her description. No one named Francine Gold."

THE INTERVIEWS (PART I)

At 400 West 12th Street, Susan Kim sits on a high stool at the concierge desk sorting mail. The desk is actually a broad marble counter closed in above and on each side of the opening. She reaches up and right and left putting residents' mail in their boxes. This is the most boring part of her job, which she has held for three years, but tips are frequent, and it is particularly nice at Christmas because the sixteen units of the condo are owned by very successful people and they are generous. Maybe more so because she knows all their secrets and she likes it that way. She has the title concierge, but basically, she runs the place. Vasili, the super, is an Albanian immigrant whose every response is "No problem." But he's a good worker and doesn't get in her face like the last one, the superstud from Ecuador who thought he was God's gift to women.

Vasili handles three condo buildings on the block

and lives with his wife and two children in an apartment in the one across the street.

Susan Kim's parents are immigrants. They'd like her to go back to teaching once she finishes her master's, but why should she? She makes double, even triple as a concierge and while she's living at home, she saves most of it. One of her residents owns a designer boutique in SoHo and is always giving her things, like last week, these black leather boots. She swings one slim leg out, flexes her foot. Elegant. The boutique guy's wife works long hours as a neurologist. She's a cold snoot, so Susan has no sympathy for her when the husband brings models to the apartment some days.

The outside door opens and a tall woman in a white shirt and black linen pants comes in. She's practically dripping sweat in Susan's nice cool lobby. The woman's clothes need ironing and her hair is in a messy ponytail. Frumpy. Right behind the frump is a skinny Latino in a cheap suit. They don't have to show Susan their IDs. She knows they're cops by their attitude. Like they can walk in anywhere. She wanted to be a cop once so everybody would respect her, but that was before she knew how grubby the job is and that they don't make any money.

"Detective Molly Rosen." The woman holds up her badge. "This is Detective Greg Noriega."

Susan congratulates herself. Right on the nose. "I'm the concierge, Susan Kim. What can I do for you?"

"You have a tenant named Francine Gold?"

"This is a condo. No tenants. Owners. The Golds are in 7W."

"She's married?"

"Yes. Adam Gold is an architect. I'm sure you've heard of him. He designed one of the new buildings just below Chelsea Pier."

"Where is his office?"

"He works out of the apartment."

"So he's at home now?"

"I believe so."

"Is Francine at home?" Noriega says. Boy, does this babe love herself.

"I don't know. I didn't see her leave this morning." Susan saw her yesterday, though, with those big dark glasses on again.

Molly waits for Susan Kim to add what she's thinking, but Susan presses her lips together so nothing else comes forth.

"What does she do?"

"She's a lawyer at Browning, Coleman. I have her office number here, if you want it." Susan sifts through the contents of a small file box, finds Francine Gold's business card, hands it to Molly.

"Thank you. See if you can get hold of her, Greg," Molly says. "I'll go up and talk to Mr. Gold." Greg steps outside to make the call.

"I'll ring him," Susan Kim says.

"No. Please don't. This is police business."

Susan Kim doesn't like to be spoken to like this, but she has a certain atavistic respect for law and order. "The elevator is straight ahead. All the W apartments are to the right when you get off the elevator."

"Thank you."

The minute the elevator doors close on Molly, Susan rings up Adam Gold. He's promised her one of the few middle-income apartments in his new building.

THE INTERVIEWS (PART II)

Molly Rosen gets off the elevator on the seventh floor, fairly certain that Susan Kim made the call to Adam Gold. She recognizes Susan Kim. Susan will not jeopardize her self-interest.

"Hold the elevator, please." A woman, her gray hair long and swingy, and a small black poodle come down the hall from the left, the E apartments.

Molly tries to catch the door but it's too late. "I'm so sorry."

"Not a problem. Those doors close too fast. We

complain, but hell, who can we complain to when we're the owners?" She smiles, presses the DOWN button. "You're not here to see me, are you?"

"Not unless you're Francine Gold." Molly holds up her badge.

"I'm Linda Reinhart."

"The writer who just won the National Book Award?"

"Yes." And about time, too. She's been short-listed for years for so many different awards. Now everything's terrific and she's creaky and cranky, too old to really enjoy it all. She's never going to do another goddam book tour either. The last one brought on an attack of asthma which she hasn't had since she was a kid. Not to mention they're badgering her for the next book and she's totally blocked.

"Detective Molly Rosen." Molly shows her ID.

"Well, at long last." Only a week ago she found Francie in a fetal position outside the Gold apartment. The prick had punched Francie in the face and literally kicked her out of the apartment. Because the milk turned and he had to drink his coffee black.

Francie wouldn't let Linda call an ambulance, so she went with her over to St. Vincent's, but wouldn't you know, that bastard figured out where they were, probably from that awful Susan Kim, and came for her.

Molly says, "What do you mean at long last?"

"I'm glad she finally filed a complaint. I hope you send that garbage to prison."

"When did you see Francine last?" But now we have our first suspect: Adam Gold.

"Yesterday morning, a little after eight, maybe closer to eight thirty. In a big hurry, too. Almost banged into Nickie and me as we came back from our walk. She had those big dark glasses on again, so you can bet Adam was up to his old tricks. She said she was late for work."

"If I have any more questions, I'd like to call you, Ms. Reinhart." She hands Linda one of her cards.

"Of course, Detective." Linda fishes for a card in her handbag and hands it to Molly Rosen.

The elevator door opens and Greg Noriega steps out. Linda Reinhart and Nickie get on. She waves to Molly as the door closes.

"Francine Gold didn't come in to work this morning," Noriega says. "The partner she works with, Norman Mosca, is pretty upset. I didn't talk to him. The receptionist whispered it to me."

THE INTERVIEWS (PART III)

A plump young woman in a lavender smock answers the door to 7W. "Yes?"

"Detectives Molly Rosen and Greg Noriega." Molly holds up her ID, as does Greg. "Are you Francine Gold?"

"No. I'm Vicky Wallaby, Mr. Gold's assistant."

"We'd like to speak to Francine." The air wafting from the apartment is more than frigid.

"I haven't seen her today." Vicky stands in the doorway like a roadblock, quite aware that she fills most of the width. He said to keep them out, that he's too busy to speak with cops about things that have nothing to do with him.

"Then perhaps you can get Mr. Gold."

"I can't disturb him. Please." If she can't get rid of them, he will deliver sharp pinches to her soft flesh when she least expects it, when she relaxes her vigil, and all the time he's smiling like nothing is happening.

"I don't think he's too busy to talk to us about his wife," Molly says, in her most reasonable voice, but she's not beyond the hint of aggression in her body language. She moves in on Vicky and Vicky instinctively gives her some space.

"Please," Vicky says. "I can't let you in. He'll . . . I—" She covers her mouth. It's the nasty pinches, the Indian burns, the less-than-friendly pressure on her neck. She got her architectural degree at Pratt and then landed this great apprenticeship with Adam Gold, working on designs for the conversion of the High Line to a public park. Or what she thought would be a great apprenticeship. Adam Gold is a sadist. She knows that now, but she needs the job for her résumé.

"Tell Mr. Gold Detectives Molly Rosen and Greg Noriega are waiting to speak to him, and that it would be wise for him to talk with us now."

"I'll take it from here, Vicky." Adam Gold's voice is thin and high. "Go back to the office and finish the layout, there's a good girl."

Vicky flees.

The detectives exchange glances. Adam Gold has ruddy skin and small dark blue eyes. With his wrestler's build and shaved head, were it not for the expensive suit and blue striped shirt, he could pass for a member of the Aryan Nation.

"Won't you come in, Detectives." Adam works at keeping his anger contained. That crazy bitch. All she does is fuck up his life. Turn on the old charm, Adam boy. "What is this about?"

Noriega has never seen a place like this except maybe in the movies. The room is huge, one wall all glass, the furnishings an impression of leather, glass, and steel. An open kitchen fit for a restaurant is on the left. The window wall would have held the view of the Twin Towers were they still standing.

"Do you know where your wife is, Mr. Gold?" Molly sees scum dressed up fancy.

"At work, of course."

"According to her office, she never came in. Did you see her this morning?"

"I worked through the night, then dozed off at my desk. So no, I didn't see her. I suggest you tell me why you're here."

"Did you have dinner with your wife last night?"

Adam's patience is wearing thin. "No. I repeat. I worked through the night. I think Francie told me she was meeting a friend." That should cover him. Last time he saw her was yesterday morning when she did it again, didn't pick up his shirts from the cleaners. Like she doesn't know she'll get punished for it. It's always her fault, making him mad. She asks for it, so he gives her what she wants.

"You were alone, then, last night?"

"No, Vicky was here until about three; then I sent her home because I needed her here early this morning."

"It might be a good thing if we sat down, Mr. Gold," Molly says. She always says this when she's about to break bad news. But somehow, she doesn't think it will make any difference to Adam Gold whether he's sitting or standing when he hears that his wife is dead.

"Just say it." Oops, careful.

"The body of a woman answering to your wife's description was discovered on the High Line this morning. Your wife's purse was found by a homeless man not far from the body."

"Oh, God." It's not what he thought. Not at all what he thought. Relieved, he sags. The spic cop grabs him. Then it hits him. Francie? Dead? "No, not Francie." He shakes himself. Jesus Christ. "Did you say the High Line? I'm working on a design—"

"Does that mean you might have a key to the gate on 18th Street?" Noriega asks.

"Vicky! Get the key to the High Line gate. It's in the bowl on my desk." Adam pours himself a shot of Jack Daniels, drinks it down. The wait is unnerving. "Vicky!"

"It's not here, Adam," Vicky says.

Molly is not surprised. "We'd like you to come to the morgue now to see if you can identify the body."

THE INTERVIEWS (PART IV)

After Adam Gold, in near collapse, identifies the body of the woman found on the High Line as that of his wife, Francine, Detectives Molly Rosen and Greg Noriega head for the offices of Browning, Coleman, where Francine Gold worked.

Noriega's hungry so they stop at a food cart on Broad Street. The heat is oppressive, though the sun keeps disappearing behind storm clouds. Molly gets a ginger ale, trying to relieve her nausea, which builds with the humidity, while Noriega works on a hot dog piled with every fixing. Funny thing, the morgue didn't nauseate her one bit but the smell of the hot dog is doing her in.

Molly holds the cold can up to her cheeks and forehead. Her swollen breasts push against her bra. Goddamit. She doesn't want this kid. What is she going to do? "Your gut feeling?" she asks Greg.

"About the husband?"

"Yes."

"He didn't do it."

"Agree." She tosses the can into a trash basket. "Finish that and let's see what her boss has to say." They are standing in front of the glass and steel tower that is 110 Liberty Street. They show their IDs at the security desk. "Don't announce us," she tells the guard, who doesn't blink. He won't. What he doesn't say is that there are some law enforcement people up there already.

Detectives Molly Rosen and Greg Noriega ride up to the thirtieth floor in an elevator reserved only for Browning, Coleman employees, clients, and visitors.

The elevator opens onto a reception area. Two men and a woman, in business suits, are waiting. The reception area is crowded now. The trio take a long speculative look at Rosen and Noriega, who return the scrutiny. All are easy to recognize as law enforcement of some level.

"Manhattan DA's office," Molly says sotto voce. "Fraud unit."

"Detective Rosen, good to see you again," Charlotte Pagan says. This is her case, and it's a big one. For her. She's up for a job in DC in the Attorney

General's office. The FBI is in the process of certifying her. What the fuck is the NYPD doing here? Easy, Charlotte, maybe it's something totally different. She shakes hands with Molly, who introduces Greg. "Marty Goldberg and Joe O'Dwyer." Handshakes all around.

"Excuse me, excuse me." An attractive black woman, until now obscured by the growing herd of law enforcement, rises from behind the reception desk. Connie Bullard is good at keeping the irritation from her voice, but she's about to lose her cool. She has enough on her mind anyway trying to get Angie off to Barcelona for her junior year, and Angie practically hysterical about buying this, that, and the other, most of which she doesn't need and Connie and Joe can't afford. And now this crowd in her reception because of that cretin Norman Mosca. "Ms. Pagan, if you all will take a seat I can help our new visitors."

Molly Rosen steps forward, shows her ID; Greg does the same. "We're here to see Norman Mosca."

"I don't have you in his appointment book." Connie puts a polite and dumb smile on her face. Well, Norman is in deep doo-doo now with people from the DA's office and the NYPD all here for his surly ass.

"We want to speak to him about Francine Gold."

"Francie?" Connie's facade cracks. "Is she okay? She didn't come in today. It's upset some partners here."

"Like Mr. Mosca?"

"I can't say. But these people were here first." She points to Charlotte Pagan and her crew, who have been listening to the exchange.

"Okay," Molly says. "We'll have a little conference and see who goes first." She leaves the desk, motioning Greg to wait.

Charlotte and Molly huddle. Charlotte says, "We're investigating a possible fraud pertaining to a nonexistent escrow account set up by Norman Mosca. One point two mil of tenants' money in a rent strike is supposed to be in that escrow account. Did you say you're here about Francine Gold?"

"Yes. Her body was found this morning on the High Line."

"Dead?" Charlotte explodes. "Damn it to hell!"

"Francie? She's dead? Oh, my God." Connie is on her feet again. "I told her—"

Charlotte Pagan and her associates are all standing. "She's our primary source."

Marty Goldberg says, "He killed her to keep her from talking."

Back at the reception desk, Molly says, "Greg, talk to this nice lady—"

"Connie. Connie Bullard."

"—about Francine. Ms. Bullard, Connie, where is Mr. Mosca's office?"

Connie presses a buzzer. "Through that door, make a right and go down the hall to the last office. His is on the left."

Molly moves. But Charlotte Pagan and her people are on her heels.

"Murder trumps fraud," Molly says.

Charlotte counters: "Our search warrant covers Francine's office and Mosca's office."

"You'll keep me in the loop?"

"Of course." Charlotte is wondering if, once she's with the Justice Department, she should hold on to her great apartment on the Upper West Side, or sell it. If she holds it, she can always come back to New York. Once you sell you can never come back.

Molly, bucking one-way traffic of secretaries, clerks, and lawyers, carrying folders, files, briefcases, knows Charlotte will be stingy with information. It's always like that.

A woman rushes from the office, last on the left. Through the open door a man's voice bellows with rage. Molly stands in the woman's path and holds up her ID. "Detective Molly Rosen."

"Oh, thank God you're here," Jeannie Lapenga

cries. "He's going crazy. Francie took stuff and didn't come in today. He's gonna kill her." Jeannie wants to hug the cop. All she can think about is getting away from Norman. He's a lunatic. He was so nice at first when they assigned her to him. Bonus every month. A crisp hundred-dollar bill. She's the only one he treats nice. Francie he treats like shit, poor thing with that abusive husband, though Francie will never admit it, always saying she bumped into a door or fell down in the subway. Only last week Jeannie tried to tell Norman that Francie has a hard life and what did Norman do but scream and yell at Jeannie and then go after Francie about how stupid and incompetent she is and how one day soon he's going to talk to the Bar Association and they'll take away her license.

Jeannie's going to Italy on her vacation next Monday to stay with her grandparents, who have a farm in Cortona, in Tuscany. There's a man there, a widower not even forty yet. He owns an olive oil business. She's getting her June check today, which includes her vacation pay. She speaks good Italian. Maybe she just won't come back.

Molly takes Jeannie's name, address and phone number, then steps into Norman Mosca's office. His back is to her as he shoves papers into the wide briefcase lawyers carry to court.

"Mr. Mosca."

He turns with a snarl, but he has the face of a whippet, long thin nose, graying temples, and the corresponding build, long, lean, ready to run. His suit is charcoal gray and fits like it was made to order. White shirt, blue patterned silk tie. Black tasseled loafers. Molly gets a rush of sympathy for Francine Gold. The husband and the boss. How unlucky can a girl get?

Norman hates women with no style and this one who is just walking into his office like she owns the place is a dog of the first order. What the fuck is she holding up practically in his face?

"Detective Molly Rosen. Mr. Norman Mosca?"

"Yes."

"I'm here about Francine Gold."

"Francie? What about her?" Fuck. That mealy-mouth cunt turned on him. He warned her if she said anything she was in deep shit. He'd set it up that way, dropped a hundred K into an account he opened in her name in the Caymans when he was there last spring. Good luck to you, Miss Goody-Fucking-Two-Shoes. They get me, they get you. Oh, wouldn't your big-shot husband love to see that in the news.

"Her body was found this morning on the High Line."

"What?" Norman sits down at his desk. "What did you say?"

"Francine Gold. Her husband identified her body about two hours ago."

If she's dead she can't hurt me. It'll all be on her. He's saved. Oh, yes. "She's dead?"

"Yes. Did you know Francine Gold's husband physically abused her?"

"No. My God, no." Adam just gave her what she was asking for, what Norman would have liked to do himself, but he doesn't hit women. "If I'd known poor Francie had domestic problems, I would have been nicer to her." Take off that look of disgust, bitch. No way should women be allowed on the police force. They've already got too much power.

"Where were you between midnight and seven this morning, Mr. Mosca?"

"Jesus fucking Christ, you think I did it?"

"Just answer the question, Mr. Mosca. It'll go faster."

He'd like to piss in her officious fucking face. "Well, I was in Atlantic City. The limo picked me up outside the office at eight o'clock last night. Got to the Taj Mahal at ten thirty and stayed in the casino all night, first blackjack, then craps. There's heavy surveillance so I'm covered from here to eternity." Put that in your twat, bitch. "Got in the limo at six this morning and was back at my apartment in the city at nine, in time to shower and shave."

"Thank you, Mr. Mosca. It would be good if you didn't leave town until our investigation is finished. I'll be going now. There are some people from the District Attorney's office waiting to talk with you. He's all yours," she tells Charlotte Pagan.

Greg's interview with Connie Bullard:

"A Robert Malkin came to the building last week demanding to see Norman and Francie," Connie says. "He was pretty hostile so Security wouldn't let him up. Norman was on vacation, but Francie was here."

"Do you know who this Robert Malkin is?"

"No. But I think Francie did."

"Why do you say that?"

"Because Francie went down to speak to him. She came back very upset. Sort of went crazy going through Norman's files. When Norman got back from vacation, they had a real blowout fight. Boy, was Norman yelling. Francie went to her cubicle and then came out with her briefcase, kissed me on the cheek, and left." Connie begins to cry. "Like she was saying good-bye."

THE INTERVIEWS (PART V)

Detectives Molly Rosen and Greg Noriega arrive at 600 East 71st Street in the midst of crashing thunder and violent flashes of lightning. Just as they enter the building, rain comes down in big splats.

They show the doorman their IDs. "Detectives Molly Rosen and Greg Noriega. Here to see Mr. Robert Malkin," Greg says. "Apartment 6B. He's expecting us."

Robert Malkin is a pear-shaped man in his seventies, an Einstein look-alike with shiny pate and kinky gray hair puffing above his ears. "Come in, come in. I'm sorry the place is such a mess. The painters just left for the day. Bella's in the kitchen. We can talk there. I tell you, I knew something was wrong with the whole escrow business." He's not normally a paranoid person and Norman has such a nice way about him. But with only their social security and his pension from Saks and Bella's from teaching, he and Bella don't have much extra. And their Dina now a widow with Jason and Judy only nine and in private school, they have to help out.

Molly edges around the canvas-draped furniture, Greg following. "We're not with the District Attorney's office, Mr. Malkin."

"You're not? Then I don't understand—Bella, they're not working on our case."

The kitchen is large and hot, in spite of the air-conditioning. The smell of butter and sugar makes Molly's stomach turn. Bella is taking a sheet of rugalach from the oven. She is a small woman with a beehive of white hair and a pleasant smile.

"Not our case?" She inspects Molly, then Greg, Molly again. "Have one, Detective. I'll bet you haven't eaten all day." Don't ask how she knows, but she can tell when a girl is pregnant like this one is. She remembers when she was pregnant with Dina. She would look in the mirror and see what she sees on the face of the woman detective. "Sit down, Detective. You have to keep food in your stomach."

"We're investigating the death of Francine Gold," Molly says. Somehow the woman knows that Molly's pregnant. How the hell?

"Francine Gold is dead? Did you hear that, Bella?"

"What did you and Francine Gold talk about last week, Mr. Malkin?"

"Why, the fraud. She said she didn't know anything about it. She just collected the checks and gave them to Norman for the escrow account."

"You're not explaining it right, Robby," Bella says. She slides the rugalach onto a metal rack. "Norman lives in this building. We're having so much trouble with the plumbing here, leaky pipes, and the landlord does nothing no matter how much we complain. So Norman suggested a rent strike. For a year we've done it. Norman set up an escrow account and we all give our rent checks to Ms. Gold. Now the landlord wants to sell the building. He'll make all the repairs if we pay him the back rent. His lawyer drew up the papers and if the landlord doesn't keep his end of the bargain by a certain date, he will have to pay us a lot of money. So we asked Norman for the money in the escrow account and he's been putting us off for three months. The fact is, we are pretty sure now there never was an escrow account."

"Ms. Gold was very upset," Malkin says. "She said she would find our money, but I didn't wait. I notified the District Attorney's office."

THE SUSPECTS

"Adam Gold's alibi sticks," Detective Molly Rosen says. She's still got the morning sickness, but saltines are helping. It is three days since Francine Gold's body was found on the High Line. "Vicky Wallaby backs him up."

"We haven't found the key," Noriega says. "He and Vicky could have done it together."

"True. Do you like them for it?"

Noriega shakes his head. "And that toad Norman Mosca. His alibi covers him, too. So what do we have?"

"One of the uniforms turned up a clerk in a liquor store on 23rd Street. A woman answering to Francine's description bought two bottles of a Côtes du Rhône around eight o'clock that night. She paid cash."

THE AUTOPSY & THE DETERMINATION

Molly's phone rings. "Detective Rosen." It's Larry Vander Roon. "Oh, yes, Larry." She listens, frowning, makes circles with her hand to get Vander Roon to move faster. "Really? You're sure? Yes, an empty wine bottle." She thumbs through the list of evidence turned up by the Crime Scene Unit. "Two empty wine bottles. And a clerk who identified the vic as purchasing them around eight that night. Well, fax me your report." She hangs up. "The tox screen came back. She had enough Seconal in her to kill three people."

"And let's not forget the wine."

"He's calling it a suicide."

"What about the beating?"

"She had plenty of old healed fractures. The contusions were recent, but not recent enough or lethal enough to kill her."

"She took off her own clothes?" Noriega answers the phone when it rings again.

"It was an unbearably hot night."

"It's Charlotte Pagan." Noriega hands Molly the phone.

"Charlotte, we just got some interesting news from the ME's office." Molly listens. "Yes. That's the story. Thanks." Replaces the phone. She has the sudden strange feeling she may cry. The walls seem to close in on her. "Come on, Greg, let's get some air."

They go downstairs. The humidity is gone and the dry heat feels good on Molly's face. They hit the food wagon down the street. Molly's hungry. Noriega's always hungry.

"They found an empty prescription bottle for Seconal in Francine's desk."

"So there it is," Noriega says, taking a big bite from his hot dog. He loves the delicious spurt on his tongue.

"Yes. They also found a paperback called *Final Exit*." Molly covers her pretzel with mustard and takes a bite. Aces. She's got her appetite back.

Ninjettes

by Kate Flora

I was threading my way between cars in the dark garage when a man coming toward me said, "Hey, looks like you dropped something." I stopped to see what I'd dropped before I recognized this as a classic attacker approach.

He was beefy and unshaven, out of place in this upscale mall lot, and his expression was an ugly mix of smirk and lust. I checked out escape routes, transferred my packages to one hand, and got my keys ready. He was close enough for me to smell tobacco and Old Spice as I clicked the lock and tossed in my packages, keeping the car between us.

"Don't come any closer. You're making me uncomfortable," I said.

He grinned and flexed his fingers like a strangler warming up. I jumped in my car, stabbing the door lock as I jammed it into reverse. He was right behind me, fist raised, his face demonic in the red and yellow glare of the lights. I hit the gas, and he became a dark blur as he dove out of my way.

As I braked and shifted, I glanced back. He crouched there like some malevolent animal, shaking his shaggy head. I reminded myself to breathe, my self-defense instructor's words in my head: Don't worry about whether he's hurt. What's important is your own safety. Keep moving. Get yourself out of there. If you're breathing you can react.

I shook all the way home, a post-adrenaline chill that went right to my bones. Inside, I dumped my packages on the table and undid my coat with shaking hands, then snapped on the oven and pulled out a rotisserie chicken and salad stuff for dinner. From behind his science magazine, Karl made an incomprehensible sound.

I thought I was fine until I stopped in Cassie's room. She lasered my face with her sharp adolescent eyes. "Mom, what happened?"

"Nothing, honey. There was just this creepy guy in the parking garage who . . ."

"Are you okay?" I nodded. "Did you tell Dad?" I shook my head.

Cassie pulled the iPod buds from her ears. "You need tea."

Blessed are those who have daughters.

Later, as I hurried past Karl, snug as a bear in his new recliner, he glanced over his copy of *Nature*. "Off to your ninjettes class?"

"Sure am, sweetie," I said. "Tonight we're practicing plucking people's heads off."

Karl would have to help Bobby, our fifteen-year-old who often got stuck on geometry, and Cassie, who was struggling with college essays. As both required hands-on assistance, he'd have to leave his chair and go act like a parent.

Communication is my specialty. Five days a week, I visit schools and community groups around the state, helping parents and teenagers learn to communicate more effectively. I'm good at helping people talk to each other. You'd think I could make it happen at home, but Karl's developed an invisible shield that deflects my words like armor. His conversation these days is mostly demands or complaints, as though as his body gets wider, his mind gets narrower.

They say women tend to marry their fathers. My mother used to roll her eyes at my father's constant demands and mutter, "Maybe it would be different if he were Winston Churchill." Sometimes, studying the back of Karl's magazine, I wondered if Mrs. Churchill was lonely, too.

I probably sound bitter. I'm not. It's just frustrating to have good communication skills and be such a failure at home. Lately I've been feeling desperately fragile. Between Karl, the house, two teenagers, and a job, I'm stretched so far I feel like I'm teetering on a window ledge.

It was good to get out for something besides errands and work. I punched the ON button and got Seeger and Springsteen. The last song I played was a Cher song about Jesse James. The idea of a woman like me sending some arrogant studlet down in flames always left me smiling.

My "ninjettes class," as Karl called it, was actually a RAD, or Rape Aggression Defense, class offered by our local police department. It was as much common sense and safety precaution as martial arts and self-defense. My friend Katie talked me into it, saying she didn't want to make an ass of herself alone. But Katie's a tough lawyer who's good on her feet and looks like you wouldn't want to mess with her, so I wondered if she'd done it for me. She always says I should get out more.

It *was* a sensible step for me. Increasingly, I found myself in far-flung parts of the state crossing scary parking lots at night. When I was standing in a gym with a bunch of nervous suburban ladies, our training had seemed distant and theoretical, but today at the mall, it had been just what I'd needed. Tonight we were practicing everything we'd learned. Police officers in their Aggressor suits were going to mug us and we were going to fight them off.

In the female officers' locker room, my classmates clustered around Natalie Burke. Natalie was a big-eyed, slender brunette, the kind of woman you think you won't like because she's too damned attractive. She had perky implants while we were scooping up our saggy middle-aged breasts and repackaging them with underwire and padding, a sculpted body with visible muscles, and a frightening amount of energy. While we dragged our sorry asses into the gym each week, mumbling our responses like a gaggle of middle schoolers, Natalie hit the floor with singeing intensity.

She wiped away tears and streaks of mascara while two women stroked her back and murmured comfort. As I joined them, Katie whispered, "Her husband just left her for a twenty-five-year-old."

I felt the instinctive anger I always felt at these stories. Karl, still attractive despite the spread, was unlikely ever to leave me. It's hard to get entangled with young honeys if you spend your life in your lab, your car, and your chair. There were young lab assistants, but anyone expecting half-decent treatment soon left unless they were as obsessed with lipids as Karl was. He looked to be the exception, though. Lately a lot of husbands were trading in their wives for younger models.

I could imagine someone youth-obsessed leaving me. My mind's nice and tight, but from shoulder to knee I'm soft as the Pillsbury Doughgirl. Natalie, though, was fit and gorgeous. Nor did the timing make sense. They'd just moved into a new house, I knew, because every week she related another construction disaster.

"He just . . ." Natalie's husky voice quivered. ". . . came home one day and said he was moving on. Standing in the kitchen, right in front of the children, he says he's finally found someone who truly understands him. Who makes him feel young again."

She drew a shuddering breath. "Who wouldn't feel younger if they didn't have to worry about homework, sports schedules, teacher conferences, plumbers, investments, and finding a retirement community for his cranky mother?"

Her workout shoes slapped the dingy tile. "I've been understanding him for twenty-five years. Twenty-five years of bullying the cleaner about his shirts. Of running in from T-ball games and showering off baby spit after moving heaven and earth to get a sitter so I could meet him for dinner in Boston looking glamorous. A quarter century of dancing to his damned piper and he dumps me. It's just not fair."

She jerked off her wedding band and threw it across the room. "Twenty years as a gym fanatic because he noticed every ounce I gained. Well, fuck him."

The shiny gold spun like a dancer on the tile, then disappeared between two lockers. The room was so quiet I could hear the small clang of metal on stone as it fell.

Natalie snatched a headband from her bag, tied back her hair, and pushed up her sleeves. "Those cops better watch out because I am mad as hell and I have got to take it out on somebody."

"What's his name?" Katie asked.

"Sterling," she said. "Can you believe it? His name is Sterling."

Infected by her anger, we followed her into the gym, lively for once. And it made a difference. When I shouted "No!" I meant it. When I punched and kicked, it was in earnest. I was thinking about the guy in the garage. How I'd hated it that some creep could get his kicks terrifying me. I got a real rush channeling my fear and anger into positive action, using my breath to keep from getting rattled, focusing my energy into a self-protective response.

I wasn't alone. The whole class was responding to the idea of men acting badly. When the massive cop in the Aggressor suit approached Natalie, I saw surprise and respect through the bars of his mask as she stomped, kicked, and punched him to the floor.

Then it was my turn. When we started the course, I couldn't bring myself to shout. I said "No" in such a quiet voice I wouldn't have deterred a three-year-old. Over the weeks my "No" had stopped sounding like an invitation to try again. Tonight I roared. When Natalie knocked that guy down and stomped the hell out of him, I was on my feet with the rest of the class yelling, "Yes!"

It was one thing to cheer the others on, another to face this guy myself. Even if he was limping a little and not showing his earlier gusto, he was nearly twice my size and probably half my age. When I began my nonchalant stroll across the gym, I felt the same clenching fear I'd felt in the parking garage. But nothing happened.

I was almost across the room when a fat, gloved hand snaked around from behind and grabbed me. I jabbed my elbow back, hard, as I seized his hand and spun around, jerking him toward me. I slapped his ear with one hand while snapping a kick toward his crotch. "Breathe," I whispered, "breathe."

Maybe he'd had enough, because he grabbed my kicking leg and dropped me hard. I scrambled back, planted my hands behind me, and kicked out at him, snapping good hard kicks at his grabbing hands. Then a second guy grabbed my shoulders, pressing me down. I gave a sudden sideways roll and got my feet under me, but as they moved in together, I cast the rules of the exercise aside. "Natalie. Help me."

Instantly, she was beside me, her feet braced and her hands up in protective, assertive fists. I curled my hands into fists of my own, and shoulder to shoulder, we faced them. "Back off. Keep away from me," I growled. The new man lunged.

"No way!" I screamed, jerking his arm so that he flew past. As he regained his balance, I should have run. That *was* the point of the exercise. But I'd called on Natalie for help. While my guy was still turning, I

rushed her attacker and hauled him off. I grabbed her
hand and we raced for the door, giggling like tweens,
crossing the black safety line just before they
reached us.

"Thanks," I said, hugging her. "You can be on my
team anytime."

"Ditto. I always forget that part about running. I
want to stay and fight."

For a moment, she looked sad. Was she thinking
about her marriage? How you can't stay and fight if
the other person's walked out and won't even give
you a chance. Sometimes they don't give you a chance
when they stay around.

I settled onto the hard wooden bleachers. The exercise had left me feeling positive that I'd been able to
assert myself. But although it was only an exercise
and I'd always been "safe," I'd felt genuine fear, real
vulnerability, powerful anger toward my attackers.
Something about that had stirred up memories of
other scary times.

I'd had a blind date once where the guy had gotten
drunk and violent. Instead of driving me home, he'd
parked on a dark side street and tried to rape me.
I'd ended up running shoeless down an icy January
sidewalk, my blouse torn, rescued by a kindly police
officer about my dad's age. He'd wrapped me in his
creaky leather jacket, given me tissues, and told me
that it wasn't my fault, repeating it in his certain, gravelly voice until I almost believed him.

That wasn't the only thing, but it was the worst. I
wanted to live in a world where women didn't have
to worry about things like this. Where I wouldn't be
thinking that I should send my soon-to-be-college-
bound daughter to this class. Where people resolved
their differences with language. But who was I kidding? I couldn't make language work in my own
home. And I was not naïve. This class had helped with
the man in the parking garage. As long as there were

men who got their kicks making women uncomfortable, who didn't respect boundaries, we needed to be responsible for our own safety.

When the two female officers who'd run the class asked how we felt, they got a chorus of "great" and "incredible" until they got to me. I told them about my mixed feelings, how I felt all jumbled up. Katie agreed, and Natalie, and another woman named Sandy, who'd had an even harder time yelling and being assertive. The officers offered sympathy but seemed annoyed, which annoyed me right back. I get impatient with people who want approved answers instead of truth.

As we filed into the parking lot, I said, "Hey, Katie, got time for a glass of wine?"

Katie looked surprised. She'd asked before and I always said no. I'd fallen into a pattern of rushing home. There was always so much to do and I could never be certain Karl had paid attention to Bobby's homework. Tonight, though, I wanted company.

"Sounds good," she said.

I turned to Natalie. "Got time for a drink?"

She checked her watch, then tossed her head. "Sure. Why not?"

From somewhere to my left, Sandy said, "Mind if I join you? I could use a drink."

It felt odd going into the pub alone. I'd never been there without Karl and the kids. When you were riding herd on coats, hats, mittens, absentminded spouses, or moody teens and outbreaks of sibling war, you didn't notice ambiance; you noticed how fast the service was.

Tonight, I saw beyond the menu and the popcorn. I noticed how homey and inviting the hanging tin lamps were. I saw all the laughing guys with their pregnant bellies pressed against the bar, not one of whom probably worried about homework or whether he looked fat. The smell of food made me hungry enough to order a burger instead of salad and to eat the fries instead of leaving them. Even Natalie was tucking into a great big burger.

"I used to think it was just guys," she said, "but sometimes a woman needs a big hunk of meat."

Sandy choked on her wine.

"I *meant* the burger."

We discussed our reactions to the course, Sandy and Katie telling stories of clients who'd been unbalanced and menacing. Yet, as I drank wine and ate forbidden food, I realized I was having fun. I liked Sandy's insightful comments, Katie's punchy iconoclasm; even Natalie, despite her brittleness and desperate sadness, was a nice person to spend time with. I admired her concern with protecting her kids from their father's neglect and bad behavior.

"If you don't mind my asking," Katie said, "did you have any idea your husband was seeing someone?" Katie does a lot of domestic work.

Natalie shrugged. "I was trying not to see it, but it was there. There was this company dinner a few months ago. The bimbo—her name's Tiffany—was wearing a skimpy dress, very inappropriate for a business dinner. She kept coming up and sticking her chest in his face. At the time, I thought it was pitiful and wished someone would set her straight so she didn't embarrass herself."

She pushed a lonely, ketchup-daubed fry around her plate. "On the way home, I suggested Sterling get one of the older women to give her some tips. He said it was just that she was so young. Laughing, you know, like we were the grown-ups and needed to be understanding. Dammit!" She dropped her fork onto the plate. "Now he's sleeping with her and I'm still supposed to be understanding."

Katie, whose nose was slightly pink, signaled the waitress and ordered another glass of wine. Natalie checked her watch again—kids at home and no spouse for backup—and got one, too. Sandy said, "What the heck." I didn't want to be the only sober one, so I caved. The extra wine led to a brownie sundae and four spoons.

We were deep into chocolate when Natalie's phone rang. "Excuse me, it's my son." She flipped it open and turned away. She listened, then said, "He what? Tonight? Why didn't you call me?" There were more staccato questions, her head tipped to catch the answers over the bar noise, until she said, "Oh, honey. I know that was hard but you did just right. I'll be home soon." She snapped the phone shut.

"Goddamn that man. Goddamn him. Goddamn her. He's lucky I don't have a gun." She burst into tears.

Sandy pushed a small packet of pink tissues with Valentine hearts into Natalie's hand. "What did he do, dear?" she asked. Her soft, faintly southern voice invited confidence.

"He showed up at the house tonight, knowing I'd be at class. I changed the locks, see, after he left. I guess he thought he could talk his way in if it was just the kids."

Her eyes traveled around the table to see if we understood. "He didn't come to see them. He hasn't spoken to them since he moved out. Not even a call on Sammy's birthday. He came to get our financial records. For his lawyer." She hissed the word "lawyer" like the guy was a real snake. Probably was. When my sister divorced, she had a snake. She said it made all the difference. "My lawyer said don't give him anything until we've made copies."

She drained her glass. "That isn't the worst of it, either. He brought her with him."

"To your house? When the kids were home and you were out?" Katie said. "That's really low."

"The kids were good, though. They wouldn't let him in, so he banged around in the garage and the mudroom, then left." She drummed on the table with her fists. "I'd like to beat his head in."

Katie grinned in that manic way she does after a

little wine. "What about *her* head? Why is *she* off the hook? She's not some innocent seduced by the wicked wolf. She went after a man she knew was married. I mean, she'd met you, for heaven's sake. Anyone with any values knows that's wrong. Now she's showing up at the house to rub all of your noses in it. Whatever happened to discretion? For that matter, whatever happened to shame?"

"It does take two to tango," Sandy said.

"Yeah," I agreed. "All these weeks we've been going to class, learning how not to be a victim, how to assert ourselves in threatening situations. What's more threatening than someone out to destroy your marriage? And who's doing the threatening? She is."

Natalie brightened. "I know where she lives. What kind of car she drives. And she never stays all night at his hotel."

"How'd you learn all that?" Katie asked. "You hire a detective?" Natalie nodded.

"So what are we waiting for?" My voice cut through their *wows*. "Maybe we should have a talk with the young lady. Point out the error of her ways." I try to speak like an educated woman, but I love clunky old clichés like "the error of her ways." And, as we know, alcohol lowers inhibitions.

They responded to my modest suggestion like I'd yelled, "Charge!"

We paid the check. Natalie called her kids. By the time we were in the parking lot, I was having second thoughts. I'm a facilitator, not an instigator, and despite the meal, company, and restorative wine, I was still jumbled. I wasn't even sure why I'd made my crazy suggestion.

"Maybe we should rethink this," I said. "What do we do when we get there?"

"No way. It's brilliant," Katie said. "It's not like Natalie's going to beat this girl's head in. Why shouldn't she have a chance to say how she feels? That's all we're going for."

Put that way, it sounded absolutely reasonable.

"I'll drive," Sandy said. "I've got a good head for wine."

If this were a movie, we'd have jumped into something big, shiny, and black. Probably been wearing leather, too. Or navy blue FBI-style jackets with NIN-JETTES in goldenrod letters. And stilettos. But this was a quiet suburban town and we were a clump of slightly tipsy matrons. We all piled into her Subaru wagon.

Natalie took the front to navigate. Katie and I dumped L.L. Bean canvas totes, an umbrella, rain boots, South Beach snack bars, and assorted audio-books into the back and fastened our seat belts. This was either going to be fun or a monumental disaster.

Tiffany lived on the first floor of a three-decker on a quiet Cambridge street. We found a parking space just one house away, and waited. Trees just leafing out overhead were a soft yellow green under the streetlights and the air coming in the open windows had the earthy scent of spring.

"I don't see her car," Natalie whispered. "She's got one of those Mini Cooper things. A yellow convertible."

"That would be hard to miss," Katie said.

"Last time she came back around eleven," Natalie said. "She'd better come soon. My oldest won't go to bed until I'm back."

"Last time?" Sandy said. "Natalie, have you done this before?"

"I came once, thinking I'd talk to her, but I lost my nerve."

"I hope she didn't see you," Katie said.

"Nope. There could have been sixteen muggers in the bushes and she just went tripping past in wobbly little heels, paying no attention to anything. I'll tell you, I could have—"

"Everybody duck," Sandy said. "There's a car coming."

Katie and I nearly knocked heads as we squinched down in the small backseat. If it was Tiffany, she must have been driving about one mile an hour. I had a crick in my neck by the time Sandy whispered, "It's her. Now what do we do?"

"Natalie talks to her," I said.

"Natalie stays in the car. She knows Natalie," Katie said. "The three of us will do the talking."

"I thought *I* was going to talk to her," Natalie said. "Isn't that why we came?"

"Mmm. But I've been thinking," Katie said. "You're in a divorce, you want to keep right on your side. You don't want her getting a restraining order, claiming you've been stalking her, do you?"

"I never thought of that."

"She's getting out of the car," Sandy hissed.

"Then what are we waiting for?" I popped upright and grabbed my door handle. We were here and the facts hadn't changed—this young woman was causing Natalie and her kids so much pain. We might as well do it.

Tiffany wore a short skirt, pink cashmere bolero over a lacy, low-cut camisole, and cute little pink high-heeled mules with black polka dots. The purse slung over her shoulder, big enough to house a small rhino, held a matching pink tennis racket. Her multicolored hair hung in an expensively nonchalant shag and her lips gleamed like pavement on a rainy night. She didn't look much older than Cassie. It was tragic how when girls were young and naturally lovely, they slathered themselves with makeup.

"Tiffany?" Sandy spoke in a ladylike, unthreatening voice.

The girl's vaguely sullen "Yeah?" reminded me of my own teenagers. "Do I know you?"

Sandy shook her head. "We wanted to speak with you about your affair, dear."

"Affair?" Tiffany gave a little bark. "What affair?" She clutched the giant satchel closer to her side, dismissing us with a scornful look. "Not that it's any of *your* business."

One of my mother's clichés, "Don't judge a book by its cover," pressed to get out. We probably didn't look like much, three middle-aged women in baggy workout clothes and clean white gym shoes. But Katie was president of the local bar association. Sandy had won awards for her work with traumatized children. And I spent my life teaching parents and teens to communicate about issues of trust and honesty and taking responsibility for your choices about risky things like drugs, sex, alcohol, and speed. What I did saved lives.

"Your affair with Sterling Burke," I said. "Family relationships matter, Tiffany. When you disrupt a marriage and come between a father and his children, that's not only selfish, it's immoral. Did you ever consider that?"

She tilted her head in an I-can't-believe-this-is-really-happening gesture. "You're joking, right?" she said. "I mean, seriously, you didn't tootle in from the suburbs to talk to me about morality." She gave a disdainful sniff, a fanny about the size of two softballs twitching under her abbreviated skirt. "Look, if some pathetic woman can't hold on to her husband, that's not my problem."

This little lightweight had a lot of nerve calling Natalie pathetic. It was hard to raise kids, run a house, hold a job, and sustain a marriage. I held on to my temper and tried to explain.

"But sleeping with a married man *is* a problem, Tiffany. It interferes with important, established relationships. Sterling's relationship with his wife. His relationship with his four children," I said. "In some states, you know, alienation of affection and adultery are still crimes."

I studied the peaceful city street, the uneven brick sidewalks and budding trees. Such an unlikely place for me to be climbing onto a soapbox. "Before you started this affair, did you consider the pain you were inflicting on his family or whether you have the capacity and willingness to be a competent stepmother?"

"Stepmother? Oh, please . . ." She rolled her eyes. Brown eyes a lot like Natalie's. "I am so not interested in children. I'm what? Twenty-five? Natalie can take care of them." Her self-satisfied smile revealed unnaturally white teeth. "I'm taking care of him. Now why don't you three witches fly back to the suburbs and stir your cauldrons or something? I've had a busy evening and I'm tired."

"If this is about Natalie's husband," Sandy whispered to me, "why are *you* so angry?"

Before I could answer, Katie said, "You stop right there, Tiffany. There's more at stake here than just what you want. There are four kids who love their dad, who miss him. A woman who loves her husband . . ."

"And I don't care." Tiffany tossed her glossy hair. "If she didn't want him straying, she should have been a better wife. She should have paid attention to his needs, instead of spending his money on fancy houses and bringing all those brats he didn't want into the world."

The Subaru door slammed. We sensibly got out of the way as Natalie marched up to Tiffany, landed an open-handed slap on her ear, ran a foot down her shin, stomped on her foot and then, sweeping her feet out, dumped her onto the pavement. Tiffany's purse landed with such a thud it might have held bowling balls.

She wore the surprised look of a baby who has suddenly fallen onto a diapered bottom. "You hurt me," she said. "You had no right."

"Having my husband leave hurt, too," Natalie said. "And *you* had no right."

The girl pulled her bag toward her protectively. "You leave me alone," she said. "What goes on between me and Sterlie is not your business."

"Sterlie? Sterlie? Oh man . . . I cannot believe you. Since when is my husband not my business?" Natalie stood, hands on her hips, breathing like a runner in recovery. Then she straightened. "All right, I'll go. Before I do, though, let's be clear. . . ."

Tiffany had wrapped her arms around her purse, waiting for us to leave. Little white iPod wires ran from her ears and she tilted her head to unheard music. Natalie jerked on the wire, unplugging her in a gesture we all understood.

"If you take my husband, you keep him," she said. "There's no sending him back when you realize what a big baby he is. And even if he says he didn't want them, Sterling is the father of four because he *insisted* we have four. They need time with their dad, so you get the kids . . . all the kids . . . every other weekend, school vacations, and half the summer. No last-minute cancellations. No weaseling out. And the dog comes with the kids, so I hope you like dogs."

"I *hate* dogs. I *hate* kids," Tiffany said. "Sterlie and me are not into any of that." She scrambled to her feet and was edging away.

"Tough shit," Natalie said. "Hey, wait a minute. Is that my tennis racket?" Natalie snatched at the bag, pulling out the racket. She pointed at the name engraved on the handle. "You steal my racket and it's none of my business? My property isn't my business?"

She swung the racket, catching Tiffany neatly on her cute little ass, remembering to follow through, which I never did. Upending the bag, she dumped out a pink iPod, pink visor and wristbands, and a pair of pink and white tennis shoes.

"Sterlie gave me those," Tiffany said.

"My iPod, my clothes, my shoes, my racket. All the stuff from my tennis bag." Natalie drove her backward with vicious swings of the racket. "Goddammit, what were you thinking? It wasn't enough to steal my husband and leave my kids without a father, you had to steal my things, too? You *had* to know they weren't his."

Tiffany, looking stricken, pressed a knuckle against her trembling lip. This was what I talked to teenagers about all the time—had they considered the consequences of their choices and were they willing to accept those consequences?

Natalie swung the racket past the pert little nose with admirable control. "I said, 'What were you thinking?' "

"He wanted me to have them." Tiffany sounded like she was about to cry. "He was so embarrassed that his own children wouldn't let him in when he just wanted to get some papers. It was really unpleasant. He knew I felt uncomfortable, so he gave me this stuff to make me feel better."

"I'll show you uncomfortable." Natalie swung toward Tiffany's head as I stepped between them.

"You're crazy, you know." Tiffany scrabbled for a cell phone. "I'm calling the police. You belong in jail."

"I'm not sure you want to do that," I said.

Worried that we'd helped Natalie commit an assault, I looked to Katie, who shook her head. "We're all witnesses that Natalie found Tiffany in possession of over a thousand dollars' worth of her property," she said. "Tiffany's a thief and that's a felony. Even if Mr. Burke gave it to her, he stole it and she was there. That makes her an accessory and a receiver of stolen property."

Katie turned toward me, as though I was the leader of this group. "Anything else?"

My mind was a jumble of thoughts about relationships, the common decency we owed each other, and sorrow that someone so young could be so selfish and could wreak so much havoc without any thought. I also knew why I was so angry and who I was angry at. Guys who defaulted on their marriage contracts and the women who, actively or passively, aided and abetted them. Including myself. My words rolled out.

"Tiffany, what you want is not all that matters. You and Sterling aren't alone in this relationship. The choices you make have consequences for five other people. You're not an innocent party, you're an active player in your own life. You have to take responsibility for the choices you make. Don't assume you can hurt people terribly and walk away untouched."

Natalie and Sandy and Katie flanked me like we were a real team, their approving glances saying I was making real sense. This wasn't just about Tiffany and Sterling and Natalie. It was about making considered choices and taking action when things weren't right. I might still be jumbled but some of the right things had been shaken loose.

Tiffany looked down at the open cell phone in her hand.

"Felony," Katie said.

Tiffany snapped the phone shut, shoved it in her purse, and went inside.

"Wow. Thank you all," Natalie said. "I never thought I'd get all this from a self-defense course."

Neither had I. "Ninjettes rock," I said.

We high-fived and walked back to the Subaru.

The People's Way

by Eve K. Sandstrom

The worst part was that Rogar was trying to be kind.

"You must see that there is no other way," he said. "The baby has to die."

Amaya pulled her legs up against her chest and laid her head on her knees, shaping her body into a coconut. She had no more words. If she spoke again, the tears inside would spill onto the hut's sandy floor, and the hard coconut husk she was using to conceal herself would crack. All her fears and her griefs and longings would be revealed to this man she did not understand and to the strange people of his clan.

She turned her face away from Rogar. She stroked the back of the tiny girl sleeping on the grass mat.

Rogar spoke again. "It's not just my people who do this. It was the same on your island."

Amaya didn't move, but she felt the air pass over her, and she knew Rogar had gestured angrily.

"Elosa says there is not enough for my clan to eat," he said. "If we had plenty, we could keep your sister's child. But we don't have food for her."

"She can share my food," Amaya said softly.

"No! You would become weak. You should bear our own child. And we need you to work. You must

219

remain strong." Rogar put his hand on her arm. Amaya did not pull away. She barely felt his touch on her coconut shell arm. Did the arm feel rough and hard to him?

"Is it kind to keep the little one if we cannot feed her?" Rogar said. "Is it kind to keep the little one if the other women here hate her? If she will be an outcast in this clan? No! It's better to put her in the water now. Better for her. Better for you. Better for all of us."

He paused, but Amaya still hid behind her hard outer husk. The silence grew between them.

Rogar sounded despairing when he finally spoke. "We cannot oppose Elosa. She is the one who decides."

Amaya spoke then. "And Elosa hates me."

"Don't be foolish!"

Amaya did not answer. What purpose was there in arguing with this man whom she knew so little, yet who had power over her, over the little one? She had thought she loved him. But he would not listen.

After another long silence Rogar stood up. "I'm sorry, Amaya. It's decided. I'll take the baby into the water as soon as it's light."

He walked softly from the hut, into the darkness.

Amaya sat motionless. If she moved, her husk would crack. She kept her hand on the sleeping baby. Little Tani, all Amaya had left of her sister, of her own clan, of her own home on the westward island. If only, if only she had not left there!

Amaya had liked Rogar's looks as soon as he and his friends had come to her island, bringing dried fish and cloth to trade. He was strong and well-made, with broad shoulders. He had smiled at her. She had been flattered that such a handsome man had liked her. And he had come from afar. If she went with Rogar, she could see other islands, meet new clans.

She had been pleased when he offered her uncle a bride-price. Her uncle hesitated, but Amaya made it clear that she wanted him to accept Rogar as her husband. Her uncle had said yes, and she had willingly gone with Rogar to his own island.

Then she had met Elosa. Elosa had hated Amaya from the moment she stepped on the shore of the lagoon. And as shaman, Elosa was one of the most important members of Rogar's clan. Her hate was serious. It had meant Amaya was shunned by all but Rogar's close family.

Rogar's mother had welcomed her as a mother-in-law should. Amaya had even thought she saw a slight feeling of exultation in her greetings. But most of the other women had been unfriendly—or perhaps fearful. They had spoken to her, but only sometimes. If they met alone in the forest, they would stop and talk. But if she met the women in a group, they would lower their eyes and pass by.

Amaya had asked her mother-in-law about it. "Why? What have I done?"

"You've done nothing, Amaya. They are afraid of Elosa."

"But she is the shaman. She is responsible for the clan's welfare."

"But the clan has had problems since Elosa became shaman. Our harvest has failed. The fish have been few. The tribe has become divided."

"But I have done nothing to cause the division."

Rogar's mother looked away. "Elosa wanted Rogar for her own daughter. When he took a bride from far away, it made Elosa fear that the people would think her foolish."

She put her arm around Amaya's shoulder. "Don't worry! Rogar wanted you! He is smart, that son of mine. Elosa will become interested in something else. Already she is looking for another husband for her daughter. The trouble will go away."

But the trouble did not go away. It grew, and it grew until it was not only between Amaya and the other women of the clan, but until it was also between

Rogar and Amaya. They had not known each other well, Amaya realized. They'd only had a few days together without the interference of Elosa. Now Rogar grew impatient, hard to please. Their lovemaking grew more awkward, instead of more comforting. Amaya felt she had ceased to please Rogar. And she had wanted to please Rogar. She wanted to love Rogar.

Amaya had hoped the ritual trip back to her own clan would help. But there they found greater disaster. Disease had come, and her uncle had died, and her sister and her sister's husband. The only one left was Tani.

The baby had grown since Amaya had left with Rogar. Now she was walking. She was staying with the great-grandmother, but the great-grandmother could not run after her. Tani would hide. When the great-grandmother called, she would laugh. But she would not come. Amaya saw that the great-grandmother could not take care of her.

Rogar had hesitated when she asked if she could bring Tani back to his clan's island. "She is a fine, strong baby," he said. "But she is just a girl. And our clan's crop was small this year."

Amaya had not pleaded. But Rogar had also seen that the great-grandmother could not care for Tani. And perhaps Tani had won him over herself, with her baby smiles and games. He had grown fond of playing with her, taking her into the lagoon to splash.

"We will take her back," he had said finally. "She is a brave little girl. She laughs when water splashes her. She will be adopted by my tribe."

But that did not happen. Elosa had hated the baby, just as she hated Amaya. She had refused to take Tani into the clan. Then she had decreed that the clan did not have enough food, and she said that the child must die.

"It is not right for this stranger child to take food from the mouths of our clan," she said. "Rogar must put her in the water."

Amaya's heart broke, but her hard outer shell remained solid. She had hidden behind it all afternoon.

Rogar had argued with Elosa, tried to convince her that the clan's resources were not so few that one tiny girl would cause others to starve. But Elosa was firm.

"You must put the girl in the sea tomorrow—as soon as the sun rises," she said.

Amaya could not argue. Rogar had spoken truly. Her own clan followed that custom, too. If food was scarce, the oldest and the youngest among them must die. It was best for the weakest to die, to allow the strongest to live.

But Amaya did not want Tani to die. She was her sister's child. She was the final link with her own clan, her own island. If Tani died, Amaya would be left among a strange people, subject to a strange husband, with no one to care about and no one to care for her. And Tani was a strong child. She would grow into a strong woman who would help her clan.

But what could Amaya do?

Amaya nestled behind her hard coconut shell and thought.

Wildly she thought of killing Elosa. She could take the club she used for breaking coconut shells. She could creep up upon Elosa's house. She could hit the witch in the head. The shaman would die.

A feeling of pleasure swept over Amaya at the thought, but it was closely followed by a shudder that shook her whole body and rattled her teeth.

No, she could not kill Elosa. Even if she managed to creep into Elosa's hut undetected, Rogar's people would guess who had done it. She would be killed. Tani would still die. Killing Elosa would accomplish nothing, except that Amaya would herself die and her spirit would be condemned to roam the sea forever, never finding rest on the heavenly island.

Could she run away? Could she steal a canoe and go back to her own clan?

Amaya could paddle a canoe, of course. Everyone

could do that. But only men, men like Rogar who had been taught to read the stars and the currents, could go so far as her native island and be sure of finding it.

Could she run away to the forest? She could take Tani and hide. She could find food for them there.

But Amaya knew that would give her only a few days. Rogar's island was not her native place. She knew only parts of it. She might be able to hide from a stranger, but she could never hide from Rogar and the men who had hunted all over that island and from the women who had gathered food all over it. She would have to sleep. Rogar's people knew where the water was, and she would have to have water. If food was scarce, the women would be looking for it everywhere. They would soon find her.

A sob bubbled up from Amaya's soul, like water bubbling from a spring. It almost cracked her coconut shell coating. She choked it back, and she did not move. But she saw no way to save Tani.

Was Rogar right? Was obeying the shaman the right thing to do? Did she have to let him take Tani into the water?

Oh, she knew it was the law, the way of the people. As Rogar had said, it was the way of her own island. Her mother's mother had become ill in the year the crop had been so bad. When she had become too sick to work, she had stopped eating. The family had grieved, but the old woman had turned away from food. She had refused water. "It is time," the old woman said. Her tongue grew thick. Her daughters keened. And in three days she had died. Everyone had admired her action.

And when the wife of the headman's son gave birth to a child with a crippled foot, the mother had wept, but she had not argued. The headman himself had taken his grandson and put him in the sea to die.

Life on the islands was hard. The strong must not be held back by the weak. That was the ancient law. Amaya knew that. If the law was not obeyed, the island clans would not be strong and clever. They would not conquer their enemies—the other tribes who wanted their territory, the fierce beasts who lived in the sea and in the forests, the very hardness of life.

But Tani was not weak! Elosa had not said she must die because she was weak. That year's crop had been poor, but there was enough. Rogar said so. His father said so. But Elosa had not listened. She said Tani must die.

Tani was to be killed because she was a strange child.

No, Amaya thought, that was not true. Tani was to be killed not because the baby was strange, but because she—Amaya—was strange. Elosa hated Amaya, not Tani. But Amaya was married to one of the clan's young warriors. Elosa did not dare attack Amaya directly. She had decreed Tani's death because that was the cruelest thing she could do to Amaya. And this would not be the last thing she did to Amaya. Elosa might not dare condemn her openly, but she would find ways. Amaya's own fate would be like Tani's.

Already Elosa had threatened Rogar because he argued with her over the baby. Amaya's presence here on Rogar's island was all wrong. She was unhappy, and she was hurting Rogar by being there. She loved Rogar, and she did not want him to be hurt because of her.

Amaya, hidden inside her coconut shell, finally knew what she had to do.

She stirred, lifting the sleeping baby and holding her close, murmuring softly. "Little pet. Sweet one. I love you. We will always be together." Standing up, she went outside, into the dark. She took the path to the beach, where the waves were high, not to the friendly lagoon.

She stumbled once on the way, but her step was firm as she walked into the water. Soon it would be over. She and Tani would both die. Rogar would be rid of them and the problems they had brought him.

Elosa would have won, true, but Amaya would have
obeyed the law. She and Tani would reach the peaceful island. The gods would bless her action.

She pictured the peaceful island as the waves
reached her waist. She clutched the sleeping baby
against her breast. Soon the cold water would waken
Tani, and she would cry. Amaya knew she must be
ready to hold her tightly then, even to hold her under
water, to make sure that the baby died first, that she
wasn't left alone in the water, frightened.

Amaya paused, embracing the child more firmly.

Suddenly, she was grasped roughly from behind.

"What are you doing?" Rogar's voice was harsh.
"You do not have to take the child into the water! I
will do it!"

"No! No! I will take her! She must not be
frightened!"

"I will not frighten her! And it must be done as
the sun comes up!" Rogar tried to take Tani out of
Amaya's arms.

Amaya clutched the child. "No! Let me take her!
We will die and leave you in peace!"

"You die? You must not die!"

"It's best, Rogar! Elosa will never allow me to be
part of your clan! She will not forgive you for mar-
rying me! There will be more trouble! It's best if I die
with Tani!"

Rogar held her and Tani tightly. His grip woke the
baby, and the little one began to fuss and cry sleepily.
When Rogar spoke his voice was low and desperate.
"No!" he said. "No! Amaya, you must live. We must
live together."

The waves broke around them and the sand shifted
under Amaya's feet. She felt as if she were falling, but
Rogar held her up.

"We must live on together," he said again. "I love
you, Amaya."

Amaya felt the coconut husk break. She was in Rogar's arms, with nothing to protect her, with no shell

to hide behind. Tani was crying, and Amaya was sobbing mighty sobs. And Rogar's arms, Rogar's love surrounded her. He led her slowly back to the beach, and there Amaya collapsed in the sand, still sobbing.

It was many minutes before she was able to speak. "Is there no way to save Tani?"

"We have to obey the law," Rogar said. "Amaya! Can you trust me?"

"Trust you?"

Rogar laid his cheek against her hair. "Yes, Amaya. Trust me."

"I can do nothing by myself," Amaya said dully. "This is your island, your people. I know you do not want Tani to die. But if she must—I trust you not to let her be afraid."

Rogar helped Amaya up and led her back to the house. Amaya did not put Tani down, but held her the rest of the night, just as Rogar held her. Finally she fell asleep.

The stirring of birds woke her, and she realized she was alone.

Rogar and Tani were gone.

"No!" Amaya jumped to her feet. "No! No!"

It was still dark in the hut, but outside the light was coming. Rogar had already taken Tani away, to put her in the water.

Amaya ran along the path to the beach. She could hear the waves pounding loudly. The tide was coming in. Ahead she saw a figure silhouetted against the morning sky.

"Rogar!"

Rogar paused, but he did not stop. Amaya ran on, until she was beside him. "Please, Rogar! There must be another way."

He walked on. "Go back, Amaya," he said. "You said you would trust me."

"Please! Please!"

Rogar did not answer. Instead Amaya heard the cackle of Elosa's voice. "The strange child cannot take food from the children of the people! Rogar knows the law, strange woman! He obeys the law of his people."

The voice brought Amaya to her knees. "Please," she said again. But this time she whispered.

"You have brought disgrace to Rogar and our people!" Elosa's voice gloated. "The way of the people must be followed!"

Amaya formed her body into its coconut shell. Rogar's mother and sister knelt beside her.

"Be quiet, Elosa!" Rogar's mother said. "Amaya is obeying the law. But a woman who likes seeing a baby put to death is no real woman!"

Surprised by her mother-in-law's sharp words to Elosa, Amaya looked up at the shaman. Elosa did not reply to the criticism, but she pointed to the surf with her heavy staff. "Rogar obeys the law!"

Amaya's eyes followed the staff, and she saw that Rogar was walking into the water. Tani was not frightened. She was laughing and clapping her hands. To her it was just another of the games Rogar had taught her to love.

Rogar did not go out very far. The waves were rolling. It would not take a lot of water to drown a tiny girl.

He seemed to be playing with Tani, and Amaya remembered he had promised to keep her from being afraid. He held her close to his body, and he ducked under the water.

But when he arose, the baby was gone.

Rogar stood motionless, the waves beating over him. Then he walked back to the beach. When he reached the edge of the water, he turned and looked back. His father joined him and placed a hand on his shoulder. Together they looked down the beach, and Rogar's father pointed.

Were they thinking where her tiny body would wash ashore? Amaya hoped so. To think of Tani not only dead, but lost in the sea—it was more than she could bear.

Then Rogar's father called out. "There! There!" He and Rogar ran down the beach.

And Rogar knelt down and scooped up a tiny bundle. He held it above his head. Amaya saw dark hair, and legs. And the legs kicked!

"She is not dead, Elosa! The sea has refused her!"

Amaya jumped to her feet and watched in amazement as Rogar walked toward them. Tani was squirming and angry. But she was alive.

Elosa shook her staff furiously. "Put her in the water again! It is the law!"

Rogar stood silently for a moment before he turned once more toward the water. Amaya again sank into despair. She watched Rogar walk through the surf, the waves breaking over him and Tani. Again he sank beneath the waves with the child in his arms. Again he rose without her and slowly walked back to the beach.

And again he and his father watched down the beach until a tiny bundle washed ashore. Once more they ran down to pick up Tani's body.

And once more Rogar brought the child to Elosa alive.

Elosa pounded her staff on the beach and screamed. "She's a demon! She must die! It is the law!"

Tani was very angry now, but Elosa's fury frightened her. She clutched Rogar around the neck and shrieked. Rogar patted and soothed her until she became quieter. And when the baby became quiet, Amaya heard other sounds. Looking behind her, she saw many people. They were buzzing with talk. And they were all looking at Rogar and Elosa, who stood facing each other. Neither of them looked around at the others.

Elosa spoke, and her voice was not loud, but it crackled angrily. "Put her back in the water, Rogar, and take her farther out."

"Are you sure, Elosa? Are you sure this is what the law commands?"

"Do you think that I—your shaman—can mistake

the meaning of the law, the law that has governed our people for generations?"

"Twice the sea has refused to take Tani. A third time—"

Now Elosa's eyes flickered right, left. Amaya knew she was considering the people gathered behind her. She took a deep breath and raised her staff. "Take her out, Rogar. Leave her for the water to take."

She swung the staff around, but Rogar did not flinch away from the stick.

"Take her out!" Elosa's final words were a shriek. "It is the law!"

Rogar turned and walked back to the water. Amaya still knelt on the sand, with Rogar's mother and sister beside her. Tears were running down her cheeks. Tani saw her there and waved, a baby wave. Then she turned to look at the approaching water—still unafraid and still trusting Rogar.

"Trust me," Rogar had said. "Trust me."

If Tani can trust him, Amaya thought, I must trust him, too. And she stood up proudly, staring after her husband.

Now the sun had moved over the horizon, and it was hard to see what was happening with her eyes dazzled by tears and by the sun.

Again Rogar walked through the surf. Again he ducked into the water, playing a game with Tani. Amaya even thought she heard the child's laughter over the sound of the waves. Then Rogar ducked beneath the water, and when he arose, Tani was gone.

Amaya did not allow herself to hope that the child would survive. No, the small one could not be lucky enough to be washed ashore three times. This time, she knew, Tani was dead. And that was good. If the child had to go into the water one more time, Amaya's heart could not continue to beat.

Rogar came through the surf, and Amaya went to meet him. She put her arms around him and laid her head against his chest.

"You tried, Rogar. You faced Elosa, argued with her. You tried your best." She looked into his eyes. "I love you."

Rogar smiled. "And I love you, Amaya. Now we had better go to Tani."

He gestured behind her, and Amaya turned to see the same brown bundle tumble from the waves.

Tani!

She and Rogar ran down the beach, and she scooped the little girl up.

Tani coughed. She sneezed. Then she screamed.

Suddenly Amaya and Rogar and Tani were surrounded by excited people.

Rogar's mother was embracing Amaya and Tani. "The witch is beaten!" she said. "This little one and my son have taken her power away!"

"What?" Amaya was amazed.

"Three times! Three times!" Rogar's sister yelled it out.

Rogar was smiling, and Amaya turned to him. "What do they mean, Rogar?"

"If the sea rejects the child three times, then the interpretation of the law is wrong," he said. "Elosa condemned the child wrongly. So Tani will live, and another will be selected as shaman."

An hour later Tani had been fed and was asleep. Other women had come to marvel at the strong little girl who had survived the sea three times. They brought gifts to the child the sea loved. Now Amaya stared in awe at the little girl.

The others were taking Tani's survival as a miracle. Were the gods of the sea showing that they loved her niece? Oh, it was easy to say that Elosa had condemned her wrongly and that the sea had rejected her. But it was hard for Amaya to believe Elosa had not condemned others wrongly, and her other victims had died. Amaya did not understand.

Outside, she heard a deep voice greeting Rogar, and she heard Rogar's respectful reply. The headman had come. Would even the headman want to behold the miracle child?

But the headman was talking to Rogar.

"The elders are going to ask you to join their council," he said.

Join their council? Amaya took a quick breath. But Rogar was young! Too young to be an elder!

Rogar sounded wary when he answered the headman. "That is too high an honor for me. The elders must command canoes. I do not have the years—"

The headman chuckled. "But you have the head, Rogar. And you have the knowledge."

Rogar did not answer.

"And you used that knowledge to benefit your people. We are rid of Elosa."

"If she had admitted she was wrong after the second time the sea refused the child—"

"But she did not." The headman's voice was brisk. "You gave her the chance to back down, to save face. She did not take it. You handled her wisely. The little one will be lucky to have you as a father."

"The little one is already lucky."

"Yes. She was lucky to have a man taking care of her who taught her not to fear the water. That is one reason we wish you to join the elders."

"But—"

"Do not say no, Rogar! The other reason is more practical."

He dropped his voice to a whisper, and Amaya barely heard his final words.

"We need all the men who understand the currents and tides as you do to command canoes."

For the Common Good

by Patricia Sprinkle

I first met Dr. Randall McQuirter in 1965 over a kosher TV dinner.

Fresh out of college, I had been hired by a private Miami hospital to welcome patients and handle complaints and requests. My boss was Angie Winters, and in those days before Medicare, when some patients stayed in hospitals for months, Angie and I were the lubricant that flowed in graceful measure between them and any irritants that might mar their visit.

Angie was a platinum blonde seven inches taller, fifteen years older, and a hundred times more glamorous than I. She had selected the navy uniforms and three-inch heels we wore, and my first day at work, she called her own hairdresser. "I'm sending you a college student. Send me back a woman." When I returned, I almost didn't recognize my reflection in the plate glass doors.

Angie gave me an approving nod and sent me to the administrator, who fixed me with a steel gray gaze. "The motto of this institution is 'For the common good.' What is best for our patients is best for all of us. Therefore, the only question you ever need ask a

patient is, 'How may I serve you?' Do you understand?"

Angie worked eight to five. She comforted grieving
families, helped choose nursing homes, and handled
our Miami Beach celebrities. I worked from eleven
until whenever, greeting new patients and visiting each
one every second day to see if they needed any special
attention. In my first week I fetched a mink jacket
and false teeth from a beach hotel after an emergency
admission, wrote a letter to children in New Jersey
(tactfully revising "What the hell's so important they
can't come see their dying mother?"), and one evening
solved the problem of an elderly man who hadn't
eaten for two days. He swore he had no appetite, but
when I saw the *Jewish Floridian* on his bedside table
and asked, "Did you know we offer kosher meals?"
he clutched my hand so hard he nearly took off a
finger.

"You got kosher? Bring me some of everything.
I'm famished!"

I went down to the kitchen, asked the night staff to
heat a kosher TV dinner, and offered to carry it to
him myself. I was halfway to the elevator when a man
strolled toward me. He had the dark eyes and hair
of a Mediterranean movie star and the god-walk that
proclaimed him a doctor.

"Why, hello!" He stepped deftly into my path. "We
haven't met but I'd sure like to."

Next thing I knew I was backed up against the wall
with nothing but a kosher dinner between me and . . .

I'll never know. I heard my name and Angie—who
should have gone home hours before—came swinging
down the hall. "I wondered where you'd gotten to.
Hello, Doctor. I need Celia up on three." She put an
arm around me and walked me toward the elevator.
When the door slid shut, she murmured, "That was
Randall McQuirter, head of our ob-gyn department.
Don't ever cross him. He's got a real temper. But
don't get stuck alone with the man, either." She spoke

so casually, she could have been offering a remedy for freckles.

"I can take care of myself." I resented her treating me like a kid sister. The doctor was closer to her age than mine. I wondered if she wanted him for herself.

Several weeks later I arrived early one morning and dashed into the tiny coffee shop off the lobby for a breakfast milkshake. Angie was having coffee with Dr. Magda Gerstein, our resident psychiatrist. Next to Angie, Dr. Gerstein looked like a toad—plump and plain, her dark hair streaked with gray, her face sallow and scarred. Her only attractive feature was a pair of intelligent dark eyes that terrified me. I kept wondering what neuroses those eyes found as they probed my soul.

When Angie saw me, she called, "Full moon last night, so emergency was crazy. Five came in after a brawl in a Coconut Grove bar. I've been running my legs off this morning. Rosa, are you guys still stitching up the Grove crew?"

Coconut Grove bars were the hangouts of Beautiful People, so Angie, of course, would handle those patients.

Rosa Marquez, our head surgical nurse, collapsed into a chair at their table, still wearing green scrubs. A cloud of dark hair fell to her shoulders as she pulled off her surgical cap. "We just rebuilt the jawbone of a young man who is lucky to be alive. *Café con leche,*" she called to the waitress approaching the table. "I can't stay but a minute, but I have to have a breather."

Not sure of my welcome in such august company, I headed to a stool at the counter. "*¡Buenos días!*" I greeted Carlos, who was wiping up a coffee spill.

The first Cuban immigrants were reaching Miami in those days, all claiming to have been wealthy professionals, executives, and the cream of Havana society. Some actually were.

According to Angie, who loved to pass on information about our co-workers, Carlos used to own one of the finest restaurants in Havana; Luis—the meds nurse up on five—had been Cuba's premier cardiologist; and Rosa came from one of Havana's richest families but had run away at eighteen to join Castro's army. After Rosa got raped by her commanding officer, so Angie claimed, she gave up the revolution and came to join her family in Miami.

I was learning to take Angie's stories with a tablespoon of salt. No way plain little Dr. Gerstein had been the plaything of German SS officers in a Jewish concentration camp, and when I asked our administrator about serving on Jack Kennedy's boat during World War II, he laughed. "Who told you that? I get seasick looking at a boat and got turned down by the army because of flat feet."

"But Angie said—"

His face softened into an indulgent smile. "Oh, Angie. She's smart like a fox, but like a child in some ways. She loves drama and wants everybody—herself included—to be larger than life. Ignore her stories and learn from her heart. Angie's got a gigantic heart."

I didn't need my friends larger than life. It was enough for me that Carlos made the best milkshake in Miami.

He also had taken it on himself to teach me Spanish so I could welcome our Hispanic patients. So far he had taught me six sentences I could rattle off with the staccato accents and speed of a native Cuban: "Good day. I am the hospital hostess. Welcome to the hospital. Do you need anything special?" If the patient responded with anything except "No," I fell back on the other two: "One moment. I am going to call an interpreter."

"Quiero un bestido de chocolate," I said carefully.

"I didn't know you spoke Spanish," Angie called.

"A little," I boasted.

Carlos laughed. The two women working with him

tittered. Rosa's dimples flashed as she hid a smile behind her cup.

"What? What did I say wrong?"

He gave me the severe look of a parent to a child. "You just ordered a chocolate dress. Dress is"—he wrote *vestido* on a paper napkin and, being Cuban, read it—"*bestido*. Milkshake is"—he wrote and said—"*batido.*" He made me order correctly before he fixed the milkshake.

Dr. McQuirter came to the counter and stood near me. "Hello, Celia." His voice was like melted chocolate, and he looked so good my knees wobbled. No wonder new mothers swooned over him. In the past month three infant boys had gone home with the name Randall. I did a quick calculation and decided our age difference wasn't too great.

"Bring your chocolate dress over here and join us." Angie's invitation was more of a command.

When I obeyed, Dr. McQuirter ambled along beside me and pulled up a chair between me and Rosa. Angie frowned.

Two minutes later the overhead pager came to life. "Miss Winters, emergency room. Dr. Gerstein, emergency room. Stat."

Dr. Gerstein muttered an oath in German. Angie pushed back her chair. "What now?"

Carver, the head orderly, hurried in and approached our table. "Emergency's got one of *those* fellows back there, nearly tearing the place apart."

"Oh, lordy." Angie looked at the rest of us. "You'd better come, too, Celia. We might need you."

The emergency room was off-limits in my job description, I wasn't on duty yet, and I still had half a milkshake left. We both knew she was simply hauling me away from Dr. McQuirter. I opened my mouth to protest, but Angie grabbed my elbow and dragged me with her.

Rosa called to Dr. Gerstein, "See you tonight."

Dr. Gerstein might be short and squat, but she moved fast. She was already out the door. Soon Angie and Carver were right behind her with me bringing up a reluctant rear.

"Magda and Rosa work at the Overtown free clinic two evenings a week," Angie explained to Carver as we hurried down the hall. "Poor folks, battered wives, prostitutes—"

Dr. Gerstein interrupted impatiently. "You are sure, Carver, it is one of *them*?"

"Yes, ma'am. He was left in the emergency room sometime during the night, wearing sweats. As crazy as things were, nobody noticed when he came in. After the place calmed down, they saw him sleeping in the corner, but presumed he was a relative of one of the patients, so they let him sleep. He woke up a little while ago and started yelling that he had been—" He looked over his shoulder at me and stopped talking.

"Fixed?" I asked bluntly. Angie gave me a chiding look. "I am an adult," I reminded her. "I read newspapers and watch the eleven o'clock news."

Dr. Gerstein, still in the lead, continued quizzing Carver. "Both testicles were removed and he does not remember a thing from the time he entered a bar until he woke up here?"

"Doesn't remember a thing," Carver agreed. "Just like the others."

I put on speed and came abreast of Angie. "How many is that?"

"Three in three weeks. The other two were left at Jackson. I guess it was our turn. Poor guys."

We turned the corner by our equal-opportunity chapel, which had icons for the religions of all our patients. I caught the eye of my favorite—a Madonna with dark hair, dimples, and kind plaster eyes—and murmured, "God knows the first one deserved it."

"How do *you* know?" Angie's eyes flashed *I share all my gossip with you*.

I wished I could take back my words. Still, fair is

fair. "His girlfriend—or one of them—had a baby here a few weeks ago. Dr. McQuirter delivered it for free." I paused to let that virtue sink in, but the look in Angie's eye pushed me on. "I recognized the man's name, Anthony Miguel Williams, because he named the poor baby Zhivago Miguel and wanted Williams on the birth certificate, even though he refused to marry the baby's mama. She cried about that the whole time she was here. You remember," I called up to Dr. Gerstein. "I paged you because she was threatening to kill herself."

Dr. Gerstein wasn't listening. She was heading to emergency like a horse to a barn. Angie claimed the psychiatrist had an internal magnet for people in trouble.

"A guy refusing to marry somebody is no reason to do what they did," Carver argued.

"He'd already had three other babies by different mamas. He bragged about that. Said Zhivago was the second son he's had this year, but the other baby was born at Jackson and his mama had to get her prenatal care at a clinic, because Anthony hadn't met Dr. McQuirter yet."

"Not a nice person." Carver finally accepted my assessment.

We stepped through the swinging doors into chaos. Somebody had ripped magazines and flung them on the floor, overturned the newspaper box, and broken the glass front of the candy machine. The telephone from the desk decorated a silk ficus in one corner. Housekeeping staff were putting the room to rights while patients and their families huddled on the far side with frightened eyes. From one examining room came curses and shouts. ". . . lawyer . . . police!"

Dr. Gerstein trotted in that direction. Angie gave me a wave of dismissal. "There's nothing you can do here. Go on upstairs and start your rounds."

I backed up and stepped on Carver. His eyes were fixed on the examining room curtain while he pressed one hand below his belt. "Who'd do such a thing to such a nice man?"

"You know him?" I asked.

"Not personally, but I heard it was Lyle Bradford."

Lyle Bradford was a big man in town. Important architect. Sat on the Orange Bowl committee. Gave money every year so Jackson Hospital could have Santa Claus for sick kids. He was even a personal friend of the governor.

"Not like that second guy who got taken to Jackson," Carver added in a voice rough with feeling. "Him, now—" He turned and headed out. "He's the one who really got what he deserved."

I caught up and trotted beside him toward the lobby. "You knew him?"

"No, but he was part of a gang that raped a girl in my daughter's high school. The other guys were nineteen and they went to jail, but because he was seventeen, he only did a few months at juvey. My daughter and her friends were terrified when he got out. They claim he's been messing with girls all his life and threatening to hurt their brothers and sisters if they told. Well, he ain't gonna be messing with any more little girls." Carver spoke with a quiet satisfaction that made me uneasy.

"I'll catch the elevator here and go on up to my office. See you later." I stepped in and pushed the button.

My usual routine was to pick up our department's peach index cards on new patients and head out to welcome them. Instead I picked up the phone and called a former high school classmate who worked in the admissions office at Jackson. "We have one of those castrated men here," I reported. "I heard it was Lyle Bradford, but I don't know for sure."

From her squeal, I deduced I'd given her a top banana for their staff gossip tree. She owed me. "What do you know about the men who turned up at your place?"

She snickered. "They are singing soprano."

"Seriously. I've read what the papers said—that they went into a bar and didn't remember anything after that—but is that all you know?"

"Well"—her voice dropped a register—"I had to take admissions information from the first one, and he said he remembered talking in the bar with a woman who looked like the Virgin Mary, but he couldn't remember which bar. He wondered if she'd put something in his drink."

"Sounds more like Bloody Mary. How did he get to your emergency room? Nobody saw anyone bring him?"

"No, he was left in a wheelchair outside. One of the ambulances found him sitting there at three a.m. in a johnny gown with a blanket tucked around his legs. It was a pretty night, so at first they thought he was a patient who had gone outside for a smoke or something and fallen asleep. They mentioned him to a nurse and she wheeled him back in, figuring she'd return him to his room. Then she discovered he didn't have an ID bracelet. About that time he woke up and started yelling. That's when they realized he'd had what we were instructed the next morning to call 'unauthorized surgery.' "

"Who was his doctor?"

"He didn't have one. Said he'd never been sick. The residents checked him out and said the surgery looked like a professional job, so they let him recuperate a few days and sent him home. Don't tell anybody I told you this, okay? He's threatening to sue us, so we aren't supposed to talk about it."

"Of course not."

We both knew there is no place more gossipy than a hospital except a police station.

"How did the second one get in? Looks like you'd have been watching the doors pretty carefully after that."

"We were. The police got a call that he was down

in Biscayne Park. They found him sitting on a park
bench dressed in loose sweats and carrying on so loud,
they thought he was drunk at first. He didn't remember anything, either, except sitting at a bar talking to
a woman he claimed was 'a gorgeous blonde with legs
up to her throat.' "

"Not my image of the Virgin Mary."

"Mine, either. He at least could remember the name
of the bar, but they were real busy that night after a
baseball game and didn't remember him. How did
yours get in?"

"Full moon night." I didn't have to say more. Anybody who works in a hospital knows a full moon
brings babies, death, and all sorts of craziness. "He
was found sleeping in a corner of the emergency
room."

"It gives me the creeps. I've never been so glad to
be a woman."

"Me, neither. See you later."

I hung up and checked my watch. I'd give Lyle
Bradford a couple of hours to get up to his room;
then no matter what Angie said (she was bound to
tell me, "I'll take care of this one," since he was, in
a sense, a celebrity), I'd go welcome him. I was dying
to hear his story.

The NO VISITORS sign didn't deter me. I was hospital
administration.

Mr. Bradford lay on his back watching a soap opera.
He glowered as I came in. "Who the hell are you?"

"A patient counselor. I came to see if you have
everything you need."

His glower deepened.

"I mean, is there something I can get you?"

He started up in anger, then sank back with a groan.
"Yeah, there's a couple of things you could get me if
you have a spare pair. Look, I'm not a freak show,
okay? I've already had another one of you in here."

"That would be my boss. I didn't know she had

visited you, so I came to say if there is anything we can do to make your stay easier, just ask. Our job is to welcome patients and handle requests or complaints."

His language blistered my ears and singed my back hair. Cleaned up considerably, what he said was, "I got a complaint, all right. Some pirate tied me up and took my crown jewels." He fingered a scrap of peach index card and squinted at something scrawled on it. "You ever hear of a guy named Randall McQuirter?"

"Sure. He's one of our ob-gyns."

He laughed, but it was not a pleasant sound. "You're kidding. He's a women's doc?"

"Yessir."

What was the matter with my tongue? Angie was always telling me that middle-aged men don't like young women calling them sir.

Lyle Bradford didn't seem to notice. He gave that rude laugh again. "Well, from what somebody told me, that's not all he is. If you see the bastard, tell him I want to see him pronto. Okay?"

"He'll be here tonight making evening rounds. If I see him—"

"You find him, you hear me?" He punctuated every word with a pointing forefinger.

"I'll tell him." I couldn't believe my good fortune. I had a patient's orders to seek out Dr. McQuirter after Angie had left for the day.

She went at five. "I am beat. Don't bother visiting Mr. Bradford. I'll take care of him."

"I won't," I assured her.

At five thirty I started lurking in the lobby. Dr. McQuirter strolled in at six and paused in the doorway to cast a quick, worried look around. He actually took a step backward as I approached to announce, "I have a message for you."

He grinned down at me. "As a pickup line, I'd rather hear 'I'm so glad you're here. I've been waiting all afternoon.' "

"I have," I admitted, trying to keep my balance under that deep black gaze. "Lyle Bradford wants to see you. He's in room 508."

"I don't know Lyle Bradford." He started for the elevator.

I followed. "He came in today. I think he's on the Orange Bowl committee."

He shook his head. "Still doesn't ring a bell."

"He specifically asked to see you. Maybe he has free tickets for you or something."

Dr. McQuirter put his right hand in his pocket. "He asked for me by name? I'll check with him after I've seen my patients. Want to meet me on five in an hour and have coffee when I'm done with him?"

"Put that in your pipe and smoke it, Angie," I said softly as I headed on my rounds.

As soon as I stepped off the fifth-floor elevator an hour later, I heard shouting. Two orderlies were sprinting down the hall. Luis, the meds nurse (who might or might not have once been Havana's premier cardiologist), dashed out of the nurses' station and headed the same way. Running in heels, I made a late fourth.

We all could hear the shouted threats. "You did this to me! I'm gonna sue you for millions! Your pretty ladies will have to work night and—"

As I reached the door of Lyle Bradford's room, Dr. McQuirter pulled a gun out of his pocket and killed the man before he finished the sentence.

By the time of Dr. McQuirter's trial, I had accrued some vacation days. I sat in the packed courtroom with other hospital personnel who didn't have to testify, grateful that Luis had pushed me toward the elevator immediately after the shooting. "You were never here. Stay out of this."

He and the two orderlies testified that Mr. Bradford had accused Dr. McQuirter of castrating him and had then threatened the doctor. The defense attorney went after the word "threatened," trying to plant the notion of self-defense. Luis refused to play. "Mr. Bradford was standing by his bed wearing only a hospital gown. Where could he hide a weapon? He was too sore to even wear boxers."

Every man in the courtroom squirmed.

The prosecutor put a police detective on the witness stand to testify they were seeking connections between Dr. McQuirter and the other two unsolved castration cases. The defense attorney managed to get that testimony ruled inadmissible—arguing successfully that McQuirter wasn't being tried for castrating Mr. Bradford, just for killing him.

On the second day, the defense started its arguments and Dr. McQuirter himself took the stand. The jury seemed unimpressed by his explanation for why he was carrying a gun on rounds that evening—"I'd gotten an anonymous threat that afternoon"—and unconvinced by his reason for checking on Bradford, who had no need of an ob-gyn and was three floors above Dr. McQuirter's other patients: "I got a message he wanted to see me."

I caught my breath. Would I have to testify after all? Heaven knew what Angie would do to me if she learned I'd been in Bradford's room.

Nobody called me. Instead, Angie was called to the stand. She testified that Dr. Randall McQuirter was an excellent doctor, highly respected and loved by all his patients and the hospital staff. She gave him a dazzling smile as she stepped down. After that, physicians, nurses, ward clerks, and even Carver spoke about what a wonderful doctor Dr. McQuirter was and how he must have been seriously provoked to do what he had done.

As we left for the day, I saw Angie in the parking lot. "You sure laid it on thick in there."

She shrugged. "Why not? He is a good doctor, but that's not going to keep him out of jail."

A good doctor? I drove home thinking about Lyle

Bradford's last words. As soon as I got in, I called another high school friend who had become an investigative reporter with the *Miami Herald*. She had established amazing contacts throughout Miami's seamier element and was so tenacious about research that her nickname was Bulldog.

"There's something odd about the McQuirter case," I told her.

"The Teflon doc? You're telling me. You think he castrated Bradford and those other guys?"

"I have no idea, but he didn't shoot Bradford for saying that. He fired after Bradford starting making threats."

"What were his exact words?"

She, like me, had taken senior English from a tyrant who made us memorize reams of poetry and famous speeches. We had gotten real good at verbatim repetition.

"First he said, 'You did this to me!' Then he said, 'I'm gonna sue you for millions! Your pretty ladies will have to work night and—' That's when McQuirter shot him."

From the silence on the other end, I knew she was writing it all down on a yellow pad. "Interesting. I'll get back to you."

She didn't get back to me, but she must have worked all night getting in touch with some of her contacts, because the next morning in court the prosecutor got permission to introduce important new evidence. The courtroom was electrified when two women testified that for several years, Dr. McQuirter had augmented his income by controlling a number of prostitutes, most of whom had come to him as adolescent patients or young nurses. The two testified that the doctor had seduced the girls—themselves included—and impregnated them, then aborted their babies (which was illegal in those days) and told them that working for him was the only way to repay their medical bills. They also testified that Lyle Bradford had been a regular patron with an increasingly nasty temper. He had broken one woman's nose and several had needed medical attention. They had all complained to Dr. McQuirter about him.

The prosecutor insisted that their testimony plus the fact that Dr. McQuirter had carried a loaded gun to Bradford's room pointed to premeditated murder. The jury agreed. They brought in a verdict of murder one and sent the doctor away for life.

Men in Miami slept easier.

Bulldog wrote a series of interviews with prostitutes. Randall McQuirter's women spoke bitterly about his treatment of them, but other prostitutes praised his methods of dealing with violent customers. Violence against prostitutes dropped. Bulldog won a Pulitzer. The Miami paper still occasionally refers to the local ob-gyn who avenged prostitutes by castrating violent johns. Another Miami moment.

But some Miami moments, like some of Angie's stories, are fabrications.

The morning after Dr. McQuirter went to prison, I arrived early at the hospital and headed to the coffee shop for one of Carlos's *batidos*. Angie, Dr. Gerstein, and Rosa were having coffee at the back corner table. Before they saw me, I saw Angie pour something from a silver pocket flask into each of their cups. They raised them in a toast. "For the common good."

As I approached the table I saw them as a stranger might: a tall blond woman with legs going almost up to her neck. A nurse who worked after hours at a free clinic and who had a cloud of dark hair and a dimple in her chin, exactly like our chapel Madonna. And a psychiatrist with a face scarred like a pirate's. As Dr. Gerstein lifted her drink, her sleeve slid toward her elbow. That was the first time I'd seen the row of numbers tattooed on her arm.

A Family Sunday in the Park: V. I. Warshawski's First Case

by Sara Paretsky

I

The heat in the attic room was so heavy that not even the flies on the screens had the energy to move. The two children lay on the floor. Sweat rose on their skin, gluing their clothes to the linoleum.

Normally on a hot August Sunday, they'd be at the beach, but Marie Warshawski had decreed that her son must remain close to home today. Normally the cousins would have disregarded such an edict, but today Victoria—Tori to her cousin—was nervous, wanting to hear as much of the grown-up gossip as possible.

She and Boom-Boom—Bernard to his mother—often spent Sundays together: that was when Tori's mother gave music lessons all afternoon in the minute front room of their South Chicago bungalow; Tori either had to read upstairs, "*Taci, taci, carissima*"—or, worse, sit primly in the front room learning from Gabriella's few good students.

In the winters, Tori followed Boom-Boom to the makeshift ice rinks where he played a rough brand of pickup hockey. No girls allowed, period, which caused a few fights between the cousins—away from the boys,

Boom-Boom made Tori help him perfect the slap shot of his idol, Boom-Boom Geoffrion.

In the summers, though, the cousins spent every Sunday together: they pooled their coins to take bus and train up to Wrigley Field, where they would climb up over the backs of the bleachers and sneak into the park without paying. Or they dared each other to jump off the breakwater into Lake Calumet, or rode their bikes past the irate guards at the South Works, playing a complicated hide-and-seek among the mountains of slag.

This Sunday, Tori was too worried about her father to violate *Ciocia* Marie's edict. Officer Warshawski had been assigned to Marquette Park: Martin Luther King was leading a march with Al Raby and other Negroes to protest housing segregation in Chicago. There'd been so many marches and riots already this summer, where Tony Warshawski had been away from home for three days, working treble shifts along with every other beat cop on the South Side. Today was going to be worse; he'd told his wife and daughter that before he left for work on Friday.

White people on the South Side had vowed to do everything they could this summer of 1966 to show King and the other agitators he'd brought with him that they should stay in Mississippi or Georgia, where they belonged.

That was how Boom-Boom's mother put it. She was furious that the cardinal made every priest read a letter to the parish on brotherhood and open housing.

"Our Chicago Negroes always knew their place before these Communists came in to stir them up," she fumed.

Her own parish priest at St. Czeslaw's read Cardinal Cody's letter, since he was a good soldier in Christ's army, but he also preached a thundering sermon, telling his congregation that Christians had a duty to fight Communists and look after their families.

Aunt Marie repeated the gist of Father Gielczowski's remarks when she dropped in on Gabriella earlier in the week. "If we don't stop them in Marquette Park, they'll be here in South Chicago next. Father Gielczowski says he's tired of the cardinal sitting in his mansion like God on a throne, not caring about white people in this city. *We're* the ones who built these churches, but Cardinal Cody wants to let those ni—"

"Not that word in my house, Marie," Gabriella had said sharply.

"Oh, you can be as high-and-mighty as you like, Gabriella, but what about us? What about the lives we worked so hard to make here?"

"Mama Warshawski, she tells me always how hard it is to be Polish in this city in 1920," Gabriella said. "The Germans were here first, next the Irish, and they want no Poles taking their jobs away. She tells me how they call Papa Warshawski names when he looks for work. And Antoni, he has to do many hard jobs at the police, they are Irish, they aren't liking Polish people at first. It is always the way, Marie, it is sad, but it is always the way, the ones that come first want to keep out the ones who come second."

Marie made a noise like the engine on the truck her brother Tomas drove for Metzger's Meats; she pursed her lips and leaned over to ask Gabriella how she would feel if her precious Victoria brought home one of *them* as a husband.

All Gabriella and Marie had in common was the fact that their husbands were brothers. On politics, on child-rearing, even on religion, they were forever in each other's hair. Maybe especially on religion. Marie had an icon of the Virgin in every room in her house. The Sacred Heart of Jesus inside her front door was a sight that shocked and fascinated Tori—the large red heart, with flames shooting out the top and barbed wire crushed around its throbbing middle ("Those are thorns," *Ciocia* Marie snapped. "If your mother cared about your immortal soul, you'd go to catechism like

Bernard and learn about Jesus and his crown of thorns.")

Gabriella wouldn't allow such images in her home and she told Victoria it was pagan to worship the heart of your god: "almost a cannibal, to want to display the heart—*barbarica!*" Gabriella didn't think like this because her father was a Jew: after all, her mother and her Aunt Rosa—who like Gabriella had migrated to Chicago from Italy—were Catholics. It was more that Gabriella openly scorned religion.

When Father Gielczowski from St. Czeslaw's came to visit Gabriella, to demand that she get Victoria baptized to save her daughter from eternal torment, Gabriella told him, "Religion is responsible for most of the torments people suffer here in this life. If there is a God, he won't demand a few drops of water on my daughter's head as proof of her character. She should be honest, she should always work her hardest, do her best work, and when she says, 'I will do this thing,' she must do that thing. If she cannot live in such a way, no water will change her."

The priest had been furious. He tried to talk to Tony Warshawski about Gabriella.

Peace-loving Tony put up his big hands and backed away. "I don't try to come between my wife and my daughter. If you were a married man, Father, you'd know that a mother tiger protecting her young looks tame next to a mother human. No, I'm not lecturing my wife for you."

After that, Father Gielczowski glowered at Victoria whenever he saw her on the street. He tried to tell Marie to keep her own son away from the den of unbelievers, but Bernard Warshawski—who was usually as placid as his brother Tony—told the priest not to meddle in his family.

Besides, the sisters-in-law only lived four blocks apart; they needed each other's help in keeping an eye on two of the most enterprising children in a wild neighborhood. Tony and Bernard suspected, too, that

Gabriella and Marie also needed the drama of their
arguments. True, Gabriella gave music lessons, Marie
worked in the Guild of St. Mary, but both led lives of
hard work; they needed excitement, and recounting
each other's monstrous deeds or words gave their lives
a running drama.

Right now, the excitement was a little too much for
everyone. The mayor, the cardinal, Police Superinten-
dent Wilson, they'd all agreed that Martin Luther
King and Al Raby had the right to march in Marquette Park. They'd also agreed that the ensuing violence might be horrific. And Tony Warshawski was
one of the officers assigned to the park.

Tony hadn't been home for thirty-six hours already.
Gabriella was worried for his safety; she and Marie
had argued about it Saturday night.

"Me, I have seen those photographs from Birmingham and Little Rock. The hatred in those faces—
I thought I was looking at Fascists from the war!"

"Oh, the press, the press," Marie said. "They want
to make good Christians look bad. They try to make
the police look bad, too, when they're just trying to
protect property."

"But in Birmingham, the police, they are going
against little black girls. Is that right, to send a large
dog onto a small child? Besides, here in Chicago, Antoni, he tells me the police have the strictest orders
to protect Dr. King and all the marchers."

"Yes, I heard Tony say that, and I can't believe it!"
Little flecks of spit covered Marie's mouth. "The police! They're collaborating with these outside agitators,
instead of looking after the community. They should
know that the community isn't going to take that be-
trayal sitting down!"

"Marie!" Gabriella's voice was quiet with fury.
"What happens if this community attacks my husband,
who is, after all, your own husband's brother? What
then? What will Bernard do if Antoni is injured in
such a way?"

Marie stalked away in a huff, dragging Boom-Boom with her. Gabriella sighed and took her daughter into her arms. "*Mia cara, cuore mio*, you must not let this hatred poison you. I must send you to your *Zia Maria* tomorrow, because tomorrow come the girls to study their music with me. These lessons, they bring the money for your education, if you are ever to go to a university, which you must, *carissima, devi studiare all'università, devi avere una vita all'esterno di queste fabbriche e questa ignoranza!*"

A life outside the steel mills and the ignorance of the neighborhood: Gabriella's goal for her daughter. But meanwhile, this adored daughter had to live in the neighborhood, and that meant, perforce, spending Sundays with *la regina dell'ignoranza, Zia Maria!*

"And do not run off to make some difficult or dangerous exploit with your cousin, Victoria, you must promise me that! I know Marie believes you are Eve in the Garden of Eden, leading her precious weak boy into danger, and me, I see him leading you too often, but truly, one must agree that together you each lead the other where no sane person would travel. On this weekend you must be like a good girl who knits and bakes and stays at home for Papa, do you hear me, Victoria? On this weekend, I give you a commandment! *Promettimelo, cara!*"

Gabriella repeated her adjuration the next day when Boom-Boom came to collect his cousin after mass. Victoria looked her mother in the eyes and promised.

They rode their bikes the four blocks to Boom-Boom's house, while Gabriella made tea and readied her front room for her students. Victoria took her new Brownie, the special present for her tenth birthday a week earlier. She had photographed her father in his uniform, her mother tending her rhododendron, her cousin in a Blackhawks jersey. Today she snapped an angry *Ciocia* Marie sweating in her hot kitchen.

Marie served Sunday dinner, roast pork loin and

boiled potatoes, that no one felt like eating in the heat. She fussed over Boom-Boom when he picked at the heavy food: was he coming down with something? Marie's brother Tomas, who was also at dinner, said that Boom-Boom was healthy as a hog.

"Stop pretending that the boy is some kind of weakling—he's playing ice hockey with sixteen-year-olds."

"Only because you encourage him, Tomas!" Marie snapped, her thin cheeks flushed pink. She had suffered eleven miscarriages before and after Boom-Boom's birth and could never believe her only child wasn't a frail scrap that the Lord might snatch from her at any second.

Boom-Boom's father, Uncle Bernie, had to work the afternoon shift at the docks this Sunday, so he missed dinner. Another of Marie's brothers, Karl, was there with his wife, who quickly changed the subject. Since she insisted on talking about the impending march in Marquette Park, it didn't help the atmosphere at the table.

Finally the children were permitted to make their escape up the steep stairs to Boom-Boom's room. The cousins lived in identical houses: four downstairs rooms, attics that had been turned into their bedrooms, unfinished basements that the fathers kept planning to fix up as family rooms on their days off.

In the small houses of South Chicago, no conversation was ever private. After squabbling halfheartedly over Tori's refusal to sneak out the window and head for the beach, the cousins lay on the floor, where it was coolest, and dozily listened to the adults in the dining room below.

With the children gone, the conversation became franker and coarser. Tomas had been fired from his job at Metzger's Meats last week, and he blamed it on the Negroes.

"But he was stealing from the company," Tori whis-

pered to Boom-Boom. "How could that be Martin
Luther King's fault?"

"He was not!" Boom-Boom fired back. "*Wujek*
Tomas was framed by the janitor, and he's a nigger
like King and all those other Commies."

"Boom-Boom! Gabriella says that's the worst word
to say, worse than 'God damn it,' or any other
swear word."

For a moment, the cousins forgot the argument
downstairs in their own fight, which degenerated
quickly to punches. Although Boom-Boom was a year
older and bigger, he was also the one who'd taught
Tori to defend herself, which she was ready to do at
a moment's notice. It was only when he tore her shirt
at the collar that they stopped, looking at each other
with dismay: what would Gabriella say when she saw
the torn shirt, or Marie when she saw the bruise on
Boom-Boom's shoulder?

In the silence that followed their fistfight, *Wujek*
Tomas's loud angry voice came up the attic stairs. "All
I'm saying is, I'm going to kill Tony."

The front door slammed. Tori ran to the window
and saw Tomas get into his car. It was a Buick Wildcat
convertible, nicer and more expensive than anything
anyone else in the family could afford. Where had he
got the money for it, everyone asked; it was Gabriella
who told Tony, while Tori was in her own attic bedroom listening to her parents, that *Wujek* Tomas stole
meat from Metzger's and sold it to supper clubs in
Wisconsin. Tony told Gabriella that was all hearsay,
so why would *Wujek* Tomas want to kill Tony?

Downstairs, Marie was demanding that Karl follow
Tomas and stop him, but Uncle Bernard said Tomas
would cool off in time, and Uncle Karl added that no
one could catch Tomas in his Wildcat, anyway.

"But he said he would kill my dad," Tori whispered
to Boom-Boom, her eyes wide with terror. "I have to
find my dad, I have to warn him."

"Tori, you can't go to Marquette Park. You promised *Zia* Gabriella you would stay here at my house all afternoon."

It was part of the ongoing battle between Gabriella and Marie that Boom-Boom had to use Italian when addressing his aunt and uncle: *Zia* Gabriella, *Zio* Tony, while Tori had to address Boom-Boom's parents in Polish: *Ciocia* Marie, *Wujek* Bernie.

"I don't care. If your stupid *wujek* hurts my dad, Mama's heart will break in half, way worse than that throbbing heart of Jesus in your doorway."

Before Boom-Boom could stop her, Tori had run to the back window. She opened the screen, lowered herself so that she was hanging by her arms over the roof to the kitchen lean-to a few feet below, and dropped. She rolled down the shingles and jumped to the ground. She ran to the front of the house, where she'd left her bike, and took off.

Boom-Boom waited an instant too long to follow her. His mother had run to the front door to screech at her niece to come back this minute, right now! and not to lead Bernard into danger. A moment later, she ran up the attic stairs and grabbed her son's arm as he was following his cousin out the back window.

II

Even half a mile from the park, Victoria could hear the screaming: ten thousand throats open in hate. The cops at the intersection, uniforms wet under the hot sun, were so tense that they shouted at everyone—old women asking what the trouble was, even a priest riding up on a bicycle—the cops shouted at them all, including Victoria Warshawski darting under the sawhorses that blocked Seventy-first Street.

She had ridden her bike the three miles to Seventy-first and Stony, where she'd chained it to a streetlight. A number 71 bus was just coming along, and she climbed thankfully on board. Her torn shirt was soaked with sweat; her throat was hoarse and dry. She had eighty-two cents in her pockets. If she used thirty cents on the round-trip fare, she'd have plenty to buy a Coke when she found a vending machine.

Seventy-first Street was blocked off half a mile from Marquette Park. Cops in riot gear were diverting all traffic, even CTA buses, in a wide loop around the park. Traffic was jammed on Western Avenue in both directions. The cops told the bus driver that no one was allowed off the bus until it got to the far side of the park, but while they were stuck in the intersection, Victoria forced open the back door and jumped out.

When the cops at Western Avenue yelled at her, she was afraid one of them was a friend of her dad's who'd recognized her. She didn't realize that every face was a blur to these hot, edgy men, but she couldn't help turning around, to see if they were calling her by name. When she did, she saw something shocking.

Uncle Tomas's white convertible pulled into the intersection. Uncle Tomas was at the wheel; another man, a stranger to Victoria, sat next to him. He was blond, like Tomas, and riding in the open car had boiled both their faces bright red, as red as the wild shirt the stranger was wearing. At first the officer tried to stop the car, but Uncle Tomas pulled out his wallet. The cop looked around, as if checking to see who was watching. He took a bill out of Tomas's wallet, then moved two sawhorses so the Wildcat could drive through.

The uniformed man was taking a bribe. This was terrible! Tony Warshawski talked about this over and over again, the people who tried to give him money to get out of traffic tickets, and how wrong it was—it gave everyone on the force a bad name.

Victoria took a picture of the cop moving the sawhorses and then of Uncle Tomas and the stranger. Tomas must have gotten someone to help him find her father. The two men would gang up on Tony and kill him, and then some evil cop would take a bribe to pretend not to see that it had happened.

Victoria started running. She couldn't beat the convertible to the park, but she had to get there as fast as she could, to find her father before Tomas and his partner did. When she got to the park, she saw this was going to be nearly impossible. The crowds were so thick that a child, even a girl like Victoria who was tall for her age, couldn't see around them. She had to fight her way through them.

People were holding up signs with horrible words on them. One said KING WOULD LOOK GOOD WITH A KNIFE IN HIS BACK, but the others! They said things that you were never supposed to say about anyone.

Victoria used her elbows the way Boom-Boom had taught her at hockey practice and pushed her way through a massive wedge of people. They were yelling and screaming and waving Confederate flags. Some of them had sewn swastikas to their clothes, or painted them on their faces. This was also very bad: Gabriella had to leave her mother and father forever and come to America because of people in Italy who wore swastikas. Even as she looked for her father, Victoria realized she couldn't tell her mother the things she was seeing—swastikas, people calling Martin Luther King by a name worse than a swear word. She hoped Tony wouldn't say anything, either. It would upset Gabriella terribly, and she and Tony had a duty to protect Gabriella from any further unhappiness in this life.

As she moved farther west into the park, she saw a group of teenagers turn a car over and set fire to it. The people near them cheered. Six policemen in riot helmets ran to the teenagers, who spat at them and started throwing rocks and bottles.

Victoria pushed through the cheering mob to where the policemen were using their billy clubs, trying to arrest the boys who'd set the fire.

She tugged on one officer's arm. "Please, I'm looking for Officer Warshawski, do you know him, have you seen him?"

"Get back, get out of the way. This is no place for a kid like you. Go home to your mommy and daddy." The man pushed her out of the way.

"Tony Warshawski," she cried. "He's my dad, he's working here, he's a cop, I need to find him."

This time the men ignored her completely. They couldn't pay attention to her—the crowd was protecting the boys, throwing rocks and cans of Coke at the officers. One can hit an officer in the head; the crowd roared with laughter when the soda spilled into his eyes, blinding him.

"The niggers are on Homan," someone shrieked. The whole mob swerved west, chanting, "Find the niggers, kill the niggers!"

Victoria followed them, her legs aching, a stitch in her side making her gasp for breath. She couldn't pay attention to her pain, it would only get in her way. She had to find Tony. She elbowed her way past the screaming adults. One of them put out a hand and grabbed her, so hard she couldn't wriggle free.

"And where are you going?"

It was Father Gielczowski. With him were half a dozen people she recognized from her own neighborhood, two of them women carrying bags of sugar.

"I'm looking for my dad. Have you seen him?"

"Have you seen him, *Father*. Doesn't your Jew mother teach you to respect your elders?"

"You're not my father!" Victoria kicked him hard on the shin; he let go of her shoulder, swearing at her in Polish.

Victoria slithered away. The crowd was so thick that the priest couldn't move fast enough to catch up with her.

"Daddy, where are you, where are you?" She realized tears were running down her cheeks. *Babies cry; you aren't a baby.*

She passed a drinking fountain and stopped to drink and to run her head under the stream of water. Other people came up and pushed her out of the way, but she was cooler now and could move faster.

For over an hour she pushed her way through the mob. It was like swimming in giant waves in Lake Michigan: you worked hard, but you couldn't move very far. Every time she came to a cop, she tried to ask about Tony Warshawski. Sometimes the man would take time to shake his head—no, he didn't know Tony. Once, someone knew Tony but hadn't seen him. More often, the overheated officers brushed her aside.

People were throwing cans and stones and cherry bombs. One exploded near her, filling her eyes with smoke. A rumor swept through the mob: someone had knocked King down with a rock.

"One down, eleven million to go," a woman cackled.

"King Nigger's on his feet, they're treating him like he's royalty while we have to suffer in the heat," a man growled.

Victoria saw the golf course on her right. It looked green, refreshing, and almost empty of people. She shoved her way through the mob and made it onto the course. She climbed the short hill around one of the holes and came on the road that threaded the greens. To her amazement, Uncle Tomas's white convertible stood there. Tomas wasn't in it, only the stranger who'd been with him back at Western Avenue. He was driving slowly, looking at the bushes.

Victoria was too exhausted to run; she limped up to the car and started pounding on the door. "What happened to Tomas? Where's my dad? What have you done with him?"

"Who are you?" the stranger demanded. "Tomas doesn't have any kids!"

"*My* dad, Officer Warshawski!" she screamed. "Tomas said he was going to kill Tony, where is he?"

The stranger opened the door. The look on his face

was terrifying. For some reason, the girl held up her camera, almost as a protection against his huge angry face, and took his picture. He yanked at the camera strap, almost choking Victoria; the strap broke and he flung the camera onto the grass. As she bent to pick it up, he grabbed her. She bit him and kicked at him, but she couldn't make him let go.

III

The battle between the cops and the protestors went on for five hours after Dr. King and his fellow marchers left the park. By the end of the day, every cop felt too limp and too numb to care about the cars that were still burning, or those that were overturned or dumped into the lagoons ringing the park. Firefighters were working on burning cars, but they were moving slowly, too.

Some patrolmen returning to their squad cars couldn't get far: women had poured sugar into the gas tanks. After going a few hundred feet, the fuel filters clogged and the cars died. When a fireman came on the body shoved under a bush, he called over to a cop uselessly fiddling with the carburetor of his dead squad car.

The policeman walked over on heat-swollen legs and knelt, grunting in pain as his hamstrings bent for the first time in nine hours. The man under the bush was around forty, blond, sunburnt. And dead. The cop grunted again and lifted him by the shoulders. The back of the man's head was a pulpy mess. Not dead from a heat stroke, as the officer had first assumed, but from the well-placed blow of a blunt instrument.

A small crowd of firefighters and police gathered. The cop who'd first examined the body sat heavily on his butt. His eyelids were puffy from the sun.

"You guys know the drill. Keep back, don't mess the site up any more'n it already is." His voice, like all his brother officers', was raspy from heat and strain.

"Guy here says he knows something, Bobby," a man at the edge of the ragtag group said.

Bobby groaned, but got to his feet when the other cop brought over a civilian in a Hawaiian print shirt. "I'm Officer Mallory. You know the dead man, sir?"

The civilian shook his head. "Nope. Just saw one of the niggers hit him. Right after we got King, one of them said he'd do in the first whitey crossed his path, and I saw him take a Coke bottle and wham it into this guy."

The police looked at each other; Bobby returned to the civilian. "That would have been about when, sir?"

"Maybe five, maybe six hours ago."

"And you waited this long to come forward?"

"Now just a minute, Officer. Number one, I didn't know the guy was dead, and number two, I tried getting some cop's attention and he told me to bug off and mind my own business. Only he didn't put it that polite, if you get my drift."

"How far away were you? Close enough to see the man with the Coke bottle clearly?"

The civilian squinted in thought. "Maybe ten feet. Hard to say. People were passing back and forth, everyone doing their own thing, like the kids are saying these days, no one paying much attention—me neither, but I could make a stab at describing the nigger who hit him."

Bobby sighed. "Okay. We're waiting for a squad car that works to come for us. We'll drive you to the Chicago Lawn station. You can make a statement there, give us a description of the Negro you say you saw, and the time and all that good stuff. . . . Boys, you're as beat as me, but let's see if we can find that Coke bottle anywhere near here."

Turning to the man next to him, he muttered, "I hope to Jesus this guy can't make an ID. The whole town will explode if we arrest some Negro for killing a white guy today."

As they picked through the litter of cups and bottles

and car jacks that the rioters had dropped, looking for anything with hair or blood on it, a squad car drove up near them. The uniformed driver came over, followed by a civilian man with his son.

"Mallory! We're looking for Tony Warshawski. Seen him?"

Bobby looked up. "We weren't on the same detail. I think he's over by Homan—oh—" He suddenly recognized the civilian: Tony's brother Bernie.

Bobby Mallory had been Tony Warshawski's protégé when he joined the force. Fifteen years later, he'd moved beyond Tony with promotions the older man no longer applied for, but the two remained close friends. Bobby had spent enough weekends with Tony and Gabriella that he knew Bernie and Marie as well; Bobby was an enthusiastic supporter of Boom-Boom's ambition to supplant the Golden Jet with the Blackhawks. He wished he could also support the freedom Tony and Gabriella gave their own only child, but he hated the way they let her run around with Boom-Boom, like a little hooligan. Thank God Eileen was raising his own girls to be proper young ladies.

"We're falling down, we're that tired, Warshawski," Bobby said. "What's up?"

Bernie shook his son's shoulder and Boom-Boom said, "It's my cousin, Tori, Officer Mallory. Victoria. She—my uncle Tomas—after lunch we heard him say he was going to kill Tony because of *Wujek* Tomas losing his job and he thought it was Tony's fault, except he also blamed it on the ni—Negroes—so Victoria took off for the park here to warn Uncle Tony and she didn't come home and we saw it on TV, the fight, and I told my dad and he said we should come here and try to find her, or anyway, find Uncle Tony, and then Dad and I, we saw you, and maybe you know, like, is she okay?"

Bobby Mallory rubbed his sunburnt forehead. "Vicki came here? God damn it, who let her do such a stupid dangerous thing?"

"She took off, sir, and my ma, she had ahold of me, so I couldn't follow."

"Which is the only good news of the day," Bernie Warshawski said. "Otherwise we'd be looking for both of you. We saw where Tori chained up her bike at the Seventy-first and Stony bus—"

He caught sight of the body under the shrub. "But—that's Tomas. Marie's brother! What happened to him? He come with the St. Czeslaw crowd and pass out?"

He moved over to kneel next to Tomas. "Come on, man, get up. You've had your fun, now get on your feet—"

Bernie dropped the shoulder in horror: Tomas was never going to get up again. When Boom-Boom started to join his father at his uncle's body, Bobby grabbed him and pulled him back.

"We gotta get a meat wagon for this guy. Bernie, give his name and particulars to one of the officers here while I get on the squawk box in the squad car. And let's see if you recognize our helpful witness. . . . Lionel!"

One of the uniformed men limped forward. Bobby introduced him to Bernie Warshawski, but when they went to look for the man in the Hawaiian shirt who claimed to have seen Tomas's assailant, he had disappeared. Just like a damned civilian—don't get involved! Or maybe he didn't want to have to explain what he'd been doing in the park all afternoon. Maybe he'd thrown the brick that hit Martin Luther King hard enough to knock him to the ground. Jesus! They'd been lucky King hadn't needed medical help.

Bobby used the squad car radio to summon a detective. When a man arrived to look after Tomas Wojcek's body and to organize a search of the grass around him, he turned his own aching body and numbed mind to the task of finding Tony Warshawski.

This morning he wouldn't have taken an overheard death threat against a cop seriously, but that was before someone had bounced a rock off his own riot helmet and squirted a can of Coke into the eyes of one of the men in his detail. If Tomas Wojcek thought he could use the cover of the Marquette Park massacre to kill Tony—but had Tony, the most peaceable man on the force, whacked Tomas in the head hard enough to kill him? Bobby couldn't picture it, unless Tony'd become as crazed by the heat and the ugliness of the mob as the rest of the cops in the park.

He got into the squad car Bernie and Boom-Boom arrived in and directed the driver to do a sweep of the park. Using the car loudspeaker, he kept calling Tony's name, or calling out to clumps of cops as he passed to see if any of them had seen Warshawski. At Homan he was directed to the north end of the park, where Bobby finally ran Tony to earth. He was pushing a last bunch of rioters into the back of a paddy wagon when Mallory and Bernie went over to him.

Tony Warshawski was a big man, close to six-four. Like everyone else today, his face was red up to the circle cut into his forehead by the riot helmet he'd worn all day: above it, his skin looked almost dead white, but when Bobby and Bernie explained the situation to him, his whole face turned ashen beneath its burn.

"Victoria? She came into this war zone hunting for me? Oh, my God, where is she? Bobby, I need a squad, I need to find her. How can I face Gabriella?"

"Tony, I'll look. You're too tired." Bernie put an arm around his brother's shoulders. "You get home, stay with Gabriella. She's just about out of her mind, worrying about you and Tori both. And Marie, oh, my God, what a day—Tomas is dead, someone killed him over on the other side of the park. How will I tell her that? Boom-Boom, did your cousin say anything that—Boom-Boom? Bernard! Bernard Warshawski, come back here this minute! Now!"

The three men looked around. Twilight was settling in; it was hard to see more than fifteen or twenty feet,

and Boom-Boom had faded into the shrubbery around
the lagoon.

IV

As soon as his dad was occupied with Uncle Tony,
Boom-Boom slipped off into the park. If Tori was still
here, she'd be hunting for Tony. If she'd left for home,
well, then she was safe, and he, Boom-Boom, could
find out what was so mysterious about *Wujek* Tomas's
death. Tomas was his least favorite uncle, mean-
spirited, prone to pinching Boom-Boom or Victoria so
hard that he left bruises on their arms or bottoms, but
it was still unsettling to see him like that, dead under
a bush. And Mama! She would cry like the world was
coming to an end. And somehow blame Victoria for it.

When Bernie had come home from his afternoon
shift at the plant and Boom-Boom told him what had
happened, Marie said, "Headstrong, how Gabriella
spoils her. No daughter of mine would run off like
that, not even a thank-you for lunch. No manners, of
course, Italian, a Jew, they don't know manners."

She hadn't wanted Bernie to drive over to the
park—they'd all seen the reports on television, the
violence, white people fighting the police—but Gabriella had telephoned, asking for Victoria to come
home; Marie had been forced to say that she'd run off.

Gabriella arrived two minutes later, still in the silk
print dress she wore to give lessons, her dark eyes two
large coals in her pale face. She had looked Marie in
the eye, spat, and turned on her heel. She announced
that she was leaving for Marquette Park at once, but
of course, Bernie told her to stay home, that he'd
drive to the park and find Tony and Victoria.

Boom-Boom headed for the center of the park,
away from the knots of cops who still lingered, keeping out sightseers, or waiting for working squad cars
to arrive if their own had been disabled. Many of the
men were lying on the grass, helmets at their sides.

Others were using their riot helmets as canteens, filling them at the fire hydrants and pouring the water over their sweaty bodies.

At the lagoons that ringed the interior of the park, Boom-Boom was startled to see how many cars had been pushed into the water. Some had been rolled in so they were upside down. He tried to guess how many men it would take to roll a car over and over like that. He wondered if the guys he played hockey with could do it.

As he continued east, toward the park entrance on Sacramento—since that's where his cousin would have entered the park—he came on a white convertible whose front end was submerged, leaving the back sticking up in the air, almost. That looked like *Wujek* Tomas's car. His body was over near Seventy-first Street. This didn't make sense. If he'd been driving, he'd have drowned in the car. Why was the car here and Tomas half a mile away?

Boom-Boom stood next to the Wildcat, trying to decide if it was his uncle's. He didn't know the license plate number, but there was a little red scratch near the bottom of the driver's door. If he could get into the water, he might be able to see it.

He was starting to untie his sneakers when a thumping from inside the trunk startled him. "If that's your ghost, *Wujek,* don't worry: I'm not here to hurt your car," he called loudly to cover a moment's fright.

"Boom-Boom?"

It was his cousin's voice, faint, tremulous.

"Tori! What are you doing in the trunk?"

"He put me there. Get me out, get me out before I die."

"Hang on, I've got to get the trunk open. Don't go anywhere, I need to find some way to smash the lock."

"I'm not moving, dodo, but hurry, I'm fried alive and I've been sick in here." Her voice ended in a gulp that sounded close to tears.

Boom-Boom looked frantically around the grounds.

He'd seen guys break into cars plenty of times—also into trunks. He needed something like a chisel and a hammer to break the lock, or— In the massive amount of junk tossed by the rioters, he found a tire iron.

He ran back to the Wildcat and managed to pry open the trunk. His cousin was clinging to the spare tire. Her feet were damp from the lagoon water seeping into the trunk from the backseat, and the shirt he'd torn earlier in the day was covered with blood and mud and her own vomit. She was shaking from head to filthy toe; it was all Boom-Boom could do to help her crawl out.

V

It was dark by the time the cousins and their fathers found each other. When Victoria saw Tony, she burst into tears.

"Pepaiola, mia cara, cuore mio," Tony crooned, the only Italian he'd picked up from Gabriella—my little pepperpot, he called his daughter. "What's to cry about now, huh?"

"Uncle Tomas said he would kill you because he lost his job," she sobbed. "I wanted to warn you, but this man, this friend of Uncle Tomas's, he picked me up and put me in the trunk. I was scared, Papa, I'm sorry, but I was scared, I didn't want you to die and I couldn't tell you, and I didn't want me to die, either."

"No, sweetheart, and neither of us is dead, so it all worked out. Let's get you home so your mama can stop crying her eyes out and give you a bath."

"What man, Vicki?" Bobby asked—the only person who ever used a nickname that Gabriella hated.

"The man with Uncle Tomas. I saw them when they—Daddy, they gave money to the cop at the intersection and he let them into the park. I took his picture—oh! my camera, he broke the strap and threw my camera away, my special camera you gave me,

Papa, I'm sorry, I didn't look after it like you made me promise."

Victoria started to cry harder, but Bobby told her to dry her eyes and pay attention. "We need you to help us, Vicki. We need to see if your camera is still here, if no one stole it. So you be a big girl and stop crying and show your uncle Bobby where you were when this man picked you up."

"It's dark," Tony protested. "She's all in, Bobby."

Victoria frowned in the dark. "It was where you come into the golf course. One of the hills where the holes are on the Seventy-first Street side of the park. I know, there was a statue near me, I don't know whose."

With this much information, Bobby set up searchlights near the statue of the Lithuanian aviators, Darius and Girenas, although none of the cops believed they'd find one small Brownie camera in the detritus left in the park.

When Boom-Boom whispered to his cousin the news that Tomas was dead and the cops needed to find the man who'd been with him, Victoria miraculously found some reserve of energy from childhood's inexhaustible reservoir. She tried to remember in her body how slowly she'd moved, where she'd twisted and turned on the walking paths, and finally cut across the grass to the golf course. Boom-Boom stayed with her; within another five minutes, they found the Brownie.

Bobby took custody of it, promising on his honor as a policeman that he'd give the camera back the instant the pictures were developed, and the cousins finally got into their fathers' separate cars. At home, they received varying receptions from their mothers: both women frantic, both doting on their only children, each showing it with tears, and then a slap for being foolhardy and disobedient. But Gabriella instantly repented of the slap and took her daughter into the bathroom to shampoo her rough mass of curls herself.

"Carissima, when will you learn to think first, to act next after thinking? This Tomas, this brother of Marie's, he was a—*mafioso—un ladro*—he stole from Metzger's Meats and sold on his own, sold the meat to restaurants in Wisconsin. He blamed the janitor, who is a Negro man, for losing his job, because the janitor reported seeing him. But your papa is telling me, Tomas also cheated his *capo* in the *mafia,* and this was a man also named Antoni. It is not such a rare name, Victoria. If you asked me, I would tell you this thing, that your papa is in danger from the *calca* in the park, but not from this brother of Marie, and then you do not get the most biggest frightening of your life. And also, then you are not giving *me* the same gigantic frightening."

And of course, as it turned out, when Bobby got the pictures developed, the man who abducted Victoria, who flung her into the trunk of the Wildcat, which he got several spirited youths to push into the lagoon, was the Tony who worked in Don Pasquale's organization. Tomas had been stealing meat from Metzger's and selling it in Wisconsin for the mob, but he'd taken more than his share of the profits. Don Pasquale sent Tony in his red Hawaiian shirt to Marquette Park to kill Tomas under cover of the riots. The don wasn't happy with Tony for letting a little girl with a camera get the best of him: he refused to post bail for his henchman.

"So you see, *carissima, è molto importante,* ask, ask, think, think, before you leap on your bicycle and turn my hair white," Gabriella finished. "Promise me, *cuore mio,* promise me this is the last time, that from now on you are turning over a fresh page, you will become more careful, more *prudente! Promettimelo,* Victoria!"

"Si, Mamma: te lo prometto," Victoria said.

You May Already Be a Winner

by Margaret Maron

"They've done what? Oh, Carlie, honey!" The white-haired man reached past the coffee cup in front of him and clasped his niece's hand in dismay. "My sister's not even cold yet and *your* sisters are already stripping her house?"

Small-boned and fair-haired, with blue eyes that were red-rimmed from crying, Carlie Baxter swallowed past her tears and nodded. "Her silver, her good jewelry. The two rosewood parlor chairs. Even Great-grandmother's dollhouse."

"That old thing? Why? They don't have daughters and you were the only one who ever played with it."

"Marsha watches *Antiques Roadshow,* and a similar one was valued at two thousand dollars," Carlie said bitterly. "When I came back to the house this morning, I thought someone had broken in. I almost called the police until Mary told me that she and Marsha had taken them for safekeeping now that the neighborhood's gone down so much."

"Well, there *is* that," Uncle Carlton conceded. "I tried to get Genevieve to sell this place ten years ago when the McNairy house was broken up into apartments and property values first started sliding, but she was so sure the neighborhood would come back to its former glory."

"She enjoyed most of the changes, though," Carlie said with a ghost of a smile. "She liked the little shops that came in, the bodega on the corner, children playing on the sidewalks again, even the signs in Spanish and Arabic."

"All the same," her uncle said, "I doubt if you'll get half the money she could have gotten ten years ago."

"Me?" Carlie asked, startled by his comment.

"You." The old man shook his head sadly. "I had no business still being her attorney and I blame myself for not making Genevieve update her will, but I never expected to outlive my baby sister."

Tears filled his eyes and Carlie felt her own eyes sting again. She had been named for this man, her mother's beloved older brother. Except for her twin sisters and their sons, Carlton Burke was her only remaining relative. A retired attorney who had taken too many pro bono cases to amass a fortune, he was almost twenty years older than Mom and the closest thing to a grandfather the three sisters ever had. Carlie adored him.

"Mom left this house to me?" She looked past the archway of the dining room where they sat to the front parlor, now denuded of its rosewood chairs and antique dollhouse, and tried not to feel a surge of hope. After her father's death, his pension and a series of part-time jobs had enabled her mother to continue living in the two-story Victorian house and finish raising Carlie. Unlike for her two older sisters, though, college for Carlie had meant student loans and working every minute she could spare from the books. Two days after she graduated with a degree in French medieval history, her mother had stepped out in front of a delivery truck without looking and was thrown into the path of an oncoming car. Both drivers were horrified and remorseful, but clearly not at fault. It was assumed that Genevieve Andrews had been on her way to the nearby bodega, full of hope and optimism, to buy her weekly lottery tickets.

Carlie had planned to work a year before going on to grad school. Instead, she had spent the last five weeks shuttling back and forth between the hospital where her mother lay in a coma and the house where Buster, Mom's elderly dog, needed daily insulin shots.

Mary and Marsha both wept and then excused themselves for not pitching in more. "Our jobs. Our sons. Our husbands. Oh, it's so lucky that you're still unencumbered, Carlie."

Trying not to feel bitter, Carlie took a deep breath. The house was shabby now. It needed paint and a new roof, and the plumbing was unreliable. All the same, if it truly was hers to sell, then maybe she could register for fall classes immediately instead of waiting a year. Or maybe she would even spend this year studying in France.

Uncle Carlton shook his silver mane regretfully. "I'm sorry, honey. You'll be lucky to get enough to pay her debts. And it's all my fault. I should have written another will for Genevieve."

"I don't understand. You just said the house was mine."

"It is. When I wrote the will after your dad died, the twins were out of college and she knew it was going to be a struggle for you to go. The house was appraised at a quarter million back then, so she left fifty thousand to each of your sisters and the rest—including all the contents of the house—to you. She thought you would end up with at least a hundred and fifty thousand."

"But if the house is only worth half that now?"

"I wasn't thinking, Carlie. Instead of a dollar amount, I should have phrased it so that your sisters each got a fifth and you got three-fifths."

Carlie had always been good at mental math.

"That's okay, Uncle Carlton. Maybe the house is worth more than you think. And even if it isn't, that still leaves me with . . . what? Twenty-five thousand?"

Again he shook his head. "Not after all her medical bills and funeral expenses are paid. Well, maybe your sisters will be fair-minded about the situation."

They both sighed then, knowing just how unlikely that was.

"Oh, Carlie, how perfectly awful for you," said Marsha when the will was read to them after the funeral two days later.

"The fair and equitable thing would be to sell the house and its contents and split anything left over after your mother's debts are paid," said Uncle Carlton.

"I wish we didn't have to take the money," said Mary, "but the boys will be starting college themselves in a few years."

It was no less than he had expected. Nevertheless, he was disappointed by their self-centeredness and fixed them both with a stern eye. "Just remember that the things you took from the house belong to Carlie, and she's going to need every penny for her own education. You must return them immediately or else pay her their worth."

"But Mom always said I was to have her silver and her diamond pin," Mary protested.

"And she promised *me* those rosewood chairs and her gold bracelets," said Marsha with a stubborn look on her face.

Under different circumstances, a widowed and childless uncle might have wielded considerable influence, but a widowed and childless uncle who barely had enough to live on? When Carlie was his favorite? They would never be openly disrespectful, but as far as they were concerned, he could whistle down the wind.

"It's okay," said Carlie, who hoped to avoid a rift with her sisters. "But I do want the dollhouse back."

"Of course, sweetie," said Mary, prepared to be gracious and sisterly now that talk of fairness was behind them.

"We'll even send the boys over to help you clear the house," said Marsha. "They can start by getting rid of all the junk mail Mom saved. Coupons and contest forms stuffed in every cranny. 'You may already be a winner!' Right. And I may already be the queen of England. Do you think she was getting a little senile?"

"There was nothing wrong with your mother's mind," Uncle Carlton said sharply.

"But all those magazine subscriptions from Publishers Clearing House? Come on, Uncle Carlton! Who needs twenty magazines coming into the house every month? She gave me three trial subscriptions for Christmas."

"I know," said Carlie, sensing how much their cynicism cut at the old man. "I told her that she didn't have to buy anything to enter their sweepstakes, but she thought that increased her chances."

"Did she honestly believe that the Prize Patrol was going to show up on her doorstep someday with a check for a million dollars?" asked Mary.

"Hope springs eternal," Carlie said lightly. "You know Mom. Remember how happy she was when the lottery finally passed last year?"

Marsha rolled her eyes. "Not half as happy as I was. No more weird magazines. My birthday card had five scratch-off cards in it this time. I actually won seven dollars."

"I won twelve with the ones in my card," Mary said smugly.

"Lucky for us that she was such a penny-ante gambler," said Marsha. "I was afraid she might get in over her head, spend her grocery money on Powerball tickets."

"No," said Carlie. "Five dollars a week was her limit. She loved checking her tickets against the winning numbers. Remember how close she came to the jackpot back in January?"

For a moment, they were united in the memory of their mother's flushed cheeks and sparkling eyes as she told them how she had held her breath when the first five numbers precisely matched the first five on her ticket. How certain she'd been that it was her lucky day.

"Eleven million dollars," Carlie sighed, thinking of France.

"The new jackpot's fifty-three million," said Marsha, equally wistful.

"Split four ways," the ever-practical Mary reminded her.

"That's still over thirteen million apiece," said Carlie, doing the math in her head. "Wonder why the fourth person hasn't come forward to claim it? It's been at least three weeks since they announced the winning number."

"Probably consulting an investment banker first," said Uncle Carlton. "Taxes are going to take a big chunk and if they don't have a game plan in place, the rest will melt away before they know it."

"I've heard that every leech you've ever met comes crawling out of the woodwork," said Mary as she gathered up her things to go. " 'I shared my candy bar with you in kindergarten, so why don't you give me a half million for old times' sake?' I read about one man who won forty million and was broke and back on welfare three years later. If I ever won, I wouldn't tell a soul."

"Not even me?" asked Marsha.

"Especially not you!" Mary's laugh was meant to show that she was joking, but Marsha still looked miffed when they left.

True to their word, Marsha and Mary sent their

teenage sons over to help, and they themselves came every evening after work to sort through the things three generations of Baxters had acquired. They even brought sandwiches and wine, and they helped dig a grave in the backyard for old Buster when he went to sleep on his rug beside their mother's empty bed and never woke up again.

"Just as well," they said. "You couldn't have taken him to your apartment."

True, but that did not stop her from grieving. Buster had been a part of her life since her twelfth birthday. She told herself she would have found a way to keep him even though her student apartment up at the university was too small to hold all the other things she wished she could keep. It was hard not to agonize over every teacup or knickknack that held its own special memory.

Uncle Carlton found a trustworthy appraiser who in turn recommended a buyer for all the furnishings. He was her rock when grief over what she was losing threatened to overwhelm her or when one of the twins wanted to take a particularly nice piece.

"Let me see," he would say, running his finger down the appraiser's list. "Ah, here we are! Dining room. Family portrait. Original gilt frame. Twelve hundred dollars."

"But that's Great-grandfather Baxter with his little dog," Mary cried. "He shouldn't go out of the family."

"You're absolutely right," he told her with an impish grin. "Offer Carlie a thousand and I bet she'll let you have it."

"Three hundred and fifty for that little cream pitcher?" Marsha was appalled.

"Made around 1912 by a well-known potter, according to the appraiser," Uncle Carlton said blandly, reading from the list. "If it didn't have that chip in the handle, it'd be worth eight hundred."

"Did you hear?" asked one of the boys as he came downstairs with a load of clothing to be donated to charity. "It was on the radio. That fourth jackpot ticket was sold right here in this city. Man! Think of walking around town with a ticket worth thirteen million!"

"Whoever bought it probably isn't walking around with it," said Uncle Carlton. "If he has any sense, he's stashed it in a safe-deposit box. A lottery ticket's like a bearer bond. You don't have to prove it's yours to cash it in."

By the end of the week, it felt as if they had barely scratched the surface, although most of the closets and cupboards had been emptied of personal keepsakes. Basement and attic were still jammed full and their father's study had not yet been touched. Except for Mom's bedroom, this was the most personal room in the house, and in unspoken agreement, the sisters kept putting off the dismantling of both rooms.

The corner bedroom was bright and airy. Organdy curtains hung at the windows, a flower-sprigged comforter covered the bed, and the carpet was bright with pink roses.

In contrast, the study downstairs had a single stained-glass window. It was small and dark with floor-to-ceiling bookcases that held nondescript paperback books of no particular value. The only furniture was a massive desk, a swivel chair and a comfortable leather recliner. Yet their mother had claimed the room as her own after their father died. She said the recliner made her feel as if he still had his arms around her. This was where she read in the evenings. This was also where she wrote letters, paid bills, and stashed receipts and proofs of purchase in the big rolltop desk. It had cubbyholes and slots and even a secret compartment that held a lock of their grandmother's hair, placed there by their sentimental grandfather. On the shelves immediately behind the desk were stacks of unread magazines and plastic boxes stuffed to the brim with more bits of paper, most of which read

"IMPORTANT!! Save this receipt! If yours is the winning number, you MUST present this stub to validate your prize."

All week Uncle Carlton had encouraged them to dump books and photograph albums and boxes of letters from other parts of the house inside the door for a more careful perusal later. Every time someone opened a drawer and found a new cache of papers, he told them a fresh tale of careless heirs who threw out stock certificates or promissory notes or valuable autographed letters in their haste to be done.

"We ought to let the boys bag up all this stuff and haul it out to the curb," said Mary, wearily surveying the messy stacks on the floor, the desktop, and the shelves around the desk.

"No," said Carlie. "Uncle Carlton's right. One of us really ought to go through it."

"Not me," said Marsha, who was as thoroughly tired of the whole process as Mary. "Besides, if there's anything valuable in that pile of trash, it would belong to you, not us."

Their sons were huffing impatiently. It was Saturday night and their plans for the evening did not include hanging around till their aunt decided what to save and what to toss.

"I agree that one should never throw papers away without examining them first," said Uncle Carlton, "but not tonight. Anybody up for Tunisian food? There's a new little restaurant around the corner. My treat."

Mary frowned. "Everything's changed so much. Isn't that where Carlyle's used to be?"

"Carlyle's has been gone for five years," Marsha reminded her.

"And good riddance," Uncle Carlton said cheerfully. "Tough steaks and soggy potatoes. This new place serves a wonderful *felfel mahchi*. Everything's made fresh on the premises, and they go easy on the *harissa* so you don't feel as if your mouth's on fire."

"Thanks, but no thanks," said Mary. "Those places never look very clean to me."

They stepped outside into a hot summer evening and as they waited for Carlie to lock the door, they noticed a crowd of people clustered around a television camera truck parked in front of the corner bodega.

"Go see what's happening," Marsha told the boys.

They were off like rabbits and back almost as fast. "Guess what? That's where the fourth lottery ticket was sold!"

"Really? One of these people?" Impossible to miss the disdain in Mary's voice.

"They still don't know who has it," said one of the boys. "But it was definitely bought here about eight weeks ago."

Marsha sniffed. "Probably by someone who can't read English and doesn't know he's won."

As they passed the little grocery store, people spilled out of the place laughing and exclaiming for the television camera. It was almost like a fiesta.

One of the new neighbors greeted Carlie by name and began to tell her their speculations about the lucky buyer.

Uncle Carlton looked pensive. "I wonder . . . ?" he murmured. Then, "No, it's too improbable."

Although he did not elucidate, Marsha glanced at Mary, whose own eyes had suddenly widened.

Shortly before midnight, Carlie was awakened by a thump from the study directly beneath the room where she slept.

She sat up in bed and listened. Only the sound of an occasional passing car broke the late-night stillness. She lay back down and was almost asleep again when another thump made it clear that she was not alone in the house.

The streetlights outside gave more than enough light as she slipped out of bed and looked around for a weapon. Nothing. And she had left her cell phone in her purse on a table by the front door. Carlie did not consider herself a brave person, but she could not cower up here while someone helped himself to whatever he could find. When she eased open the door into the hallway, she saw her father's old leather golf bag at the top of the stairs. She carefully pulled out the nine iron and tiptoed down the stairs.

The door to the study was open a narrow crack and the desk lamp was on. There was movement by the desk and she heard a drawer squeak open, then the rustle of papers. Moving closer to the door, she cautiously pushed it open and froze in surprise.

"Mary? Marsha?"

Her sisters must have jumped a foot.

"Carlie! You almost gave us a heart attack."

"Then we're even. I thought you were burglars. What are you doing here?"

"Mary lost an earring," Marsha said, "and we came back to look for it."

"In the desk?"

Mary gave an impatient shrug. "In the desk, on the desk, under it. Who knows? I remember that when I was looking at the books over here, the back of my earring felt tight. I must have loosened it too much and—ah! Here it is!" she said triumphantly although Carlie thought she saw the earring flash in her sister's hand before she actually plucked it from the floor. "I'm sorry we woke you. I thought we could just slip in and out without disturbing you. You run on back to bed now and we'll let ourselves out."

"That's okay," said Carlie. "I'll watch to make sure you get to your car safely."

Marsha started to argue, but Mary said, "Thanks, sweetie. And maybe you'd better put the dead bolt on. You never know. The next person might be a real burglar."

Uncle Carlton arrived early the next morning to take her to breakfast. When Carlie told him of her midnight adventure, he immediately called a locksmith he had once represented. Even though it was Sunday morning, his old client came out and changed the lock within the hour.

"But why?" Carlie asked. "I'm only going to be here a few more nights at the most."

"Humor an old man," he said when the locksmith had finished his work and handed him two new keys. "I'll keep one; you put the other one on your key ring. And promise me you won't have duplicates made for your sisters."

"But—"

"No buts," he said sternly. "Now come along. I know where there are fresh bagels and the best coffee in town."

When they returned an hour later, Mary and Marsha were cooling their heels on the front steps. Both were furious.

"You changed the locks? Why?" asked Marsha.

Before Carlie could answer, Uncle Carlton said, "That was my doing, girls. We don't know how many keys Genevieve might have given out over the years and I'd be derelict as Carlie's attorney if I didn't take this simple precautionary step to be sure that no one removed anything until she had signed off on it."

Carlie voiced her surprise at seeing them. "I thought you were taking the day off."

"We decided that if you could keep going, we could, too."

"That's nice," said Uncle Carlton.

"Actually," said Mary, "we have a proposition for you, Carlie."

"Proposition?"

"You have everything from the house that you want to keep, right?"

Carlie nodded. "I guess so."

"You've been down here so long, you must be dying

to get back to your own apartment, so why don't you let Marsha and me finish up here?"

"Oh, no, I couldn't possibly do that," the younger woman protested.

"Sure you can. Everything's on the inventory sheets. We won't take a single thing on it without paying you full value."

Carlie clasped their hands impulsively. "Thank you, Marsha. Mary. But really, there's not that much left to do. Another big push by all of us and we could be done by the middle of the week. If the boys will bag up the papers, Uncle Carlton's offered to go through them at his house."

The old man rubbed his hands in anticipation. "Once the papers are cleared away, I'm anxious to see if I can find all the secret compartments in that desk."

"Compartments?" asked Mary.

"There's more than one?" asked Marsha.

"At least two that I know of," he told them cheerfully. "Genevieve showed me how to open them years ago but something she said makes me think there may even be a tiny third one."

The twins exchanged glances; then Mary said, "Marsha and I have talked it over and we've decided it was selfish of us to let Mom's will stand. You were right, Uncle Carlton. The only fair thing is to sell the house, pay her debts, and then split whatever's left three ways."

Carlie was incredulous. "Really?"

"Really," they assured her.

Uncle Carlton beamed at them. "There now! I just knew you girls would come through for your sister." He pulled a folded legal paper from the breast pocket of his jacket. "Let's go right down to the bodega and make it official."

"Bodega?" asked Marsha.

"Official?" asked Mary.

"The owner's a notary public. He'll witness your

signatures and I'll give your waiver to the county clerk of court when I file the will. I drew up this form last week, hoping you'd do the right thing for Carlie."

Before they could protest, he herded the three sisters down to the bodega where they showed the bemused owner their driver's licenses. He carefully examined each in turn as they signed the document, then carefully embossed it with his heavy seal and signed his own name and date on the proper lines.

"In the legal world, it's a truism that you never really know someone until you've shared an inheritance with him. For the rest of your lives," Uncle Carlton told the twins, "you will always be glad you treated your sister so fairly. Genevieve would have been proud of you."

Carlie glowed with happiness at the thought of France and of registering for fall courses. "Are you sure you don't mind if I head back this afternoon?"

"We're positive," they told her. "Go!"

"All right," she said, giving them more hugs. "I will!"

"And you don't need to stay, either, Uncle Carlton," said Marsha. "We'll take care of everything."

When the house sold two months later, Carlie came back to town to sign the final papers and pick up her share of the money. The sale had brought more than Uncle Carlton expected and even after all their mother's debts were paid, each daughter wound up with thirty-six thousand.

"Remember that lottery ticket that was sold at the bodega?" asked Carlie as she and her uncle lingered over dinner that night. "No one ever cashed it in, did they?"

"There's still plenty of time," he replied. "Another three months, anyhow."

"You're going to laugh at me," she said, turning her wineglass in her slender fingers, "but on the drive back to school, I started thinking about how that ticket was bought a couple of weeks before Mom's accident, but the winning number wasn't announced till after she was in a coma. It made me wonder if that was the real reason Marsha and Mary came back to the house that night and were rummaging through the desk. That maybe they thought Mom was finally a winner.''

"And you were worried that you'd exchanged a few thousand for thirteen million?" asked her uncle.

"Crazy, I know," Carlie said with a rueful smile.

"Not at all," he said. "It could have happened that way. After all, someone has to win, and it's logical that your sisters would consider it when the ticket was bought at her store and no one came forward with it. It would have been all yours if they hadn't agreed to set aside the will and share the estate equally. They certainly checked every shred of paper twice, and I'm afraid your father's desk was rather the worse for wear after they finished hunting for its secret compartments with a crowbar.''

Carlie shook her head. "I thought Mom was the only gambler in the family, but the twins gambled that the winning ticket was in the desk and you gambled that it wasn't.''

"I never gamble," he told her. "Except on sure things. There was only one secret compartment in that desk.''

"But— You mean you tricked them into signing that agreement?"

"Guilty as charged," he said happily. "It was for their own good, too. Now they won't spend the rest of their lives avoiding you because they treated you shabbily. And in all fairness, they weren't terribly angry with me for getting mixed up about the desk. They put it down to encroaching senility.''

"You sly old fox." She patted his hand affectionately. "Thank you. For my inheritance *and* for my sisters.''

"Genevieve sent them lottery tickets in their birthday cards. What about you, my dear?"

Carlie shook her head. "My birthday's not till October."

"A pity." He reached for the wine bottle and divided the remainder between their two glasses. "My birthday was last month."

"I know," Carlie said sadly. "The day after Mom's accident."

"When the card came, I was so upset and worried about her that I just stuck it on my desk and never gave it another thought until after the funeral when the twins said that she had started sending lottery tickets in their cards instead of magazine subscriptions."

Carlie stared at him, openmouthed. "You mean—?"

Her uncle nodded, then lifted his glass with an upward glance to the heavens. "Your mother was always a winner in my book."

Dies Irae

by Dorothy Salisbury Davis

BRUTAL MURDER! She could still, at ninety, remember the bold headline in the *Hope Valley News,* and she could remember listening from the top of the stairs to her mother and father arguing in the kitchen about whether or not they would go to the funeral.

"Margaret, you don't even know if they'll hold a wake for him."

"Wake or no, they have to bury the man, don't they? You'll go alone if you're going, Tom. I knew he was trouble from the night I first laid eyes on him—a mouth like a soft prune and eyes you'd think were going to roll out of his head . . ."

Yes, she could remember the very words, for they were her mother's and therefore her own.

All three of them, her mother and father and the girl she was then, went to the funeral.

There were people there she didn't even know, and she had thought she knew everyone in Hopetown. She was her father's daughter in that; you couldn't get him away, talking to everyone he met on the street. Her mother would always wait in the car. Her mother's two cousins, first cousins—she called them Aunt Mary and Aunt Norah—stood next to each other beside the

grave but with room enough between them for another grown person. Maybe there was, she had
thought, and tried to imagine what Denny would have
looked like with half his head blown off.

Father Conway always prayed as though he had a
train to catch. Ed McNair, the sheriff, was there, and
several deputies. Her father wasn't wearing his deputy
sheriff badge. Donel Rossa was there.

When the gravediggers loosened the straps to lower
the coffin, what flashed through her mind was the
story her mother once had told her of the man who
brought his wife, coffin and all, home to Ireland and
buried her on land he claimed was stolen from him.
She'd never found out if it was a true story or one of
many her mother made up. In time she had asked her
Aunt Mary if it was true, for the sisters had come
from the same village as her mother on the coast of
the Irish Sea.

"She could as well as not have made it up," an
answer the very ambiguity of which she had somehow
found satisfying. She had discovered you could tell the
truth with a lie. That may have been the moment
when she first knew she was going to be a writer.

The sisters could barely have been more different
from one another. Norah, the older, was thirty-four,
tending to fatten as she grew older. She smiled a lot,
but it never seemed to mean much, on and off. Mary
said if she ever laughed it was under her breath. Mary,
having met with a lifetime's share of troubles, tended
at thirty-two to make fun of both her sister's and her
own foibles. Rheumatism was already hacking away
at her joints; she was more bone than flesh anyway,
and her very blue eyes were sometimes shot red with
pain. The devil trying to work his way in, as she put
it. Norah was convinced he had already made it.

It was late on a morning of early August heat when
Mary saw him come out from the shade of the last

elms that arched Main Street. He stopped at the mail-box by Norah's walk and seemed to study the names. Norah's was first, Mary's scratched beneath it as though it was an afterthought, which, in a way, it was. After deciding, perhaps, which of the women it was he saw in the field between house and barn, he came directly to her. He stepped with care to avoid the potatoes she had forked from the ground. He was un-shaven, and younger than she had thought at a dis-tance, and for an instant she felt she had seen him before. He was young-old or, better, old-young. His clothes weren't shabby, but they'd not been in a wash-tub for a while. Nor had he. But his kind was not uncommon on the road, men without work, some wanting it, some not. The grain harvest, then silo-filling, were soon ahead.

"You're Mary O'Hearn, are you, ma'am?"

She looked hard at him—something familiar again—and he moistened his lips before saying more.

"You're welcome to a cup of water there at the pump," Mary said.

The pump with the well beneath it stood a few feet from the faded red building she had converted from barn to the house she lived in. Beyond the pump, and shrouded in rosebushes, was the outhouse she still used. Norah had indoor plumbing.

His eyes shifted from the pump to the outhouse, then back to her. "Would it trouble you if I asked to use the wee house?"

It would, but she nodded, and dug the fork into the ground to lean on while she waited for him to go and come back. Cows' eyes, she thought, dark and murky. If he was Irish, and she felt he was, a Spaniard had got in there somewhere. Black Irish, they called them with his looks at home.

When he came back he asked, "Don't you re-member the skinny runt of a kid that sang at your wedding? That's what they used to call me, Skinny-runt."

Mary grunted, remembering not the child, but the man beside her with tears in his eyes when she suddenly looked up at him. She could still hear the high, sweet trill of song, but what she had always seen, remembering, was the tears. "What was it you sang?"

"The 'Ave Maria.' That's what I always sang, the 'Ave Maria.' "

"And your name?"

"Denny. Dennis O'Hearn, the same as yours. It was my father's brother Michael you were married to, may he rest in peace."

There was almost mockery in the sound from her throat. Neither peace nor prayer came easy to her. "Your voice has dropped a notch or two since then."

"I was afraid it wouldn't ever," he said.

She gave a snort of amusement.

She brought him a cup of tea with bread and jam where he sat on the bench by the door. By then, she was sure, Norah would have a crick in her neck, trying to see what was going on.

"Bring your cup." She led the way into the house through the kitchen and into the room she called her parlor. The house was cool and dark, more walls than windows. She lit the one electric lamp and moved it to where it cast light on the portrait above the couch.

"That's him," Denny said, looking up at the tinted photograph, life-size, head and breast of a young policeman in his high-buttoned uniform. His mustaches bristled and his eyes had spark. "I wouldn't think I'd remember him so well, but I do."

Mary turned off the light and they went outdoors again without speaking. He knew when to keep his mouth shut, Mary thought. Within months of her marriage to Michael O'Hearn, he was killed in the line of duty. She squinted in the sudden sun to have a longer look at Dennis. "I don't see any resemblance at all."

"My mother's name was Castillo."

So she'd been right about the Spanish strain.

By midafternoon he had picked all the potatoes

she'd harvested in two days' digging. It was easier for her to dig them up than to pick them and she'd have paid a boy from the town a nickel a bushel. She put off deciding whether to offer him the sixty-five cents. She watched him wash his hands and face at the pump and shake himself dry. She thought of the dog she no longer had. He wiped the dust from his shoes, one leg against the other. City shoes, she decided, even though they were high-laced, broken in a hundred miles south on the streets of Chicago.

"Have you no baggage?" she asked.

"I left a carryall with the stationmaster. I've to pick it up before dark."

"The mean bastard," she said. "It would kill him to turn on a light if there wasn't a train coming in."

He went back into the town before suppertime. And about time, Norah thought. She had watched, off and on, the whole afternoon and almost ruined a pattern trying to watch and use the scissors at the same time. As soon as he passed her house—a queer-looking dark fellow, half Indian, she thought, with the reservation a few miles north—she went across to where Mary was washing the smallest potatoes.

"Have you lost your senses, taking a stray like that into the house? And letting him use your convenience."

"Convenience!" Mary mocked.

"You could catch something from the likes of him."

"I could, and wouldn't that surprise you?" Mary gave her a bark of a laugh.

"Not in the least," Norah said, fairly sure she was being made fun of.

"I'm thinking I'll fix a cot for him in the back kitchen."

"So he's coming back, is he? And why not? The hospitality of the house. And never a word to me, Mary."

"Amn't I telling you now?"

"When you've already made up your mind. There was a piece in the paper last week if you ever read it, a man's watch stolen right from the table where he was asleep in his bed."

"My old clock wouldn't bring much," Mary said. Then she told her sister, "You can't call him a stray, Norah. He's Michael's nephew, his own brother's son."

Norah sucked in her breath, needing all of it. Michael, more than ten years dead, ought to have been out of their lives, but he never would be—a man she had never met, never wanted to meet, married to a sister she was sure she had saved from the streets after he died. Many times since she wished she hadn't and near as many times said so to Mary when goaded by her. Out of this roiling memory, she cried, "Did you invite him to come? Did you know he was coming?"

"What a crooked mind you have," Mary said. "I didn't know who he was till he told me. He sang at my wedding. A wisp of a boy then, he sang like an angel. Even Michael cried. His name is Dennis— Dennis O'Hearn." Mary lifted her chin saying it.

As though he was a child of her own, Norah thought with another surge of anger. She was as barren herself as Mary. More so, an old maid.

The two Lavery sisters had been brought over from Ireland, one after the other before either was twenty, by the childless couple from whom Norah inherited the farm, lock, stock, and barrel. It was not written into the bequest, but confided to the priest as well as to Norah, that it was hoped she would take care of her sister if ever she returned in need. Mary had run away within a year of her arrival. She was not greatly missed. Except by the farmer who had grown too fond of her.

Norah could see the change come over Mary. It was always like that with her after she had been mean. Mary touched her toe to the mound of potatoes the size of marbles. "Will you take a handful of these for your supper?"

"I will. They're sweeter by far than the big ones."

"Aye. Why shouldn't they be, coming to you for nothing?" She knocked the soap from the dish by the pump and filled it. "Bring the dish back the next time you come." When Norah was halfway along the path, Mary called, "Listen for the telephone in case I ring you later."

Mary was never without a drop of whiskey in the house. She kept a small flask of it under her pillow to ease the pain at night. Everyone knew but nobody told in the town where she got it. It would be a sad day for her when Prohibition ended, and the end was in sight. They'd be shipping the real thing in from Canada, and it wouldn't be half as good as what she got from Donel Rossa.

Rossa belonged to the first generation American Irish who farmed the rich soil of southern Wisconsin. His principal crop was corn, which he sold to a variety of consumers, some, no doubt, to members of his family said to have connections with the Chicago underworld.

Something Mary kept hidden in her heart was that soon after Michael was killed she began to receive, like clockwork and wherever she was, a pint every month marked "holy water." Since her coming back from Chicago, it was delivered by Donel himself, and if ever she mentioned paying him for it, he'd say, "Ah, Mary, Michael O'Hearn was a fine man. It comes to you with his pension." God and Mary knew the pension could take a supplement, but whenever question of where it was coming from bothered her, a tweak of pain put her conscience if not her bones at ease.

Donel was older than the sisters, closer in years to the old couple who had brought them over. Mary hadn't become close friends with him until she moved out of Norah's house, saying she'd rather live in the barn. The barn was an empty shell by then. Norah had auctioned off livestock, equipment, everything but the barn doors. And since Donel had had a hand, along with Father Conway, in bringing Mary back to where she wasn't wanted, he'd undertaken to help make the barn livable.

He was the first one Mary phoned to come round that night after supper. "I've someone here I want you to meet. Come and bring the missus."

"And I'll bring a smile," he promised.

A smile: his word for a bottle. As though she hadn't expected it.

Norah, as usual, put off going over for as long as she could stand not to go. She wanted them to wonder what was keeping her and at the same time suspected they wouldn't miss her if she didn't show up at all. They never tired of singing the old songs over and over, and she could hear the thump of Mary's stick on the floor as she beat time. When there was a quiet minute she imagined them passing the bottle to all there except Margaret and Tom's lump of a girl pretending to be asleep on the couch. Norah got her shawl from the hall stand, went out the front door and locked it behind her. You never could tell at night.

She moved with caution along the path, guided only by her memory of it in daylight. Rossa's voice was the loudest. It always was. She didn't like him. He treated Mary better than he did his wife, for one thing, but closer to the truth of it, Norah was sure he did not like her. She could never forget the look he had given her when she clapped her hands at news of Mary's marriage. The smile on his face had seemed to say, *So now it's all yours, all yours.* He'd been right, of course. And he was the one who came to tell her Mary's husband was dead, so soon. She would swear it was his cold eye that kept pity from coming over her. Now as she neared the barn, she tried to listen

for a new voice among the familiar. The Angel Ga-
briel couldn't be heard over Rossa and the thump of
Mary's stick.

Dennis O'Hearn wasn't bad-looking when you saw
him up close, she decided, but she would never have
taken him for an Irishman. There was a hangdog look
to him, big sad eyes that reminded her of the dog
Mary wanted to bring into the house when they lived
together. Now he picked up on a tune Margaret
hummed for him and put the words to it. Norah had
not heard it before, a nursery song, nor had she heard
a voice like his, deep and dark and soft as velvet. Her
love for music was the truest thing in Norah's life. It
drew her to High Mass on Sundays, and prompted her
to buy a piano as soon as she had money. It stood
mute in her living room save for the few chords she
had taught herself to play so that she might know
there was music in it.

It was strange the way Dennis O'Hearn's and her
gaze met and locked as though their eyes had got
accidentally tangled. He wiped his mouth with the back
of his hand to hide a smile, she felt. And she sensed
her color rising to the roots of her hair. She caught at
the foot of the girl stretched on the couch. She'd had
to push it aside to make room for herself. The young
one pulled her foot away so fast Norah almost lost
her balance. She flashed her a smile when she'd rather
have pinched her. The upstart mimicked her smile
back at her.

The room was stuffy and smelled of the men, sweat
and tobacco smoke and the cow barn, and a whiff of
Mary's liniment. Mary called this one big room her
parlor. Norah always thought it resembled a gypsy's
nest. To be sure, she'd never seen one. But, for example, instead of a door to the kitchen, the frame was
hung with a curtain of beads Mary had bought off a
peddler's wagon. The beads rattled if a wind came up
or when someone passed from room to room. Mary's
nook of a bedroom was to one side, chopped out of

the kitchen. If Dennis O'Hearn roamed through the house at night, it occurred to Norah, Mary would hear him part the curtain. Would she call him in to the side of her bed and ask him to rub liniment into her knees? Surely not. But Mary was that way. She was as easy with men as she was with women.

The songs they sang came, most of them, out of *The Golden Book of Songs*. Norah had a pristine copy of it on her piano at home. Mary's copy looked like an old prayer book that had lost its covers. She tried to picture how this lot would fit in her parlor, where the piano took so much of the room. Mary, when first she'd seen it, let out a whoop. "Holy Mother of God! It looks just like Reverend Mother!" They wouldn't fit at all, Norah decided. They just didn't belong there.

"Can you sing 'Mother Machree,' Dennis?" Rossa asked. "I don't think it's in the book. 'There's a place in my heart which no colleen can own,'" he started, not waiting for Dennis to answer. Suppose Dennis could play the piano, she thought. There were people who played by ear and he might. He picked up on "Mother Machree" and he knew the words by heart. Before he could finish, Rossa demanded "That Old Irish Mother of Mine."

"Give me a minute," Dennis said.

"Let the man wet his whistle," Mary said. "Isn't there a drop left in the bottle?"

Rossa sent his wife out to the car for the spare he kept hidden there.

"Norah." The girl's mother leaned toward her. She'd seen what happened between her and the upstart, but that wasn't on her mind at all. "Do you remember the queer woman at home who'd come out on the castle grounds just before dark? She'd sing 'The Last Rose of Summer.' Don't you remember? A veil round her head so you couldn't see her face. But every night she'd be there . . ."

"You know better than ask Norah about something

back home," Mary said. "She'd turn to salt if she said the word 'Ireland.' "

That was Mary.

"I remember—I remember the roses on the castle grounds," Norah said. "And the wreath they sent of them for our mother's funeral."

"Oh, for the love of God!" Mary said, out of patience.

Dennis sang "The Last Rose of Summer."

There was no beat Mary could thump to liven "The Last Rose of Summer" and she felt the party turning into slop. She pulled herself up from her chair and announced she was going to fire up the kitchen stove and make tea. She swiped at the curtain with her stick and set it jingling.

"I think I'll go home now," Norah said. "It's been such a grand evening."

Dennis was on his feet before she was. "I'll walk you home, Miss Lavery," he said.

"Then you don't need to come back," Mary snapped, quick as a dart.

You could hear the chirp of the crickets.

"Oh dear, dear me," Rossa said then.

Tom Dixon added treacle. "Stay a while longer, Norah, and we'll all go out together."

Mary would have as soon seen them all go out then. A man as fond of the military as Tom was known to be, you wouldn't have thought such an appeaser.

But it was Dennis O'Hearn who set things right again. "Please come back and sit down, Aunt Mary. I know how to fire up the stove, and I'll put on the kettle for you."

"Denny, will you put the kettle on?" took on a familiar ring in the next few days, and finding that it pleased her, he brought her a cup of tea every morning as soon as he heard the creak of her bedstead. It was what he had done for his own mother till the day she died.

"She never wanted more than a half cup. She'd send me to spill it out if there was more, and it had to be hot as blazes. Then she'd let it cool off before she drank it."

"She wanted you more than she did the tea," Mary told him.

Denny shrugged. If it was so he didn't understand it.

Mary did not lie long abed on these harvest days—or many others, for that matter—but with morning tea and afternoon tea and the cup she would say she was perishing for in the evening, she learned enough about Denny to know why he had come to her. The last of four boys and by ten years the youngest, he could remember his father saying he should have drowned him the day he was born, the runt of the litter. Until he discovered, when Denny started to school with the sisters, that he had a voice the nuns called sacred. "He'd hire me out for weddings or funerals for a dollar or two. He'd give me a nickel and spend the rest before my mother got her hand out."

It was not the first time Mary had heard a story like it.

"Would you like to hear me sing the 'Dies Irae'?" he offered.

"I would not."

Most of Mary's necessities were obtained through barter, and while she was frugal she was not miserly. But Denny wasn't long with her before she began to calculate the toll it took of her preserves and garden produce to bring home a pound of bacon. The first time Donel Rossa stopped by after the night of Dennis' arrival, she broached the possibility of finding a job for Denny in the valley.

"So you've decided to keep him," Rossa said. "You're a soft touch, Mary."

Mary caught something in his tone too intimate for her taste. "Did you have something to do with him coming, Donel?"

"Whatever makes you ask a question like that?"

"It struck me he might be something else that came with my pension."

Rossa found a place clear of their feet to spit. "You're sharp as a tack this morning, Mary."

"I should be. I've sat on a few."

Rossa laughed. He toed the spittle into the ground. "You know, Mary, the holy water is going to run dry. I'm not saying the state'll go dry. God forbid. The Dutchmen have a powerful thirst for their beer, and they've a throttle on the legislature."

Mary pulled him over to the bench and hung on to his arm. "Sit down here and tell me what you're saying." She was never long on patience.

"It's time I'm thinking about, time and change. I have a horse that climbs the fence whenever I start up the truck. He goes wild. But any day now I'll go out and see him nuzzling the radiator and the next thing you know, he'll be willing to go tandem with it. It's what the wear of time does to man and beast."

"You're an old fart, Donel." Only Mary could say it with affection. She pointed to where Denny was crawling from one currant bush to another, at the bottom of the field. "He'll be coming up from there any minute. I sent him back to strip them clean. Now he'll be counting every currant he puts in the basket."

"Have you sent him around the town to make inquiries?"

"He'll need more starch in him for that," Mary said.

"Well, there isn't a hell of a lot of that in the family . . . Ah, now, Mary, I've offended you," Rossa said, for her chin shot out. "Michael had the heart of a lion. What about Norah? Isn't there work she could put him to?"

"She'd eat him alive!"

Rossa changed the subject in a hurry. "The nuns brought him up pretty well, didn't they?"

"He can do his sums," Mary said. "He's not a child,

you know, and he's strong as a bull. He was digging ditches for the city of Chicago till they ran out of money."

"I hate to tell you what that qualifies him for on the farm, Mary."

She grunted. "And isn't the world full of it?"

Denny came up as Rossa was about to leave. His face was as red as the currants. "Do you want to do a day's work for me on the farm now and then?" Rossa asked him. "A dollar a day and your grub."

"On the farm," Dennis said, as though to be sure.

"Didn't I say on the farm? Would I be sending you to Australia? And you'll have to walk the five miles or hitch a ride on the road."

"I could pay Aunt Mary for my keep," Denny reasoned aloud but in no hurry to take up the offer.

Why? Mary wondered, when half the country was out of work. And why the "Aunt" Mary, which had been dropped after the first day?

"That's the idea, lad," Rossa said as though to a child.

It wasn't starch Denny needed. It was yeast. But Mary was pleased, too, at the prospect of getting him out from under her feet now and then, as long as it wasn't to Norah.

Norah had no great opinion of herself, though most people thought the opposite. Trying to get Denny out of her mind, she kept at the sewing machine until her eyes were bleary and her foot going numb on the treadle. She excused her back-and-forth trips to the window as the need to relieve cramps in her leg. She said the Hail Mary every time but she knew very well that her true intention was to catch sight of Denny going about his chores. She even numbered his trips to the outhouse, and noted when he carried Mary's pot with him, though it turned her stomach to think of it. Not often, but often enough to give her a surge of pleasure, and only when Mary was not in sight, he'd send a little salute her way—the tip of his fingers to his forehead to her. Sometimes she left the window open and sang while she worked, harking back to songs of her childhood even as Margaret had to "The Last Rose of Summer." It wasn't true that she despised Ireland. That was Mary belittling her. It was Ireland that let her go. Mary was the one with a passion for America.

But this was Norah's busiest season. The hand-me-downs were patched and freshened at home, but in most Hopetown families the oldest child got a new outfit at the start of the school year, and as often as not Norah was chosen over Sears, Roebuck to provide the girls' dresses. No one, at least to Norah's knowledge, ever remarked on the similarity between Norah's new dresses and last year's fashion in the Sears catalogue.

The morning Rossa came by and talked with Mary and then with Denny, Norah guessed rightly what it was about. She intercepted Denny on his way into town for Mary that afternoon. "Will you be going to work for Donel?" she asked outright, to be sure of a yes or no before Mary interfered. "He's a hard man, Dennis."

"I was thinking that myself and I'll have to walk five miles before starting the day's work."

"Doing what, do you know, Denny?"

"It's on the farm. I made sure of that."

Where else? Norah wondered, but before she could ask, Mary was at the barn door shouting to him.

"Amn't I waiting for the sugar? Get on with you, man."

Dennis went on and Norah sought out Mary in her kitchen. "I've sugar enough to let you have five pounds, Mary."

"He'll be back in time." She was picking over a great basin of currants, her hands stained bloodred. "Thank you, anyway," an afterthought.

Norah settled on a kitchen chair she almost overflowed. It creaked with her weight.

"You're fading away to a ton," Mary said with pleasure.

Where the inspiration came from Norah would never know. The thought just came up and out. "I've decided it's time to get rid of all those things of theirs in the cellar." "They" or "theirs" always referred to the couple who had brought her over from Ireland. "There's some I kept for you, if you remember, when you first wanted a place of your own. You might want to take a look at them now."

A little twitch of Mary's nose betrayed her interest and Norah pressed on. "The wash boiler—pure copper—I ought to have sold it," she began, "and the mirror. It wouldn't hurt you to take a look at yourself now and then."

As soon as the jelly was sealed in jars, Mary took Dennis with her to Norah's. They went first to the cellar door, but Norah waved them around. It was his first time in her house, and she didn't even ask him to wipe his feet.

Dennis' great dark eyes took in everything Mary gave him time to see. She nudged him on with the knob of her cane. He wasn't a dumb animal, Norah thought, but she smiled and bit her tongue. Above all she wanted him to see the piano. Mary shoved him past the parlor door.

Norah had to lift the door to the storage room where it sagged on the hinges and scraped the floor.

"Maybe I could fix that," Denny said.

"Some rainy day when Mary has nothing for you to do."

"That'll be the day," Mary said, but by then her curiosity was picking up and she was the first into the room, where there was only a whisper of light from the ground-level window. Norah pulled the electric switch. Mary let out a squeak of pleasure at things she thought on sight she had a use for. Then she settled down to a careful selection. One glance at her own

reflection eliminated the mirror. Nor did she want
Norah's junk. Denny figured the most in her calculation, of course. The clothes wringer, for example,
would have to be fastened to the sink board in the
kitchen, where the only running water in her place
came in. She'd not have needed it for her bits and
pieces, but laundering a man's wear could put a terrible strain on her knotty hands. Denny carted the
wringer to the cellar door. Norah, her arms folded,
watched. With an eagle's eye, Mary thought. "Couldn't
you go and sit down somewhere?"

"I'd be willing to help," Norah said.

"Isn't that what I'm talking about?"

On Denny's next trip between the storeroom and
the cellar door, he brought back an old kitchen chair
he'd seen near the furnace. He even dusted it with his
bare hand. Norah sat.

"God save the queen!" Mary cried.

Norah's eyes and Denny's met, even as at the party,
but not this time by accident. What she felt was like
an electric shock. She was sure they had struck a bond.

Mary thumped her stick against a humpbacked
trunk that stood beneath the window.

Norah snapped out of her reverie. "Leave that!"

Mary all but clapped her hands. "Is it the bones of
a lover?" She'd read the story long ago. "Watch out
for yourself, Denny!"

She was enjoying herself, Norah thought, making
fun of her. That was Mary. Her own thoughts turned
to what she could do or say that might engage Dennis.
There wasn't much left in the room—the big wardrobe, the mirror, some picture frames she'd thought
she'd use, but hadn't, the trunk, full enough, but not
of bones, and the rusted garden tools even Mary
wouldn't want. And here among them, half shrouded
by an old umbrella, where she herself had hidden it
one winter's night, was the old man's shotgun.

Mary hobbled to the outside door with a yardstick
to measure whether they could get the wardrobe out

that way. She had begun to think of making a room of his own for Denny. There was room enough in the barn, sure.

Norah got up and took the chair back herself to where it had come from. When she returned she saw that Denny had discovered the gun. He was bent over, trying to see it better, but not daring to touch. "Aunt Norah?" He looked round, his eyes jumping out of his head.

"Not now," she said, and chanced a wink.

He winked back.

There was no way Denny could transport the big cupboard from house to barn without help. Mary cursed the rheumatism and Norah refused to make a fool of herself trying. It was decided between the sisters that the wardrobe could wait till Donel Rossa's next visit. Mary and Denny left by the cellar door. Norah locked it, turned off the light, and went upstairs. She wasn't sure what had happened to her, but whatever it was had never happened to her before.

Mary put up her first crop of tomatoes by the end of the week. Dennis kept the kitchen range at top heat under the copper boiler, and though Mary denied her need for the clock, just to be sure she set the alarm for each step. The sweat ran down both their faces, and when a great drop fell from the tip of Mary's nose into a bowl of tomatoes she cackled, "Sure, they needed more salt."

In the evening they sat at the kitchen table where Mary marked labels "Mary's Best" for the jars she would seal with a final turn before bedtime. Hope Valley Market would take all she could provide. Through the open window they could hear an occasional car go by and the singsong chatter of katydids, and closer overhead, the frantic buzz of an insect caught on the sticky tape that dangled from the light. Sometimes music wafted their way from Norah's radio.

Dennis tilted back in his chair though she'd asked

him not to do it. He sat upright suddenly and, pinching his nose, began to sing, " 'I'm just a vagabond lover . . .' "

"My God," Mary said, "where did you learn that?"

"From the radio. Didn't you ever hear Rudy Vallee?"

"I'd just as soon not," Mary said. "Try it without the clothespin."

He grinned, cleared his throat, and sang it in his own voice. The voice of the child she remembered was gone, but there was a deep, sad music in what she heard.

"Do you miss the city, Denny?"

"No."

"Neither do I," she said. It seemed many yesterdays since she'd come out from Chicago on the train with Donel Rossa to Norah's chilly welcome.

Both sisters were alongside the road when the threshing combine on its way to Rossa's came rattling through town and stopped for Denny. Men aboard the last rig gave him a hand up, and all of them waved at Norah and Mary, who watched until the blinding sunrise washed them out of sight. Children, up at dawn to follow the caravan through town, went home to breakfast and the sisters turned into their own walkways. Mary resented Norah's being there, but it was not in her heart to part without a word.

"Will you have a cup of tea? The kettle's on the back of the stove."

Norah would rather have gone home. More and more she felt the presence of Dennis to be everywhere in Mary's house. She even avoided seeing the cot where he slept in the back kitchen. But what she said was, "Let me close the front door and I'll be over."

"Oh, for the love of God," Mary said. Doors were anathema to her.

Norah pulled a chair out from the kitchen table.

"I'm leery of that one," Mary said from the stove.

"I can't break him of the habit of teetering on the back legs of a chair. You'd think they were rockers."

"I won't teeter," Norah said. The chair creaked when she sat down. "And I won't be staying more than a minute."

Mary brought the teapot and swirled the tea before she poured it. It was on the tip of her tongue to say *This'll put hair on your chest*, but she held it back. She was trying to cure herself of saying the common things like it she had picked up God only knew from where.

Norah helped herself to sugar. Whatever milk Mary had was always on the turn in summer. She could have kept it in the well like the couple used to. "Did you want the old trunk in the storeroom badly, Mary? I could empty it out."

"What would I be putting in it?"

"And what will you put in the cupboard when you get it over?"

"Won't he be getting clothes one of these days and needing a place to hang them?"

Norah was sure now she shouldn't have come. She felt hurt, pushed out. She wanted to push back. "I've been going through the things I've kept in the trunk all these years—I was thinking I'd make a rag rug of them someday but I never did—her petticoats and his flannel shirts. The shirts would fit Denny, you know. I could shorten the sleeves for him."

Mary's face shriveled up like an old woman's and the spittle sprayed from her mouth before she could speak. "Keep his filthy shirts to yourself. They're all yours. Do you think I'd let him put them on his back?"

"It was a long time ago, Mary."

"If it was forever, would I forget it?"

"I know how you feel."

"You know how I feel! There's more feeling in this teapot than in you."

Norah struggled to get up. "I don't have to take

this from you, Mary. I could turn you out if I wanted and nobody'd say I did wrong. It wasn't my fault he made a strumpet out of you. Didn't you beg them to bring you over? 'I'll do anything that wants doing,' you wrote. I read them your letters—she couldn't read—and I remember him sitting there laughing to himself. 'Isn't she the lively one now?' he'd say. He treated me like dirt from the day you arrived. The two of you making fun of me behind my back. I never told on you. I never complained to her, but she knew. She'd sit at the sewing machine and cry to herself."

At the mention of tears her own eyes filled, not at what she remembered, but at the feeling of emptiness building inside her. "I'm trying to help you if only you'd let me. I've tried ever since the day you came back. Even Father Conway says I could not have done more."

"Nor cared less," Mary said. "Will you go home out of here, Norah? You're like a great, fat hen, scratching everything into your nest. Cluck, cluck, cluck. Can't you leave him and me alone?"

"You think you own him body and soul," Norah blurted out. "You'd hire him out to your bootlegger friend, but you wouldn't let him wash a window in my house."

Mary put her hand up to shield her face. Norah looked about to strike her. And Norah had never wanted more to hit her across the mouth. But she pulled back and made her way toward the door. She stopped and looked round at a burst of laughter from Mary.

"Oh, my God," Mary shouted. "You're in love with him!"

Norah quick-smiled. "You can't say that, Mary. Haven't you always said, 'Poor Norah. She can't love anybody except herself'?"

Rossa stopped for a word with Mary when he brought Denny back on his way into town. "I was wrong about him, Mary. He's not all muscle. He's got a brain up there. And get him to sing 'Home on the Range' for you."

"Aren't you the one," Mary said, sparing herself having to thank him.

Christopher Columbus could not have had more to tell returning from America than Denny coming back from Donel Rossa's farm.

"Did you learn how to milk a cow?" Mary asked.

"And how to squirt milk in the cat's mouth," Denny said.

Mary remembered learning to milk and the kick of the cow who didn't think much of how she went about it, and she thought of Norah's going on about how she had begged to be brought over. She'd known when she landed she'd never go back. In steerage, sick as a dog all the way.

And him threatening to send her back if she didn't give in to him. "Lie down on the bale there and turn up your arse." She'd never got over it, even with Michael. And Norah saying, "I know how you feel." Norah had gone home and pulled down the blinds on the windows that faced the barn. When she came out of the house it was by the front door and she never looked across. Nor had she hung a stitch on the clothesline.

"I didn't get to do much milking," Denny said. "It's terrible hard on the wrists, you know."

"Is it now? Would you teach your granny to milk ducks?"

Denny told things in spurts. He'd have told them better, Mary thought, if they'd had a tune to them—how the men on the wagon took the pitchfork away from him and made him load the sheaves by hand. "I couldn't get the hang of it, you see. They said I'd be murdering them." And Mrs. Rossa's pies: "The look of them made your mouth water. Only she'd made a mistake and put salt instead of sugar in them. You should've seen Donel. I thought he was going to hit her. But he put his arm around her at the last minute, and told the men, 'I'll make it up to you,' and he sure did. Two bottles. He told me after he was taking an awful chance. One of the ones he didn't know could've been a spy, a Revenue agent."

Rossa had kept Dennis a day and a night after the combine pushed on to the next farm, and to hear Denny tell it, nothing as wonderful had ever happened to him before. He discovered Rossa's collection of guns that he kept locked in the harness room. Rossa was a hunter. He showed Denny how to load and carry a shotgun, and had taken him out at dawn that very morning to shoot at the crows where they were cleaning up grain left in the harvest stubble.

"I told him about the gun in Norah's storeroom. You didn't even see it, I bet."

"I've seen it," Mary said.

"It's a shotgun, Donel says. I knew that myself when I seen his. He says if Norah would let me borrow it, he'd help me clean it up and oil it. And he'll take me hunting with him in the fall. They hunt small game with it—squirrels and rabbits. He told me you can make a better rabbit stew than Mrs. Rossa."

"Once in my life," Mary said. "Once in my life. Donel skinned it for me and I pretended it was an old rooster."

Denny pulled his chair closer to hers. He wet his lips. "Would you ask Aunt Norah for me?"

She should never have taken him over there, Mary thought, but she'd been all over that with herself. And she ought not to have made fun of Norah, blurting out that she was in love, though she didn't believe it for a minute. From the way Norah was carrying on since, Mary wasn't sure what was going on with her.

"I'll have to think about it," Mary said. She'd begun to feel sorry for her sister, the boob, the big, blubbering boob. "There's enough to do in the onion patch to keep you busy. And for God's sake take off the clothes you're wearing and soak them in the tub."

"I will," Denny said. "I sweated a lot. Donel says

we should keep the gun ready just to fire off and scare the Revenue men if they come snooping around. He says they might."

"I said I'll think about it," Mary said.

How many times in those three days had Norah said, "How dare she!" and attacked with fury every chore she could put her mind to. She scoured the kitchen and bathroom sinks, the toilet bowl, the front steps. She finished the last of the schoolgirls' dresses, folded them, and called round for them to be picked up. Her anger fed on memories of one good thing after another that Mary had spoiled for her. Even the piano. The dead piano in her parlor— Mary's joke.

But her anger and her feeling of shame wore down, and that morning when she heard Rossa's truck pull up to the barn, she looked out through the crack of daylight between the blind and the window frame, and watched Denny's return. She pulled up all the blinds and boiled an egg for breakfast.

"I could have done this myself," the girl said, wanting to hand in the dress without a hello or how-are-you when Norah opened the door. Margaret surely taught her better.

"Come in and let me look at you," Norah said.

"Dad's in a terrible hurry."

"No, dear. You are." Norah smiled and backed into the house. "I know your father." Tom Dixon was a great talker. Mary got to know more about what was happening in the town from an hour with him than Norah learned reading a month of the *Hope Valley News.*

The girl had little choice but to follow her indoors.

"If you had more time," Norah said, "I'd ask you to play your latest piece for me."

"When I pick up the dress, maybe," the thirteen-year-old said. She was even less fond of Norah's piano than of the one at home. She could kick hers and the place she'd kicked wouldn't show.

"You'll have to put the dress on, dear, if I'm going to pin it up."

"Mother said . . ."

Norah stopped her. "Elaine, I know how to alter a dress."

The girl took the dress into the bathroom and put it on.

Why they named her Elaine, Norah would never know. From a poem Margaret had read, she remembered. Or was it after someone in Tom's family? He was English. She certainly wasn't Norah's notion of an Elaine. No wonder they called her Lainie.

What was her hurry? Norah wondered when she let her out of the house and watched her lope across the way. Did the girl hate her that much? Norah did know she was fonder of Mary and her ramshackle house. It struck her then: Denny.

Lainie burst into Mary's kitchen. "She's spooky!"

"That's enough," Tom said.

Mary chuckled. "I think it myself sometimes." She turned up her cheek for a kiss. "Is it you that's growing or me that's shrinking?"

"Where's Denny?" the girl asked.

"Didn't I tell you?" Tom said to Mary. He was right. The girl had reached the age where one word said it all: boys.

"I've fixed him a jar of tea. You can take it down to him in the far field and make him share it with you."

"You have the devil in you, Mary," Tom said.

She gave that rattle of a laugh. "Sure, it's broad daylight."

And the blinds were up next door. Wouldn't Norah be watching with the frozen heart of a chaperone? Mary pushed their tea things out of the way. "I've a question or two for you, Tom. You're wearing your badge, I see."

"If I didn't the sheriff would take it from me."

"I thought maybe something was up. The Revenue men going round, say. Or is Donel filling Denny's head with goblins?"

"I'm on the side of the Feds. I have to be," Tom said. "It's the law."

"Would they be after Donel, do you think?"

"I'm not in their confidence, Mary."

She let it go. "Wouldn't you think they'd have more to do in this country than put and take laws like that one?"

"It's a country for and by the people," Tom said. Scratch a veteran and find a patriot. Mary could beat time to it.

"You know Donel's put down money on a building in town," he added.

"Is that a fact?" she said, all ears.

"I've heard he'll be opening a business of some sort, a big one."

"And quitting the farm?"

"The farm's quitting a lot of us these days, Mary."

Mary envisioned the main street of Hopetown as she had last paid it attention. Vacancies galore.

"What kind of business, do you think?"

"It's a ways off," Tom said.

"He plans ahead," Mary said. She was thinking of Donel's palaver about the horse and the truck. "And he has money. Sure, that's what makes the mare go, Tom. Money makes the mare go."

"I'll put the dishes in the sink for you," Tom said, getting up.

"Leave them. There's something I'd like you to do for me while you're here: Give Denny a hand with a cupboard he's to bring over from Norah's."

She made her way to the telephone and gave it a mighty crank.

"Are you feeling better, Norah?" The very tone of Mary's voice, the purr of concern, put Norah on guard.

"I'm doing fine," Norah said.

"Ah, that's good news. I was worried about you," Mary chirped. "I was wondering if you felt up to it, while I have Tom here, could him and Denny pick up the cupboard? I can't count on Donel these days."

"I'll go down and unlock the door," Norah said.

"Would it be less trouble if I sent Denny ahead for the key?"

"I said I'll go down." She'd send Denny ahead for the key, taunting her, that's what it was, Norah thought.

She was sure of it when all four of them crowded down the cellar steps. The girl giggling and Denny coming down backwards to give her his hand. A gentleman!

"Hey! It's creepy in here," the girl squealed.

"Couldn't we have more light?" Mary called. "Tom wants to look at your furnace while he's here."

Denny opened the storeroom door for her, where she pulled the switch that lit up the whole cellar. Denny seemed to light up with it, as though she had conjured the light for his delight. She could not conceal the pleasure of looking at him, but she turned on Mary. "Is that light enough for you?"

"Ah, Norah, you're still not yourself. It's Denny made me come along and speak to you for him. I think he's afraid of you, God knows why." She gave a swipe of her hand at Lainie, who'd crept up, never wanting to miss anything. "Go there with your father, girl. He'll need your advice." And to Norah, "Can we come in for a minute?" Her stick ahead of her, she was already in the storeroom. Canny as a scavenger, she saw the gun, but didn't let on at first. Then: "There it is!" She looked up at her sister. "It's the gun, Norah. It's been on his mind ever since we were here. If I'd known at the time, I'd have said something."

Norah's brief shock of pleasure went dead. She felt let down by Denny, betrayed, him letting Mary in on the little bond she'd thought between him and herself. Afraid of her? Mary's nonsense. Nobody was afraid of her. He was shy. That's what she loved about him.

He stood there holding his breath, waiting for the next word.

"What about the gun, Denny? Can't you tell me yourself?" She didn't want to hear any more from Mary.

"Aunt Norah," he started.

"Just plain Norah, Denny."

He nodded. "Could we borrow it, Aunt Norah?"

"Who's the 'we,' Dennis?"

"Mr. Rossa and me. He'll help me clean it up and take me hunting with him in the fall."

Norah did not like Donel Rossa. She didn't trust him—all his trips to and from Chicago, and his "holy water," his "smiles" as he called them. He was in the business, she was sure. Why he coddled Mary, she never knew, but she did know how he treated her. Like she was a crook, like she'd befuddled the old lady into leaving her everything. In truth, he made her feel about herself the way she felt about him.

"Have you ever fired a gun in your life, Denny?"

"I have—in the amusement park in White City. I shot down the whole row of ducks and I took the prize. It was a kewpie doll I gave to my mother."

"Oh, my God," Mary said. "Tell her about the crows in the field this morning."

Denny repeated the story much as he'd told it to Mary. He wasn't sizzling, Mary thought, but he was holding his own. And so was Norah. Mary could see her guard going up. She was afraid of losing something, of something being taken away from her, and she didn't like Donel, Mary knew.

Tom and the girl had come to the door.

"Rossa knows guns," Tom said. "He'll teach you proper. I'm not a hunter myself, but I know one when I see the gun in his hand."

"Dad won't even shoot a fox," Lainie said. "I'm a better shot than he is."

The bold thing, Norah thought. Next she'd want to go hunting with Denny and to hide in a duck blind with him.

"Could I show you, Aunt Norah?" Not waiting for leave, he darted across the room and took the gun in hand. He brushed away the dust and broke the breech. Not easily. It needed his strength.

"Empty," he said of the cartridge chamber. "You must never take a chance." He locked the gun again and held it crosswise to himself and waited.

They were all waiting. Except Mary, who had neither patience nor use for guns, especially this one. She was determined Denny could become the apple of Donel's eye. "What good is it to you, Norah? Couldn't I have taken it the day we were in here cleaning out for you?"

"You could not," Norah said. "Shall I tell you why?"

"There's no need." She turned round to the door. "Come on, Denny, let's go home."

Norah spoke out so that all of them would hear. "You may borrow the gun, Denny, if you give me your word as a gentleman, it stays in this house when you're not out hunting with it. But you must give me your word."

"I do," Denny said with such fervor it made Mary laugh.

She laughed, but with no great pleasure. Norah had won something though she wasn't sure what. Her back was to them when Denny put the gun back from where he had taken it.

"Thank you, Norah," he said, up close to her face.

Norah thought it eloquent, that soft, rich voice. Simple and eloquent. "We'll have a key made for you, Denny."

His smile went through her.

Tom was already testing the weight of the cupboard. He had rarely visited the sisters that they did not end things with a quarrel between them. He wanted away. "Let's go, Denny. I want to get home before the cows come in."

Lainie was there first, lifting the other end of the huge pine box with its clattering doors. "Lay it down flat and you could put a couple of bodies in it," she said to her father just above a whisper.

"Never mind," he said. But he let her help. He always said she was more help to him than ever a boy would have been.

Denny wanted to telephone Donel that very night and tell him he'd be able to go hunting with him in the fall.

"When you next see him, it'll be time enough," Mary said, and when he drooped like a spent daisy, she explained, "Donel Rossa has more on his mind than teaching you how to shoot rabbits."

"I know that, but I could start working on the gun by myself. It's terrible rusty." He suddenly brightened. "I know what I'll do—I'll go in town to the hardware store and they'll tell me what I need."

"I'm sure they will," Mary said. "And maybe they'll tell you how to pay for it."

A storm blew up in the night and set the beaded curtain rustling. Old bones, she thought. That's what it was made of. She hadn't listened to it much since he had come and she had a terrible premonition that she was going to lose him. It was a new kind of pain, as though she needed it. She reached for the flask under the lumpy pillow. She was going to lose that, too.

Rain came with the wind and in the morning she knew they were not going to pick a second round of tomatoes or plough under the potato field. She also knew that one thing she had to do about Denny was keep him busy. She waited for him to come up from emptying the slops and wash the bucket at the outdoor pump. By the time he came in he was soaked to the skin. From the storage bin under the sofa she brought out a checkered wool shirt of Michael's she'd intended to wear herself someday. The someday had never come. "It'll keep you warm hunting ducks," she said. "Put it on for now."

At the first break in the weather they went out to the padlocked back door of the barn. "This is where the cows came in," Mary said, and Dennis, with his nose in the air, said, "I can tell."

Piled along the cement frames where once there had been stanchions were several sheets of beaverboard and the lumber they had not used in carving a place of her own for Mary. Donel had been generous and he dreamed big dreams. She would remind him, when the right time came, of how they'd planned a second room, and maybe a second stove off Mary's parlor. She pointed out to Denny the slit of light in the roof, a boxed vent to where a chimney pipe might be raised.

It was her dream at the moment, not Denny's. He wandered off. He was a city boy, sure, and he'd met cows for the first time in his life at Donel's, and he'd caught the smell of them here.

She was startled when he called out to her, "Aunt Mary, someone's standing in the doorway."

As she turned to see the man, he greeted her, "The top of the morning to you!"

"Oh, my God," she muttered. It could have been Donel with his make-believe Irish, but it was not.

He was holding an open wallet for her to see his identification. When she reached him she saw little except the government insignia, for her heart started to pound. She thought he was from Immigration. She'd never lost the fear of being sent back.

"What is it you want, mister?"

"My name is Spillane. I've orders to search the premises for corn whiskey, ma'am. You've nothing to fear if you're clean, Mrs. O'Hearn."

He stretched his neck to see behind and beyond her into the cavernous barn and he took a good look at Dennis when he came up. Whoever he was, his pale eyes had no warmth in them and he had stoked her fear. She disliked him on sight.

"What kind of name is Spillane?"

"It's Irish, as Irish as yours."

"And you a Revenue man," she said with scorn, the full use of her tongue restored.

He put the wallet back in his pocket. "So you're one of *those* Irish women," he said. "I have a warrant in the car if you want to see it."

"Never mind. Take him around, Denny. And be sure to show him the still."

"Where, Aunt Mary?" Denny had missed the point.

"Oh, for the love of God, go where you like, Mr. Spillane, and take care you don't miss my bedroom."

He did not miss much. He went to his car and brought a flashlight. A touring car with the windows all open to let out the stink, Mary thought. He'd be losing his authority soon. Maybe that was what ailed him. But he made Denny lift the cover from the mouth of the well. He searched its depth with the beam of the torch. He looked up at Mary where she watched from the back stoop and he'd have heard her laugh. He reached out and snatched the cup from where it hung by the pump and threw it into the well.

"May you die of thirst," Mary shouted and went into the house.

When he was gone, Mary poured herself and Denny cold tea from what was left in the breakfast pot.

"What did he mean by one of those Irish women?" Denny wanted to know.

"Why didn't you ask him?" Mary snapped. She'd known exactly what he meant: They should never have been given the vote. Not, of course, that she had ever used it.

"He didn't talk much. I didn't like him either, Mary."

"Did he say anything to you at all?"

"Yeah."

"Well, what?"

" 'Where'd you get those great, big beautiful eyes?' "

"The bastard," Mary said.

"Yeah. Now can we call Donel?"

Donel came in the afternoon. He heard them out, but he shook his head. "Did you have to make an enemy of him, Mary?"

"Was I to make a friend of him, then?"

"It's what I've been doing all my life, and I eat three square meals a day." He dropped his voice. "They're all over the place, so do me a favor, Mary, if he comes back, give him a cup of tea."

"I know what I'll put in it then, him pouring the last drop in my bottle down the sink."

"You've had worse things happen to you."

He was out of patience—short of time, she realized, and he hadn't offered to replenish her holy water. She saw a glint of anger in his eyes. She wouldn't want him for an enemy, either.

"And I've had better!" In spite of herself, she couldn't yield the last word, but she rang a good change on it with a nod toward Denny. "Till this one."

Denny grinned. "Donel," he said, "I got the loan of the gun."

Donel grunted as though to give his memory a jog.

"I plan to clean it up myself," Denny went on, "and be half-ready at least, when we can go hunting."

"That won't do at all," Donel said. "It's not a musical instrument. It's a weapon."

"I know," Denny said.

"You think you know. That's worse than not knowing at all."

"I'll learn."

Mary was proud of the way he said it.

Donel said, "That's better. Let's have a look at it while I'm here."

"I have to keep it at Norah's," Denny said, "but I'm to have a key."

Mary's eyes and Donel's met, for they shared a deep and silent association with the words. When Mary had run away to Chicago, she found a haven and employment with a friend of Donel's to whose house Donel had a key.

"He'll make friends at Murray's Hardware," Mary said. "They'll get him started."

Donel looked at his watch. "I'll take you in town with me now and introduce you to Murray. If you can bring the gun, he'll know what you're talking about."

"I will," Denny said. "I'll ask Aunt Norah. It's a single-barrel twelve-gauge shotgun."

"It'll do," Donel said without enthusiasm. It was one of the cheaper guns on the market. "And where in hell did you get the shirt you're wearing?"

Norah made a quick choice of where to hide when she saw Rossa stop and wait in the truck for Denny to come to her door. She wasn't ready yet. She listened as Denny rapped and called out her name. The note of concern was endearing. She sat on the cushioned lid of the toilet and waited to hear the truck pull away. In a snatch of memory she heard Mary's cackle: "God save the queen."

The bathtub, she thought, staring at it, was big enough for him to flop over in. He'd splash and grin. She thought of getting a bar of Lifebuoy soap.

Denny knocked on her door again late in the afternoon. He had come back on foot carrying a brand-new canvas knapsack.

"I must have heard you in my sleep," Norah lied. "I lay down with a headache after my lunch, and wasn't I dreaming of you?"

"What was I doing?"

"You were playing the piano," she said. "It's just come back to me now."

"You were dreaming, all right," Denny said.

They went down through the house to the cellar, and Norah pointed out a workbench near the coal bin he could use.

"Couldn't I take it over there to work on?"

"You could not."

While she watched him unpack the knapsack she listened for a telephone call from Mary or the rap of her stick on a window. "Isn't Mary feeling well?"

"She's all right."

Which told her nothing. "I wondered if it was a doctor I saw stopping in this morning."

"Not for Aunt Mary. She thinks they're all quacks."

He'd been given instruction, Norah thought, on what he could say and what not. She was furious, not so much at what she might be missing, but at the idea of Mary's taking advantage of his innocence. She had made up her mind from what she'd seen of Mary's visitor that morning that he was on a mission from Donel Rossa. He might even be bringing her the monthly holy water. He looked like a bootlegger and his long-nosed car suited the notion.

"Will you save your tin cans for me, Norah? Donel says I should set them up on the fence posts in the far field and practice."

"You know this is all my property, Dennis."

"Oh, I do. Donel said I should ask you."

"I'll save you the tins."

"Thank you, Norah." His smile was like honey.

It would do for the day, she thought. "You'd better go now. She'll be waiting for you."

"She will. She'll want to hear."

"To hear what, Denny?"

"About Donel's construction business. Mr. Murray shook hands with him. It's going to be great for Hopetown—for the whole valley."

Norah smiled. "How nice!" she said.

"Mary! Come outdoors quick!"

"Quick!" she mocked.

And when she got to the stoop: "Look!" he insisted.

"I can hear them," she said.

Fading fast into the morning mist even as their cries grew dimmer, the Canadian geese were going south.

"Would God they were coming back." She drew her shawl tighter. "For God's sake put your shirt on, Denny. You'll catch your death of cold."

"I won't." He still washed, naked to the waist, at the pump by the well. He shaved at the kitchen sink.

They had eggs for breakfast that morning, and though she knew he was only half listening, she told him, and probably for the second or third time, she thought, of how as children she and Norah waded in the stream at home, groping the sand with their toes for duck eggs. Whoever found one got the top when her father opened it for his breakfast the next morning.

"Did you and Norah fight over it?" He was listening after all.

Donel stopped on his way into town. He was a little early, due at the lawyer's office within the hour to sign the final papers. The teacup trembled in his hand. He put it down. "I'll be glad to get this over with," he said.

"Will you have a drop from my bottle to settle you?" Mary said.

"Not on your life, macushla."

He had brought her the last "smile."

He stretched out his hand and held it steady, but his teeth were clenched. He took up the cup again. "I'm clean, Mary." He toasted her—or himself—with the lukewarm tea: "Slainte."

Let Norah ridicule him all she liked, Mary thought, but they would never know a man more Irish.

Norah was on the lookout. She had been from the moment she heard Rossa's car drive into the yard. The family car, no less. He sometimes drove her and

Mary to Sunday Mass in it. Lately he'd been driving it into Hopetown. It was more befitting a businessman than the Ford truck. She knew Denny would be going back to the farm with him—to shuck corn and then to go hunting with him in the morning.

He would come soon for the gun and take it away for the first time. And what would she have left? A bag of tin cans with holes shot through them. She caught a whiff of her cologne. She'd used too much of it. And dreamed too much. She'd worn out a paltry thrill remembering it. Only once had she come even close to telling him she loved him.

He'd been at the cellar workbench that day, his back to her, and what she told him was of her love for music and how beautiful she thought his voice was. When he seemed to stiffen, she thought it safer to talk about the piano and how she'd hoped someday to even play it herself. She'd been pleased at the moment for what she said then: "But it's my heart and not my head that's musical."

And Denny, looking around to her in the expectant silence: "Couldn't you sell the piano?"

"I don't need the money, Denny."

"Aunt Mary would have," he said.

Denny came out from the barn with Rossa. He put his knapsack and a box of Mary's preserves, no doubt, in the rear seat of the sedan. He stepped back and watched Rossa drive off. Without a glance her way, he went back in to Mary.

He would not come till the last minute, waiting for Rossa to return and hurry him away.

She watched the traffic coming into town, not a car a minute, but picking up these days. She couldn't believe it had anything to do with Donel Rossa's new enterprise, Hope County Construction. County no less.

She moved away from the window and then went back to straighten the curtain. By sheer chance she saw the black long-nosed touring car drive past the house and on into Hopetown. When she thought about it, she wasn't a bit surprised.

In the late morning she heard Dennis open the cellar doors. She called down to him to leave them open, that she would close them when the sun was gone.

"I didn't want to bother you," he said at the bottom of the kitchen stairs. "Donel didn't think he'd be this long. Mary says it's the lawyers that's holding things up."

"Ah, yes, what Mary says." He was like a silhouette between her and the shaft of daylight. "I'm coming down," she said.

"You don't need to, Aunt Norah."

He didn't want her to. He wanted to go off, gun in hand, without even a thank-you-very-much. "I'm coming down."

He lifted the storeroom door for her when she went in to switch on the lights. "I was going to fix this for you, wasn't I? When I come back from Donel's."

She followed him to the workbench. "What if Rossa doesn't come, if something happened to change his mind?"

"He'd let us know," Denny said. He took the gun from the rack he had built for it and broke it to be sure the chamber was empty.

"You are such a foolish boy, Dennis. You believe everybody. The Revenue agent in the rain that morning: I could have told you the truth about him. But Mary spat at me when I even mentioned him."

"That bastard," Denny said.

"No, Denny. He's worse. He's a gangster. I would take my oath on it. And isn't he back today for the celebration?"

"He's back?" Denny questioned as though he didn't understand her.

"You don't forget an automobile like that, Denny. When Donel left here this morning, it came by right after him. What an odd coincidence, I thought at first and then I realized: Of course, they're going to the same place."

Denny groped his jacket pocket and brought out a cartridge. He loaded it into the open gun and closed it.

She was a second or two understanding what he had done. "He doesn't need you, Denny. He's one of them."

"You're crazy," he said.

He edged her aside, when she tried to block his way to the door. "It's Mary needs me, don't you understand?"

"No, I don't understand and I never will. You can't have the gun, Denny. It's mine. I want it back."

She tried to take it from him, but he was by far the stronger. She tried to twist it free.

The explosion rocked the house. Smoke and debris clouded the air. She knew she was losing consciousness, but now she couldn't let go of the gun. It was frozen in her hands. And her hands were wet with blood, her sleeves, her breast saturated. She could taste it. So much blood.

Then nothing.

When the girl, Lainie, got home from Denny's funeral, she put the Mass card in the box of clippings she was saving from the *Hope Valley News*. It didn't belong there, and yet it did. It would always carry her remembrance of the lone high voice from the choir loft singing the "Dies Irae," Day of Wrath, and the single sob it brought from her aunt Mary.

For as long as she lived, Norah would say that she had killed Denny—in spite of the coroner's finding that his death was most probably caused by a bullet fired from the cellar doorway an instant before or an instant after the gun in her and Denny's hands exploded.

Mary swore she had seen Spillane when she started

over at the sound of gunfire. So she, too, bore willing guilt. But it was Donel who could beat his breast the hardest.

Norah had been right. Spillane was a low-level member of the Chicago gang Donel had been in business with for years. He had thought he was breaking away from them that fall. "The boss" thought so, too. He suspected at first that Donel was tying in with another gang and using Mary's place for storage. Spillane investigated even the well. Donel no more than Mary doubted his claim to be a federal agent.

When the news of the construction business came out—Hope County Construction—"the boss" wanted a part of it. Donel refused. As he told Mary, he was clean. He thought he was, but Spillane caught up with him before he reached the door of the lawyer's office that morning. The boss expected him to postpone the contract signing and expand the partnership. The boss promised he would get well paid, whichever way he played it. Donel told him to go to hell.

Why Denny and not Mary if Spillane was his killer? It was probably the boss's decision. Denny was Michael O'Hearn's nephew, and Michael had been killed—in the line of duty—in an exchange of gunfire that also killed a young and promising member of the gang those many years before.

Spillane was never found, dead or alive.

About the Authors

P. M. Carlson
P. M. Carlson taught psychology and statistics at Cornell University before deciding that mystery writing was more fun. Her novels have been nominated for the Edgar, the Macavity, and the Anthony. Two Bridget Mooney short stories were finalists for the Agatha. Her latest novel, featuring Deputy Sheriff Marty Hopkins, is *Crossfire* (Severn House). She was president of Sisters in Crime in 1992–93.

Barbara D'Amato
Barbara D'Amato has won the Carl Sandburg Award for Fiction, the Agatha twice, the Anthony twice, the first Mary Higgins Clark Award, the Macavity, and others. She is a former president of Mystery Writers of America and Sisters in Crime (1994–95). She and her husband have written several musical comedies, which were produced in Chicago, London, and Toronto.

Dorothy Salisbury Davis
Dorothy Salisbury Davis was born in Chicago in 1916. Author of twenty novels, thirty-some short stories;

Grand Master, Mystery Writers of America, 1985; Lifetime Achievement Award, Bouchercon, 1989. Member of original board of Sisters in Crime.

Susan Dunlap

Susan Dunlap has written nineteen novels and numerous short stories. Her series feature Berkeley police officer Jill Smith, forensic-pathologist-cum-private-investigator Kiernan O'Shaughnessy, meter reader Vejay Haskell, and, most recently, stunt double Darcy Lott in *A Single Eye.* Her day jobs have ranged from social work to legal assisting, teaching hatha yoga, and being part of a death penalty defense team. She was president of Sisters in Crime in 1990–91.

Kate Flora

Recovering attorney Kate Flora is the author of seven Thea Kozak mysteries, a suspense novel, and the Joe Burgess police procedural mystery series. Her true crime book, *Finding Amy,* was a 2007 Edgar nominee. With two other mystery writers, she is a partner in Level Best Books, which publishes anthologies of crime stories by New England writers. She is an MFA candidate in creative writing at Vermont College. She was president of Sisters in Crime in 2002–03.

Linda Grant

Linda Grant is the author of the Catherine Sayler series. Sayler, a San Francisco private investigator, specializes in high-tech crime, taking cases that range from sabotage in a genetics lab (*Lethal Genes*) to sexual harassment in a software company (*A Woman's Place*). Three of her six books have been nominated for Anthony Awards. She was president of Sisters of Crime in 1993–94.

Kate Grilley

Virgin Islands resident Kate Grilley was the president of Sisters in Crime in 2003–04. Kate is the author of the Anthony and Macavity Award–winning Caribbean mystery series featuring amateur sleuth Kelly Ryan. Writing as Kate Borden, she is the author of the Peggy Jean Turner/New England mysteries. In 2006 Kate was the Malice Domestic Toastmaster.

Carolyn Hart

Carolyn Hart is the author of thirty-nine novels. Her newest title is *Set Sail For Murder,* seventh in the Hennie O series. Coming in 2008 are *Death Walked In,* eighteenth in the Death on Demand series, and *Ghost at Work,* first in a new series featuring the late Bailey Ruth Raeburn, an impetuous redheaded ghost who returns to earth to help someone in trouble. Carolyn was president of Sisters in Crime in 1991–92.

Libby Fischer Hellmann

Libby writes the award-winning Chicago-based mystery series featuring documentary producer and single mother Ellie Foreman. There are four novels in the series, starting with the Anthony-nominated *An Eye for Murder.* Libby was president of Sisters in Crime in 2005–06. Her next release, *Easy Innocence,* is a stand-alone PI novel set in Chicago.

Sue Henry

A past president of Sisters in Crime (1997–98), Sue Henry lives in Anchorage and has traveled widely in Alaska for the last thirty-three years. Her first mystery, *Murder on the Iditarod Trail,* featuring sled dog racer Jessie Arnold and state trooper Alex Jensen, won both the Anthony and Macavity for Best First Novel of 1991. Besides the series that followed that book, she now writes a spin-off series featuring Maxie McNabb, another Alaskan character first introduced with Arnold in *Dead North.* Sue has lived in Alaska for thirty-seven years and, before retiring to focus on writing, was an administrator in the field of adult basic education for both the Alaska State Department of

Education and the University of Alaska–Anchorage, where she also taught writing.

Rochelle Krich
Rochelle Krich's first mystery, *Where's Mommy Now?* won the Anthony Award and was filmed as *Perfect Alibi*. The author of five stand-alones, five Jessie Drake mysteries, and several short stories, Rochelle (www.rochellekrich.com) writes a series featuring LA tabloid journalist Molly Blume ("A sleuth worth her salt," *New York Times Book Review*). *Grave Endings* won the Mary Higgins Clark and Left Coast Crime Calavera awards. Rochelle is currently working on *Mind Games,* a stand-alone. She was president of Sisters in Crime in 2006–07.

Charlotte MacLeod
Charlotte MacLeod was the cofounder and former president of the American Crime League. She was the Guest of Honor at Bouchercon and Malice Domestic. She received the Lifetime Achievement Award at Bouchercon and Malice Domestic, and has received five American Mystery Awards, two Edgar nominations, and a Nero Wolfe Award.

Margaret Maron
Margaret Maron is the author of twenty-three novels and two collections of short stories. Winners of several major American awards for mysteries, her works are on the reading lists of various courses in contemporary Southern literature. She has served as president of Sisters in Crime (1989–90), the American Crime Writers League, and Mystery Writers of America.

Claire McNab
Claire Carmichael McNab is the author of more than fifty published books in many genres, although her favorite has always been mystery fiction. She is proud of her dual citizenship of two of the greatest countries

in the world—Australia and the United States. Claire also counts as one of her most rewarding experiences her term in 2000–01 as president of Sisters in Crime, followed by her ascension to the title of goddess, as she's assured past presidents of the organization are known.

Annette Meyers

Annette Meyers was born in Manhattan, grew up on a chicken farm in New Jersey, and came running back to New York as fast as she could. With her long history on both Broadway (assistant to Harold Prince) and Wall Street (headhunter and NASD arbitrator), she is the quintessential New Yorker.

All of her books—the eight Smith and Wetzons (contemporary), the two Olivia Browns (1920), and the stand-alone *Repentances* (1936)—are set in New York.

Using the pseudonym Maan Meyers, Annette and her husband, Martin, have written six books and multiple short stories in the *Dutchman* series of historical mysteries set in New York in the seventeenth, eighteenth, and nineteenth centuries.

She was president of Sisters in Crime in 1996–97.

Sara Paretsky

Sara Paretsky, who helped start Sisters in Crime, is the creator of V. I. Warshawski. Among her awards is the Cartier Diamond Dagger for Lifetime Achievement from the British Crime Writers Association. She was president of Sisters in Crime in 1987–88.

Nancy Pickard

Nancy Pickard is a founding member and former president of Sisters in Crime (1988–89). She is the winner of the Agatha, Anthony, Macavity, Barry, and Shamus awards, and is a four-time Edgar nominee, most recently for *The Virgin of Small Plains*. She lives in Kansas.

Medora Sale
A past president of Sisters in Crime (1998–99), Toron-tonian Medora Sale has written fourteen mysteries as well as various shorter works. Eight of these are set in the Middle Ages and have been published under her alternate name, Caroline Roe.

Eve K. Sandstrom
Eve K. Sandstrom is a fifth-generation Oklahoman. She is the author of fourteen published mystery novels and several short stories, most of them set either in Oklahoma or in her second home-state, Michigan. She writes the Chocoholic mystery series under the name JoAnna Carl. She was president of Sisters in Crime in 2001–02.

Patricia Sprinkle
Patricia Sprinkle relies on her Southern upbringing to write three series of Southern mysteries and occa-sional short stories, but this story is based on several years spent in Miami. She currently lives in Smyrna, Georgia, and enjoys reading, working with children, seeking justice, and doing nothing. She was president of Sisters in Crime in 2004–05.

About Sisters in Crime

Founded in 1986, **Sisters in Crime** is an international organization of women writers of crime and mystery, with 3,400 members in forty-eight chapters worldwide. It includes Edgar®, Anthony, Gold Dagger, and Agatha Award winners and nominees, as well as national bestselling authors. For more information and a Sisters in Crime membership application, visit www.sistersincrime.org.

Copyright Notices